D0272226

It should be noted… how easily men are corrupted and in nature transformed, however good they may be and however well taught.
Machiavelli

The best rulers are those about whom people know nothing but for their existence.
Lao Zi

THE MASTERSHIP GAME

THE MASTERSHIP GAME

Scott McBain

HarperCollins*Publishers*

702702
MORAY COUNCIL
DEPARTMENT OF TECHNICAL
& LEISURE SERVICES
F

This novel is entirely a work of fiction. The names, characters and incidents portrayed in it are the work of the author's imagination. Any resemblance to actual persons, living or dead, events or localities is entirely coincidental.

HarperCollins*Publishers*
77–85 Fulham Palace Road
Hammersmith, London W6 8JB

Published by HarperCollins*Publishers* 2000
1 3 5 7 9 8 6 4 2

Copyright © Scott McBain 2000

The Author asserts the moral right to
be identified as the author of this work

A catalogue record for this book
is available from the British Library

ISBN 0 00 225919 2

Typeset in New Baskerville and Photina
Typeset by Rowland Phototypesetting Ltd,
Bury St Edmunds, Suffolk

Printed in Great Britain by
Caledonian International Book Manufacturing Ltd,
Glasgow

All rights reserved. No part of this publication may be reproduced, stored in a retrieval system, or transmitted, in any form or by any means, electronic, mechanical, photocopying, recording or otherwise, without the prior permission of the publishers.

For men pursue their goal (which is generally the acquisition of glory and wealth) by very different means: one is cautious and another impetuous, one uses violence and another cunning, one is patient and another quite the opposite; and yet all of them may succeed with their different methods.

Machiavelli, *The Prince*

PROLOGUE

POWER CORRUPTS. THE GREATER THE concentration of power the greater the corruption.

Never was this more so than at the beginning of the twenty-first century. For the first time the world witnessed immense power becoming concentrated in a very few hands with the rise of supranational companies, the federalisation of Europe and the integration of world trade. These developments brought benefits to most of the citizens of the world in terms of greater material wealth. They also brought the threat of dictatorship on a global scale.

While the concentration of power was dangerous it was the dramatic increase in the flow of information that made the mixture lethal for, in a paradoxical way, it meant that the truth was often more difficult to determine. At the onset of the new millennium, mankind was receiving a huge and expanding amount of knowledge about itself and the planet. This raw pulp was circulated around the globe by the supermedia (the new buzz word for the closely integrated networks of press, television, satellite and supernet) whose legions of commentators and pundits were all too anxious to distort the facts to achieve their real purpose – the good story. After all, the truth was rarely so interesting. But behind the picture lay a cost that few had anticipated. The people soon began to realise that this information, and the truth itself, were being manipulated to secure financial and political gains for the few at the expense of the majority. The result was that society began to distrust the foundations on which democracy was built.

Governments were the first to fall from grace. Politicians traded in economic and political data long before its official release. Facts became a commodity to be repackaged and distorted by the spin doctors for monetary gain. Truth and virtual reality became indistinguishable.

Who really told the people the truth? The US Congress, the Russian Duma, the European Parliament, the Japanese Diet – did these contain honest men? The man and woman in the street thought otherwise. They felt the corruption and they saw, albeit fleetingly in the shadows, hands passing money under the table.

Meanwhile, the incestuous interactions between the supermedia, the technobarons and the stock market became ever more prominent. They moved from each other's pockets into each other's beds. The people knew that they were being fooled by those in whom they had put their trust. As a result, the twenty-first century became an age of deep cynicism and disbelief.

So what was the truth and who would tell it? This became an acute problem not only for the masses, but also for their leaders. From whom could presidents and prime ministers seek accurate and balanced advice? Their own ministries and think-tanks, while claiming to give them objective opinions, were pursuing hidden agendas or were secretly controlled by multinationals and criminal organisations. In despair, leaders turned to the international advisory bodies and institutes. Yet, in time, most of these also succumbed to peddling the half-lie for money.

Of the few remaining institutes that gave unbiased advice the most important was the College. Founded on a remote island off the west coast of Scotland in the thirteenth century this secretive organisation had long been the pre-eminent consultative body to the leaders of countries. Impartial in its dealings with the outside world since its establishment, it had only one task – *to advise the leaders of all nations in the cause of peace.* It was from the College that the great and the powerful sought advice to solve the most intractable problems of society. Civil wars, environmental disasters, border disputes, major geopolitical issues – at sometime or another the head of every nation beat a path to the College gates to obtain an objective view of the best means of resolution. In secret.

On its small island the College jealously guarded its integrity. No ordinary institution, it had no students, it set no exams and it sought no finances. Of the eighty persons that comprised its Fellowship, each had demonstrated outstanding abilities. Once appointed, the post was for life and the Fellows were made financially secure, to pursue such work as they and the Master determined, subject to one restriction: their connection with the College and all that occurred within its confines was secret.

What of the Master? Although the general public was aware that he existed almost nothing was known of the one who wielded the highest power. The Master remained in the realm of speculation, an enigmatic figure, brilliant, solitary and remote. Yet of his influence on global affairs there was no dispute. Even Pope Julius IV quipped in a papal audience that:

While St Peter holds the keys to the Kingdom of Heaven, the Master holds those to the corridors of temporal power.

As the twenty-first century unfolded and organs of government as well as institutes across the globe became paralysed or ineffective, the College alone remained above it all – a pure source with which the leaders of countries could raise the issues that troubled them and receive objective advice in confidence. Yet these leaders, as they witnessed the disintegration of their own societies, anxiously pondered how much longer the College could withstand the tide. What would happen when it too fell? What also of the Master? Who could succeed this mighty guardian that secretly protected the affairs of men?

However, none of them knew of the Mastership Game, nor of the path to the truth.

THE NATURE OF POWER

CHAPTER ONE

A prince, therefore, who does not recognise evils at their commencement cannot truly be called a wise man; and yet this gift is given to few.

Machiavelli, *The Prince*

IT WAS A POLITICAL CRISIS that caused the new President of the United States and the Master to meet. Although this meeting did not affect the Mastership Game, nor its contestants, it did affect the President. It caused probably the most powerful man in the world to reflect on the true nature of power and who should best wield it and, in that way, the Master touched the life of the President as he did many millions of others, whether or not they knew it.

However, before the Mastership Game began there was a political crisis and a corpse.

Jack Caldwell, special adviser to the US President, was there when it started. Like all great political disasters it was unanticipated, although it came at a time when politicians should be most careful of treachery – at Christmas, the season of goodwill.

'Jack, the President wants to see you immediately.' The press secretary's voice was tense and hurried.

Jack got up from his desk and walked along the corridor. He was a tall, lean man in his early sixties, with grey hair and an impassive face. He had worked in government a long time and had been senior adviser to a number of presidents. There were few things about the political system that he didn't know, and people trusted him and relied on his judgement. Passing along the corridor he glanced out of the window on to the White House lawn. It had been snowing heavily and the President's two young daughters, Jessica and Karen, were building a snowman in the garden. They ran about, giggling and laughing, full of the joys of life. Jack smiled. He was reminded of the Kennedy years, with a photogenic president, a beautiful wife and two young children. President Davison was every bit as clever and photogenic as President Kennedy had been. He also could become a great man, in time.

Further down the corridor a door was opened. A female clerk appeared.

'Sir, you should go in right away,' she told him.

By God, Caldwell reflected, as he walked into the Oval Office, the country needed an honest president. The United States political system had been mired in crisis during the last few years as had those of many other nations. A Congress seething with corruption, the previous president impeached for receiving financial payoffs (Caldwell had never advised him) and a Government that people joined to squeeze money from and not to serve – the last few years had been bad and the disgust and cynicism of the American public with the political process profound. Which is why they had voted in the forty-three-year-old Davison as President of the United States by a massive margin. He'd been in office ten months and he'd already trodden on many toes – those of powerful people who sought to prevent him exposing their corruption by finding a weakness in his own armour. It was inevitable. Still, Davison had the support of the US voters and that continued to matter in politics. Just.

'Jack, come and sit over here.'

Jack followed the President's outstretched hand and sat down on the sofa. Opposite him were three other individuals. He knew all about them. Joe Buchanan, the formidable Vice President, a thickset man from Nebraska. Beside him, the National Security Adviser, Paul Faucher, who stomped the corridors of power, leaving people in no doubt of his authority nor of the consequences of opposing him. Finally, William Olsen, the bespectacled and enigmatic Director of the CIA, in his late fifties and coming up for retirement. They were as thick as thieves. The atmosphere in the room was tense. Caldwell noticed that there was no military presence, which seemed curious.

'Mr President, this is very serious indeed,' Faucher angrily continued a discussion already under way. 'In fact, it's probably the worst breach of national security we've had.'

President Davison, sitting in an armchair between the two sofas, looked at Caldwell. The famous wide grin was missing. Absent-mindedly he drew a hand through his thick mane of dark brown hair in which flecks of grey had started to appear. These palpable signs of age gave him an added air of dignity and would do him no harm. Davison remained a handsome man with a wonderfully relaxed manner.

'You'd better tell Jack, Paul.'

Faucher turned to Caldwell. It was not difficult to dislike the Security Adviser, but he was a shrewd political operator, and in politics the President sometimes had to work with strange bedfellows: the good, the bad and, in Faucher's case, the downright ugly.

'It's basically this.' Faucher slapped a folder on the table. 'Last night we received information from a highly placed source in the Russian Government. They've got hold of some top-secret information: blueprints of our nuclear launch sites in Japan and Turkey.' He hesitated, 'That's bad. But the really bad news is that the source is a secret cabinet paper.' He shifted uncomfortably, as if perched over a slow-burning flame.

Caldwell was stunned. 'Is it genuine?'

'Oh, it's genuine, all right,' snorted Faucher with a dismissive wave of his hand. 'Our Russian mole sent a copy back to us. You'd have thought he was in our cabinet room reading the fucking thing.'

Buchanan said 'It can only have been leaked by someone at the top.' He dropped his voice, 'Within the cabinet. Someone very close to the President. That means we have a traitor in our midst.'

There was silence. 'How much time before the media gets it?' asked the President.

Faucher glanced at his watch. 'At a guess, four to five hours. We all know the Russian Government itself leaks like a sieve. Besides, rumours are already starting to spread on the Supernet. We'll have to admit it soon.'

They looked at the President. Davison was unruffled. A strong nerve was one of his great attributes. He reflected on the problem. Then he leant forward in his chair, his face decisive.

'We should do three things. First, Joe,' he turned towards the Vice President, 'I want you and Paul,' he nodded to Faucher, 'to find out as a matter of top priority how this information came to be leaked. Second, I'll call an emergency cabinet meeting for this evening. Third, we need to take the sting out of the media coverage from the start.'

'Tell that to Congress,' said Olsen sourly. 'The military have just spent billions of dollars modernising these sites, and those in Japan never officially existed. It will start another arms race. Congress will be baying for blood.' His anger was becoming volcanic.

'I know, I know,' said Davison, abruptly stemming the flow of Olsen's angst. He rose from his chair. 'And I want someone to feed a question to me at the press conference this afternoon. By tonight we must discover where the leak came from and how the documents got to the Russians.'

Davison glanced at Jack. Their eyes briefly met in understanding. It was a crisis, albeit manageable. They still might be able to squash the story. Yet, if very sensitive cabinet papers were being passed to the Russians, what other secrets might be leaked?

That afternoon, at the end of the annual gathering of the Association for American Industry, President Davison gave what appeared to be an impromptu press conference. However, it had been carefully scripted an hour before. He stood at the podium, his appearance relaxed, his wife, Christina, by his side. A lovely couple. The questions came up nice and easy, slow balls from the pitcher.

'Mr President, what about the state of the economy and inflation?' 'What about the oil slick off the coast of Miami?' 'What about the stock market disaster in Brazil?' 'Will you be making a trip to Russia later this year to see President Barchov?'

President Davison delivered his answers with a touch of wit and, now and again, a flash of that brilliant grin. It was impressive. Caldwell had seen him perform hundreds of times before but it still charmed him. He was the most natural orator he'd seen. The question came, right at the end of the session when the media machine was lulled into relaxation.

'Mr President, is it true that a spy has leaked details of US missile bases to the Russians?'

President Davison grinned slightly. *Sow the seeds of doubt from the start.* 'Well, you know, we live in a world of conspiracies and alien intervention.' The audience laughed, recalling last week's newspaper article in which an eccentric Congressman had asserted that the White House was infiltrated by aliens. 'Sure, we've heard of this rumour and we're following it up.' *Sow more doubt.* 'We think it may be out-of-date information on old missile sites.' *Then cover yourself.* He shrugged, his body language indicating the allegation was of little worth even as he said the opposite. 'Still, we're giving it serious attention.'

Before another question could be asked one of the President's spin doctors said loudly, 'OK, that's it, folks.'

The President turned to go. At that moment, while the world's cameras were still focused on him at the podium, his five-year-old daughter, Karen, ran to him, gently prompted by an unseen hand. Suddenly, the President caught sight of her. He reached out and caught up the giggling red bundle into his arms. At home, fifty-eight million Americans watched this display of parental affection on their TV screens and there was not a motherly or fatherly heart that did not feel a great warm glow. With a brilliant example of what the word spinners called the 'spontaneously choreographed event', the nation forgot what had been said and saw only the proud family man whom it trusted.

President Davison, his arms around his daughter, gave that great wide grin. The State of the Nation was strong. He personified it. The smile, the carefree manner, the common touch. God bless him, God bless America.

Of course, the illusion was shattered when they found the body.

'I don't believe it!'

It was early evening. The President had returned from the Association gathering. The full cabinet sat before him and two rows of anxious faces gazed down the table. The Chairman of the Joint Chiefs of Staff was apoplectic at the news of the leak. People had discovered his toys. He would have to play with something else.

'I just don't believe it,' the President said, flatly this time.

His National Security Adviser, Paul Faucher, stood his ground. 'I'm sorry, Mr President, but the leak came from the US Embassy in Paris. The secret services are sure and it's been confirmed by our top-level contact in the Russian Government. That narrows things down. In fact,' he glared at the assembled company, 'there's only one man who could have had access to that sort of information. Only your senior political adviser could have received those cabinet papers and taken them to Paris.'

'No. Now you look,' said President Davison, pointing a finger angrily at Faucher, his voice cracking slightly with emotion. 'Ambassador Pearlman's as honest as the day he was born. I appointed him. I've known him for years. It's inconceivable that he's a spy.'

The cabinet was silent. They appreciated the consequences of what the President was saying. If the best friend of the President had leaked secrets to the Russians, the President himself would be in very great trouble. Could it really be so?

They all knew Dan Pearlman. He was a homespun man from

Montana ranching stock who had become a multimillionaire in the cattle trade. Although he had acquired a patina of sophistication, his simple philosophy, great patriotism and personal courage shone through. He was as homely as James Stewart and he personified the real heart of America.

'Well,' Davison paused, knowing he had no choice. 'I'll order the Ambassador to return to the States immediately so you can question him. In the meantime,' he inclined his head towards the Vice President and his Security Adviser, 'continue your investigations. I want every detail: who else could have gotten access to these cabinet papers, how they were transmitted to the Russians and when. Let's meet again tomorrow morning, seven o'clock. This cabinet meeting's over.'

He got up from the table. 'Joe,' he called back the Vice President, 'could I have a word with you? And with you, Jack?'

They sat together in a small side room. President Davison looked at his advisers. He trusted only these two in a world where politics made no friends. He reflected that he had also trusted Dan Pearlman. Betrayal usually came from those closest to you.

'We have a crisis on our hands,' he said quietly. Caldwell could see the deep sadness in his eyes. 'But I don't want Dan Pearlman to be thrown to the wolves until he's had a chance to speak in his defence. Is that clear?'

Even as he spoke a thought sprang to President Davison's mind. Why had someone leaked those particular cabinet papers and not others? They were so politically sensitive that their release would cause maximum political damage. But to whom? To the United States? Or to the Presidency? Davison opened his mouth again, but he couldn't voice his suspicions. Certain secrets could not be told. They were too personal.

They could bring down the President.

Dan Pearlman took the phone call at home in the huge Parisian apartment that was allocated to the US Ambassador. Though in his late sixties and in good health when he put down the phone he felt much older. He had faced many adversities in his time and his affable countenance belied a steely determination. Already he was preparing for the worst. The tornado was fast approaching and it was coming directly towards him. Flight was not in his nature, though. He would stand. He was more worried about his wife.

'Dan, keep calm. It'll all work out,' he muttered as he climbed the stairs to the bedroom where Ingela was preparing for an official dinner.

Life had been good to Ambassador Pearlman and he was the first to acknowledge it. He had come from nothing. His parents had been small-time ranchers, people who had known real hardship and suffering in the 1930s, and who had imbued in him honesty and the will to work. By middle age Dan was a rich man and he had been content. However, luck was to give him more than he had bargained for. At the age of sixty-three, when his beloved first wife had died of cancer, he had anticipated a single and lonely life for the rest of his days. But fate was to decree otherwise.

He entered the bedroom. Ingela had just finished dressing. She was a Swedish beauty with long blonde hair, a well-proportioned figure and a striking face. Dan had met her at an old friend's dinner party one night four years ago and it had lead to a whirlwind romance and marriage. Course, Dan knew what people thought – that he was an old fool, that Ingela, who was thirty years younger than he, had married him for his money, that she wanted power, that she was very ambitious.

'Yep,' Dan had replied to those close friends who'd had the balls to raise the subject with him, 'all that. Women are always attracted to money and power, always have been.' Then he'd deliver the punchline: 'But she also loves me.'

Now he sat down heavily on the bed and studied his wife while she put on her diamonds. Did she still love him? He believed so. Of course, he'd heard rumours but he'd ignored them. They didn't matter, her love for him did. She'd tell him in her own good time and he'd forgive her. That was just the way he was and Dan Pearlman wasn't changing at his age. Not for the world. The world would have to change a little for him.

'Honey, the President's ordered me back to the States immediately,' he said. He informed her of what an old cabinet friend had just phoned to tell him.

Ingela received the bad news with utter incredulity. 'They think you're a spy? What total lies,' she said spreading her painted fingernails. 'You're the most honest man I've ever met. Anyway, why would you want to leak cabinet secrets? What could you possibly gain from it?'

Dan said, 'Well, I didn't do anything, that's for definite. Which can only mean one thing: someone's setting me up.'

'Who?'

'I don't know, honey, but I'm sure going to find out.'

Ingela started violently. Lines of fear and alarm spread across her face.

'Will they come here?'

'Yep,' said the Ambassador. 'There'll soon be teams of CIA men crawling all over the place looking for evidence.' He waved his hand dismissively. 'But I'm safe. I've got nothing to hide.' He rose to his feet. 'My flight's at six tomorrow morning. We'll continue with the dinner party tonight, no point in letting people down.' He kissed her, a tired old man. 'Don't worry. We'll win. See you downstairs, darling, in a few minutes.'

Ingela watched him depart. When she was certain he'd gone she went to a locked escritoire. She sat down and quickly penned a letter, tears welling up in her eyes. Her own endgame had arrived unexpectedly.

The dinner party was a great success and the guests very much enjoyed themselves. Dan was a good raconteur and Ingela sparkled as always. No one remotely thought that anything was amiss. It was on her last trip to the kitchen that Ingela casually requested her Filipino cook, Marcella, to post a package for her. Unnoticed by anyone else she popped it into Marcella's old leather shopping bag and then hurriedly embraced her farewell.

That night, as events in Washington were already beginning

to spin out of control, Ingela waited until her husband was sound asleep. She slipped out of bed and put a gown over her satin night-dress.

'Goodbye,' she kissed the reclined figure tenderly on his forehead. Dan Pearlman was a good man; she couldn't have wished for better. 'I loved you,' she said, half to herself and half to him.

She made for the door, passed along the landing and went upstairs where more bedrooms, presently empty, were set aside for Ambassadorial guests. Her movements were slow and languid.

Opening a window in one of the bedrooms, Ingela stepped out onto a narrow ledge and ascended the ladder of a fire escape. Sometimes, there really was no solution, she reflected. People's capacity for cruelty and evil had always surprised her but she had learnt to accept it as an ineradicable feature of humankind. That was it, they wouldn't change. Ingela stood on the roof ledge. An icy wind blew in her face. About her, the lights from a myriad buildings and the passing traffic punctuated the Parisian night. Four storeys below was the enclosed courtyard of the Embassy. She was not alone. Millions of people were close to her. Yet she had never felt so alone in her life. No one could help her now.

Slowly Ingela opened her arms, her decision and her utter despair complete. She looked down at her body. She had given it to various men. None more so than to Dan, and to the other individual, the one whom she had also loved. Ingela knew that Dan was wrong. These people didn't just want to bring him down. There was something more. They had tried to blackmail her for too long.

'Mother,' she said in Swedish, her first tongue. She opened her arms in greeting and stepped out over the edge. She was free at last.

'Ambassador, you must get up.'

At four in the morning they woke him. Drowsily, Dan Pearlman turned over in bed to see the frightened faces of his

Deputy Chief of Mission and two other members of staff.

'Please come with us.'

They hurried him along the corridor and down the stairs, refusing to tell him what had happened. Pearlman passed outside into the quadrangle. Then he saw Ingela. She appeared serene as she lay there, her blonde hair blossoming out in the snow, her face beautiful in the lamplight. The impact of the fall had left no external mark apart from a small pool of blood that seeped out from the left side of her head. Dan approached his wife, shuffling now like an elderly man. Her blue eyes were open and as Dan closed them he wept, for they saw far beyond him, into an uncorrupted world. Not even his love could have held her back.

'Ambassador, you must come inside.'

Now they had the corpse.

When the news broke, it was the political scandal of the decade. The headlines said it all:

SECRET CABINET DOCUMENTS PASSED TO RUSSIANS.

WIFE OF US AMBASSADOR TO FRANCE COMMITS SUICIDE.

MAID POSTS PACKAGE. COULD HAVE BEEN LETTERS. DESTINATION UNKNOWN.

Both Pearlmans were very close friends of the President. The excited press dug deeper. More scandal emerged. Ingela Pearlman had had an affair with a prominent person – but who? The hunt was on. The media, the commentators, the pundits, they loved it and the bloodlust was in their eyes as they smelt the kill and the money to be made from it all. Disclosure was in the public interest of course – they'd tell the public that.

Faring even better than the press were the arms manufacturers. Russia, China, Pakistan, Iran, Iraq, alarmed by the public disclosure of the nuclear launch sites, and facing internal military demands to counter the threat, soon announced plans to supplement their own arsenals.

Of course everyone knew the truth, didn't they? Someone close to the President had handed over US secrets to damage US interests. It was so obvious. The politicians, quick to notice a change in the wind, began to distance themselves from the President, and even Vice President Buchanan started to tiptoe away, loudly protesting his loyalty to his boss all the while. Finally, the cabinet waited for the Attorney-General to administer the death blow: 'Mr President, I think that you should consider the possibility of . . .'

Meanwhile, in the midst of all the treachery, a nation felt sad and disappointed as they watched the tragedy unfold before their eyes on TV. For they knew two simple truths the press had disregarded – that good men were also human and that judgement should be suspended until the full facts were known.

However, they also were sure that, when the letters were discovered, the President would fall.

It was on the morning of the third day after the death of Ingela Pearlman that Jack Caldwell walked into the Oval Office. President Davison was looking out of the window. His face was taut with stress and he had aged visibly over the last few days. Davison knew someone was out to destroy him but it wasn't clear who – the Russians? Ingela? People in Washington? It didn't matter now, for the letters would seal his fate. The President had slept with a spy.

As Jack crossed the deep blue carpet towards the desk that symbolised the heart of the nation, he knew that, if this President were to fall, there would be profound implications for the democratic system of government in America. For one President to be impeached was a disaster, for his successor to be brought down would undermine the whole structure. If this happened then those who desired power, but could not attain it by legitimate means, would penetrate into the very heart of the American political system. Caldwell knew what he had to do.

'Jack . . .' President Davison slowly turned from the window. His dark brown eyes focused on Caldwell. These last few days had been instructive. He had been reflecting on power and its true nature. Power, and the lust for it, corroded men and women like an acid. It bit into their souls and made them evil. For power, they would betray, lie and conceal. The greater the power, the more so. President Davison knew that now. He saw it in those closest to him who would bring him down even as they protested their allegiance. It had also affected the President himself, blinding him so that he could no longer see the solution to his own problem.

'Jack,' he hesitated. 'I have decided to resign.'

Caldwell shook his head slowly.

'No,' he said. 'You should go to see the Master.'

CHAPTER TWO

The sage is always skilful at saving men,
And so no man is uselessly cast away.
The sage is always skilful at saving things,
And so nothing is uselessly cast away.
This is called the hidden wisdom.

Lao Zi

THE SNOW, DRIVEN BY A bitter wind, gusted across the bleak Scottish island. The President glanced out of the car window. It was late afternoon. Following a NATO conference in Paris they'd flown to Scotland and then taken a chopper from the mainland to the island of Tirah. Now they were on the final leg of the journey to the castle in the centre of the island where the College was located.

Davison watched the snowflakes blow against the windowpane of the car. A former president had told him how much he had enjoyed these trips to the island during his presidency. It had given him time to think, to get away from the sterile politics, the intrigue and the interminable bores. President Davison wondered about the hundreds of others who had come here over the centuries, as if on a pilgrimage, to find answers to things they themselves could not.

'Another twenty minutes or so, Mr President.'

The voice of Jack Caldwell broke through his reverie. It had been wise to bring Jack with him for, at least, part of the way. Jack had met the Master in his work for previous administrations. That would help break the ice.

'Mr President?'

Davison flicked a switch in the car. The booming voice of the head of his secret service agents came on the line.

'They've cleared the road to the College, sir, so it should be a smooth ride.'

'Thanks, Tom.'

There was a slight clunk as the presidential car drove off the camber of the helipad. Other cars lined up in front and behind it, forming a small convoy. Then there was a roar of engines and the shouts of the secret service men into their wires.

Davison was oblivious to his surroundings. It was two days before Christmas. He could imagine his daughters running around the White House, wide-eyed with excitement and unaware of the unfolding tragedy. He thought of his wife, Christina, and what he had confessed to her the night before. He also thought of Ingela Pearlman. He could still feel the taste of her, her body scent and her gentle laugh. Why had she betrayed him in this way?

'I hope it's worth it, Jack.'

Caldwell smiled grimly. 'It will be, Mr President.'

Davison knew that his National Security Adviser and the Vice President had bitterly opposed this trip. They had warned him that the College was no supporter of the US. They were probably helping the Russians, they had insinuated darkly. Besides, the College was much too mysterious and too powerful for its own good. No point in giving them even greater insight into US domestic problems to use against the country when occasion demanded. Well, today, Davison would find out for himself. Perhaps they were jealous, since only leaders of government could get access to the Master to discuss affairs of State. Despite his worries, Davison was full of anticipation at meeting a man whose reputation and mystery fascinated him.

Before them was a narrow road that led into a tract of forest. On either side the fir trees swayed with snow. The presidential car began its journey, the slush thrown out to the sides by its wheels. After a turn in the road the ferry and the helipad beside it were entirely lost to view. Davison listened to the monotonous swish of the windscreen wipers. In the distance the forms of two mountains loomed, their peaks obscured by fog.

'I think they should get an airport or, at least, let us land at the College.'

Jack Caldwell laughed. It was the first time he had laughed for many days. It was normally a breezy and confident laugh. This time it had an edge to it.

'Mention it if you like to the Master, Mr President, but I'm not sure he'll agree. Allowing helicopter access was a special extension to the UN-approved exclusion zone for Tirah, which only provided for a ferry to the mainland. The College guards its privacy very carefully. Even if Tirah had an area large enough for an aircraft landing strip I suspect the Master would veto it. Besides,' his voice became sombre again, 'a short car journey is always good for reflection.'

Davison nodded. The forest had closed in on them. Outside the car there was a cocoon of whiteness, another world. Could the Master really help? How could he know anything more than the President? And yet . . .

Without turning from the window, Davison said, 'Jack, the last Secretary General of the United Nations gave me some advice when he left office a couple of months ago. He patted me on the arm in that avuncular way of his and said, "Remember one thing. When the chips are really down, consult the Master".'

'That's about right, Mr President,' Caldwell replied.

Davison turned from the car window to scrutinise him. 'Yeah, but I still can't believe he knows as much as they say he does – state secrets, details of our missile sites and military hardware, things like that.'

'Not all of our secrets,' said Caldwell evenly. As a member of the College he didn't want to disclose too much. 'I suspect he knows most of them, though. He has access to people and information that others can only dream of, and he's been meeting world leaders on a confidential basis for over thirty years. I imagine the Master is the only person alive who has visited both the Vatican's secret archives *and* those of the Chinese Communist leaders in Beijing. Being above the political fray, and the confidant of the great and the powerful, the Master learns things not even the CIA can extract out of people. I was told by a previous president that visiting him was rather like going to confession and that, like a priest, he never betrays secrets.'

'Never?' asked Davison in a sharp tone. 'Are you sure?'

'Yes,' said Caldwell, 'from all that we know about him. In the case of this man I am certain the answer is "never".'

'I hope you're right, Jack.'

President Davison shook his head wearily and turned back to the scenery outside. A jumble of thoughts flickered through his mind. Would his wife leave him? She said she wouldn't but would she feel the same when the story broke and she came under pressure from the media? And what about his kids? How do you explain these things to young children who only have unconditional love for you? Once he told them, the dad they knew would have perished, to be replaced by a more suspect, more unreliable, figure. An ex-president, a fallen father. Davison sighed.

The forest gave way to a rocky mountainside. The vegetation was sparse, mainly heather and gorse. They were approaching the centre of the island and soon the College would come into view. Davison cursed himself for his foolishness. Love and power were strong aphrodisiacs. Unfortunately, they didn't mix.

'Pass me the briefing notes.'

Davison glanced at them again, quickly turning the pages. As President of the United States he was privy to a lot more information about the College than before his election. The general public and the press knew about the island of Tirah but they had never visited it. The College was the stuff of legend, and the story still amazed Davison. A college, established in the medieval ages by a famous Scottish leader, to provide impartial advice to the leaders of all nations that might request it, hidden away on a remote island – how could it possibly have survived throughout the centuries? Yet it had, and prospered. Today, it was the greatest, and most secretive, advisory body in the world. Davison was glad Jack had persuaded him to come. At least he would see the place for the first, and possibly the only, time in his life. Something to tell his grandchildren about. He tossed aside the memo and stretched out his legs in the car.

'How exactly does the College operate, Jack? I still don't have a feel for it.'

Caldwell raised his eyebrows slightly. 'I don't think anyone outside the College does. We know very little about how it's run internally apart from the fact that its head is the Master. He is assisted by five Arbitrators, senior fellows of the College who are appointed by him to help with administration. In total there are no more than eighty Fellows at any one time. We also know that the Master is the supreme executive, judicial and legislative head of the College.'

'Who appoints whom?'

'The Master appoints the Arbitrators; they appoint the Fellows. The Master also appoints his successor as far as we can ascertain. That's about all we know, I'm afraid.'

President Davison felt none the wiser. 'Yes, but how does the College collect its information? And how come they can find out so much about us?'

Caldwell bent forward. 'Well, it's rather like the Freemasons, Mr President. The Fellows never disclose their identity to the outside world. Their normal employment will be in the top government posts of countries or in research institutes, universities or international bodies, you name it – anywhere where there's power and decision-making on a national scale. They are the eyes and the ears of the Master and the Arbitrators.'

'And the Master? He's the only one with a full understanding of how it all knits together?'

'Yes,' said Caldwell. 'You see, he sits at the centre of a huge information-gathering system they've been building up over hundreds of years. In addition to information supplied by the Fellows and the leaders of nations, we're sure the College has long had the ability to tap into any military or commercial computer around the globe. Even the Fellows, I suspect, only know a small part of what goes on inside the web. In that way the College maintains its secrecy and it is virtually impenetrable. It's a very clever system that predates the way terrorist cells operate today, so that the betrayal of one does not destroy the whole structure. It's all based on the medieval concept of a great wheel of being, like the planets rotating about the sun, except that, in this case, the sun is the Master, the very centre of power.'

Caldwell went on to explain that the College, in advising the leaders of countries 'in the cause of peace', didn't just track wars and military activity around the globe. It monitored all areas of human endeavour. Genetics, human rights, crime, environment, space, medicine, economics, politics, stock markets, you name it, the College had databases on it and, through the Master, provided advice to the heads of all countries, of whatever political persuasion, big and small. In that way the College had a vast, albeit intangible, influence in the world. It was a sort of benign guardian that covertly altered and moulded the direction of mankind. If any human institution knew about power, its use and abuse, it was this one. 'We reckon their computers are probably even more sophisticated than our own.'

President Davison looked at him slyly. His wide grin made a brief appearance. 'So you could be a Fellow, Jack?'

Caldwell returned a self-deprecating look. 'Who knows? The Head of the CIA, the Chief Justice of the Supreme Court, the Chairman of the Federal Reserve – they could all be Fellows. Only the Master can reveal who the Fellows are and, to our knowledge, this has never happened.'

Davison tapped his fingers against the armrest of the car. He was thinking of what he would say to the Master. Who was the more influential, the Master or the President of the United States? He began to question the supremacy that he had implicitly assumed. How much did his own people ever tell him anyway?

'Do you think the College misuses its power, Jack?'

'Difficult to prove,' replied his special adviser. 'Personally, I don't think so. The College was originally set up to promote peace and I guess they've held on to that principle throughout the centuries. Yet so much depends on the Master and the integrity of the College. Like all human institutions it cannot be made perfect. Get one rotten apple and the whole system could collapse. That said, we suspect the way the College is structured means that there are checks and balances and that the corruption would have to get to the very top, to the Master himself, before the system could be brought down. The Mastership is a bit like the Papacy, the holding of enormous influence at its apex, with a direct line to everybody of importance, with the possible exception of God.'

'I hope they choose the Master well,' said Davidson drily. Then almost as an aside, 'Can we get more info on the College?'

Caldwell knew what Davison was really trying to say. Could the US Government infiltrate the College and subvert it, just a little, so that it would look upon the US with especial favour? Just as they had done to almost every other think-tank and advisory body around the world. Other presidents had asked him the same question about the College, some countries had even tried it, but none successfully.

'That would be a problem.' Caldwell explained that, although the CIA had detailed satellite pictures of the College and of Tirah, they were of little use. One needed to get inside the system and that was very difficult, like trying to get into a closed order of monks, though the Fellows could marry these days if they wished.

'Besides, Mr President,' Caldwell coughed politely, 'as you'll be aware, in 1860 the US Congress legislated to protect the integrity of the College, including its property and information. So does the charter of the United Nations. Any president that plotted to break in, or to bribe the Fellows, would be very foolish. Once the College found out the shutters would come down. The bond of trust would be gone and you'd be the loser.'

'Of course,' said Davison hastily. 'It was only an idle question.'

By way of an added warning Caldwell told him of a plan some years before by a previous US administration, in league with the CIA, to get someone appointed a Fellow. Despite their best efforts it had proved impossible. Caldwell waited for the message to sink in, his face never betraying the slightest intimation that it was he who had forewarned the Master of this particular attempt. The system had many subtle and discreet ways of protecting itself. Davison nodded, chastened by the implied rebuke.

Their journey was almost over. Before them large castle walls appeared and the car began to ascend a steep mountain slope. Davison eagerly peered out. 'It must be unique.'

Caldwell replied, 'Only in some ways. The idea's not new. The Ancient Greeks had a famous temple at Delphi. People would go there and ask the Oracle, a priestess, about the future. Since every important person came to consult her, she knew more than anyone else about what was going on. As a result, her predictions were amazingly accurate. Well, the Master is rather like the Oracle. Someone once told me that he never lies and that you always depart from his presence wiser than when you came.'

'So he'll know who gave the secrets to the Russians?' The voice was cynical and despairing.

Caldwell scrutinised the President. The young, open, face. The engaging smile that had won a million hearts. The most recognisable human being in the world. And so very, very human.

'I think so,' he said quietly.

The College was located near the centre of Tirah. Built on a rocky outcrop it stood above the forests of fir and pine trees that surrounded it, with an almost uninterrupted view of the island save to the west, where sight of the Atlantic was obscured by the mountains of Mullach Coll and Mullach Mor, great peaks that rose to more than six hundred metres above sea level. The College had all the hallmarks of a medieval castle: sheer walls with no footholds so that the place seemed to grow out of the rocky promontory on which it was built, windows set deep into the stonework so that they were hidden from view and battlements made from massive blocks of granite. Indeed, it had been a castle before the Lord of the Isles had ceded it to the Fellowship. Then things had changed. While the exterior had retained its ancient and foreboding appearance, the inside of the castle had been considerably altered over the centuries and it now appeared like the interior of an old university, with stonework and features of a softer and more appealing hue.

A single road led to the College. It tailed off just outside the castle walls into a small parking area. A guest – for no one could land on Tirah without the permission of the Master – then ascended a steep flight of stairs and crossed a flagstone bridge to the only entrance to the castle. This comprised a stone arch with large oak doors that always remained open during the day. Having gone under the arch, the visitor would pass through two courtyards.

The first courtyard, the larger, was almost rectangular in shape, wide and spacious. There was a great fountain in its centre and cobbled pathways around it. In each corner of the courtyard stood pine trees which had been planted long ago and were protected from the full onslaught of the wind by the height of the battlements. Around the perimeter was a variety of buildings faced with limestone, their backs built into the outer walls of the castle. They had been constructed in the fifteenth century and their features included leaded windows, winding stairways and walls covered with ivy. Here the Fellows resided when they stayed at the College. Overall, the first courtyard had an academic and monastic feel about it, tranquil, contemplative, remote.

At the far end of the first courtyard a narrow corridor led into a second courtyard. This was smaller and more picturesque than the first. It comprised an extensive garden with a large pond in its centre, full of ancient carp. To the right was the Great Hall where the Fellowship dined and, close by, the College library, an elegant building with a marble façade modelled on the Parthenon although smaller in form. Both these buildings were situated near the outer wall of the College and were obscured to a considerable extent by tall trees and shrubs even in winter. To the left of the second courtyard was a reception hall. Limestone-faced and similar in design to the buildings in the first courtyard, it contained rooms where the Master received visitors.

While the first courtyard was tranquil the second had an aura of unreality about it, as if the narrow corridor led into some mysterious inner abode accessible only to the chosen few. Both courtyards were aesthetically pleasing, especially so in contrast to the bleak exterior of the castle. Indeed, to visitors they often appeared to view like precious jewels hidden away in a rough-hewn box. These two courtyards seemed to constitute the entirety of the College and for all persons, bar one, they did.

For the Master alone – the pivot around which the institution revolved – the secrecy of the College persisted even in the physical layout of the buildings. The second courtyard terminated at the base of a high wall that was identical in shape and size to the outer walls of the castle, so that it appeared for all the world that nothing lay ahead. It was almost impossible to contradict this since both the mountainous terrain and the forest of fir trees surrounding the College prevented anyone making a circuit of the castle's exterior. Nevertheless, this was an illusion.

Set in a corner of the wall at the westernmost part of the second courtyard was a locked door almost obscured by trees and ivy. Behind that lay a third courtyard, the innermost sanctum of the College, a secret place where the Master alone had his rooms. As a result, the third courtyard was invisible and the College, even as it physically stood, remained shrouded in secrecy, reflecting the nature and aspirations of its occupants.

President Davison, together with his bodyguards and Jack Caldwell, stood on the threshold of the medieval corridor leading into the second courtyard. Framed by an arch, the narrow entrance disclosed the large garden beyond. It was covered in snow apart from a single cleared path. President Davison glanced at his minders.

'You stay here.'

There was an awkward silence. The security men shifted uneasily on their feet, their suits concealing their microcom units.

'We're obliged to accompany you everywhere, sir,' said one of them firmly, 'for your own safety.'

'Not here,' said President Davison. 'And that's an order.' He stepped into the passageway. 'Come on, Jack.'

The President and his senior adviser strolled through the College garden until they were out of sight of their protectors. Davison sat down on a stone bench by the pond, his thick wool coat wrapped about him. Caldwell sat beside him.

'This is very difficult to explain.' The President gazed across the frozen pond. For a single moment they both felt the stillness and serenity of the place. 'Jack, it's possible those cabinet papers were leaked to the Russians via me.'

There was a long silence. Then Davison sighed. 'Ingela and I had a sexual relationship. If she was a spy she could have gotten access to cabinet papers I left in my rooms. She was unhappy about our recent parting, but I'd never have believed she'd betray me or her adopted country. She killed herself before I could talk to her.' He paused then continued, his voice racked with despair: 'Folly is a gift given to us equally by the Gods, Jack. If I could change the past, I would. But I can't.'

So that appeared to be it. Betrayal by someone very close to the President. Just as the media suspected.

'I think that the package everyone's looking for contains letters I wrote to Ingela,' the President confided. 'They are intimate. You see, I trusted her completely.' In his mind's eye Davison saw himself walking over the ice in the pond before them, great cracks appearing beneath his feet.

Caldwell heard the words of the President but said nothing. He was already aware of all that Davison had told him. 'Who do you think has the letters?' he asked.

'Either the Russians or people in Washington. Whichever way, I think it is over,' said the President sadly. 'There's nothing more to be done. The letters will seal my fate if they are ever published. Congress won't forgive an affair with a spy.'

Caldwell nodded.

'Do you think the Master has the answers now?' said the President.

Caldwell looked at him, then up at the still sky.

Symes, the elderly manservant, knocked discreetly on the study door then passed within. In a corner by the window was a large desk illuminated by an antique table lamp. On it many papers were spread out. Symes knew from a glance that the Master had worked throughout the night. He frowned. He had long ceased to be amazed at the extraordinary ability of the man to digest and assimilate information in a multitude of languages. The Master was getting older, however. He could not continue to work at such a pace. Symes brought yet more papers, this time from the Indian Government about the worsening situation in Kashmir. More papers, more problems, more urgent requests for meetings from world leaders. What if the Master were no longer to be there – who would take his place? Who would hold the ring and advise the leaders of nations in the cause of peace?

'Master, the President of the United States has arrived.'

The Master looked up from his desk and nodded. He was a tall, well-built man with slate-grey eyes and hair that was turning white. However, it was his face rather than his physical presence that drew attention. A large forehead, firm cheekbones and an aquiline nose, coupled with an imperturbable expression, gave him a presence and definition that commanded attention. It was a face that would not have been out of place in the Renaissance, that of the ruler of an Italian state or one of the Medici. A face that resonated a knowledge of power and its exercise.

Symes continued 'The Fellows' Banquet will be at eight o'clock this evening.' He saw the Master glance at the documents which Symes had brought him and place them to one side. Symes waited. He knew that his next piece of news would surprise even the head of the College.

'Master, there is a further meeting today. The Senior Arbitrator would like to speak with you urgently. He also asked that no one else be informed of this.'

The Master raised his eyes from his work. It seemed to Symes that his expression bore a look of sadness, perhaps a realisation that something was coming to an end.

'Symes?'

'The rules of the College permit the Senior Arbitrator to request such a meeting on special occasions,' continued Symes. 'This has not occurred previously during my time at the College. However, it would seem . . .' His voice trailed off somewhat nervously. He felt as if he had betrayed the Master by not warning him of this demand earlier. Yet the Senior Arbitrator's words had been both specific and peremptory.

The Master said in a neutral tone, 'Please tell the Senior Arbitrator that his request is granted. The meeting will be in my rooms immediately after the Fellows' Banquet.'

President Davison and Jack Caldwell sat in a large drawing room in the second courtyard. It was light and airy. The decoration was Louis XIV, all gilt and gold, with large paintings and fine antiques. Visitors to the College were invariably surprised by its rich interior, having witnessed the castle's foreboding appearance and the spartan landscape of the island. A fire burnt fiercely in the grate. It seemed unnecessary since the room was already warm. A door opened.

'Mr President.'

President Davison shook hands with the Master for the first time. He noted that the handshake was strong and firm. So this was the guardian of many secrets.

The Master turned to the other visitor. 'Mr Caldwell, we've met before.' The voice was mellifluous.

Caldwell glanced towards the President.

'Thanks, Jack,' said Davison. 'You can go now. I'll catch up with you outside.'

The Master and the President sat down. Symes poured coffee and departed. President Davison contemplated his companion, a quarter of a century older than he. The Master's visage was lined and his face had a patient and unruffled air about it, as if disinterested and remote from the outside world. Yet President Davison had met all manner of men over the course of his political career and he knew that appearances could be deceptive. The most distant of men were often the most self-interested. Why should the Master be any different? And what advice could he really give him? None, he imagined. He wouldn't, he couldn't, know enough. Almost certainly it had been a wasted journey. The President decided to adopt the same manner he employed with his cabinet, firm but brusque. What the hell, this man was only another adviser, a kind of civil servant, though there was no payment for the advice.

'You've read the background paper Jack sent you on the leak of the cabinet documents?' Davison asked.

'Yes,' said the Master. 'I've also talked with President Barchov.'

'He won't return my calls.'

'The Russian premier is very much his own man,' commented the Master. He glanced out of the window for a moment, then back to the President. 'I believe that part of your problem is resolved.'

'Really?' Davison was surprised at the authority with which the Master spoke.

'Yes,' said the Master. 'As you already know, President Barchov has the blueprints of US nuclear launch sites in Turkey and Japan. He plans to make an announcement about them today.'

So it was the Russians that were going to bring him down. Davison had been right after all.

'To help you,' continued the Master.

The President stared at the Master, utterly taken aback. Finally, he said in an amazed voice 'But why should Barchov want to help me?'

'Because the cabinet papers were not leaked by a Russian spy,' said the Master simply. 'They were released by people in your own administration as part of a plan to remove you from office.'

Davison said nothing. Then, 'Who?'

'President Barchov tells me that their secret service received the documents from a US Embassy official stationed in Paris.' The Master mentioned a name, not Dan Pearlman. 'It is clear, though, that the papers originated from people within your own cabinet.'

'Who?' The President's voice was dry and husky.

The Master wrote down two names. President Davison read what he had written and drew in his breath sharply. 'My God,' he said, almost in a whisper. 'Have you proof?'

The Master nodded and continued, 'President Barchov sent this for you to read.' He passed some documents to Davison. 'I have translated them for you since it is best if these documents remain here. As you can see, it was a well-planned operation. We have most of the names. There are still some further details to check. You will be sent additional information tonight to confirm them. I would recommend that you act quickly, Mr President. This matter is very serious and there are powerful interests in the United States and Russia who are against you.'

'Is Caldwell trustworthy or with them?'

The Master observed him keenly. 'He won't betray you.'

'And Olsen, the CIA chief?'

'Likewise. I suggest you replace your bodyguards as soon as possible on your return to Washington.'

'What did these people intend?'

'To have you resign the Presidency. Two weeks later you would have perished in an air crash.' The words were stark in their simplicity and devastating in their effect.

The conversation was utterly different from what Davison had anticipated. Now he knew what Caldwell meant about the Master. For here was no adviser, no official. Here was a man who spoke like an oracle, the voice quiet and yet compelling, the tone one of absolute assurance, the face serene and untroubled. Here was a man telling the President of the United States what had really happened and what would happen. Was it true? In silence Davison read the papers and the translation of the hand-written note from the Russian President. As he did so he knew that the Master was telling the truth and this would soon become evident.

The terrible tension and personal fear that had been with him over the last few days began to dissipate. The truth was not what he thought it was. Ingela had not betrayed him after all. He sat back in his chair to listen to the counsellor, spellbound, as if in the presence of a wise old friend.

'You'll be wondering why President Barchov should want to help you,' continued the Master smoothly. 'He believes that nothing would be gained from allowing you to be removed from office. If you fall, the political situation in the United States will become very unstable. Ultimately, this will be of no benefit to the Russian Government nor to any other government for that matter. It seems that the conspirators' intention was to force a transfer of power in Russia in the future as well.'

The Master paused, allowing the gravity of his words to sink in. Then he said, 'As a result of his own concerns, President Barchov wants to inform you of his plans in advance. In one hour's time he will hold a surprise press conference in Moscow. In it, he will officially invite you to Russia for a summit meeting to discuss a further reduction in nuclear weapons. He will also indicate that he believes the leaked cabinet papers are part of a plot to damage US-Russian relations and that they are of no real worth. Finally, he will publicly identify the US official in Paris who passed on the documents. For your part he expects you to act decisively. Here is a translated text of his speech.'

Davison nodded grimly and then scanned the proffered paper. A flicker of the great grin emerged.

'Your handiwork, Master?'

The Master made a dismissive movement with his hand 'Perhaps a word or two. If you announce a summit and visit Russia within the next few weeks it will enable Barchov to isolate those more hawkish members of his cabinet who are strongly in favour of increased expenditure on nuclear weaponry and will use the stolen cabinet papers to support their case. President Barchov wants both his country and yours to win, but not the militarists in his cabinet nor the traitors in yours. You see, Mr President, these two people are part of a powerful association of interests in the US and Russia. They've been receiving kickbacks for some time from military contracts, particularly those relating to nuclear weaponry. They wanted you replaced since they feared you would find out about this matter. So they decided on a pre-emptive strike.'

'They were going to do this for money?'

'Partly. Knowing the date of your death would enable them to make huge profits on the international stock markets. What they ultimately wanted was power. The power of the US Presidency.'

It seemed to Davison as if victory could be snatched from the very jaws of defeat. Almost.

He pondered on this. The Master's advice was like no other he had received before and it cut to the heart of the matter. Where was the catch, though? What favour did the Master want? Abruptly, the President asked 'Is this being done to weaken the United States in some way? Are you helping Barchov? '

The Master's eyes showed quiet amusement rather than anger or an absence of truth. 'I am on no one's side, Mr President. I am simply trying to achieve an outcome that enhances peace. The College only gives advice. Whether you follow it is for you to decide.'

Davison ran his hand across his chin. Even if he trusted Barchov to keep his word a solution was still impossible for other reasons.

'You seem troubled,' said the Master. He placed his coffee back on the tray. 'Personally troubled.'

President Davison frowned. He may as well discuss it with the Master now. The world would soon learn of it when the letters were published. 'Ingela Pearlman sent a package of letters to someone. Do you know whom?'

'Yes,' said the Master.

Davison looked at him. He could scarcely breathe.

'She sent it to me,' said the Master, 'because she trusted no one else. She told me she was being blackmailed by the same people in Washington who are seeking to have you removed from office. With the package she enclosed a note. She told me the letters were from a person with whom she'd once had an intimate relationship. She could not bear to destroy them but she knew that, on her death, all her belongings would be searched. So, she sent the letters to me. She asked me to decide what to do with them.'

There was silence. Then President Davison said in a hollow voice. 'What will you do?'

The Master motioned towards the fire. Only now, on a table close by, did the President notice there was a package.

'Mr President,' said the Master dispassionately, 'I have not read these letters and I am quite sure none went to the Russians. Nor, in the current circumstances, do I see how their disclosure will assist in the cause of peace or in the political stability of your country.' The Master rose from his chair. 'I believe these letters should be returned to the person who sent them to her. I think that's what Ingela Pearlman really would have wanted. Perhaps, you may be able to assist?' He paused. 'I'll leave you to decide on this.'

There was silence. Davison knew he had been wrong about the Master. If anyone knew about the nature of power and its wielding it was this man.

The Master said, 'You must excuse me. The Fellows' Banquet is taking place tonight and I must attend it. Perhaps you might like to stay here for a few moments to gather your thoughts. By the fire.' He walked towards the door.

'Master?' The tall and slightly stooped figure turned.

'If I can ever help you,' said President Davison, 'you have only to ask.'

The Master replied gently. 'Thank you. Help is the basis of all advice.'

* * *

The presidential motorcade swept out of the College. In his car Davison and his faithful aide were listening to the news, beamed in by satellite. President Barchov had just spoken. The Russian bear was as forthright as usual. True, they had received some US cabinet papers with details of nuclear secrets but they knew it was disinformation, a fake sent by a disaffected employee to sour US-Russian relations. Some Russian officials were also involved. They would be dealt with. There was no crisis. However, it was time for another summit on arms reduction. He invited President Davison to Russia for talks and to sample Russian hospitality and good vodka. It was the age of co-operation.

President Davison switched off the satellite link.

'What did you make of the Master?' asked Jack Caldwell.

The motorcade entered the forest. Staring out of the window, Davison thought of the letters he'd placed on the fire. He understood now why the fire had been lit. The Master had already foreseen the outcome before he had walked into the room to meet the President. And had Davison really gone to see the Master? Or had the Master arranged for the President to visit him, to solve a problem that Davison could not? He stole a glance at his companion. Jack would never tell him if he was a Fellow, of course.

'What was it you said about him?'

Caldwell frowned. 'I'd heard it said that he was rather like the Oracle. You always depart from his presence wiser than when you came.'

President Davison gave his great grin. He was back on form; and going back home to his wife and kids.

'Jack, I think you deserve a Christmas present for that,' he said.

Other people received presents that Christmas. They came early. On Christmas Eve, the National Security Adviser, Paul Faucher, was fired for leaking cabinet secrets and receiving kickbacks. Before a full inquiry could be started Faucher committed suicide.

Two weeks later the nation was saddened to learn that Joe Buchanan, the Vice President, was to retire from office on the grounds of ill health. It seemed his heart was somewhat dicky. Poor old Joe, said the media. He had been under such stress recently – what with standing loyally by his President and then discovering that his friend, the National Security Adviser, was a crook.

With the departure of the Vice President, the rumours about Ingela Pearlman and the President soon died down. In fact, the cognoscenti among the media were soon saying that she'd been having an affair with Paul Faucher and *not* the President. Trust them to know.

As for Davison he went on to become one of the great US presidents of the twenty-first century.

With his wife by his side.

THE COLLEGE

CHAPTER THREE

The best rulers are those about whom people know nothing but for their existence.

Lao Zi

THE ISLAND OF TIRAH, OR the Land of Wisdom, was located in splendid isolation more than one hundred kilometres off the west coast of Scotland. A small dot set in the Atlantic, it measured no more than twenty kilometres in length and six in breadth. Possessing no indigenous population and having only one bay, it was insignificant in all of its features bar one, the presence of the College.

This isolation and insignificance of Tirah had long since prevailed. For the island had generally been overlooked while Celts and Vikings ravaged the coasts of Scotland for more than a thousand years, fighting their scattered conflicts and gaining little despite the bloodshed. It was not until the eighth century that a small castle was established on the island as part of the domain of an ambitious laird, the Lord of the Isles, who held sway over most of the other islands off the Scottish coast. It was soon abandoned, his successors concluding that any marauders were most welcome to this barren outpost. The centuries passed and the island, together with its two mountains and the large loch near its centre, remained undisturbed apart from the visits of gannets and other sea birds who stopped off on their way to and from Iceland. Successive lords only dimly remembered that the island belonged to them and none ventured there.

Then, in 1165, Margaret of Beauvais married Donald, Lord of the Isles. They had a son, James. It was a period of great factionalism and slaughter in Scotland and Donald was soon killed in battle, leaving a grieving widow and a young child. By the time James came of age the fighting had moved elsewhere and he went on a crusade to free a land so saturated with blood that it was difficult to call it holy. Outside Jerusalem, James was cut down in battle. Lying alone in a lazaret for the dying, his wounds suppurating and his fighting spirit broken, James decided that he would do something for God for once, instead of asking God to do everything for him. He vowed that, should he ever see the rugged coast of Scotland again, he would cede one of his islands so that there could be founded on it a College of 'learned people' whose sole task it would be to

advise the leaders of all nations in the cause of peace.

By the grace of God, James, Lord of the Isles survived and he returned to his native country from the Holy Land. When his own son came of age James gave up his title and for the remaining years of his life he dedicated himself to developing the castle on Tirah. There, on an icy day in December 1217, the College was established under his Mastership with only twenty disciples. Few thought that it would survive the death of its founder. However, fate, or perhaps God, played a hand. For when James died, recognised by all as a man of saintly disposition, the great nobles of Scotland gathered at his funeral. In a rare moment of solidarity these fearsome fighters and rough-hewn men swore on the Celtic cross in the churchyard of Iona that they, their kinfolk and their clans would ensure that the 'vow' of James was upheld 'in the name of Scotland and of peace.' So are great acts performed through simple faith.

Large sums were raised and this tribute, which was never sought but was freely given for the love of another man and his works, spread among a Scottish population that had always remained free and independent in spirit although not in power.

The fame of the College passed abroad with the Scottish migration. Over the centuries money to fulfil the 'vow' soon became a standard clause in the wills of the rich and the poor of many nations – of people who would never set foot on the shores of Tirah but who kept faith that its Master would guide their leaders in the paths of wisdom and of peace.

James had stipulated in the founding statute that the Fellows should never number more than eighty persons, that they be blessed with great gifts and that they be ruled by a Master. All these tenets were strictly adhered to. Also, that of *secrecy*. For James had required that all that went on in the College should be kept secret, as should the advice that the College gave. He felt that if the College were to show off its talents to the outside world it would soon become proud and arrogant and the Fellows would compete to outdo each other. As a result, down the centuries the members of the College never disclosed their affiliation, though in the case of some outstandingly gifted individuals like Joachim di Fiore, Roger Bacon, Jane Gascon, Duns Scotus, Pierre Rochelle, Isaac Newton, Athanasius Kircher and Robert Boyle, it was manifest to all and sundry that they had belonged to the order and probably had also held the Mastership in their time.

In memory of the founder a Fellows' Banquet was held in late December every year, an event that had been observed since the establishment of the College. It was the one occasion when all the Fellows assembled, if possible, at the bidding of the Master since they generally did not reside within the College during the course of the year, though they had rooms to which they could return whenever they desired.

Thus, the College continued throughout the centuries, steadily growing in influence and power, but ever shy of revealing its own greatness.

After his meeting with the President of the United States the Master returned to the third courtyard and to the Master's Lodge. He did so by means of an underground tunnel to which only he had access. Ascending a long flight of marble steps to the upper floor of the Lodge he began to dress for dinner. Outside, the chapel bell tolled for the Banquet.

In the Great Hall of the College a fire burnt fiercely in the grate, lighting up the stained-glass windows, the delicate wood carvings and the medieval wall paintings. Long trestle tables, sawn from wood cut down at the dawn of the Renaissance, bore the heavy weight of silver settings and flagons of wine stood on side tables ready to be replenished the moment their contents had been drained. Little had changed in the hall since its establishment and its traditions continued down the centuries. Here was the heart of the College and a visible reminder of the antiquity of the foundation, stretching back to the medieval ages.

The Hall began to fill up. Within a few minutes the Fellows sat in their allotted seats, their black gowns wrapped about them. There were a few absentees, people like Jack Caldwell whose presence at the feast would have alerted the US President to his true role. Then there was silence. It was not until the clock chimed the final stroke of eight that the voice of Symes rang out.

'All rise for the Master.'

The commanding figure passed into the hall, his golden gown swaying slightly as he walked. All eyes turned to him, the living embodiment of the institution to which their lives were dedicated.

'The Fellows' Banquet will commence.'

The annual dinner was an opportunity for the Fellows to discuss among themselves the nature of the work on which they had been engaged. In that way they learnt a little more of the huge spider's web of information and contacts that the College had spun over the centuries in its endless interactions with the leaders of nations in the world outside. Since they remained Fellows for life, over the years the labyrinthine structure of the College's secret activities gradually became more apparent to them and they appreciated its true greatness, particularly if they were appointed by the Master to become one of the inner circle of the College, one of the Arbitrators. For a clear perception of the College and what it stood for was like a vision, at first seen through a glass, darkly, then in great light.

Although much was discussed at the Fellows' Banquet, by tradition, of the labours of the Master no mention was made even within the confines of the College. The Fellows could only guess at the extent of his influence, safe only in the knowledge that it effortlessly eclipsed their own.

'Tanya!'

Sitting at High Table with the five Arbitrators, the Master heard the brief shout above the din in the body of the hall. He looked up. He noticed that one of the Fellows, Tanya, was laughing merrily. She blew a kiss to someone at another table. That would be Sebastien Defrage. They seemed very much in love.

The Master began to seek out the other three Fellows to whom he needed to talk. It was difficult to miss Rex Boone, his massive bulk rising up from one of the benches like the prow of a ship, as he argued some point of nuclear physics, gesticulating wildly. Then there was Andrew Brandon, sitting at a table near the back of the hall, chatting with an earnest-looking woman who was an expert on space exploration. Poor Brandon, he had never recovered his happiness after the death of his wife. Finally, the Master's eye caught the slim figure of Ivan Radic at a table not far from his own, sitting with other Fellows involved in secret service activities. The Master had worked with Ivan to determine the truth behind the conspiracy to topple President Davison. It had been an impressive performance on Ivan's part. His contacts with the Russian intelligence services had been very helpful. Here was a man likely to achieve great things.

'The first speech will be given by the second Arbitrator.'

There was silence as the man immediately to the Master's right at the High Table began to address the gathering. This time the Master did not listen. His thoughts, for once, were elsewhere. What would James, Lord of the Isles make of it all, if he could return? Nearly eight hundred years had passed since he had established the foundation and, throughout the centuries, the College had tried to continue his noble aspirations.

The Master looked at the Fellows assembled before him. They were not academics; these people were quite different. Although they were gifted and had achieved high honours from the universities of their home countries, they had sworn to dedicate their lives to an institution for which they worked in secret and which would never publicly acknowledge their contribution; this in addition to undertaking onerous and demanding employment in the world outside.

'Master.' Symes was at his elbow. He muttered discreetly. 'I have a message. The President of the United States will shortly announce that he will fly to Russia next week for arms talks. He wanted you to know in advance.'

The Master nodded, then his train of thought continued. The College would have to change in the future. The threats they faced in this new century were unlike those of any other. With a global concentration of power in fewer and fewer hands the College remained one of the last bastions to provide unbiased advice. However, the pressure from the outside world to break, and destroy, this sanctuary of wisdom was becoming ever greater. To withstand the onslaught would require a Master with great wisdom and skills. An individual who understood power, its true essence and its fiendish subtlety.

Each of the people in this Hall wielded great power in the world. A hidden power. It was even more so in the case of the Arbitrators and himself, as the supreme authority in the College. The Master watched the Fellows as they observed the speaker and then him. He knew their thoughts. They desired to stand in his place, to be at the apex of it all, to see the innermost secrets of mankind spread out before them as if on a mountain top. Their desire for such influence was understandable. Yet, in their quest for the greatest of power, people would do the most terrible things even as they pursued it. The Master knew this; he himself had experienced it. Yet, how could he tell the Fellows of this, and of an outcome which he had already foreseen?

The Master directed his eyes around the Hall, at the faithful Symes and the other retainers who tended the College so well, just as their forefathers had done, then at the Fellows and the Arbitrators. Could he leave all this? It was now that this institution most needed his help. In these critical years ahead, when the College would have to fight for its own survival. To give up his power now could be disastrous. Yet the decision was not his. It belonged to another.

In the Great Hall there was silence. Then Symes announced: 'The Master will give the closing address.'

The Master rose to speak.

After the Master had delivered his speech the Banquet was over, though many of the Fellows and Arbitrators continued to sit and talk. Symes led the Senior Arbitrator through the third courtyard, to the Master's Lodge, and up to one of the drawing rooms on the second floor. The Arbitrator sat at a long polished table and waited. His speech was prepared.

He glanced about him. On the walls hung portraits of Masters of the foundation down the centuries. Gleaming silver lay on a dresser and rare antiques were set out on side tables. On one he noticed a beautiful Chinese puzzle box.

The Master entered the drawing room and drew out a chair opposite him. His face had changed little over the thirty-five years that the Arbitrator had known him. Despite being in his late sixties the strong features remained and the Master's eyes were as attentive and alert as ever, a window on the very remarkable intelligence that lay behind.

The Master waited in silence. Aware of the long history of the College he knew what the Arbitrator was going to say was in accordance with a formula that had been used before. What the Arbitrator said did not take long and the Master made no remark throughout.

When he had finished his speech the Arbitrator rose to go. At the door of the drawing room he stopped.

'We await your decision, Master. It must be given within the next three days.'

The Arbitrator walked down the panelled corridor. He

wondered whether he would ever see the Master again. He had wanted to spend time with him, to discuss the past and to savour the memories of so many years. However, there was no time. One crisis gave way to another and he knew that the Master was indispensable. Almost.

Meanwhile, the Master sat quietly as he listened to the departing footsteps, his mind turned towards the next labour of Hercules presented to him. This time it was not a problem from the world outside. No beleaguered president would call at his door, no ruler of a nation at war. This concerned the College itself. His head bowed in weariness, the Master reflected on the words of the Senior Arbitrator. The Mastership Game had begun.

The ultimate game of power.

THE PLAYERS

CHAPTER FOUR

Human appetites are insatiable, for by nature we are so constituted that there is nothing we cannot long for, but by fortune we are such that of these things we can attain but few.

Machiavelli, *The Discourses*

December. The College.

REX BOONE WAS PLEASED, MIGHTILY pleased. The Master wanted to see him. He passed down the winding lane to the boathouse located a couple of kilometres from the College, breathing in great scoops of early morning air. It was good to be noticed. Not that there was much danger of missing Rex. A giant of a man, with the shoulders of an ox and the physique of an American football player, he was difficult to avoid. His agile bulk, coupled with close-cropped blond hair, a great slab of a face and a jawbone that brooked no opposition, made him the epitome of a sportsman. Rex was as impressive physically as he was intellectually. Even on the battlefields of Troy he would have been impressive.

'Jenkins, I'll row for an hour or so,' he bellowed to the stout figure of the boathouse keeper on the opposite bank, who waved back at him.

'Very well, Dr Boone. There's a lot of ice in the loch.'

Rex grinned contemptuously. Fuck the ice. Arriving at the waterside he eased his huge muscular frame into the small scull, brushing snowflakes from the boards. Of course, there would be patches of ice in the loch but nothing he couldn't handle. In fact, there was nothing Rex couldn't handle. Or so he believed. He flexed his massive arms and shoulders, toning them. Long had he wanted to be a Fellow of the College. That he had achieved two years ago. Then, out of the blue, yesterday, a few days after the Fellows' Banquet, he had received from Symes an invitation to dine with the Master. What an honour. He imagined it would be just the two of them. An interesting tête-à-tête. Perhaps, it was to discuss his latest text on nuclear physics. What next?

'I'm going up to Cairn Druar and back,' he shouted to the boathouse keeper.

The scull shot off from the bank. Above him the frost gripped the overhanging branches, defeating the warming rays of the sun as they weakly penetrated the clouds. On the mountains a great blanket of snow spread out like a shroud and in the loch itself there was the slow, sluggish movement of the icy water. Rex loved it. It was a quintessential part of the north of Scotland that he had always dreamt of. Rugged countryside, bitter winters, a harsh wilderness. And for him, rowing. The great sport of the individualist.

The scull headed for the centre of the loch. Rex glanced back at the boathouse. He was happy. He was a winner.

Tanya drew in her breath. She released it again in short, shallow, gasps as she felt him shudder and climax inside her. Pressed back against the pillows, she dug her fingernails hard into his buttocks while she felt her own body race and tremble. She closed her eyes and, for a few brief seconds, she let her body overwhelm her mind. For those seconds she felt beyond time, beyond cares, sheltered and protected in a warm blissfulness.

It was slowly and reluctantly, like a baby drawn from the womb, that she returned from the outerworld, back to her room at the College. Back to Sebastien. Back to reality with a lingering sense of happiness and well-being. She lay there, her mind gradually readjusting to the present. Fellows of the College had their uses, she reflected idly. At moments like this she could forgive Sebastien anything, despite having lived with him for over two years. Tanya grasped a sheaf of black hair and raised Sebastien's tired head from the pillow.

'Have you forgotten to tell me something?'

'I love you?'

'Try again'

'You were wonderful?'

'Again.' She tugged his hair. She liked what she saw before her: a handsome, expressive face, with dark brown eyes, a boyish look and a small scar to one side of his forehead. He would have done well in films, she thought, as the phantom lover. It was a pity he was so demanding in reality.

'It was the best sex ever.' His voice assumed a cruel tang.

'Again,' Tanya tugged harder at his hair.

Sebastien lay back on the pillows. 'Well, give me a clue.'

Tanya giggled and pushed him away from her, prodding his nose with a finger. 'Think, idiot.'

Sebastien peered at Tanya lazily. He said nothing. He was still half in a dream world. His eyes ran down the length of her body, caressing her nakedness and stroking its slim outline. He focused on one of her lush breasts pressed into the white satin sheet, the reddened nipple almost hidden.

'Sebastien?' Tanya raised his head again. His mocking eyes met hers. 'You *have* forgotten to tell me something, haven't you?'

'Have I?'

He stared at Tanya. Long dark hair, a rounded Italianate face with the slight tint of an olive complexion, a full mouth and firm cheeks. His lover was thirty years old and at the peak of her physical attractiveness. Experienced, mature and sensual. Sebastien felt the warmth of her personality and her love for him.

'You did receive an invitation from the Master?'

'What invitation?' Pause.

'Sebastien, you didn't? Really?'

'No.' He conveyed just the right tone of puzzlement and annoyance.

Her cheeks flushed. 'Oh, Sebastien, I'm sorry. I didn't mean to tease.'

Sebastien had her. He turned away. He loved her room, the modern works of art splashed with warm colours and rich tones. He knew that, if he pressed the bedside switch, the curtains would swing back to reveal the stark beauty of the mountainside of Mullach Mor.

'Well, let me guess,' said Sebastien, casting his eyes back to the beauty before him, his voice disappointed and faintly sardonic. 'You received an invitation to dine with the Master and you never told me.'

Tanya hesitated. As usual, Sebastien had guessed right. 'Sebastien, I'm sorry. I thought you'd also received one and were teasing me. Honest.' She touched his firm and muscular body, stroking it with her fingertips.

'It doesn't matter.' Sebastien looked at her with a subtle blend of hurt and betrayal. He buried his head back in the pillow.

'Sebastien, I said I'm sorry,' replied Tanya, somewhat aggrieved. 'I didn't mean to tease. I thought the Master would have invited you as well.' There was no response. Damn, he would be disappointed, he was so impossibly competitive. How could she make it up to him? Sebastien soon found the answer between the bed sheets and her slender legs.

Following their second bout of lovemaking, Tanya went into her bathroom and stepped into the shower. Sebastien lay back on the pillows. He smiled.

'You bastard.'

She had found the Master's invitation to Sebastien. By the shampoo. Just where he had placed it.

It had been a hectic day at the studios. Completely hectic. Sabine Striker, the prima donna of German TV, swore. They'd be rolling the cameras in a couple of minutes. Yet her principal guest still hadn't arrived. His flight had been delayed. She tossed back her sleek golden hair and vowed this would be her last series with Deutsche Telefunken.

'Kristal!' she brushed aside the powderman and seized the series co-ordinator by the arm. 'Where is our guest?'

'I don't know, Sabine.'

'Well, find him. Don't just stand there. And for Christ's sake, where's the producer? Where's George?'

Sabine moved forward relentlessly. The cameramen and the flunkies parted before her like the sea. Her face was fixed in grim determination. She'd kill him. Why did TV producers always have affairs at the critical stages of filming? It was not the affairs she minded, but it was bloody impertinence of her ex-husband, George, to fixate on the tits of a Dutch TV researcher just when they were doing the final part of the series. Wait until she got hold of his favourite cameraman, the Pole with an unpronounceable name and a voice like ground glass. She'd teach George a thing or two. She sucked hard on her pen. About her was a frenzy of nervous activity.

'Sabine Striker?'

'I'm busy,' she snapped. She turned round. Instantly, her face and persona changed. She cooed.

'Oh, I am sorry. You must be Ivan Radic.' He was more lithe than she thought, otherwise he matched the photo: light brown hair, moustache, thin lips, well-defined face, almost angular. Sabine logged him in the filing system of her mind, just as she did everyone. Suddenly, she realised that she had missed one small feature, small, but for her, important. The narrow face and cold blue Slavonic eyes combined to provide a starkness in his features, a hint almost of cruelty. Sabine liked that. A splash of hardness and sharpness. Like thirties avant-garde furniture. Uncompromising.

'I'm sorry, Mr Radic.'

'Ivan.'

'Ivan.' Sabine slipped her hand round his waist and the expensive leather jacket as she guided him to the set. 'I'm sorry, filming starts in a couple of minutes and it's a live TV show. We haven't time for a practice run.'

'That's all right.'

Cool as a hitman. Sabine was impressed.

'OK, would you like to sit here? Let me tell you the format. I give a short intro and then we go straight into a discussion of the East European economies. On the video screen we'll have Professor Leo Tiederman from the Mannheimer Institute and Boris Juvenko from the Hungarian University of Technical and Economic Affairs.'

'No problem.'

The stagehands disappeared, the lights dimmed, the cameras rolled. Sabine sat in her chair, straightened her leather skirt, and delivered the pouting smile that had made her the most popular current affairs commentator in Germany.

'Good evening. This is the last programme in our series on the world's economies. Tonight, we'll be discussing the financial situation in Eastern Europe and the effect that the turbulence in the Far Eastern markets is having on it. First, a report on the state of unrest in Romania.'

Sabine glanced across at Ivan while the film clip was being shown. She'd forgotten to ask him how good his German was. She'd better start with Tiederman when the clip was finished. Within a few minutes she began to regret it. The learned professor bored on with the precision and monotony of a drill.

Abruptly, Sabine interjected. 'And, Mr Radic, from the Institute of Foreign Affairs. Do you agree with Professor Tiederman that we are likely to see continuing large balance of trade deficits in Bulgaria and the Czech Republic?'

There was a delay. Sabine's eyes widened in concern. Perhaps, he hardly spoke German at all. What a disaster! The viewers would scream. She would have to try to translate. She opened her mouth. Then Ivan spoke. It was in impeccable German without a trace of an accent. Quickly, he showed that he had a command of the subject matter. A command both comprehensive and hypnotic.

After a minute Sabine sat back to listen. Actually to listen, instead of just pretending to listen. She felt a frisson of pleasure. The audience would love it. Tiederman was not only a total bore, he was Germany's greatest economic guru and tonight a man years younger than he was coolly explaining the flaws in his analysis and taking him apart. It was just too delicious, too erotic. Sabine moved her split skirt a little, so that the viewers got a full view of her legs. They liked that and so did she. It kept up the ratings.

'Are you saying, Mr Radic,' Sabine said coyly, 'that you think Professor Tiederman has paid too much attention to macroeconomic factors when considering the Bulgarian economy, particularly its military sector?'

'I think so.' Ivan's voice was quiet and incisive while he dissected the professor's arguments, to conclude that there was little meat on the bones.

Sabine continued to listen. His was a soft voice, the tone soothing and so reasonable that it seemed almost churlish to disagree. Sabine shifted in her chair again and readjusted her skirt. She couldn't remember whether she'd put knickers on. Well, who cared? It was past ten. Besides, that was what the viewers really wanted to see.

'Thank you, Mr Radic.' Sabine almost kissed him in appreciation. She turned to the video monitor. 'Could I have the view of Mr Juvenko?'

The academic gave his opinion. Sabine had mentally switched off since she knew the rest of the programme would be a doddle. She looked across at Ivan, cool and self-possessed. A wicked thought entered her mind.

'Mr Radic, do you agree with Mr Juvenko?'

'I'm afraid not.'

'Oh really?' Sabine opened her eyes wide and flashed a smile 'Please do tell us why.'

Inside, she laughed while Ivan dismembered Juvenko's analysis as well. It was too good for words, the perfect ending to the series. One genius and two idiots who thought they were geniuses. Ivan was such a dish. She wondered what he was like in bed. Was he into leather and neoprene? She hoped so. She liked his jacket. It went well with her skirt.

'And, Mr Radic, what do you have to say about the fall in the Slovak coal output by twenty per cent over the last four months?' Dare she ask him out after the programme? Sabine glanced at the stubby figure of George behind the TV cameras, his hand perched on the backside of the Dutch girl. Damn him. Coquettishly, Sabine ran her fingers through her hair while she gave an adoring look at Ivan. It would get the gossip columnists speculating. She wanted a man; she wanted Ivan. And what Sabine wanted she invariably got.

The programme finished. They rose from the sofa and Sabine shook Ivan's hand. 'Thanks, you were marvellous.' She wondered whether he was a member of the College. Of course he would never tell her if he was.

'Wonderful!' The stubby figure of George magically appeared from across the studio floor. Tottering behind him was a leggy blonde. She had difficulty maintaining the equilibrium of her silicone breasts which were intended to progress in the same direction as her body yet swung alarmingly to the sides, like an excited compass needle at the pole. Ivan gave ground as she veered dangerously in his direction. 'The discussion was wonderful,' said George, thumping Ivan on the back. 'And you, Mr Radic were exceptional. We must have you on the programme again. Come out and celebrate with us.'

Ivan looked at Sabine and then at George. It was clear that the reference to 'us' was designed to exclude his ex-wife. Ivan's lipped curled momentarily before he gave a gracious smile. 'Another time, perhaps. I'm afraid I have to get back.'

Sabine guided him to a stage door and out into the frigid air. A limousine was waiting to take him to the airport. She shivered, her small nipples hard under the satin blouse. 'Thanks again,' she said, and giggled. 'You really were very good. Professor Tiederman will never forgive you.'

Ivan's eyes gleamed with humour. 'It was a pity. I just couldn't agree with him. He couldn't relate the analysis to the facts.'

The limousine arrived. Sabine caressed Ivan lightly on the arm as he got into it.

'Can't you stay?' The words came out in a rush.

'I'm sorry, I really do have to go.' Ivan smiled at her in an affectionate manner.

'Another time, perhaps?'

'I'd like that,' he said.

The car drew away from the kerbside. Ivan waved goodbye. It was a shame. Sabine was a lovely girl. He was glad she'd got rid of her husband. She deserved better. There were two things, however, that Sabine didn't know about Ivan. Two things that prevented him from having a deeper relationship with her that evening.

The first was that Ivan was homosexual.

The second was that he had an invitation to dine with the Master.

'We think they are holding them here, at the riverside, which makes it difficult. Flying in troops is not possible.'

The UN military official stubbed his finger at the map of the Democratic Republic of Congo, formerly Zaire, on the table. They were in a ruined hut, the grass thatch having fallen in. It was stiflingly hot and flies swarmed about them incessantly. Neither Andrew Brandon nor the official bothered to look down at the floor which was saturated with cakes of dried blood. From the smell they could tell that the corpses would only have been removed a day or so before.

'How many do you think they have?'

'About ten women and twenty children.' Captain Garnaud scratched his nose and inspected Andrew. Swatting the flies away from his face with his hand, he continued, 'They're probably in a bad state. The last lot they raped, both women and children. The rebels have promised to slit their throats if the Government doesn't release the local rebel commander, Musawena, by five. They'll carry it out, of course.'

'Of course.' Andrew regarded the captain. He was a thin Frenchman with a pinched face and a nervous tic at the side of his mouth. He smoked incessantly. Andrew noticed the faint tremor in his hands. He guessed the captain had been in the jungle of the Congo for no more than three months. Within six, Andrew reckoned, he'd either be dead or have gone mad. He made a note to recommend that he be recalled.

'What time do you make it now?'

Garnaud glanced at his watch. 'Four thirty. They have thirty minutes more to live. The Government will never release Musawena. Poor sods.' The Frenchman trod his Gitane on the ground and rolled up the map.

Andrew went to stand by the entrance to the hut. He looked outside. A few days before it had been a village clearing. Now there was nothing but the embers of buildings still smouldering in the bright sunlight and silence. A brooding silence as the trees and the wildlife bore witness to the massacre perpetrated by the rebels. Over two hundred people had once lived here, a small and bustling community. Today, the majority lay in makeshift graves. The murderers had waited in the warm afternoon sun until the children had come back from school along the jungle track. Then they'd gathered the village together in the church and systematically massacred them. Even a woman in the throes of giving birth to a child had been killed – a child born to die before she had breathed in the warm, sunlit air.

'I don't think there's anything we can do,' said Captain Garnaud. He had given up within minutes of arriving at the village clearing, as soon as the rebels who were holding the hostages had told him that, if the UN soldiers interfered, they'd be killed as well. Suicide was not his scene, and it wasn't his war.

'No,' said Andrew simply. 'I don't think there is. I'll go to the village. Alone.'

Captain Garnaud's face was a picture of disbelief as the words sunk in. He half laughed. 'You're mad,' he said. 'They'll kill you without a shadow of doubt. Look, I've seen this all before.' He spread out his hands in a sympathetic gesture. 'It's not your fault. They're going to die anyway.'

'Maybe,' Andrew shrugged, 'but I'll go.' He went to his Jeep and took out a satellite phone. Then, slinging a jacket over his shoulder, he walked into the jungle.

The captain watched him depart. He shook his head. Madman. Two hours previously he'd phoned the UN base in Kapanga. He'd told the administrator for the area that the rebels had refused to release their hostages or to talk with the UN any more. Instead, they had withdrawn to the river station and announced they would kill anyone who came near. In reply his colonel said they'd send help. Half an hour later a solitary man had arrived. Captain Garnaud had contemplated him as he got out of the military Jeep. Australian, medium height, sandy-haired, rugged complexion, about thirty-five, no trace of a military gait. Although Captain Garnaud had greeted Andrew with the impeccable good manners born of long experience working in a multinational organisation, privately he knew it was a joke. This man was a makeweight, a UN consultant, and the UN were simply trying to show that they'd done what they could as they prepared for the inevitable recriminations. He'd seen it all before in his time in Africa. Even with fifty legionnaires they wouldn't be able to free the hostages. Now Andrew wanted to go and get himself killed. Oh well, people did crazy things in the Congo.

After Andrew departed Captain Garnaud sat down on a bench in the centre of the former village to wait. His four men sat beside him. The captain scuffed his boots in the dirt and smoked another cigarette. They chatted among themselves to fill the time. He knew the rebels would kill Andrew and he wondered how. Would they split his head open with machete blows to the skull? Or just shoot him in the back? He guessed the former. They wouldn't waste bullets. Not these guys. Fifteen minutes to go.

Twenty minutes later Andrew appeared. Behind him walked eight women and many children. Andrew led one of them, a small boy, by the hand. They stopped at the bench.

'These are all the hostages,' said Andrew. 'Please take them to the displaced persons' camp in Kapanga. This boy's name is Obedi. He has a slight knife wound, so he'll need hospital attention. I'll be back in five days. I have to go now.' Andrew put the satellite phone in the back of the Jeep and drove away, leaving the astounded captain and his UN colleagues to watch his departure in a swirl of dust.

That night Captain Garnaud went into the displaced persons' camp at Kapanga for the second time. He knew it was pointless talking to the women. They would tell him nothing. So, he sat down by the hospital bed of the seven-year-old Obedi, who had a bandage swathed about his right arm. It was sweltering under the canvas and the only light came from the hurricane lamps. Obedi was awake on his makeshift bed, staring up at the ceiling. He seemed alert and glanced at the captain with mild interest.

Garnaud took his time before he started to talk to him. First, he produced some chocolate from his pocket and gave it to Obedi. Then he chatted with the nurse. Finally, he settled down by the bedside and got to the point. After some more chocolate Obedi described the situation matter-of-factly. The white man, Andrew, had walked down to the river station. He had sat on the ground in front of the rebels. He had made one phone call. Then another. Then another. After the third phone call the white man took the women and children with him.

'How interesting,' said Captain Garnaud. So who did the white man phone? More chocolate. Well, Obedi had been nearby and had overheard. He didn't know who the white man made the first phone call to. The second though was to the President of the Congo and the third was to the supreme leader of the rebels. After the third call the rebels let them all go. Which is why Obedi thought that telephones were such a great thing. They solved all problems.

'How very interesting,' said Captain Garnaud. So who had the white man made the first call to? Couldn't Obedi remember? No, he couldn't, not even with more chocolate. However, it was strange how the white man ended the first phone call. Obedi remembered that. He had said, 'Thank you, Master.'

* * *

Andrew stared out of the window. He listened to the drone of the aircraft's engines. Below him, the African jungle stretched out. Tomorrow, the scenery would be so different.

Tomorrow, he would dine with the Master.

THE MASTER

CHAPTER FIVE

Therefore, the sage does not fail in anything
since he does nothing;
Does not lose anything since he holds nothing
Therefore the sage's desire is to have no desire,
And he doesn't value rare goods.

Lao Zi

IN THE PORTER'S LODGE AT the College, Symes looked at the list of the Master's dinner guests. There were five Fellows: Rex Boone, Ivan Radic, Andrew Brandon, Sebastien Defrage and Tanya Johnson. Symes put down the list and consulted his watch. It was time. Eight o'clock. They would be waiting by the door in the second courtyard. Doubtless, they would also be intrigued at the prospect of dining with the Master in his own rooms, for he rarely ate with the junior Fellows and when he did the dinner was invariably a formal one in the reception building in the second courtyard. Those who had seen the third courtyard and the private rooms of the Master were few even among the Fellows, though this was accepted as an inevitable part of the secrecy that surrounded the College and its inhabitants.

Symes left the porter's lodge. He walked along the gravel path into the first courtyard then into the second. The place was silent, all the other Fellows having departed for Christmas after the banquet. The snow crunched under his feet and the stars were out in abundance. Symes could not remember a precedent for such a dinner in December once the College had broken for Christmas. Not in his time and he had become manservant to the Master when he took office, nearly thirty years before.

Tanya snuggled into Sebastien's shoulder as they stood waiting for Symes.

'I feel cold.'

She looked across at Rex. He said nothing, although she could see a smile play across his lips in the light from the lamppost. Tanya smiled back at him and wondered what he was thinking. She had met Rex at an international symposium on nuclear energy four years ago, before he had become a Fellow of the College. She was there in her official position as a consultant to the European Computer Union, advising on computer modelling for complex calculations, including simulated nuclear explosions. And Rex was there to give an address in his capacity as an adviser to the Global Forum for Nuclear Research. Tanya had listened to him and had found his speech the most lucid and intelligent of the entire symposium, delivered with a deft touch, a dry wit and a supreme confidence in his own abilities. However, it was not Rex's ability that had attracted Tanya. She had liked him then and there as he stood at the podium. Something about his sheer bulk and size that was both comforting and gentle. Like a huge sofa one could sink into and feel protected. Tanya had long wanted another human being to assuage the feeling of loneliness she had always felt since the acrimonious divorce of her parents when she was a young child. Someone to be there for her but for her to remain free. An eternal contradiction. Rex in the form of a huge sofa. She had not been wrong.

They had slept together that night and every night throughout the duration of the symposium. On the last day Tanya had left, not ready for the more permanent relationship which Rex had passionately sought to impose on her. She had told him early that last morning they were together, after they had got up and she had showered his seed from her. Rex had said he understood and had carried on packing, but she could recall the look of pain and disappointment on his face. Much as she liked Rex, Tanya did not want marriage or children at that stage. Besides, there were added complications. She had just been invited to join the College and she was cautious with everyone, careful to give little away about herself. It was an essential part of her nature, too deep to change. Her freedom came first.

So, their paths had diverged and Tanya had remained without a male companion until she met Sebastien when he joined the College over a year later. Rex came on the scene once more, as a new Fellow, a few months after that.

'What are you thinking about?' asked Sebastien.

'Nothing really,' said Tanya mechanically. She looked away from Rex. She had never told Sebastien about their relationship and Rex had promised not to do so either. Sebastien would not have understood and he would have become jealous. She had hoped that Rex and he could have become friends but they had too much in common. Both were fiercely competitive and their paths rarely crossed, even as Fellows of the College.

Sebastien looked across the courtyard. 'Here comes Symes.'

Tanya remained deep in thought. Or did their competitiveness lie in the fact that they both recognised Rex's attraction to her? She didn't know and it didn't really matter. She liked Rex and she'd always remain on good terms with him. But she loved Sebastien. Passion was one thing, love was quite another. She was sorry if Rex still loved her, since she couldn't reciprocate. Not now.

'More guests,' said Rex, in a rather disappointed voice. His private tête-à-tête with the Master was postponed.

Soon, the final guests arrived. Andrew and Ivan emerged in the second courtyard from out of the darkness. Ivan looked about him, curious. He knew them all. A strange combination of Fellows for a dinner party he thought. He wondered what the Master wanted to talk to them about. There was Rex, a physicist; Tanya, a computer expert; Sebastien, a specialist in financial markets; Andrew, a UN consultant on military matters; and his humble self, a spy masquerading as a political theorist and economist. All in their thirties and single, all with very different personalities. Then there was the Master. It was going to be interesting conversation that evening. Rex, of course, would talk loudest and Ivan himself would just observe.

'Please follow me.' Symes stepped forward into the light.

In the western corner of the second courtyard and at the very back of the garden there was a bower of laurel trees. Behind these lay the wall of the second courtyard. It was identical in all its features to the outer wall of the College. However, in between the trees and the wall, and scarcely visible to the naked eye, was a path that led to a sturdy oak door. Symes led the small group down the path, pressed an electronic combination to open the door, and beckoned them in.

None of them really knew what to expect, though others had spoken of the beauty and size of the third courtyard. They passed along an arcade of carved limestone until they stood at its mid-point. Before them lay the Master's Lodge – a magnificent Elizabethan building with its black exposed beams and heavy leaded windows. From its centre protruded a large bay window bearing the College coat of arms: a dove straddling crossed swords. In front of the Lodge was a box garden, its hedges no more than knee high. It was set out in the form of a maze. Enclosing the corners of the box garden were a number of cherry trees presently denuded of their branches and labouring under great quantities of snow. None of this would have been visible to the Fellows in the darkness but for the light thrown out by a series of cast-iron Japanese lanterns set into the wall of the cloister. They gave off a ghostly hue. The view was both mysterious and enchanting, like the domain of a wizard.

The Fellows had no opportunity to gaze further since Symes hurried down the path to the entrance doors. Any surprise the guests had at the outside of the Master's residence was soon to be beggared by the vista within. As they entered a panelled reception area a great span of marbled steps ascended before them. Furniture, tapestries and paintings of outstanding rarity and exquisiteness filled every available space. They stopped to stare. Symes noted this delay with anxiety.

'Please follow me or we will be late.'

He led them up the winding staircase without leaving them a minute to gaze at the magnificent paintings, jade figurines, porcelain and other works of art that greeted their ascent. At the top of the first flight of stairs they alighted on a spacious landing. Ivan noticed that the flight continued upwards to a second floor and he followed it with his eyes. However, his attention could be distracted no more. Symes ushered them across the landing and knocked discreetly on the casement doors. Then he beckoned them in.

They came face to face with the Master.

'There's something I'd like you to look at.'

Andrew's mind had wandered from the conversation as he relaxed in an armchair in the Master's sitting room, a glass of brandy in his hand. He was not drunk but his senses had been pleasantly dulled by the excellence of the meal, the vintage wines and the repartee at the dinner table. He felt content. At the same time the ambience of the evening had subtly heightened his perceptions. Narrowing his eyes so they became slightly out of focus he became conscious of the colours about him. The orange of the fire, the blue white of a Ming vase, the subtle green of a Fabergé glass orchid stem and the deep burnished brown of the mahogany panelling. His introspection brought with it a deep feeling of wellbeing and calm.

The more Andrew contemplated the matter the more he realised that his serenity emanated from the Master's domain. For this room had been laid out in accordance with the Master's personal wishes and not for show. As a result, it was not just the exquisiteness and rarity of the *objets d'art* that awoke Andrew's senses, it was the care with which they had been assembled, giving the clear impression of a detached and aesthetic mind in harmony with itself.

'Perhaps, you might be interested in this?'

The Master's voice startled him out of his reverie and Andrew immediately refocused on the group sitting around the fire.

From a side table the Master had taken a small box which he handed to Sebastien. Then he sat back in his chair, the grey eyes fixed, almost inquisitorially, on the younger man. Sebastien felt the same sensation he'd experienced many years before when he was an undergraduate about to take his first exam: trepidation mingled with an overweening confidence in his own abilities. He examined the object for some minutes. Tanya, who was beside him on the sofa, smiled encouragingly.

'I've seen one of these puzzle boxes before. In a museum, in Washington,' Sebastien began. 'I believe this is a Chinese lacquer box of the late seventeenth century. I say Chinese because of the characters on the lid and late seventeenth century since the face of the box contains a seal from the time of the great Emperor Kangxi.' He hesitated. 'Given its exquisiteness I suspect it was made by the mastercraftsman Chang. Probably one of the last he crafted since it was only in the final period of his life that he changed from painting city scenes to those of the countryside on lacquer boxes.'

There was silence in the room. Rex Boone looked across at Sebastien in admiration. Just what he would have said. A clever bastard. Handsome, quick-witted, and oh so ambitious, that was how Rex saw Sebastien. Always ready with a word, always so fluent and glib. Rex swivelled his gaze to Tanya and their eyes met, fleetingly. He knew he was still in love with her. How difficult a thing love was, he reflected. You could never quite get it out of your system. Still, he'd liven things up a bit. Hurriedly, he tried to recall what he'd read about Chang's puzzle boxes years before. Not much. So, employ a little bit of deception. That was the thing if you got really stuck. Never let on you don't know. It always fooled them, although he doubted it would this time. Not the Master.

'May I . . . ?' He leant across and took the antique in his massive hands. It was less than half the size of a paperback book.

'I think Sebastien's right.' He glanced at his colleague and imparted a generous smile, to reveal the full range of his strong white teeth. 'I also think much more can be said about this box.

It's a great piece of work. It's a Chinese puzzle box and a very rare one at that. Chang, for a limited number of clients'

'Mainly members of the Chinese imperial family.'

'Er, that's true,' said Rex, acknowledging Ivan's comment. Ivan was bound to be right. Besides, it was dangerous to contradict the person who would almost certainly have the greatest knowledge of this subject. Rex continued: 'Chang transformed ordinary jewel boxes into those that could only be opened by solving the puzzle contained in the painting on the lid. As can be seen, the sides of this box are made up of different layers of wood, each of which has indentations along its length. Small metal pins must be inserted into one or more of these indentations to open the box, since it operates by way of a lever mechanism inside. The key, though, to the number of pins and their precise location lies in the painting. It's virtually impossible to find the solution by trial and error alone, since the number of possible permutations is immense and the number of pins to be inserted unknown. The only other way is to smash the box, which was done by some of Chang's less intelligent clients to discover the jewel or other precious treasure hidden inside.'

'I believe Chang used to insert a jewel in these puzzle boxes in accordance with the relevant birth year of the reigning Chinese monarch,' said Tanya. 'A pearl for the first year, jade for the second et cetera.' She smiled at Rex affectionately.

'Oh, I wasn't aware of the fact.'

'Tanya's right,' said Sebastien, keen to emphasise Rex's lapse. 'May I see the box again?'

'Just hold on a minute,' said Rex, raising his hand in a peremptory fashion. There was a long silence while he focused on the painting, trying to decipher the puzzle on the lid. As he did so, his memory raced. Long ago he'd analysed Chang's Chinese puzzle boxes since he'd been intrigued whether they could be approached from a mathematical viewpoint. On that occasion, as now, he could find no solution. Not that he was surprised. It seemed clear that he was looking at the work of the greatest exponent of the art and one that was undoubtedly fashioned at the very height of his powers. He glanced across at the silver-haired figure in the hope of assistance, but the Master was staring intently into the fire, seemingly lost in thought. No one else was forthcoming.

Eventually, with a glum sense of defeat Rex passed the *objet d'art* to Ivan. Rex had failed. He felt the bitterness of being less able than he'd supposed. He vowed to remedy it somehow.

Ivan took the Chinese puzzle box and turned it over in his delicate hands. He caressed the lacquer and ran the tips of his fingers across the indentations. Then he inspected it closely through his rounded glasses.

'I have no doubt this box is by Chang. No one else could have fashioned such a beautiful work of art. This is the finest piece I have seen.'

'Yes, but what's the key to the puzzle?' said Sebastien. Hell, why did the Master want them to discuss this box? Surely, he knew all about it? What was the point of playing games with them?

'That's difficult,' said Ivan. 'The key lies in the painting on the lid. The scene is a pastoral one, of mountains with a river wending its way between them and eventually disgorging itself in the form of a waterfall. There are six mountains in all. The river winds behind four and then flows out between two others until it falls as a cascade. Small trees are located on the slopes of the mountains, some with three branches, others with five. Finally, there are Chinese characters written at the four corners of the box. They are in the hanzi script and symbolise the following: Death, Success, Life and Eternity. There are many mathematical possibilities inherent in this picture.'

'The mountain spaces could represent depth, the trees height and the branches width,' said Rex.

'Depth?' said Sebastien. 'Surely the mountains represent height?'

'They could do, but the spaces between the mountains are valleys and can represent depth,' said Tanya. 'You have to read into the picture more than meets the eye.'

Rex grinned at Tanya. Clever girl. That's why he loved her. A lateral thinker. Her best side.

'Quite so,' Ivan replied. 'Or, for our purposes, movements up, down and along the sides of the box. The Chinese characters also have numerical equivalents, Success being equated with the number six, Death with four, Life with three and Eternity with nine. The answer to these puzzle boxes is not just a mathematical formula; it's also a philosophical one.'

Tanya glanced at Ivan and took the box from him. He had a reputation for being a strange person, secretive and aloof, although there was no doubting his analytical genius. Why was he always so cold to her? Was it that he didn't like computer experts? Or women?

'The real difficulty,' said Tanya, 'is in determining their order. Look at the second tree with three branches. It is situated on the mountain slope between the first two mountains. Does it mean the first pin is to be placed two up, three along and one down? On what side, though? Above the tree is the Chinese character for Life which also has a numerical equivalent of three. Does this mean that the pin is to be placed on the third side of the box, going from the top in a clockwise direction?'

Tanya contemplated the Chinese puzzle but the answer eluded her. Eventually, she passed it on. 'What do you think, Andrew?'

After a few minutes studying the box Andrew said, 'Ivan has pointed out that the Chinese characters have a philosophical significance as well as a numerical one. I agree. The choice of such symbols was often dictated by the philosophical leanings of the maker of the box. In the cosmic order of things, as Chang saw them, perhaps Life came first. Success, the fulfilment of man in this world, comes next. Then Death, the termination of all earthly things, after that. Finally, Eternity. Thus, these four symbols, perhaps, represent the four sides of the box, Life at the top and the others in a clockwise direction. Yet, there is the difficulty. Did the maker believe in that order? Perhaps he believed that all things stem from Eternity, including Life and

Death, which states are eventually subsumed into the whole again after many cycles. If so, the cycle commences with Eternity, Life, Success then Death, which merges into Eternity again for another circle to commence, so that each time existence progresses towards a higher stage of fulfilment. To understand the order we need to understand the maker.'

They continued to analyse the box, each determined to prove to the Master their genius. At last, reluctantly, and not with a little anger, most of which they were able to conceal from the others, each admitted defeat. Each felt that he or she had undergone a test and failed to pass. Sebastien frowned and stared at the ceiling in frustration. The others continued to ponder the painting on the box lid while Rex, his massive frame dwarfing the armchair in which he was stretched out, gently tapped his heels on the floor, relieved that the others had also failed to solve what he could not. The Master sat motionless by the fire, deep in thought. Andrew glanced at him, the sage in the centre of the circle.

Ivan broke the silence. 'Well, Master. What is the secret?'

For a moment it seemed no answer would be forthcoming for the figure continued to gaze at the fire as if he hadn't heard. Then the Master looked up.

'I believe,' he began quietly, 'that puzzles may be equated with life itself. The key appears so simple yet the puzzle is usually only solved after enormous effort. Life, too, seems simple yet unforeseen difficulties and hazards trip us up on the way and make it fraught with confusion and despair. For the craftsman Chang it was, perhaps, the same. I have spent many hours considering this puzzle and the life of the man who fashioned this remarkable work of art. Still, I do not know the solution.'

His audience listened with astonishment. If the head of the greatest institute of learning in the world did not know the answer how could they?

The Master continued, carefully weighing his words: 'All problems have a solution. That I have always believed. When people declare there is no solution it simply means that they cannot see one. The limitation lies in themselves. Through the rigidity of their minds or the imperfection of their vision they are blind. **The solution itself is neither confused nor complex.** It is the beholder who brings confusion to the object beheld and, by failing to discard his or her desires and prejudices, the search is usually in vain. People who wish to find the solution and the path to it must first consider themselves and analyse their own thoughts. In that way they can reflect on the situation with the unclouded clarity of a mirror.

'What do we know of the maker of this box? Little. The life of the mastercraftsman Chang was shrouded in mystery. Certainly his origins were humble and the recognition of his great genius was slow to be appreciated. Indeed, he seems to have actively thwarted his fame, being content to live in obscurity. Although he was renowned for his artistry in making lacquered writing boxes, it was not until late middle age that he began to fashion his first puzzle box. When they finally appeared they were an enormous success among the Chinese literati of his day, not only on account of their extraordinary beauty but also for the ingenuity of the puzzle that lay within. The elite clamoured for them. Chang produced remarkably few, each more difficult than the last. Sadly, through loss and human destruction, fewer than ten still exist, most in museums.'

The Master stopped for a moment to reflect. He continued, 'After only a brief period of fame, Chang began to retire from the world – saddened, perhaps, by the greed and ambition surrounding him. Other accounts say that he was suffering from a mortal ailment. He hid himself away in a monastery determined to live out his last days in solitude. There was only one person who could bring him out of his mountain retreat and that person did. The Son of Heaven, the Emperor of China, the most powerful of rulers, Kangxi. He was captivated by Chang's lacquer boxes and he ordered a search to be made for the craftsman throughout the length and breadth of the land. The frail old man was brought to Beijing. There, in the Forbidden City, the Emperor ordered Chang to make for him one last puzzle box. The most beautiful and the most difficult of all.'

The Master sat forward and held up the Chinese box to the firelight.

'This is the box that Chang made.'

Tanya looked at the rapt faces of her companions while they sat with the Master, like disciples around a teacher. Were they looking at the box or at the Master for the solution?

The Master continued, 'You are probably wondering how this work came into my possession. Emperor Kangxi bequeathed it on his deathbed to a previous Master for having rendered assistance to him. So it came to me. When I say that I do not know the key to this Chinese puzzle, my words need some qualification. I believe that I know the answer. However, my belief is founded on the knowledge that, if I am right, I shall never be able to prove it. I shall try to explain. Throughout his life Chang depicted scenes from the lives of others. What might a man do when his own last days are fast approaching? What small reminder might he wish to leave behind as a token of his own earthly existence? Look closely at the painting, especially at the river. See how it commences at the top left-hand corner of the box, a small rivulet, growing in size as it approaches the first mountain. Then it's lost from view to emerge once more, greater in volume this time. It disappears again. Eventually, it streams out as a great torrent flowing between the largest mountains in the centre of the picture. What might a simple explanation be? Was not Chang depicting his own life? An obscure birth, an uncertain path to middle age, at last, the full flood of his brilliance? But where does the greatness lead? Nowhere. The waterfall just hangs there, suspended. At the bottom of the picture there is nothing. No spray, no rocks, no pool. Nothing.'

'Nothing,' said Ivan abruptly, 'that can't be the answer. The puzzle box must disclose some secret. It cannot be pointless.'

'I didn't say pointless,' said the Master, 'I believe that the secret to this box is one of personal perception. For me, this box discloses an inner beauty that we, as human beings, endlessly seek to represent in our life and our art. After all the complexity, simplicity. As with life, the beholder is convinced there is a secret to be disclosed, a puzzle to be solved. Perhaps, there is none. Whoever said there should be? It is *we* who assume that this box is a Chinese puzzle box. This supposition arises from our preconceived notions. We have failed to see the solution because our own perception is faulty. I believe the answer to this puzzle lies not inside the box, but in ourselves. For me this box and its beauty alone is sufficient and it contains no greater secret.'

'Yes, but if what you are saying is correct,' said Tanya, 'and this is not a puzzle box after all, it cannot be proved. It can only be proved by destroying it, to see what is inside.'

'That may be so,' said the Master. 'And in that way Chang fulfilled the Emperor's request to create the most difficult puzzle of all. **For to understand the meaning of the box, perhaps, is to understand ourselves and our own desires.**'

After the Master spoke the clock in the sitting room struck twice. No one had noticed the passage of time, so enthralled had they been by his words, and angry with themselves for failing to provide a simple and yet profound solution. They began to rise from their chairs, ready to depart. The Master did not seem disposed to move. Instead, his face assumed a deeper gravity.

'Although it may surprise you, I have not invited you here tonight to talk only of the Chinese puzzle box. To each his own quest.' He paused.

'I have invited you here tonight to offer you the Mastership.'

THE GAME

CHAPTER SIX

The security of a republic or of a kingdom, therefore, does not depend upon its ruler governing it prudently during his lifetime, but upon his so ordering it that, after his death, it may maintain itself in being.

Machiavelli, *The Discourses*

IT HAD BEEN AN EXTRAORDINARY evening and it promised to become more extraordinary still. Ivan listened to the words of the Master in astonishment. All thought of the Chinese puzzle fled from his mind. The offer of the Mastership. A position of unrivalled power. The greatest prize of all. Surely, it could not be? He drew forward in his chair, noting that the others had the same eager look of anticipation on their faces as he doubtless had on his own. The Master placed his hands together. With the fire flickering across his visage he seemed like a monk at prayer.

'At the Fellows' Banquet I said that the burdens of the Mastership are great. For the Master not only has obligations to the College, his primary duty is to the world beyond. He must advise without seeking to influence unduly. He must also be aware that any advice he gives may have a profound effect on his audience. This combination of power, and the need to apply it with restraint, is a terrible burden which becomes all the more wearisome as the years go by. There must come a time when the Mastership passes to another.'

He paused. The logs crackled in the fireplace. Rex Boone bent forward excitedly.

'Master, are you going to retire?'

The others looked at him. Ivan's lip curled slightly in amusement. For all his ability, Rex was just a little too keen. Tanya glanced at Sebastien. Surreptitiously, she squeezed his hand. He didn't look at her, his eyes fixed intently on the Master.

The Master answered, 'I would be grateful if you would let me finish.' He paused and then said, 'It is often thought that the Master elects his successor. However, this is so only in form, for there is a contest for the Mastership.'

There was an audible intake of breath.

'The most senior Fellows of the College, the Arbitrators, establish both the terms of the contest and those who participate in it. Over this the Master has no control. The contest is designed to test the capabilities of the participants to the full, since true worth will only manifest itself under the most trying of conditions. The Master must be fully conversant with the ways of the world, including the use and abuse of power. If that were not so the College, and all that it stands for, would long since have fallen into decay. Yet, if the world is permitted to intrude too much the streams of wisdom will become tainted and both the College and the Mastership will fail.' The Master sighed. 'It is a knife edge that must be walked and to do so requires all the skill and finesse that human ingenuity commands.'

The Master continued, 'By order of the Arbitrators each one of you has been nominated to undertake this contest for the Mastership. You have the freedom, though, to decline the nomination at this stage. Do any of you wish to do so?'

There was profound silence as those who sat around the fireside struggled with their ambition and their desire: The Mastership. To be the confidant of the leaders of all nations, the guardian of some of the most fascinating human secrets. What power. What would they not give for it?

Ivan spoke first. 'What is the nature of the contest?'

'It cannot be divulged until you have accepted the nomination,' said the Master.

'I see.' Ivan gave an enigmatic smile. He glanced at Andrew, a glimmer of comprehension in his eye. There was a slight cough. Everyone looked at Rex who was normally so talkative, waiting for him to say something. He remained silent, a brooding expression on his face, like a person who has heard bad news and is beginning to appreciate its significance. He stared into his brandy glass, swirling the contents around in the bottom. Then he took a large swig.

Sebastien said, 'When must we decide?'

'On New Year's Eve. We shall re-assemble here. By then you must decide.'

The conversation was at an end. Ivan rose to inspect an Assyrian tablet on a side table. The Master continued to sit in his chair by the fire, his visage expressing no emotion. The Fellows could not divine his thoughts.

'Master, I can't accept this.'

Rex's words exploded in the silence like a pistol shot. He shook his head angrily and stood up. His jaw was clenched. 'Are you saying we have to agree to take part in the contest before we are informed what it involves?'

'Yes. That is the procedure,' said the Master.

'That's crazy.'

Andrew asked, 'Who knows about this contest?'

'Only the Arbitrators and ourselves.'

Sebastien whistled under his breath.

Meanwhile, Rex had crossed the room to look out of the large bay window at the stars. His huge frame was hunched as though he was about to ward off an attack. He turned back to the assembled company.

'This is unacceptable. Madness. Don't you think so?' he scowled.

'Oh, I don't know,' said Ivan in a neutral tone. 'It seems quite a good idea. Darwin's principle of the survival of the fittest and all that.' He turned back to the Assyrian tablet; the Master had better antiquities than the British Museum. At the same time he was thinking furiously: The Mastership? What would a person not do to obtain it?

'Well, I ain't entering any contest without knowing more about it. No, sir,' said Rex. His drawl was insistent. 'Are you prepared to accept this? Andrew?'

Andrew shrugged in a noncommittal way. He still felt tired from his trip back from the Congo and he needed time to think. The whole evening had been momentous. Further, great decisions always involved the paths of good and evil, this one particularly so. What exactly would the contest entail?

'Tanya?'

'I don't know, Rex.' Why was he behaving like this? He was worried. Or did he just appear to be worried? Tanya watched his body movements. If so, why was he acting? Who was he trying to convince? The Master, or them? Rex focused on Tanya almost quizzically for a moment, then turned his eyes away. Was he trying to tell her something?

'Sebastien?'

'I'd calm down if I were you, Rex.' The tone was smug and condescending, exactly as Sebastien had intended it. Rex scowled at him, his physique silhouetted against the bay window like a malevolent presence.

'Until I receive an explanation of the contest I refuse to accept the nomination.' The tone was suspicious.

The Master observed him, not unkindly. Then he calmly replied, 'You have until New Year's Eve to decide. Now, goodnight.'

Symes led them down the marble stairs. The Master walked to the window. He watched them depart in the darkness as they followed the dim glow of Symes' lamp. He knew their minds would be focused on the same thought.

There could only be one Master.

The Master's dinner guests passed out of the third courtyard. Once more they stood by the pond, back in a place that was familiar to them. However, everything had been changed and they felt lost. Everything had been changed by the Master and by the third courtyard, and it had been changed irrevocably. It was as if they had been given a sudden insight into a world much more mysterious and more powerful than their own. Their little cosmos had been shattered and they were being offered their heart's desire at a time when they had least expected it.

Symes bade them goodnight, unaware of the momentous events that had occurred during the course of the evening though he noticed that they were surprisingly silent and subdued. The small group broke up.

Sebastien and Tanya began to walk back to Sebastien's room in the first courtyard. Her mind was in a whirl. It was as if a magician had cast a spell and suddenly offered her something so incomparably wonderful that it stirred the deepest wellsprings within her. To be at the centre of it all. With the Mastership and its access to world leaders, she could mould and influence the lives of huge numbers of people on the planet, secretly directing things from behind the screen. For good, of course; and to fulfil her own wishes. But at what cost?

Tanya knew that Sebastien would accept the nomination. Of that there was no doubt. He was the most ambitious person she knew, even among the ambitious. He had to win, it was an essential ingredient of his being. What about her? If Tanya had to choose between the greatest thing that she could ever wish for and her love for Sebastien, what came first? Would she compete against him? She half knew the answer but she dare not admit it, not even to herself.

'Tanya,' Sebastien stopped, 'is it OK if we don't sleep together tonight? I need time to be alone. To think about what has happened this evening. So much has occurred.'

'That's all right.' She felt disappointed but she understood. They kissed.

'Sebastien,' she said, 'I love you.' She meant it.

'I love you too,' he said.

Tanya watched Sebastien depart, swallowed up in the darkness. Had his reply been too automatic? Did he really mean it? Would he give the Mastership up for her? She stood in the courtyard, lost in thought.

'Sweet dreams.'

Tanya started, the deep voice was so near. She ran her hand through her hair. 'Oh yes, goodnight, Rex. Sleep well.'

Rex bent close to her, inhaling the scent of her tantalising perfume that reminded him of more passionate days. They kissed. Tanya watched him depart also. She felt both happy and disturbed. Happy, since her wildest dream might come true. Disturbed, by the words Rex had whispered as his mouth lightly brushed past her ear.

'Take care, Tanya. Things are not as they seem.'

Rex returned to his rooms, well pleased with himself. He chuckled. It was like a rowing competition, everyone out for themselves, and Rex already had got off to a head start. Yet, there was still something that puzzled him about the contest. He glanced at his watch. It was almost three in the morning and he needed some sleep. Tomorrow, he would make a phone call to the States. It would take a day or two to locate the material, but it was important information he needed before he made a final decision on the Mastership. It was too dangerous to phone from the island in case the College monitored the call. Rex made himself a cup of coffee and sat down by his giant computer screen to wait. For a fish to bite.

He thought of Tanya. He was worried about her. Should he be? She was capable of looking after herself. His mind idled. She was beautiful and talented, and he had always wanted her for his partner and wife. It seemed, though, that Sebastien would beat him to her. For a man like Rex, who was never accustomed to lose, that was a very galling thought; and it was all his own stupid fault. When they had met at the symposium and had slept together Rex had pushed things too far with Tanya. On their last night they had gone out to dinner. They had been so close. Tanya had told him of her childhood and her desire to remain independent. Rex had listened to her, captivated by her conversation, feeling content and in love. Then he'd wrecked it all. Suddenly, he had babbled on like a fool and talked of their living together, of marriage and of children. With the sheer force of his personality and his impulsiveness he had sought to overwhelm her with his love and desire. He began discussing a firm relationship when it had been clear she wanted only friendship at that stage and nothing more serious. It had been a bad error, like a mathematical equation that did not balance. And the following morning, after they had made love for the last time, she had delivered the death blow – kind but cruel.

In truth he had never got over it, for Rex still did not truly appreciate the fruitlessness of being in love with someone who did not love him. When he'd become a Fellow of the College, Tanya had already been going out with Sebastien. Rex's infrequent meetings with her at various conferences around the world thereafter had been friendly yet distant. In his heart of hearts, though, Rex had no doubt Tanya retained affectionate memories of him and that she would return to him one day – when Sebastien had deserted her for younger prey or when she grew tired of him. Besides, with the contest for the Mastership everything would change. For Tanya would be competing against Sebastien and in this game no holds would be barred. Friendship and love were invariably displaced by power. It was the way of the world. How well did she really know Sebastien anyway?

'Rex Boone.'

The e-mail message flashed up on his screen. The first fish had bitten. It was not Tanya.

'Essential we meet tomorrow to discuss something to our mutual benefit. On the mainland. Town of Erris. 7.30 p.m. Crossed Hearts Hotel. Ivan.'

The message faded from the screen. Rex sat back in his chair and pondered. So, Ivan did not want to meet at the College. He preferred the mainland. Very wise. Perhaps he also thought something was amiss. But then Rex could be wrong after all. He should not be too precipitate in passing judgement on the contest. Things could be simpler than he'd supposed.

Rex closed his sleepy eyes. Already, in his dreams, he was rowing down the loch to Cairn Druar and back. The others were rowing as well. However, he was far out ahead.

* * *

It was six o'clock in the morning. A thick fog rose from the mountains and began to dissipate in the light of dawn. Andrew stood on the bridge of the ferry as it made its first journey of the day from Tirah to the mainland. He had hoped to catch a helicopter, which would have made the trip in forty minutes. However, they were grounded owing to the fog, a not uncommon occurrence this early in the morning. It was biting cold and he shuddered. He looked back towards the island.

Only a few hours before he had been flying from the Congo for dinner with the Master and soon he must return to Africa to complete his work there, whatever happened. However, those few brief hours with the Master had changed so much. Would he take part in the contest?

He gazed at the wash made by the vessel's propellers and at the island's only port, just visible in the distance. Behind it, ranks of fir trees swept up the steep hillside and covered the flanks of the two mountains almost to their summits. Hidden away in the centre of the island lay the College. It contained so much mystery and Andrew was sure it contained even more than had been disclosed to them. A Chinese puzzle in itself.

Would he take part?

Andrew had become a Fellow five years before. After leaving the military he'd joined the UN and worked on a peacekeeping mission in Taiwan at the time of the aborted Chinese invasion. There he had met Amy, a wonderful Taiwanese girl who was a TV newsreader, and married her.

Just after his marriage, the Arbitrators had approached him with an invitation to become a Fellow. Secretive as always, the College's first meeting with Andrew had been a clandestine one at the offices of the Eastern Military Alliance in Tokyo, the head of which was an Arbitrator. Andrew had been surprised and delighted that they thought him worthy of such a post. He had agreed without hesitation and had never regretted it. To be able to work quietly in the background with the College to try to bring peace to disturbed regions of the world and to alleviate the sufferings of others was, he believed, his destiny.

It had been a good decision and, with the devastating death of Amy in a car accident a year later, it had been the only thing that had kept him going. Relentlessly, he had pushed himself to fulfil both his demanding job with the UN as a consultant on military affairs as well as undertake all the various projects the College had allotted to him – investigation and review of government and mercenary activity in Burma, report on the civil war in Kashmir, cease-fire negotiations in Burundi, information on the assassins of President Laurent in Mali, and others. In these he worked with other Fellows at the College who were also engaged in monitoring military activity world-wide – on one occasion with Ivan on the secret war in Yemen, and once with Rex on the Kazakhstan nuclear disaster. Rex had been impressive, Andrew had to admit that. He'd soon worked out that the explosion had been a case of negligence at the plant. With that evidence, the Master had ensured that a border war between Kazakhstan and its Russian neighbour, whom it had falsely accused of sabotage, was averted.

Andrew watched as a black guillemot circled overhead.

Of the other contestants, Andrew knew little about Sebastien. They'd never worked together though this was not surprising. The College covered a huge range of activities and each specific project was strictly controlled to prevent information leakage, with perhaps just one or two Fellows collating information and working with one of the Arbitrators or, more rarely, with the Master himself.

Andrew also knew little about Tanya. His expertise in military matters and hers in computer programming had not come together in a project yet. That said, he had talked with her on a few occasions at the Fellows' Banquets and had enjoyed her good company. Of the five contestants, she was probably the most brilliant in terms of sheer technical expertise. Almost certainly she had helped in the programming of the College's computers and she would know much more that he did about its internal goings-on. It was a pity they couldn't work together, but Tanya would obviously work with her partner, Sebastien. A very strong combination. Still, only one of them could become Master and he doubted whether their relationship would last.

Would he take part?

The Mastership was the very pinnacle of success. That said, the competition would be fraught with danger, for it was no ordinary game and the Mastership no ordinary post. Standing in the centre of it all, the Master saw the pace of human history as it passed before him and he could probably influence it to a greater extent than any other living being. For such a prize people would be prepared to forfeit their moral principles, Andrew was quite sure. And he suspected that the most formidable opponent in the end would not be a man but a women. He thought of Tanya.

So, would he take part? Would he? The inner voice was insistent, seeking to drive out other thoughts.

Andrew decided that he would wait on the Scottish mainland until New Year's Eve before returning to Africa. This would enable him to attend the College and to declare his nomination if he did decide to throw his hat in the ring. He had left a message with Symes, informing the Master where he would be. In the meantime, assuming that he would take part, was there anything he should do at this stage to ensure success?

The island was soon lost to sight.

After dinner with the Master, Ivan Radic returned to his rooms in the first courtyard. Taking off his dinner jacket he hung it up carefully before going into his library. He stood there for a minute, gazing with pleasure at the multitude of books before him, at the large standing globes, at the engravings of ancient cities on the walls, at the small Greek and Roman statuettes that gracefully adorned the mantelpiece and side tables. Walking across the library floor, he loosened his shirt and placed his cufflinks on a desk. Finally, he parted the heavy velvet curtains and drew up a chair so that he could gaze at the stars. Ignoring the lateness of the hour, Ivan contemplated the universe.

A contest for the greatest intellectual and, possibly, the most powerful position the world could bestow. The Mastership. A game of chess that would be played out on a human chessboard in which there could only be one winner. What the Master was offering them was power, enormous power. And to gain power one must understand its nature and the means by which it should be wielded.

Ivan reflected on his fellow contestants. He had no illusions about their great abilities. In particular, Rex, whom Ivan was sure would be a contestant despite the histrionics. Yet, Ivan also knew that each one of them, somewhere, would have an Achilles' heel, a fatal flaw, that could be exploited. Something in their psychological make-up or their past. They would not be human otherwise. Obtaining information on their backgrounds would be difficult, though, for the College went to considerable lengths to help the Fellows disguise the fact that they belonged to the institution and many of their personal details were carefully 'lost' or erased from public computer files, to prevent inquisitive people from learning too much about them. Only a computer expert might be able to delve into the records and piece things together. Ivan had no doubt Tanya would do so. What interesting secrets would she find out about him? People were rarely as they seemed.

Of course, Ivan knew some basic details about his colleagues and the work which they did in the outside world, keeping the fact that they were Fellows carefully hidden. He knew that Rex was a physicist who worked for an international body on global nuclear energy programmes, both civil and military, reports on which he secretly passed back to the College; and that Andrew was a consultant to the United Nations on military issues. The clever Sebastien was an adviser to the World Bank with a comprehensive knowledge of global financial systems and money markets. Then there was Tanya, whose talent lay in computer programming and analysis. An impressive array of abilities and skills between them. They were also people capable of achieving whatever they had set their hearts on. Yet, Ivan was sure that, in the end, skills and abilities would not be crucial components in this competition for, in games of power, what really mattered was who you were. And, given this, it seemed clear in the final analysis that he, Ivan, would win the Mastership, whatever the nature of the contest.

Why? Well, the answer was simple. Because Ivan knew himself and where his strengths lay. Ivan recognised that, unlike Sebastien, he had no great skill in manipulating people and directing them to achieve his ends. Unlike Rex, he had no supreme confidence in his intellectual and physical abilities. Unlike Andrew, he had no military and tactical prowess and, unlike Tanya, he did not have a loving and loveable personality that could secure the co-operation and help of others. Yet Ivan knew that he had one gift and a very rare one at that.

Ivan possessed an intellectual objectivity scarcely touched by emotions such as love and fear, guilt or remorse. For him, these human frailties were great imperfections, blights in the apple that oppressed the spirit and made it blind to the deepest insights of man and his relationship to the universe. Instead, Ivan consciously lived in a mental vacuum in which feelings and sentiments scarcely penetrated. His was the mind of the clinician: objective, dispassionate, cold and pristine. His was the conception of the purist, his the thought process of Machiavelli. Less affected by human frailties than his colleagues, Ivan had a rare advantage over them when it came to power and its wielding – he was a gamesplayer extraordinaire.

Leaving his library Ivan went into his sitting room and sent an e-mail to Rex. It was clear from Rex's antics that evening that he wanted to start the game straight away. Enthusiastic as always. Just a little too enthusiastic. Fine, let's play.

For others on that same night, life progressed in other ways, no less mysterious. In Germany, the TV presenter Sabine Stricker lay half asleep, her leg astride her Polish cameraman. That night she had discovered he not only had a voice like ground glass but the sexual pump and swell of a church organ. What more could she ask for? He'd invited her out just after she'd bidden

Ivan farewell. Of course, her ex-husband George had been furious. But who cared? Strange how life turned out. Sabine kissed the tattooed arm of her companion and her hand inched towards his groin. If only she could remember his name. . .

A world away, in the displaced persons' camp in the Congo, young Obedi was lying in a hospital bed, wide awake. He was waiting for the return of the mysterious man with the telephone. He wondered whether you could talk to God on it.

CHAPTER SEVEN

It should be noted . . . how easily men are corrupted and in nature become transformed, however good they may be and however well taught.

Machiavelli, *The Discourses*

IN HER ROOM AT THE College, Tanya stretched out in bed and yawned. She knew it was late in the morning since strong light peeped through the blinds. Slowly, her mind began to engage. Had the previous evening been a dream after all? Had they really had dinner with the Master and been offered the Mastership? Tanya felt a soft thud on the bed and a bundle of fur nestled beside her thigh. Gemma, her Persian cat, had arrived. Cats were an adequate compensation for men, Tanya reflected. They kept you warm and they didn't get excited at the first sight of flesh.

'Come on, Gemma, it's time to get up.'

Reluctantly, Tanya pulled back the duvet and stood up. She wandered into her study and eyed the treadmill warily, as did Gemma, who stroked against her legs. Not this morning. She would go for a run later. Probably Sebastien would join her. They could run to Mullach Coll and back. Tanya switched on the news and went for a shower. Afterwards, towelling her hair, she passed into the kitchen. Settling down with a bowl of muesli, she watched the television headlines. It appeared as if the US and Russian Presidents were going to reach a historic agreement on a reduction in nuclear weapons in the Western hemisphere.

It was a good ending to the disaster that had affected the US Presidency only a few days before. Tanya wondered whether the Master had been involved. Probably. She flicked on the recorded phone messages.

'Tanya. I've decided to go away for a few days, to think things over. I'll see you on New Year's Eve if you decide to accept the nomination. Take care.'

The curt words of Sebastien cut through the television announcer's voice like a knife. Tanya turned off the recording machine and put down her breakfast bowl with a gasp. Something within her set off an alarm bell. Quickly, she picked up the phone and contacted the porter's lodge. Symes answered. He confirmed that Andrew, Sebastien, Ivan and Rex had all left the College earlier that morning, at different times, Ivan and Sebastien by helicopter, when the fog had lifted.

'Bastards,' she muttered as she put down the receiver. A rush of adrenalin shot through her. They had left without her. Why? Was it something to do with the contest for the Mastership? Damn them and damn Sebastien. Hadn't both Rex and Sebastien also told her to 'take care'? Did they know something she didn't?

Resolute, Tanya hurriedly finished her breakfast. She must find out where they'd gone. That might be difficult to determine. Yet there's was one thing in her favour. As an expert in computer programming she could access most computers round the world without difficulty. Which meant that she could probably access Rex's computer remotely, and the code to Sebastien's she already knew. That would be useful. People who go places often leave messages. They should have thought of that. But why had they left so soon? Was the game more deadly than she thought?

'You stay here, darling.' She gave Gemma a cuddle. Cats were more dependable than men *and* they always stayed close to the milk. As she went out the door, Tanya realised she'd taken a decision without really thinking about it.

She'd take part in the Mastership Game, come what may.

*   *   *

The journey from Tirah to the mainland usually took a couple of hours, though this depended on the seas. They were invariably high at this time of year and they could add another half-hour to the journey, as would occur today. Rex didn't mind. He wanted time to think and to prepare for his meeting with Ivan, who always went by helicopter. Besides, the lurch of the ferry as it passed through the stormy waters of the Atlantic gave him the feeling of progress – a sensation of forging ahead.

'Nice to see you again, Dr Boone.' The watchman, one of the hereditary posts in the hands of the island, nodded to him as he passed down the gangplank onto the mainland.

Rex nodded back. No one ever got on or off the ferry without the College knowing about it. Not that it was important. The Master could as easily find out from Symes or the other porters whether Rex had left the College. More difficult would be to determine where he was going.

Two hours later his car journey had taken him to Erris, a small fishing town further down the west coast of Scotland. Rex went to a guesthouse not far outside it. He didn't want to draw attention to himself. It had taken him longer than expected since the weather had deteriorated badly overnight and many of the smaller roads had become impassable due to a blizzard. Rex wondered whether Ivan had managed to get to Erris and to the hotel. He imagined his calculating friend would have broken his neck to do so, so keen would he be to talk with him. Ivan obviously had a plan and he intended that Rex should be part of it. It could be an interesting proposition. That said, someone else might have an even better one.

Rex consulted the clock on the bedroom mantelpiece. Time to make the phone call to the States. The call was brief. After that, and a hasty lunch in his room, Rex sat down to pen a letter. It was a difficult missive to write and he spent a lot of time choosing his words carefully. Even writing it was risky. He could have made a wrong assumption and he was in danger of neglecting his own inner voice to trust no one. As he wrote, he stared out to sea, deep in thought, many questions flowing through his mind. Why had the Master decided to offer them the Mastership? He had told them that the office became all the more wearisome as the years went by and that there was a time when it should pass to another. But was that the full story? Could it be that something had gone badly wrong? Something connected with the US Presidential scandal or another matter he was dealing with? Was the Master being forced to resign and, if so, would he really renounce his power so easily?

While Rex wrote he also reflected that he would have to give up, at least temporarily, his work as an adviser with the Global Forum for Nuclear Research. That was not a problem. He often took time off to pursue projects for the College.

Rex had still not finished his letter when he left for the hotel to meet Ivan. As he was quitting his room he caught sight of himself in the mirror. He paused for a moment to adjust his collar. Rex liked what he saw and he forgave himself his few seconds of self admiration. Everyone had a right to congratulate themselves sometimes. Rex knew that he had the stamina and competitiveness to go the full distance; he could win. Besides, in a race it was often useful to put the others off right at the start. His intentional ham acting would have got them puzzled and concerned. He closed the bedroom door. Already he was thinking of the Mastership and what he would do.

Rex decided to walk since he needed a breath of fresh air. He put on a thick anorak. Stepping out of the guesthouse, he started towards the town a couple of miles away. The storm had abated slightly and he breathed in the icy wind as his feet crunched through the snow. His only regret was that he had not had the opportunity to fit in some rowing that day. It would have taken the tension from him. Still, his afternoon's work would reap dividends, he was sure.

Or would it? Rex would have been dismayed to learn, not twenty minutes after his departure from the guesthouse, that his bedroom received a guest, and an uninvited one at that. After unpicking the lock someone entered the chamber and stood there, inspecting its layout and the few possessions that

Rex had brought with him for a night's stay in Erris. Finally, the letter Rex had been working on was taken up from where it lay on the desk, half covered by a writing pad. It was carefully read. There was silence, then a slight sigh. The letter was slipped into a pocket. It would never be sent.

It was far too dangerous.

'Do you trust the Master?'

They were seated in an inglenook by the fire. In the hotel of the small town of Erris the guests swirled about them, like ships in a squall, full of post-Christmas spirit. The landlord, a bluff figure of a man, held court behind the bar and a group of young singers, giggling nervously, threatened to unleash their discordant voices on the dinner guests. Rex sat back and laughed.

'Well, I've got one thing right so far, Ivan. I'd guessed you'd invited me here to talk about the contest for the Mastership. Otherwise, I'd have underestimated your generosity.'

Ivan examined his visage. Freckled complexion, wide eyes, and a flat nose – a face that gave away nothing and had the malleability of concrete. Rex's face was compatible with his cranium, thought Ivan. It would only concede information with a reluctance bordering on death. Still, it was imperative to try.

'Well, you were interested enough to come,' he said in a reasonable tone of voice.

'Perhaps,' conceded Rex. 'First things first. Who's paying for this dinner?'

'I will,' said Ivan reluctantly. He suspected Rex was going to make it an expensive chat.

'That's my man,' said Rex. He loved a sportsman. He told Ivan to talk no more while he analysed the menu. After some minutes weighing up the various culinary delights, he beckoned a waiter to the table and ordered the fois gras and a large fillet steak with a bottle of Chateau Latour. For dessert the lemon soufflé. Finally, cheese and biscuits and a 1960 Warre's port.

'That's a good year, isn't it, Ivan? You know all about these things.'

'I believe it is,' said Ivan sourly.

'Better make it a bottle in the case of the port,' Rex said to the waiter. He was enjoying himself. Ivan would be hoping he would give something away when drunk. Of course, he wouldn't. He could drown a battleship. 'Now where were we?' he grinned pleasantly.

Ivan made small talk until Rex was deeply embedded into his main course, his mouth turning the food like a combine harvester. Then he said in his most persuasive tone of voice, 'I think we can help each other in this contest.'

'Um, I doubt it.' Rex shook his head. 'But carry on.' The steak was delicious. Would it be too much to order another? It was the cold that gave him such a big appetite. He beckoned the waiter over and requested a second helping.

'You'd be surprised,' said Ivan in his soft voice. Rex turned his attention back to him. Ivan's face always reminded him a little of paintings of Cardinal Richelieu: narrow, angular and with enigmatic eyes. Rex imagined Ivan would have few scruples in getting what he wanted if he desired it enough. Was the Mastership something Ivan really wanted? Rex would stake his life on it.

Ivan continued, 'Rex, I'd like to ask you something. You seemed reluctant to involve yourself in the contest last night. Of course, I didn't believe it for a moment.'

'No?'

'No,' said Ivan, unperturbed. 'Not for a moment. What you wanted was to see how we would react, and how the Master would react.'

'Really?' Rex dispatched his second steak and carried on munching contentedly. 'Pass the asparagus.'

'Yes, for me, your atrocious play-acting was designed to determine one thing,' said Ivan. 'You wanted to know whether any of us had heard about the contest before.'

'Uh huh? Why you do think that?' Rex poised over his food. Outwardly, his expression gave nothing away. Inwardly, he was moderately impressed. Ivan had hit the bull's-eye first time.

'And,' continued Ivan smoothly, 'that tells me that you *know* something about the contest for the Mastership.'

'Eh?' said Rex. He was right again. Damn. Where was the waiter? He could do with some more potatoes as well. He turned away.

'What you know relates to how the contest will be played. And what you know is not good news.'

Rex put down his knife and fork. Three bull's-eyes. He was impressed. 'Well,' he said brutally, 'so what, Ivan? Suppose this were true, what's your proposal? Get on with it. I don't have to be a nuclear physicist to work out that you want to make a deal.'

Ivan smiled, a razor-thin smile. Yes, it was time to get to the point. 'Rex, the assignments we normally undertake for the College are no beds of roses and there are risks. This game, though, is much more hazardous and of a different order of complexity. Probably the most difficult task we'll have to face in our lifetimes.' Ivan stopped and ate a morsel of salmon, less from desire than to add to the dramatic effect. 'There's an added problem in that all of us want to win. So, I propose a degree of cooperation, at least in the initial stages. An alliance. The important thing is to reduce the odds. A wise move as you'll doubtless appreciate. I think we could work together as a good team, whatever the contest for the Mastership is.' He hesitated fractionally. 'Both you and I also know that Sebastien and Tanya will work as one.'

'You sure?'

'Oh, yes. Quite sure,' said Ivan smoothly, 'even though you're in love with her.'

Rex Boone sat back, genuinely astonished. Was it so obvious, or an inspired guess? How could he possibly be aware of their short-lived affair four years ago? Yet Rex knew he should never underestimate Ivan the spy. Working with the secret services he must know a vast amount. Perhaps the College also used him to keep an eye on the other Fellows? Rex glared at a small group of singers. They had gathered in the dining room and now began a rendition of an old Gaelic song. It sounded like a patient undergoing heart surgery with a vacuum cleaner. Rex grimaced. He turned back to Ivan.

'Well, what's your proposal?' he demanded.

'Whatever the contest is, we work together to beat the others. Then it's you against me and may the best player win.' Ivan's eyes gleamed with suppressed excitement.

'You want the Mastership?' said Rex in a surprised tone. They both laughed.

Rex inspected the dessert they had brought him. Sebastien would never help him and deep down he knew that Ivan was almost certainly right. Despite hope against hope Tanya would tie her colours to Sebastien's mast if it came to the crunch. So he needed a back-up strategy. Andrew? An unknown quantity: a military background, a man who often worked in Russia and the Far East, monitoring, Rex suspected, arms shipments. And Ivan? What attributes did this Croatian with a British passport have? A very logical mind and a dispassionate temperament. He was also rumoured to have very good connections with the secret services of a number of countries, particularly the US and Britain. A useful ally, a dangerous foe. However, to Rex, there was one overriding consideration that would seal any temporary co-operation. Rex did not want Sebastien to win. The possibility of Sebastien becoming Master of the College was quite unacceptable to him; so too was the possibility that Rex would ever give up his Fellowship. That meant he just had to be the victor.

Rex continued to eat his dessert as he mused over the matter. When his plate was empty and he pushed it away from him. His lips formed into a tight smile. Not a smile of pleasure at the excellence of the food, but the smile of an executioner about to make his guest appearance on the stage. Rex would deal with Ivan later.

'Ok, agreed. An alliance, but leave Tanya to me.'

'Fine,' said Ivan equitably, though he had no intention of doing so. He would try and outwit her first. Sebastien and Tanya would be too strong a combination. 'Now, tell me what you know about the contest.'

Rex nodded. 'When I listened to the Master speaking last night it jogged my memory. I'd come across something about a contest for the Mastership before, from a former Fellow of the College who'd taken part.'

'When? And what happened?'

'That's all I can tell you now. There's some further information I need.' As Rex spoke, his voice was audible only to Ivan, drowned out by the cacophony of the singers. Rex and Ivan ignored them, they were too engrossed in their own thoughts. Yet, had they glanced up at that moment it would have repaid them handsomely, for they would have seen a person looking attentively in their direction, a figure whose departure was as silent as its arrival.

'Rex,' Ivan spread out his hands in mock supplication, 'this is pathetic. It really is. All you've told me is that there have been previous contests for the Mastership. Doubtless, that means the present Master took part in them. Anyone could have guessed that. Can't you tell me a little more? Otherwise our meeting's been a complete waste of time.'

'Sorry, that's it for now,' said Rex. He threw down his napkin and stood up, dwarfing the small table at which he'd been sitting. 'Thanks for the hospitality, Ivan. The meal was delicious but I have to be off. There's nothing more to say at this stage. And there's someone I have to talk to. So I'll forgo the cheese and the port. That will save you a bit on the bill, anyway. You should be pleased.' Rex turned away.

'I think we should discuss this matter further, Rex.'

'No.' The tone was definitive. 'We'll keep in touch. I'll contact you.' He grinned at the obviously startled Ivan and quit the restaurant.

Ivan remained at the dinner table while he finished off his glass of wine. Despite a lack of hard information, he was not at all disappointed. Rex seemed to be as easy to read as a book. Too easy, which suggested Rex could be playing him along and that he had no real intention of co-operating. But then neither did Ivan. So, what had he learnt? Clearly, Rex knew something very important about the contest for the Mastership. And that information he probably had on, or near, him. Yet, Ivan didn't believe for a moment Rex would tell him where it was and so he would have to use other means to obtain it. He wondered who Rex was going to talk to. The Master, perhaps? Something about the game? Ivan crossed to the restaurant window and peered out. He watched Rex's massive figure plodding down the driveway like some gargantuan bear. Then Ivan paid the bill and also left.

Not a bad meeting, he thought, as he stepped onto the hotel porch. Rex had already given away much. Lucky guess about his being in love with Tanya. That would come in very useful. He wondered whether Sebastien knew.

Rex peered ahead, focusing on the fog lights of the oncoming cars as they cautiously plied their way along the road. The blizzard had worsened and visibility was down to a few yards. He turned down a side road. The guesthouse was less than ten minutes away. He glanced behind him. Nothing. He was becoming too suspicious. He should receive the information from the US by tomorrow at the latest.

He dug his hands deep into his anorak pockets. As he trudged along sleet battered against the uncovered part of his face and his eyes narrowed in defiance against the onslaught. He couldn't remember such bad weather in years. An inauspicious start to the contest? Rex didn't believe in such things. He focused his mind on the Mastership. Perhaps, he'd given away too much? No, he thought not. What he had done was to find out quickly whether any of the others knew about the nature of the contest and it was clear that they didn't. He'd keep Ivan on side for the moment, of course. As for the others, they were in for the shipwrecking storms. Rex trudged round a corner, exultant. He knew that he must act quickly. The learning curve in this game was very steep and every minor slip would be exploited. It was time to make himself scarce until they appeared before the Master again on New Year's Eve. Then Rex would have something to say to the Master. He wondered how he would take it. Rex battled on against the elements, his mind preoccupied. He'd post the letter to Tanya tonight.

Soon, the entrance to the guesthouse was just around the corner. It was here that Rex reached the most exposed part of the road. The wind howled and the force of the gale held him back. Momentarily, he glanced down, sensing ice under his feet. Then, above the noise of the wind, he heard an unnatural roar. Rex turned round and peered back into the snowstorm. Suddenly, from the opaque cloud, a vehicle emerged. It hurtled directly towards him, its speed increasing. With a cry he sought to avoid it. Hastily, he stepped to the side of the road. However, nature and fate had conspired. He slipped.

'Fuck the ice!'

In the final surreal seconds before he felt the full impact of the car, Rex could see himself in his mind's eye. Once again he was sculling across the waters of Loch Moyne, the College in sight. There he was, way out ahead. This time, however, to his consternation, the scull suddenly seemed to lose direction and the oars broke in his hands. Other sculls, phantom boats, swiftly passed him, leaving him dead in the water. He was losing the race and his boat began to sink. Sadness overwhelmed him.

There was a mighty thud as Rex's body hit the front of the vehicle. Then it slewed across the bonnet and was hurled into the verge with terrifying speed. Rex groaned as he lay in the snow. He felt blood frothing over his lips. Slowly, he turned on his side so that he could see the heavens. As he lay there Rex recalled the face of the driver. His expression contorted with anger and sadness. He had been too slow after all. Betrayed.

'Tanya,' he murmured.

Snowflakes alighted on Rex's face while his blood leeched from him. Reluctantly, and in agony, he died. The blizzard and the vehicle carried on.

Andrew was mountaineering on the mainland of Scotland. As he climbed, his figure a small speck against the formidable backdrop of nature, he thought about the contest for the Mastership. Now he reflected on it, it was perfectly consistent with the structure of the College that they would have some form of competition for the highest position of all, and that it would be conducted with the utmost secrecy. About the contest, though, there lurked an unmistakable and powerful scent of danger. Despite this and the fact that his instincts, which normally served him so well, warned him not to, Andrew knew that he would take part. Like a climber long accustomed to reaching the peaks of so many mountains, he could not resist the fatal attraction of the highest one of all – even though the chance of coming back alive receded with each footstep forward.

Methodically, Andrew began to climb and in a couple of hours he had progressed far up the rocky mountainside. He knelt down to tighten his laces. As he did so, he gazed out over the landscape. Suddenly, he saw something below. Then the mist obscured his view. He strained his eyes, trying to relocate the movement. There was nothing. Frowning at the sense of unease that came upon him, Andrew carried on. He passed a small mountain hut and pressed ahead, up the tortuous path. He'd not proceeded for more than an hour before he realised a storm was coming in fiercely from the west and, if he was to get back safely, he would have to hurry.

Reaching the summit Andrew caught sight of a panorama of mountains spread out before him, wreathed in whiteness. The weather began to deteriorate rapidly. As he swung his eyes back down to the valley, far below, through a gap in the clouds he saw the figure of a person outlined against the snow. Then another. Andrew extracted his binoculars and focused them on the figures. They seemed to be scanning upwards with powerful binoculars as if trying to seek him out. Andrew was puzzled. Was someone looking for him? Who else knew about the contest for the Mastership? While Andrew continued to watch, one of the climbers made towards the mountain hut below him. The other disappeared from sight.

Andrew began to descend. It wasn't unusual for there to be

other climbers on the mountain at this time of year. Despite this, for some unexplained reason, he sensed that all was not well. Soon he had arrived back at the hut. He was scarcely twenty paces from it when the door was flung open and a man rushed out. Taken by surprise Andrew started back. The bulky figure halted just before him and hastily removed his snow goggles. Andrew recognised him as one of the mountain guides.

'Andrew. Thank goodness we've found you. I'm afraid it's terrible news.'

A white slip of paper was handed to him and he read the message.

'Rex Boone killed in a car accident. Funeral tomorrow. Your attendance required. M.'

On the island of Tirah the granite-built chapel was situated at the base of Mullach Mor, in sight of the sea. A couple of miles inland lay the College. Betwixt and between there was nothing save for a road that snaked across the landscape like a lifeline, hidden at times within the forest. In complement to the scenery the chapel had a forlorn air about it as if it was rarely visited. And so it was, for here the College held services of remembrance for departed Fellows. There were only a handful of attendees; few at the College had been notified of Rex's death and returned. The service was brief and simple. The Master gave the memorial oration. As expected, he said all the right things: a man of great promise . . . the tragedy of his untimely death . . . an irreplaceable loss to the Fellowship . . . the uncertainty and unpredictability of life. In the course of his thirty years as head of the College, the Master had, doubtless, uttered similar words before though none could fail to detect the deep sombreness in his voice.

While the Master spoke Ivan glanced around the little church. The rays of winter sun flickered in the stained-glass windows and were gone. The candles cast a tenuous glow in the gloomy recesses of the nave. On the walls memorial tablets and plaques bore testament to the centuries. And in a graveyard in Erris, inside his coffin, the massive frame of Rex Boone that had breathed life and emotion so strongly only a few days before began its slow process of decomposition. Alone. Already his link with the College was severed and the secret of his Fellowship taken to the grave. To the outside world a moderately well-known physicist had died in a car accident while on holiday in Scotland. Sad, but these things happened. End of story. Not even the supermedia could make much of it.

Tanya sat at the back of the chapel. She also thought of Rex, but in a different way. Of the last kiss he had given her. Of his passion and of his hope for more. She closed her eyes but no prayer came. Before her she could see the Rex of long ago, when they had been lovers. As he guided her to the bed. As he gently undid her blouse. As his mouth suckled on her breasts. As he penetrated her. The immediacy of Rex and of those dormant emotions was so overwhelming that Tanya forced her eyes open with a gasp, to fix them once again on the simple cross on the altar. She must not remember him in this way. Not here. Despite this, while the Master continued to speak, Tanya's thoughts inevitably turned once again to a relationship that had never been and now never would be. Poor Rex. He had always wanted so much and he had wanted it all at once. He could have become Master. Yet this is what had become of his ambition – a death in the snow. Was it an accident or did the desire for power make people do evil things? Tanya knew the truth in her heart.

'So how exactly did he die?' asked Sebastien.

Ivan and Sebastien were standing outside the chapel after the service had ended, chafing their hands in the cold. They walked towards the lichgate.

'The Erris' chief of police told one of the Arbitrators that Rex was returning to a guesthouse in which he was staying,' said Ivan. 'The car struck him as he walked along the roadside. He died instantaneously. The time of death was not certain but it was probably near midnight. They've no other details as yet.'

'And the driver?'

'Hit and run. The driver may not even have known Rex had been struck, the weather was so atrocious. Death by misadventure, that's the verdict so far.'

There was a pause. 'Must be difficult for Andrew,' said Sebastien. Although Ivan and Sebastien had little liking for each other, the occasion was conducive to a sense of shared grief and mutual confidences. Andrew had left the chapel and started to walk towards them, drawing a thick overcoat about him as he regarded the bleak, clouded, sky.

'Why?'

'His wife died in a car accident a few years ago. In Taiwan. Must bring back the memory.'

'Yes,' said Sebastien. 'Tragic.' He changed the subject. 'Where had Rex been that night?'

'No one knows,' lied Ivan evenly. 'Probably in one of the bars. The police told the Arbitrator that he'd had a high level of alcohol in his blood. The drink may have affected his balance, don't you think?'

'Yes.'

Ivan and Sebastien regarded each other. Suddenly, a thought, sharp and intense, darted into Sebastien's mind. Fearful that it might be seen, he averted his eyes to gaze across the sea. However, it was too late. In the split second that their eyes had met they both realised, with shock, that their thoughts had been identical.

'I must go,' said Sebastien. He nodded to Ivan and to Andrew, who had just reached them, then he hurried away. Tanya had been studiously avoiding him, doubtless in punishment for deserting her that night the Master had told them of the contest. She could be very unforgiving at times and Sebastien didn't want her to leave the island before he'd talked to her. However, as Sebastien passed through the lichgate, another thought dominated his mind.

Sebastien had seen Ivan having dinner with Rex the night he died, so he knew that Ivan had lied. One point to Sebastien. Yet Ivan had detected from his look that Sebastien knew he, Ivan, was lying. This meant Ivan was now aware Sebastien had also been in Erris. One point to Ivan.

Sebastien smirked. So where had Andrew been when Rex died?

Tanya shut the door carefully behind her. The others would soon be back from the funeral and she wanted to be out of the College by then. Entering Rex's apartment in the first courtyard, she hesitated. She could still feel his spirit there, grieving and despondent. Tanya surveyed the art that decorated the walls, the great splashes of colour by Monvillet and Chagall, and the strange wooden figures from the South Pacific islands. Above the picture rail were oars decorated with the details of countless rowing competitions, national and international, that Rex had won when he'd been younger. The air in the room was still, expectant. Tanya half anticipated Rex to appear from the bedroom at that very moment and to lean against the doorframe, his light blue eyes gazing at her and then towards the bedroom as he invited her to share with him their bodies once more. Yet for all his strength and all his ability Rex had lost the greatest contest of the body – that of life. He had been outwitted at the start. Too premature.

She mustn't waste time. Tanya hurried into Rex's study. It was clear to her from his curious behaviour at the meeting with the Master that Rex had known, or suspected something, about the contest for the Mastership and that information must be somewhere. Rex's study was piled high with files and computer disks. On the desk in front of her was the very powerful computer Rex used, its great screen staring at her blankly.

Tanya extracted a long schedule of numbers from her pocket and a small hand-held calculator, which she plugged into the back of the computer. Then she turned the computer on.

First, she needed Rex's password. She had spent the last couple of days working on it, ever since she'd heard the news of his death. She had not dared enter his room but had tried to access it remotely from her own computer with no luck. Now she decided to risk an actual appearance. She had to know for sure that Rex had died accidentally.

Nervously, Tanya flicked back her hair and pulled the chair closer to the desk. Given his work on secret civil and military nuclear energy programmes, almost certainly Rex would have made it impossible for people to access many of his files, although discovering the password to get into his computer shouldn't have been too difficult. It had proved otherwise so far. Perhaps he'd changed it recently?

Suddenly Tanya stopped and glanced about the room with a sense of alarm. Those objects on the floor – had they been moved? And what about the books strangely positioned on the desk. Had other people been in?

When a Fellow died the College always went through his, or her, apartment. Documents of importance were transferred to the library; other papers and any personal effects were destroyed, to efface the connection with the institution. The people who did this were in the employment of the College and they acted under the authority of a Fellow specially designated by the Arbitrators for the task. They were nicknamed the 'cleaners'. Had the cleaners been in? Or had someone else, one of the other contestants? With a dreadful sense of foreboding, Tanya's hands raced across the keyboard, typing in formulation after formulation, numeric and alphabetic.

'Rex. Come on. You must help me,' Tanya whispered.

Nothing. Finally, a face flashed on the screen. It was of a child. Tanya sat back, puzzled. This had not happened before although, of course, when accessing his computer remotely, she'd not seen his screen. The drawing was of a babe in arms, like Jesus, swaddled in clothes. It was meaningless. Tanya tried more combinations. The child's face disappeared. It reappeared again as she typed in more numbers. Tanya looked anxiously at her watch. She was not going to make it. Her fingers tapped the keys with even greater speed. More combinations, more permutations – nothing.

'Think, Tanya, think,' she said out loud to herself. The face of the child reappeared. She stopped typing with a gasp.

'Oh, Rex.'

Now Tanya understood. Rex had been leaving a message – and it was a message for her. So what was the password to access it? It must be something that linked her and Rex. Something that he knew she could work out, but sufficiently remote to preclude others. What could it be? Think. Think. In agony she tried to recall as the seconds ticked by. At last a thought came to her. When she had slept with Rex that last night of the symposium he had asked whether she ever wanted children. Tanya had been emphatic that she didn't. She was too busy with her own life and with fulfilling herself. Rex had asked her whether she was sure, since he would love to be a father. She had laughed. Quite, quite, sure. She had told him about Gemma, her Persian cat, and she had said, 'Gemma will be my only child.'

Tanya typed in 'Gemma' and 'child'.

Nothing. She tried various other combinations. Nothing.

Then, 'Gemma – only child.'

The screen opened and Tanya looked transfixed at the message that appeared on it. *Her message.* Yet it was too late. Outside, in the corridor, there was the sound of footsteps. Tanya started up in fear as she heard the tread coming ever closer. However, her eyes dragged back to the message on the screen.

'Tanya. I'm leaving the island for Erris tomorrow. If you read this message something will have gone badly wrong. You will probably have also decided to take part in the game. I knew you would, but trust no one. This contest is much more dangerous and difficult than you think. I'll write from Erris if I can. To delete all files on this machine, type in the word 'Farewell'. And Tanya, I have always loved you. And I always will. Rex.'

There was a PS: 'Find out about Max Stanton. Try Boston Newspaper and Periodicals Library, Room 6B, by computer link if they have one. Tell no one else.'

Stifling a cry, Tanya could hear the sound of footsteps just outside the door. What should she do? Would Rex want her to delete all his files now that he was dead? But what if there was information in them that she could use to help her win the game, or to find his killer? She agonised. Then, with tears in her eyes, she hurriedly typed in 'Farewell'.

There was a slight electronic beep as the combination to Rex's room was pressed. Tanya watched as the door swung open. Standing behind it, she remained deathly still. As she held her breath, she raised a bronze ornament in her hand. Whoever it was seemed reluctant to cross the threshold, perhaps sensing her presence. After an age the footfalls of the intruder slowly made their way to the sitting room and into Rex's study. The door closed. At that very moment, Boone's computer screen blinked for the final time and the thousands of computer files contained in its memory dissolved. All of Boone's analytical genius faded into the absolute, leaving nothing behind. Trying not to make a sound, Tanya stepped out into the corridor. She felt traumatised, not only as a result of Rex's final message, for she appreciated now that he'd been murdered, but because she'd also seen the back of the intruder's head.

It was that of the Master.

CHAPTER EIGHT

My words are very easy to understand, and very easy to practise. But no one under heaven is able to understand them or to practise them.

Lao Zi

New Year's Eve.

SYMES ENTERED THE MASTER'S STUDY late in the afternoon. He expected to see its occupant at his desk, engrossed in his work as usual. However, Symes was surprised to see that he was standing by the window gazing out at the snow-covered mountain of Mullach Mor. When he turned Symes could see a great tiredness in the Master's face, and his cheeks had a pallor his manservant had not noticed before.

'Master, the prospective Fellow has arrived. Shall I show her into the main reception room?'

'Yes,' he said. 'The people for the other appointment at seven o'clock should be taken to the library when they get here.'

'Very well, Master.'

Somewhat nervously, Susan Corelli stood up as the Master entered the reception room. She was fascinated to meet a man about whom so little was known and who had an aura of legend about him. She'd been sure she would be intimidated to appear before one so powerful and august. However, when she regarded his face, her fear dispelled. He was taller than she had expected, and his presence was augmented by his full frame and silvery hair. Yet his eyes were friendly and his bearing without ostentation.

He crossed the room and shook her hand. He regarded her very directly without any embarrassment or dissembling.

'Hello, Susan.'

'Master.'

'I know it's a little cold but I thought we might go for a stroll in the College. Everyone else is away for the New Year.'

'I'd like that.'

They walked down the stairs to the ground floor of the reception building and then out into the garden, where the paths had been cleared of snow. The Master studied his guest. He already knew all about her. The College had been keeping an eye on her for some years. She was a pretty woman, slim and petite, with auburn hair, chocolate-coloured eyes and a firm and determined chin. Thirty years old, unmarried with a boyfriend, she worked at the Global Forum for Nuclear Research in Washington. Rex Boone had recommended her. She'd worked for him.

They walked in silence for a minute while the Master let his guest adjust to her surroundings. Susan stared about her avidly, mesmerised to see the interior of the College for the first time. The very thought of the institution had held a magical fascination for her for so many years – the idea of becoming a Fellow, one of the elect, being her dream and the height of her intellectual ambition, as it was for so many others. Today, she had discovered that the College and the island of Tirah were for real. She was actually here, though even now the place retained a mystique and an aura. Her eyes absorbed the ambience and the buildings, almost desperate to touch them in case they disappeared from view. Down the centuries millions of people throughout the world had given money to sustain it all, based only on a simple faith – a faith that somewhere in the world there should be an institution without partisanship dedicated to peace. What if the College were to fail? How terrible it would be. And with its fall how much else of civilisation would it bring down?

'I believe you talked with the Arbitrators a few days ago?'

'Yes,' said Susan with a warm smile, her heart full of gladness. 'I met the Senior Arbitrator in New York. He took me to meet two of the other Arbitrators. I gave the oath of secrecy and they invited me to become a Fellow of the College. I was thrilled to accept.'

'Do you understand the nature of the College?'

'I think so,' said Susan. 'The Fellows are dedicated to assisting the Master in his dealings with world leaders and to undertake such tasks as the Master and the Arbitrators appoint for them. Also, that the College has only one purpose – to work for the cause of peace, without regard to national allegiances, political affiliations or territorial boundaries.'

They stood before a stone bench beside the pond. Only a few days before, President Davison had stood there with the faithful Jack Caldwell.

'That is correct,' said the Master. 'But let me tell you what it will mean for you in particular.' He paused. 'Susan, we have selected you since we believe you will be able to carry out the terms of the founder's wishes. Your work for the College will be onerous. Besides your current employment as a physicist at the Global Forum for Nuclear Research, with the other Fellows you will continuously monitor the development of all nuclear programmes throughout the world on behalf of the College. Any useful information you receive during the course of your employment you will remit to us. It will be processed here at the College and details passed on to the Arbitrators and to myself, to be used when necessary. You will also be sent on various assignments from time to time. These may be quite hazardous.'

'In what way?'

'Well, for example, some time ago Rex Boone visited a new nuclear reactor in Romania. Ostensibly he went as an adviser to the Forum. However, in fact, the College had asked him to go since we'd received some disturbing information via the secret services in Russia. Rex discovered that there were major design faults in certain parts of the plant which the manufacturers were trying to cover up. He prepared a secret report, which he sent back to the College. We brought this to the attention of the Romanian Government and helped them get World Bank funding to remedy the situation. Rex was in considerable physical danger from the manufacturers of the plant when in Romania, since they stood to pay out hundreds of millions of dollars in compensation and they were prepared to go to any lengths to hide their mistakes.' The Master hesitated slightly. 'That said, the College will do whatever it can to ensure your safety. Our influence is not inconsiderable.'

It's immense, thought Susan.

The Master continued, 'As a Fellow you will have great influence and power in terms of the position that you hold and the secrets you are privy to. Further, most of your actions and decisions will be left to your own discretion. We are sure that you will not fail us.'

'I won't,' Susan promised. 'But how will I square that with my bosses at the Forum? Won't they want to know what is happening from time to time when I disappear off on projects? Won't they get suspicious? '

'That will not be a problem,' said the Master. 'The Head of Forum is also a Fellow.'

Susan laughed. 'I see. The College has its tentacles everywhere.'

'Yes,' said the Master. 'It has. It is at the heart of everything. It must be, to be effective.' He continued, 'Your status in the Forum will change. You will become an adviser to it, in order to have more time to work on College matters.'

Susan digested all this information and then said, 'Can I ask you some more questions?'

'Of course,' replied the Master. 'It's to be expected.'

'Why was I selected?'

They strolled down another pathway and stepped across the threshold of the main entrance to the Library, past large oak doors. Susan was initially surprised at the apparent lack of security. Then she recalled that no one could even get on to the island without the permission of the Master and that an intruder would be easily recognised.

'Before we appoint a Fellow, the Arbitrators undertake background research,' said the Master, 'to determine that they are the appropriate kind of person. This includes evaluations by other Fellows, an analysis of their personal history and a thorough consideration of their character. Only a very few people are suitable. They must be prepared to subordinate their own desires and wishes to those of the College and not to misuse the privileged position given to them. They must also be prepared to work in absolute secrecy – rarely knowing the uses to which their labour is being put and recognising that their input may only be a small part of the jigsaw. They must also accept that, in the world outside, they will never attain the highest political or corporate positions. There are only a few people prepared to do this.'

'Only eighty.'

The Master smiled slightly. 'That's right. The founder chose the number well. Only a few people.'

Susan looked about her at the library. It was like no other. On the ground floor where they stood there were no books. Instead, the library comprised a high-ceilinged room supported by bulky Grecian columns that stretched back into the distance, the whole being much larger in size than appeared from the outside. Before them was a central corridor inlaid with pristine white marble. On each side were rooms partitioned by thin, opaque glass. The Master went to one side of the library and ran his hand over what seemed to be nothing more than a pedestal and a plinth of black marble or graphite. It gleamed and pinpoints of light appeared on the control panel. The Master pressed a key. The glass suddenly became transparent. Susan saw that most of the rooms had inside them nothing more than a white marble desk and a black chair. They started to walk down the corridor.

The Master said, 'Books and documents are held on the first floor and in the basement. This floor contains only review rooms and the computers.' Then he continued with their prior conversation. 'For the first year or so, Susan, your time here will seem strange. However, as the Arbitrators will have told you, the post is for life and you can return to the College whenever you wish, an apartment being made available for your personal use. You will be given details of other Fellows who interconnect with your field of study. Financially, you will be secure for the rest of your life and the College will do everything it can to assist you.'

They stopped by a side door. It opened when the Master glanced towards a light source at eye level. They both stepped into the room. After they had done so, the glass became opaque once more. It was as if they were in an isolated chamber now, as silent and bare as a monk's cell save for the marble table and chair which faced a wall of silicone. Approaching the table the Master ran his hand over another graphite slab set into the marble. A keyboard appeared. As it did so the white wall shimmered and there was projected onto it a massive screen as high as a human being. A spinning disc in a multitude of colours started to form.

'A quantum computer,' said Susan.

'Yes,' said the Master. 'These computers are rather more advanced and sophisticated than the computers you will have seen at the Global Forum for Nuclear Research. The College has two, which were built and are maintained by the Fellows. They can secretly access almost every computer in the world. They also connect into all libraries and institutes. One of the computers is available to the Fellows for their research.'

Susan wondered what the other computer was for. For the Master to communicate with world leaders in secret? For storing even more information? But on what?

The Master continued, 'All the information you acquire which will be useful to the College can be inserted into this computer's databanks wherever you are in the world and in whatever language. You can also access it whenever you like.'

The Master passed his hand over the graphite slab and the screen disappeared. They walked out of the room and back down the corridor. The Master said, 'You asked why you had been selected in particular. The person who had been undertaking the work you will now be doing, died recently. His name was Rex Boone.'

'I worked with him a number of times at the Forum,' said Susan. 'He was a brilliant man. It was such a tragedy he was killed in a road accident. I'd no idea that he was a member of the College.'

'He was,' replied the Master. 'He was also a great loss to us. The Arbitrators have decided that you should take his place.'

'It's an honour,' said Susan. She paused, to gather her thoughts together, before continuing: 'What is done with the information we insert into the computer?'

'It is used by myself and the Arbitrators,' said the Master, 'in particular, in my discussions with the leaders of over two hundred countries around the world. For example, we seek to warn them in advance of potential environmental and natural disasters. In your field we do everything we can to ensure that nuclear energy is utilised for non-military purposes and that it's properly controlled and inspected. In the case of human rights we can often secure the freedom of political prisoners in return for providing help and information in other fields. We do all this by directly talking with the leaders of nations on a confidential basis, so that they can claim the credit for any breakthroughs or, in the case of difficult problems, so that they can be discreetly resolved out of the critical eye of the media. There's always a solution. Perceiving and formulating it is the key.'

They stood on the steps of the library once more and started down the pathway towards the first courtyard. Susan realised that her introductory meeting with the Master was rapidly coming to an end. Just how much influence did he have? It must be colossal. Was the recent release of a famous Libyan dissident due to the Master's influence? The sudden opening up of Burma? The provision of aid to Iran after its disastrous civil war? The unification of Korea? Did the Master do these things or did he persuade others of the merits of doing them?

'Master, why doesn't the College influence countries more and make them act for the common good of humanity? With all this knowledge and power you could control nations.'

The Master shook his head 'That way evil lies. The College controls nothing; we seek only to advise. If we start to interfere in the politics of individual countries, if we only support the principal world powers, if we became a hugely bureaucratic institution then, in the end, the College will become as bad as any other dictatorship – except that it will be an intellectual dictatorship. The purpose of the College is not to dominate, nor to impose our will on the outside world. It is to seek to advise humanity as a whole and to be impartial in all our dealings. The College itself does not have a political agenda.'

'But why must the College, and everything about it, remain secret?'

They passed into the first courtyard.

'This has been so ever since the beginning,' said the Master. 'What would happen if it were otherwise? The members of College would start to compete among themselves. Then the world's press and media would come to the island and try to influence things. Finally, the leaders of the world would no longer trust in the confidentiality of the institution, nor be safe in the knowledge that our advice is given only to them and in secret, to make of it what they will. If this happened, the College would soon become corrupted and it would fail. You see, this institution only survives by virtue of its unobstrusiveness. It does not try to compete, only to inform.'

'But it has huge power, knowing all the secrets of countries.'

'It does,' said the Master, 'however, what it ultimately seeks is insight, not power.'

Susan did not bother to ask the Master what would happen if a Fellow disclosed secrets relating to the College. The Arbitrators had already made that clear to her. They would be immediately expelled. Not only would they lose the privilege of being at the very centre of things, as well as their financial security, they would be required to return all information to the

College and have no further part in its affairs. Susan had no doubt that the College had quite enough influence to ensure this happened. Also, to prevent any disclosure to the public – not least since the College's archives and its dealings were declared inviolate by the UN charter and national laws. Having the College and the leaders of the world against him, or her, would make life very difficult for a former Fellow unprepared to co-operate. Susan wondered whether the College would actually go so far as to physically liquidate those who betrayed it. Perhaps not the thing to ask the Master at this juncture. So, she switched to another tack.

'Master, so much is failing in the world outside,' she said. 'Ordinary people are worried about our institutions of government. We are moving towards dictatorship of the greedy and the corrupt on a huge scale. Even the US Presidency seemed as though it was about to collapse not long ago. No one trusts the supermedia and what we are being told these days. People want the College to step into the political arena, to discard its veil of secrecy and to tell everyone the truth. They say that the College must throw its weight against the global corruption and be seen to be taking a leading role.'

'And it will not,' said the Master, 'although the same request has been made for the last eight centuries. That is not the purpose of this institution. Our power must always be a hidden power. If not, the College would soon become worse than the institutions people complain of.' He fixed his gaze on her. 'Have faith,' he said, his tone gentle but firm. 'Very difficult times are approaching but the College will stand until the end, even if all else perishes. For it comprises more than individuals. It is an ideal, and for that humanity will always continue to strive, long after you and I are gone.'

'But surely, people try to infiltrate the College?' Susan said. 'How do you prevent them from destroying this institution?'

'The College does what it can to protect itself,' replied the Master. They stood by the fountain in the first courtyard, its ice as bright and clear as glass. He spoke more deliberately. 'Of course, it is possible for a Fellow or even an Arbitrator to seek to use the institution for his, or her, own ends. No one can design a perfect system and, sometimes, the arts of deception are very great. However, this is very rare and there are ways in which the College seeks to protect itself from corruption and internal decay. Sometime or other people reveal their true nature.'

'Even the Master?'

Susan smiled at him provocatively as she said it. She liked him. She could feel that she was in the presence of a remarkable human being and she felt his humility and his greatness. Yet, in the world outside, the rumours were growing that, at last, the College itself was failing and that it was working for individual countries rather than for peace. Had not Paul Faucher, the former US National Security Adviser, declared in a suicide note that the Master had been behind the efforts to bring down President Davison, even though the President himself had vehemently denied this? Had there not been calls in the UN to revoke the privileged status of the College? How could she prove if the Master really was as he seemed?

'Yes, even the Master. He also could seek to impose himself and his own selfish desires on the College, for all human beings are subject to cravings, the assertion of power especially, and all things eventually fail. It is the nature of things in this world.'

Finally, they stood by the porter's lodge and Symes came out to collect Susan. When she returned again it would be as a Fellow of the College. She would begin to work inside the system.

'I have one further question,' said Susan. 'Can a person resign?'

'A Fellow can resign,' he said slowly, 'but that has not happened for very many years. You will discover when you work at the College that its inner mysteries will become revealed over time. It is like an unfolding for everyone, even for me.' He changed tone. 'However, if a Fellow does resign he or she can never return to the College and the vow of secrecy continues to the end of their lives. Perhaps, you were asking, though, whether the Arbitrators or even perhaps I, as Master, can resign?' He inclined his head slightly. 'The answer is no.'

They shook hands and Susan prepared to leave. The Master then said 'Susan, we would like you to help us with one thing straight away.'

'What is that?'

The Master lowered his voice. 'Rex Boone died suddenly. We are sending people to the Global Forum for Nuclear Research to help clear his desk. We are very interested in what he was working on just prior to his death – any information that he might have collected, especially about the College and its internal workings. We would like you to assist us. One of the Arbitrators will get in contact with you on your return to Washington. It is urgent.'

'Fine,' said Susan enthusiastically. Today was the greatest day of her life. 'I'd be delighted to help. Goodbye, Master.'

'Goodbye.'

Susan watched as the Master departed into the second courtyard and then was lost to sight. As he walked she noticed that his back was slightly bent. Like a pilgrim bearing a cross.

Andrew, Ivan and Sebastien gathered in the Master's library in the third courtyard. Symes told them that the Master would be along shortly.

Where was Tanya?

The three contestants contemplated the rows of books before them – their spines glowing in the subdued light given off by the lamps on the mantelpiece. The library covered a wide spectrum of human learning. Scientific tomes nestled alongside philosophical tracts. Serried ranks of law books stood next to works of literature coined in a multitude of languages. Politics and religion were placed together on the same shelves, their mutual antagonism only faintly alleviated by texts on psychology and economics interspersed between them. These bookcases, stretching from the floor to the ceiling, contained the pabulum of an enormously well-read mind, one that had relentlessly searched through the annals of human history and thought in an attempt to understand a little of that strange creature, man. What had the Master discovered after all his learning? What secret insight did he have into the human mind and its deepest wellsprings? What of man's cravings for success, for power, and for glory?

Ivan did not know. One thing he did know, however: in his heart he admired and he envied the Master. He envied him his power, his learning, his books, his rooms, his seemingly effortless genius. And, above all, he envied him the Mastership, the crucible of his talent and the bedrock of his success. Furthermore, he was sure that this same envy beat strong in the hearts of his companions.

Where is Tanya? wondered Sebastien. Had she chosen not to take part after all? It seemed so. He was glad at her decision since he didn't want to compete with her. It would have hurt them both and he had no doubt who would have won. Yet he didn't want to lose her. He wanted her to stay with him while he undertook his quest, to give him her encouragement and her love. Sebastien studied the others, a faint smile on his lips, as he thought of Tanya. They must realise the two would work together in the contest for the Mastership. What would Andrew and Ivan do about it? Sebastien had no doubt what he would do in their situation.

Just then the library door opened and Tanya entered the room. Sebastien grimaced. Despite her immaculate dress, which showed off her figure to its best effect, and the radiant smile she freely delivered to all of them, Sebastien could tell she was furious with him. Tanya went to sit on a sofa beside Andrew studiously avoiding Sebastien's gaze. He would make it up to her somehow, though he knew it would take more than an apology. Sebastien began to say something, but conversation was precluded by the entry of the Master into the room.

'I assume that each of you has decided to accept the nomination.'

His eyes passed from one face to another.

They exchanged uneasy glances, reluctant to reveal their ambition in such a naked fashion.

'Yes,' each answered.

'Think on this carefully, for once you have chosen you cannot turn back. You will no longer be members of the College and you will not be able to return unless you become Master. In any case your oath of secrecy remains.'

'Yes.' The assent was made by all of them without hesitation.

'Very well,' said the Master.

They watched him keenly, knowing what he was going to say would have a momentous significance for them.

The Master began, 'As I previously indicated to you, the terms of the game for the Mastership are established by the Arbitrators and I am as obedient to their commands as you are.' From a drawer the Master took out a sealed letter. He broke it open and read out its contents.

> 'The next Fellows' Banquet will be held on Christmas Eve at 8.00 p.m. The contestant who appears before the Arbitrators in this room at that hour, and who has previously placed the sum of twenty million dollars, gained by his or her own efforts, into an account nominated by the Arbitrators, will become Master.'

There was complete and utter silence. A dumbfounded silence. The Master watched them. He knew what they were thinking. An involuntary groan escaped Andrew's lips. It was quite impossible. He could not believe his ears. All his thoughts had been bent towards the belief that this contest for the Mastership would be one of the mind, a contest of intellectual prowess, not this, the grubby sale of the office to the highest bidder. Andrew noticed the stunned faces of his companions. They also, for once, were unable to hide their surprise behind an intellectual veil. The contest was not as they had supposed; the very opposite. What would the College want twenty million dollars for? It was ludicrous, the foundation was very wealthy. Yet what possible explanation was there? Were the Arbitrators mad? Or had the College, like so many institutions, at last fallen victim to greed and the Mastership was now being sold to the highest bidder – just as the Romans had sold the imperial purple? Andrew's face reflected his dismay. It must be impossible. He must have misheard or been caught in a foolish reverie. Yet he knew he hadn't. He brushed his hand across his brow, his eyes blazing with anger and contempt – anger at himself for his ambition and contempt for the Master. Did Rex Boone die for this?

Sebastien was the first to recover. He gave a wry smile. They were now caught up in a game the winning of which involved the opposite of what they had imagined. Very clever. The Arbitrators were not mad. So they must have decided on this for a reason, and he was sure that he knew what it was.

'How do we make this money?' he asked.

'That is for you to decide.'

'Legally or illegally?'

'That is for you to decide,' said the Master. 'It is your choice. You have undertaken this contest and your future path must now be determined by you and you alone.'

Ivan said nothing, anxious to keep his thoughts to himself. Manifestly, the College did not need the money. As a result of the 'vow' it held huge sums in trust. So why the requirement to make twenty million dollars in one year? Why such a large sum? Had Rex discovered that the College was engaged in something suspect? What? Nuclear secrets? Paying off some debt? More importantly, who would get the benefit of this money – the College, the Arbitrators? Perhaps, even the Master? Were they buying him out?

Tanya cleared her throat. Her complexion had become very pale. She said in a slightly husky voice, 'The letter says by our "own efforts". What does that mean?'

'It means,' said the Master, 'that you cannot obtain the direct assistance of any of the governments, companies or institutions you work for in the world outside to make this money. Nor can you simply borrow the money or be given it by a third party. You have to make this money yourselves using your own abilities and skills.'

Clever, thought Sebastien. Or else he'd simply get the American or Brazilian governments to help him become Master in return for later favours. Of course, he could ignore this prohibition but he'd have to be careful. He knew that Fellows worked in the highest echelons of government around the world. Perhaps, he could steal the money? There was a possibility. Still, there was plenty of time to determine how he'd get hold of it. With the death of Rex Boone, he reckoned he was the front runner. Who was his greatest competitor? He eyed Tanya, Ivan and Andrew. He would work with Tanya, to reduce the odds. That left Andrew and Ivan. He'd put his bet on Andrew. Military man beats political tactician. Philosopher beats spy. And yet . . .

There was silence while they pondered their fate. Making twenty million dollars legally in a year was almost impossible, thought Tanya. Yet, the pre-requisite wasn't so stupid after all. It put them all at square one, regardless of their skills and connections. No one had an in-built advantage and they ran great risks if they acted illegally. Not only would they not have the protection of the College, languishing in some foreign prison would prevent them reappearing at the next Banquet. Tanya scrutinised the Master. What did he think of this contest? Was he not shocked by its mercenary flavour? His expression gave nothing away, which disturbed her even more. What had he been doing in Rex's room? Did the Master know the circumstances behind Rex's death? She shivered slightly. Perhaps she and Sebastien should work together after all. Should she tell him now of her decision?

Ivan cleared his throat. 'It says "the contestant". What happens if more than one person appears?'

The Master replied firmly, 'What the Arbitrators have stipulated is for you to interpret as you will. They will vouch no further explanation.'

'I see.' The only way for Ivan to guarantee victory was to ensure he was the only one to appear on that day. Was that the intention?

The Master continued, 'There's one further matter. As I

indicated, you are now on your own. No one at the College – including the Arbitrators and the Master – will provide you with any assistance in this contest. From this day hence you are no longer Fellows and you will not be allowed within its precincts until the day on which you must appear before the Arbitrators. Perhaps you will begin to appreciate the seriousness of the task ahead. It is one that you have chosen. Goodbye and good luck.'

With that he gravely shook their hands and led them to the door. Downstairs, Symes escorted them out of the third courtyard for the second and last time. He had no knowledge of what had passed between them.

The Master went to his study and sat down at his table. In a few minutes he had a meeting with China's premier. Then the President of Mexico would arrive to discuss the latest bloody uprising in the Chiapas region. After that he had more appointments and calls until late into the night. The work of the Master was endless. Yet all human things had their finality . . . and their price.

He sighed. What price the Mastership?

CHAPTER NINE

To have little knowledge is yet to gain, to have much knowledge is yet to be perplexed.

Lao Zi

January. The Congo.

ANDREW DROVE INTO THE UN displaced persons' camp in Kapanga, a small township in the south of the Congo. Two weeks had passed since the contestants had quit the College and started out on their competition for the Mastership. Andrew had immediately flown back to Africa to wind up his work with the United Nations so that he could begin his quest. Before leaving the Congo for good he went to see how those villagers whom he'd rescued from the rebels a month ago had fared. His final journey of the day took him to a ramshackle hospital at the back of the camp.

'Where's your phone?' said Obedi in Swahili. He contemplated the sandy-haired man with his sunburnt face and receding hairline. It wasn't an ugly face, but it wasn't handsome. Yet the dark blue eyes remained very much alive in the somewhat worn and weather-beaten complexion, and that was important to Obedi. For when the vitality left the eyes it meant that the person had given up and he knew from experience to keep away from such people. If you want to survive, stick close to survivors. His sister had told him that. Unless it was family. In that case stay with them until the bitter end. For after family, there was no one.

'I haven't brought my phone with me.'

'Oh,' said Obedi and squinted at Andrew. They were sitting on a small wooden bench just outside the hospital. Obedi dug his toes into the yellow dirt. All about them was the noise of people scurrying to form queues for the next handout. Andrew had discovered the seven-year-old in the middle of the commotion, sitting calmly on the bench while he contemplated the tragic world around him.

'How are you feeling?'

'Better,' said Obedi. 'They give us food here. And my arm's much better.' He fingered the bandage which had been put on that morning. The white cotton was already discoloured with dirt and dust.

'Good,' said Andrew. 'And what about your sister?'

'She's OK. She's looking after the infants.'

'I see.' Andrew waited for Obedi's questions as he watched the crowd stampeding and fighting for food, every person out for him- or herself, the men fighting the hardest. Humanity that had reduced itself to a state lower than that of cattle.

'How long are you going to stay?'

'A few more days,' said Andrew. 'There's another group of people the UN want to move into this camp. From the north. I may have to help them.'

'Oh,' said Obedi. He shifted his position on the bench a little to keep his injured arm from the full force of the sun. 'When will the fighting stop?'

'I don't know,' said Andrew. 'Soon, I hope.'

'Will you make it stop?'

'That's what I'm trying to do.'

'With the men on the phone.'

'Yes, with the men on the phone.'

'Then what will you do?'

Andrew said, 'There's something else I have to attend to.' He couldn't explain to the child that he was involved in a contest for one of the most powerful positions in the world, the position of a man who was even now trying to stop the fighting in the Congo and in so many other places.

'Will you come back?'

'Yes, I will, but not for a while.'

Obedi nodded slowly. 'When you come back will you come and see me? If I'm still alive?'

'Yes. I will come back and see you,' Andrew said. He patted him on the head affectionately. 'Now, I think I ought to talk with your sister.'

They got up and walked to the hospital entrance through the mêlée of people.

'There she is.' Obedi pointed to a thin child, probably no more than fifteen. She had on a simple red dress and no shoes. The dress was too mature for her childish figure, stunted as it was by malnutrition, with small breasts, a pinched body and puny limbs. She'd probably given most of her food to her brother. Obedi's sister viewed them with doleful eyes. She was looking after a group of infants playing hopscotch on crudely marked out squares in the dust.

'What's your sister's name?' said Andrew.

'Shisvannah.'

'Fine. Go and get some food now.'

Obedi went off to get food while Andrew sat down beside the girl and began to converse with her. As Andrew had suspected, Obedi and his sister had no family and no relatives. They'd been killed in the massacre of the village by the rebels. Andrew gave her some money and told her to keep her brother close to her. He would return to see them when he could. He'd also ask the UN officials to keep an eye on them – though he knew this would be of little worth since they had thousands of people to care for. Andrew told Shisvannah to go and get some food. He would look after the children.

He propped himself against the wall of the hut, exhausted. The rebels had moved their lines far into the south of the country, contrary to the UN-brokered agreement, and there had been renewed fighting and many casualties. Even with the influence of the Master it was unlikely a cease-fire could be agreed this time. And what was Andrew doing here? The contest had already started and he'd make no progress on that in the Congo. Twenty million dollars was more than the entire wealth of the district. Andrew watched the small children playing in the dust. What would become of Obedi and his sister? As orphans their chances of survival were not good, and they had already lost a lot of weight. Andrew placed his head in his hands. His mind was in a whirl.

'No, you can't jump into that square.'

'Why not?' said the little child.

'Well, you just can't. You have to hop into this square.' The older girl, all of six years pointed it out and prodded the young one in the chest. 'Go back and start again.'

'Why?'

'Because that's how you play it.'

'But I want to go into this one.'

'Well you can't.'

Andrew watched the two children squabbling before him. Suddenly, it was as if a veil had been lifted from his eyes. Hopscotch and the contest for the Mastership had one important thing in common. The Master had referred to the contest for the Mastership as a game. And all games have rules. The Master had also told them what the rules were. To obtain twenty million dollars and to appear before the Arbitrators on a certain date. However, Andrew realised, the contestants had failed to ask a crucial question. They had failed to ask the Master what the other rules to the contest were. Rules dealing with questions such as when the contest had to be held, how many contestants there had to be, how the contestants were selected. For the Mastership Game, like any other game, could only exist if it was regulated in all of its aspects. So what were the other rules? More importantly, where were they?

To the last question Andrew knew there could only be one answer: in the College, for the secret to this game would be hidden as securely as possible.

He got up to say farewell to Obedi.

Holland. Rotterdam.

Andrew sat in the grimy office on a rickety plastic chair. The warehouse, of which the office comprised the front part, was situated in an alleyway in a run-down area of the Rotterdam docks. A casual observer would not have given the place a second look, not least since it bore the faded markings of a container company on its stout walls and therefore seemed like all the other wharf buildings, shabby and somewhat neglected. But it was not the same, for appearances could be deceptive and they usually were in the case of military warehouses.

Behind the far wall of the office lay numerous locks and gates; and behind them was an impressive arsenal of weapons. It had been assembled by one of the leading groups of Dutch mercenaries who sold their skills and services to the highest bidder. Andrew had had contact with them for many years, just as he had with a very large number of organisations, military and terrorist, around the world. It was all part of his work as a Fellow to help the College and its Master assess the military strength of countries and their capacity for war. All threads in the spider's web.

'Andrew!'

The Dutchman shook his hand and plumped himself down behind a battered metal desk. He was a bulky man, with heavy shoulders and a paunch. This, and his receding ginger hair, fleshy cheeks and rather bulbous nose did not hint at any military connection. Rather, it reflected the countenance of a butcher. Or a down-to-earth priest who had enjoyed too much of his parishioners' hospitality. Yet he headed the mercenary group. Andrew had known the Dutchman for a long time and knew all about his mercenary operations. On his side, the Dutchman knew little about Andrew apart from the fact that he was a consultant to the UN who had the uncanny ability to pop up in the world's troublespots. Who Andrew really was the Dutchman didn't care although he had his suspicions. Normally he would, he would care very much, but in Andrew's case he made an exception. A few years ago, in the bush in Papua New

Guinea, Andrew had saved him and two of his wounded companions from being disembowelled by the winning side. Not a pleasant prospect and for saving his life the Dutchman was prepared to accord him his complete trust and a very big favour waiting to be repaid. A favour Andrew now intended to cash in.

'Pieter, I need your help. I want to visit an island.'

'Good, you could do with a holiday,' said the Dutchman in his accented English. He got up. 'Let's go for a walk.' He grabbed a packet of Russian cigarettes. He had been to the Urals recently.

They sat down at the waterfront on large bollards, watching the oil tankers coming in. It was drizzling and a light mist hung over the water.

'I need to get on and off the island without being seen. So I want to acquire some of your equipment. The best you have.'

The Dutchman nodded and lit a cigarette. Dying from smoking was the least of his problems. 'OK. It can be arranged. When?'

'Three weeks' time.'

'Tell me more. What's the name of the island?'

Andrew hesitated. 'I'll tell you in a moment.' He began to explain about the island of Tirah without divulging its name. It was a particularly difficult place to visit in secret for various reasons. First, it was in a remote location. Second, the island was only accessible by ferry at its one port; or by helicopter at its one helipad. However, neither of these means of access could be utilised since they were watched. Third, the very steep cliffs of the island and the strong ocean currents swirling about it prevented the approach or landing of vessels other than at its sole port. As a result, the topography of the place made unannounced visits extremely difficult – which was exactly why the Lord of the Isles had selected it on which to found the College. Andrew had concluded that the only way he might be able to get in without detection was by air and at night. The Dutchman grunted at this news.

'Will they have equipment to detect aircraft in their airspace?'

'No doubt,' said Andrew. 'But I guess it'll only be in the upper airspace and not below a certain height, say two hundred metres. There'd be too much interference otherwise. If it was a small chopper coming in low just above the cliffs I don't think they'd be able to pick it up. Especially if it comes in from the northwest of the island where the mountains are. That said, it will be a hazardous journey at this time of the year since the sea winds will be particularly strong. I'd need a very experienced pilot. One that can fly blind.'

'Go on,' said the Dutchman. He was committed to nothing yet. Not even to a man who had saved his life.

'I think the chances of getting on and off the island undetected in this way are good. Also, it will be unexpected. There's no reason why anyone would want to visit the island in secret apart from entering the principal building on it, a castle.'

'A castle? Who lives there?' The mercenary's curiosity was aroused. It sounded like a prison complex. Was Andrew trying to spring someone from jail?

Andrew explained that no one lived on the island apart from those in the castle. At this time of the year the number of occupants would be small, less than thirty, including staff. He also explained that getting into the castle was the real problem since there was only one entrance and he had never seen any detailed maps of the place. He suspected they didn't exist.

The Dutchman was astonished. 'There must be some. The Russian or US military are bound to have them for every island on the planet.'

'They may do,' said Andrew, shaking his head, 'but they won't show much. It's not the surface that's important. It's underneath. Underneath the surface is a warren of tunnels.'

'Sure? You've been in them?' The Dutchman stubbed out his cigarette and watched a tanker pass by.

Andrew confessed he hadn't. However, the third courtyard was occupied by only one man, who entered and left it secretly. Since his route was not overground it could only be underground. The tunnels would have been built long ago. Andrew was quite sure they existed. The Dutchman studied him carefully as he explained all this. A third courtyard. It didn't sound like a military installation. Perhaps it was a hospital or a research institute; and who was this mysterious man in question? Was Andrew planning a hit?

Andrew continued, 'The castle has three courtyards in total. As you can imagine, the third will be the most difficult to get into unnoticed. In fact, it's probably impossible.'

'And where do you have to go?' asked the Dutchman with a grimace.

Andrew smiled. 'The third courtyard.'

'It follows,' said his companion grumpily. 'I knew you'd take the easiest one. Apart from the tunnels, are there other entrances?' They started to walk down the quay. The Dutchman kicked a Coke can into the water. Not a prison. More like a military installation.

'The only entrance I'm aware of is a door into the third courtyard,' said Andrew, 'but I've already discounted it. I don't know the electronic combination and it would be the most obvious one to watch.'

From his time at the College, Andrew knew that all their apartments could only be accessed by means of electronic combinations. The entrance to the third courtyard was the same. He was aware of no such devices in the first and second courtyards, which suggested to him that the College trusted in its general impregnability. However, he also knew that he should assume nothing. The third courtyard was unknown and mysterious territory.

'So,' said the Dutchman, 'what do you propose?' he glanced at his watch. He'd have to go soon. They had a consignment of bazookas coming in from his Chinese friends and they always wanted immediate payment.

Andrew explained that the plan was not to enter the castle by way of the main entrance nor through the first or third courtyards. Instead, he would get into the second courtyard and proceed to the third via an underground tunnel which he was sure must exist. Any direct entry into the third courtyard above ground was too risky. To get into the second courtyard though meant that he would need to ascend the cliff face, and then the granite of the castle walls. For that he required climbing equipment like the US special forces used.

They spent some minutes discussing whether the Dutchman could supply and the likely cost. The Dutchman confirmed that he could with some reluctance. He was becoming more cautious. It looked as if an assassination was being planned and his estimation of Andrew was undergoing a rapid reappraisal. He was not sure he wanted to get involved.

'So what about the person in the third courtyard?' the Dutchman asked casually. 'How do you know he'll be there?'

'I hope he isn't,' replied Andrew, 'but I can't say for certain.'

He had selected a day to enter the College when he thought the Master would be absent: the day of the G10 meeting in Chicago, 26 February, when the world's most powerful leaders got together to discuss the world's economies. Almost certainly the Master would attend to have private discussions with them. What if Andrew was wrong about this? What would happen if he were found in the College and couldn't get out? He would have to deal with that problem when it arose.

'Anything else?' enquired the Dutchman.

'No. The rest's up to me.' Andrew stopped at the end of the quay.

'Which means that you're not going to tell me. I see.' The Dutchman chuckled as they started to walk back to his office. 'Things really are secret.'

'Exactly,' said Andrew. 'Apart from the loan of a chopper I need equipment to detect spaces between walls.'

'Done. Anything else?'

'Electronic jamming devices. The best on the market.'

'And?'

'That's it. And I need to get on and off the island the same night. So I'm looking for a pilot in whom I can have complete confidence. Anyone in mind?' Andrew had a noncommittal expression.

'You mean me?' said the Dutchman sarcastically, lighting

another cigarette. He must try to cut down. Perhaps just two packs a day after all.

'Yes,' said Andrew, 'since you're the only one I trust to keep this secret.'

The Dutchman clicked his tongue against his teeth. He didn't like the sound of it but he owed Andrew a favour and he always repaid. 'OK,' he said finally. 'But I want to know the name of the island. If it's Papua New Guinea, no bloody way.' He couldn't stomach the natives again.

'It isn't,' said Andrew. 'It's off the west coast of Scotland.'

The Dutchman pulled a diary from his pocket and searched in its atlas section for a map of Scotland. He read off the names of some islands. After each one Andrew shook his head. There was a pause. He raised his head sharply.

'Shit,' he said. 'You don't mean Tirah?'

'Yes.'

'But that's impossible to get to.' The mercenary's face registered his consternation. No one even knew what the place looked like.

'Not impossible. Almost impossible. I'll give you the co-ordinates to guide you in.'

The Dutchman stopped outside his office and focused on Andrew. 'Now why do you want to go there?' he asked with a puzzled expression. 'I always thought you might be a Fellow. So why would you want to break in?'

'My secret,' said Andrew. He smiled. 'I may just be trying to get home.'

The Atlantic storms smashed against the island of Tirah throwing up great clouds of spray with a deafening roar. Its cliffs rose up sharply and majestically from the ocean floor to more than four hundred metres above sea level. The Dutchman couldn't see them in the darkness. However, he knew from the chopper's avionics they must be very close. He slowed down the chopper.

It had been a hair-raising journey. They'd set off from the far north of Scotland with the wind blowing at gale force seven. This had increased to force nine as they passed in the darkness right out into the Atlantic, to approach the island from the northwest.

The helicopter had been severely buffeted by the wind and several times when the engine started to whine dangerously, the Dutchman had proposed that they turn back. On each occasion Andrew had shaken his head and pointed out it wasn't much further, as if by way of comfort. They carried on but the Dutchman felt a small knot of fear beginning to develop and expand in the pit of his stomach. He knew from professional experience that there was a point beyond which they should not push their luck and that they were passing it. The chopper was not built for such hard wear and they could easily go down. Even if they survived the crash, two minutes in the sea and they'd perish from the cold. The Dutchman began to view his previous mercenary expeditions more favourably in light of this trip. Maybe Papua New Guinea wasn't so bad after all.

'One minute to the drop zone.'

'Have you got the coordinates right?'

The Dutchman grimaced. 'You'll have to swim if not.'

He lifted the nose of the chopper and they ascended, the machine battling against the wind. The Dutchman had supposed from the helicopter's electronics that the island was a few hundred metres in front of them. Suddenly Andrew shouted out a warning, but it was too late. As the Dutchman switched on a headlight to guide himself in, he caught sight of the cliffs. They reared up in front of the cockpit, awesome and frightening to behold, like a monster risen from the depths of the sea. They were far too close. In an instant the chopper was caught up in a vicious mini-tornado of wind that swirled about the cliff face, and it was violently twisted around and upwards. Then they were inside the vortex. The helicopter started to free fall into white space, the blades whirling aimlessly.

'Shit!' The Dutchman fought with the controls, trying to thrust the machine away from the landmass, but there was nothing he could do. They continued to free-fall. In the milliseconds that followed they watched, like passive viewers of a film, while the jagged and indented edges of the cliff face flickered only metres away from the chopper window. The first flecks of spray appeared. Unable to break free, the helicopter hurtled towards the waves which smashed against the rocks below with a thunderous roar. The Dutchman shouted again, his voice icy with fear. No more freedom fighting in this world.

'We've had it.'

With a final desperate wrench at the controls he slewed the machine completely on its side. There was nothing else to do. They were facing death in any case. With a mighty judder the engine began to cut out and the chopper blades skimmed the waves. The electronic lights faded and the glass window at the back of the helicopter cracked with the pressure. Time to say goodbye. The Dutchman even caught himself praying -- something that would have surprised his ex-wives. Suddenly, as if by a miracle, the chopper was thrust up and far out over the ocean, caught in another swirling mass of air that bounced off the island at speeds greater than 200 kilometres an hour. It was like being on a roller coaster without brakes or harness. No fun when it was upside down.

'Jesus Christ,' said the Dutchman after a minute, feeling the perspiration in his flying suit. 'I think we're still alive.' His prayer was instantly forgotten.

Andrew said nothing as he viewed the flickering dashboard. Then he replied in a neutral tone: 'We need to go further to the north, and higher. Go behind the mountain of Mullach Mor. Its six hundred metres above sea level so you'll need to ascend. And be careful of the stacs. Veer round them. The wind will be too high to pass between.'

In front of their gaze five needles of rock, the stacs, appeared out of the ocean. Once part of Tirah, they had broken away millions of years ago. Clip them, or land on them, and the sightseeing would be over in an instant.

'Isabel,' the Dutchman muttered under his breath as he thought of his new girlfriend, 'I just want to go home.'

Ten minutes later they reached the western slope of Mullach

Mor. The chopper hovered a couple of metres from the ground. Andrew pushed out his equipment. He turned to the unhappy pilot, his face sprinkled with rain. 'Thanks, Pieter. Five o'clock this morning. Same coordinates. I'll put up a beacon. If I'm not there, just leave, OK?'

'Too bloody right.' The Dutchman fumbled for another cigarette.

'Good luck,' said Andrew. He inclined his head towards his colleague in farewell and said conversationally, 'I think the weather will get worse.'

With that, he disappeared into the darkness. The Dutchman made no reply to this useful observation. He headed back to the mainland and a very large drink. Perhaps he'd try marriage a third time. Less risky than this.

Andrew located his equipment and slung it over his shoulders. Five kilometres to reach the College. It was pitch-black and there was no sound apart from the wind and the deep boom of the waves. He could have shouted at the top of his voice and a person next to him wouldn't have heard. Extracting a torch from his pocket he set off.

The snow and ice had gone from Tirah and had been replaced by persistent drizzle, so that Andrew's feet squelched through the mud. He passed around the back of Mullach Mor and through a thick forest of fir trees. After two hours' hard trek, the castle loomed up before him.

Andrew stopped for a moment to catch his breath. Then he shone his torch up the rock-face. It was almost smooth, even before the granite blocks of the castle walls began. Great runnels of water gushed down it. While he extracted ropes and pitons from his bag, Andrew remembered incidents from his past: a treacherous night climb in the High Andes in Peru many years ago with a small group of US Special Service men to investigate the strength of the Shining Path guerrillas, a solitary trek in the jungles of Borneo to warn of an assassination attempt against a local politician that threatened to unleash an inter-tribal war;

and a terrible journey across the mountains into the remote Kingdom of Bhutan, in which one of the Fellows had died from exposure and Andrew had been sure he himself would perish. Yet he'd enjoyed the rigour of it all, and pitting his wits against the elements so that the College might learn of things to fulfil its obligation to promote peace. Andrew shook his head ruefully. Now he was trying to break back into the College, a place that he could never revisit unless he became its Master.

Andrew commenced his ascent. It was more difficult than he'd supposed, even for an experienced mountaineer, and on more than one occasion he lost his footing badly. The noise of the wind hid the sound as he drove pitons into the rock and then into the granite face. Finally, more than one hundred metres up, Andrew reached the battlements and looked over. Below him was the second courtyard and the garden. Close to the outer wall was the back of the library. Andrew scrutinised the battlements. As he had guessed, it was impossible to reach the third courtyard by walking along the top of the wall for crossed spikes of an ancient construction had been set into the granite. That left him only the possibility of descending into the second courtyard. He began to pay out cord, fairly sure there would be no thermal or movement sensors on the castle walls since the rain and snow would have precluded their use, nor in the garden below given that all the Fellows had access to it. The third courtyard he was certain would be quite different. It would contain a minefield of detection devices. Therefore, Andrew had to think of a way of getting into the third courtyard that no stranger would be aware of, for he believed the Dutchman had been right in saying it was impossible for anyone to get into the College undetected. Unless, that was, one was a Fellow and knew the layout.

The library comprised two floors and a basement. Its clean, limpid beauty was visible from the gleam of lights on the ground floor, signifying that various Fellows were researching in the quiet of the evening as they mined the libraries and computer databases of the world. Andrew frowned. The library had only two entrances, with large oak doors: one at the front; the other at the side of the building, which was only used by the staff. Once these doors were closed Andrew reckoned it would be impossible to get into the place without setting off alarms, and he had only fifteen minutes.

Hastily, he climbed down the inside of the castle wall and entered the library through the side door after carefully checking that no one was about. Then he made his way up a narrow spiral staircase. He decided the safest place to hide until the library closed would be on the first floor of the library since he could see no lights there. Its long hall had numerous doors leading off it into separate rooms, each room packed with books and data relating to a particular field of study. From these, other rooms led off, each diminishing in size since the library had been built on the prevailing philosophy of the sixteenth century that knowledge was like a tree and should branch out. In any one of those small rooms Andrew could secrete himself. Stealthily, he crept up the stone spiral stairs, part of the original fabric of the building.

As he neared the top, a loud voice just below him on the stairs exclaimed, 'Good evening.'

Andrew shrank back against the wall and waited until the discussion between one of the Fellows and a librarian on the ground floor ceased. Had they decided to ascend the stairs at that moment they would easily have detected him. He listened intently to the voices. One was of the Custodian, the other an Arbitrator. What was the latter doing here? Could it be, in the absence of the Master from the College, one of the Arbitrators took his place? Where would he stay – in the Master's Lodge? It was something Andrew had not counted on. Silently, he debated whether to proceed. He had no real choice; he had come so far. Whatever the risks he must continue.

The voices finally faded away into the distance. Crouching down, Andrew ran along the corridor and hid himself in a side room. He waited. Within a quarter of an hour the Custodian of the library had turned off the lights and the oak doors had thundered shut. An eerie silence prevailed. Andrew was left alone with the works of Fellows of ages past and the spirits of those who had laboured on them. He rose from his cramped location and made his way down the steps to the basement.

Andrew had determined that the basement of the library was his best chance for getting into the third courtyard. Almost certainly there was a tunnel from the library to the Master's Lodge. It was also not difficult to hazard a guess where it might commence since, at the back and behind the Custodian's desk, were certain rooms reserved for the Master's private use. Quickly, Andrew stripped off his immersion suit and put on felt shoes that would leave no mark. Carrying various items of equipment he had brought with him, he went downstairs, with only a pencil beam of torchlight to guide him.

In the basement, at the door to the Master's rooms, he inserted a small device in the keyhole. The scanning laser measured the space in the lock left for the key and produced an outline on a thin sliver of plastic. Within minutes it had hardened sufficiently for Andrew to insert it in the door and enter the room. That was the simple part over and done with.

The side room was rectangular in shape and seemed to be for storage. It was lined with bookshelves filled with documents marked for the attention of the Master. There was nothing dreary about the place though, for paintings were carefully positioned on the walls and antiques lay among the shelves. In one corner was a gorgeous silk rug on which stood two Chinese Yüan dynasty vases of great beauty. Yet Andrew had no time to gaze at these things; what he sought was before him. Under an old limestone arch worn steps led down to beneath the ground level of the library. Andrew took an electronic sensor from his pocket and turned it on. Stealthily he passed through the arch and down the steps. Before him was a large tunnel which he supposed from its direction could only lead to the Master's Lodge.

Andrew started to walk down the tunnel, holding the sensor out at arm's length before him in one hand, the torch in the other. The passageway was neither dank nor claustrophobic. On the contrary, like a museum corridor, it was beautifully decorated. On the walls were pictures of former Masters while delicately carved tables bore a profusion of antiques, in wood, in jade, in stone and in porcelain. In many cases they were hundreds of years old. Indeed, before his gaze was a veritable storehouse containing some of the most spectacular *objets d'art* Andrew had ever seen. Where had they come from? Gifts to past Masters? Objects stored here for their protection by Governments while war raged outside? He had no idea and no time to question.

After progressing along the tunnel for some several metres, Andrew came to a divide in the road. One path went straight ahead to some steps and then through another arch. The other path led off at a right angle. Andrew was sure he was now directly under the third courtyard and that the first path led on to the Master's Lodge. He knew he should go ahead since time was running out. However, his curiosity got the better of him and he turned right to investigate the second path. Worn flagstones reflected its great age. It must have been one of the first parts of the College to have been built. Andrew stepped quickly over the flagstones. Finally, the cave opened out into a cavern. What Andrew saw in the torchlight made him catch his breath.

Before his gaze was a mausoleum. Here, under the third courtyard, was the burial place of the Masters. Like a child in a daze, Andrew began to walk among the marble sepulchres. Tombs going back to the very foundations of the College lay on the floor of the cavern, each bearing in white marble the full name of those individuals who had held the supreme title down the centuries. When a new Master was elected his personal name was never used again and often the Fellows themselves could not recall the names of holders of the post in past centuries. They were simply known as the Master, for everything was done to preserve the anonymity of those who held the highest office of all. Similarly, there was scarcely a ripple on the surface of College life when a successor took over on the demise of the incumbent. Thus, a Fellow of the College who, perhaps, once occupied the post of a very senior official – a professor or a researcher outside – quietly retired to become Master of this, the most remarkable institution in the world. Yet in death, their real names and their dates were recalled once more – to be known only to God and to their successors in that great office.

Andrew wandered among the tombs, reading the details of those individuals who had once held the Mastership, many of whom had been touched by genius. He knew that time was rushing by. Despite this, the mystery and antiquity of it all entranced him. At the back of the mausoleum and set aside from the others Andrew came across the last resting place of James, Lord of the Isles, the first Master. It was a marble sepulchre remarkably unadorned save that, on its top, it bore in alabaster the reclining effigy of a man dressed in a simple robe. The image was so real in the torchlight that Andrew almost thought it would rise up and address him. And below, carved into the white marble base, were engraved James's final thoughts to the world, written for eternity:

'Peace and compassion.'

Andrew sat down and pondered before the tomb for a while. A feeling of grief came upon him. How sad this saintly man would have been to learn that the great institution of the Mastership to which he had dedicated his life could now be bought and sold. For the moneylenders were truly within the temple. The College, which had held firm throughout the centuries while so many other institutions had decayed, had fallen victim, at last, to greed and into evil ways. The nature of the contest evidenced this decline. If Andrew became Master he would seek to change this. Yet, to become Master he ran the risk of taking the same path of evil for which he castigated the College and its Master. Perhaps, he should stop now. It was probably too late anyway. So many institutions in the world outside had declined in the last few years, it was irrational to expect the College to be able to withstand the onslaught for much longer. In his mind's eye Andrew saw a great colossus slowly pitch over and topple into the dust. Poor James, he thought. All things pass, and all greatness fails.

Quitting the mausoleum Andrew approached the arch that led into the Master's Lodge. His sensor detected an electronic field just inside. Andrew began to set up the sophisticated devices the Dutchman had given him to deactivate the system temporarily. As he went through the field, his body tensed, waiting for the sound of an alarm, the closing of a door or the fall of a trap. Nothing happened. Swiftly, he passed into the Lodge and then, via an anteroom, emerged from a door into the hall.

To his right was the main entrance to the Lodge across whose threshold Andrew and the other contestants had passed the fateful day they sought to be nominated for the Mastership. To his left, the marble staircase which wound its way upstairs. From his pocket Andrew drew out a boxlike device, the size of a mobile phone. It was a void indicator for detecting spaces behind walls. Then he got to work. There were many rooms and in less than two hours he must start back for the rendezvous if he wanted to get off the island before dawn.

Andrew began with the dining room, then moved on to the other rooms on the ground floor. Minutes ticked by and the device gave no response. It seemed that Andrew was mistaken after all and there were no hidden recesses as he'd supposed. He went upstairs, entering the sitting room in which they'd sat when the Master first told them about the Chinese puzzle box, then the study, then a reception room. Finally, at the end of the corridor, he came to the library. It was here they had assembled when they had told the Master of their decision to take part in the contest.

The library was a beautiful chamber with a marble fireplace, on each side of which stood a bronze globe and an armillary sphere. The rest of the room was taken up with bookcases. They stretched from floor to ceiling, apart from one wall which was covered with panelling. Within each of the panels was an embossed coat of arms of a former Master. While there was no sign of a concealed entrance the indicator noisily informed Andrew that, behind the panelling, was a large space.

How to get in? Andrew sat on a chair and contemplated the scene before him. On the supposition that the Master used any hidden passageway frequently the entrance shouldn't be too difficult to find nor involve him in removing large quantities of books. Therefore, it must have something to do with the insignia. He examined them minutely. He pressed one and then others. There was no response. Finally, more by luck than design, he touched the coat of arms of a Master in the sixteenth century in whose period of office the room had been converted into a library. Silently, part of the bookcase slid back to reveal a dimly lit corridor sloping steeply downwards. Andrew allowed himself a brief moment of pleasure in finding the secret recess, then he quickly proceeded down the corridor.

The sight before him took his breath away. He came out onto a narrow ledge of rock. Below him was a vast natural cave located deep within the bedrock of the mountain. A stone staircase beneath his feet spiralled down to the bottom of the cave, on various levels of which rooms had been carved out of the rock by human hands hundreds of years before. The Lodge itself comprised a veritable mystery with an inner casing, like a puzzle box.

Andrew went down the steps, glancing into the rooms on each level as he did so. On the first level was a computer room. Now he knew where the second quantum computer the College possessed was located. What did the Master use it for? To hold information on the College and Fellows, past and present? To communicate directly with world leaders? Andrew had no time to speculate. The book that he sought would not be contained in its memory, it would be far older. There were more levels, some leading into huge halls full of information and documents.

At the fourth level Andrew entered his Aladdin's cave. Just inside the entrance was a beautiful marble fountain into which water gushed from out of the mountain rock. Beside the fountain was a door. Andrew guessed that it probably went outside the College. Perhaps there was an underground tunnel leading to the port or to elsewhere on the island which enabled the Master to disappear and to emerge unseen. Andrew rested for a moment and sipped some of the cold water. Then he entered the library, the hidden library of the Masters.

Although the College had a magnificent library, it had long been rumoured among the Fellows that it also possessed a collection accessible only to the Arbitrators and to the Master, one that contained some of the rarest books in the world. It was these on which Andrew now gazed. The room was large, like a baronial hall. It contained beautifully carved shelving with wooden steps leading to the upper stacks. In the middle of the room were a few desks and chairs – rather like the library of an ancient university. But this library was more spectacular still, for it stretched far back into the mountain and it contained row upon row of books, most beyond price. Andrew wandered the length of this room and on into others. As he did so, he realised that he was looking at the wealth of civilisations, many of the works known only by references in other works or not known to have existed. The aphorisms of Aldricus, volumes from the great encyclopaedia of Qianlong, Becker's astronomical observations, the secret edicts of Charles V, the De Rerum Animarum of St Bernard of Clairvaux. Hundreds of Greek, Roman, Aramaic, Coptic, Sanskrit and Hebrew manuscripts. A hundred thousand more texts. Where had they come from? The library at Alexandria? The library of the Caesars? The Vatican library? Andrew didn't know. However, he was sure that the College was a custodian of those great treasures – works thought to have been destroyed by men in ages past during their endless battles and internecine wars. Somehow, miraculously, the College had salvaged what it could, to preserve them for the future. For humankind.

Andrew wandered through the rooms, agonised. What he would give to spend time here, to delve into the past, into lost thoughts and writings. However, he knew he must ignore them. There was only one book he must discover. Feverishly, he searched for any material or documents relating to the College itself. Eventually he found them in one of the side rooms of the hidden library.

In addition to maps and architectural drawings on the walls, and a large collection of diaries and notebooks by former Masters arranged along the shelves, there were two bound texts located on a table. One bore a reference to the Arbitrators. Andrew ignored it and turned to the other. It was a tall but slim text, bound in black leather. In gold it bore on its face the insignia of Pierre Rochelle, one of the greatest of Masters. Inside the cover was the firm signature of Rochelle followed by that of every one of his successors framed in a red spiral around the simple black letters of the title, *Regulae Magistrati*, the Rules of the Mastership.

Andrew began to read. He was staggered by its contents. For it had been written in the fifteenth century and amended from time to time by succeeding Masters and Arbitrators. It dealt with every contingency concerning the Mastership. He skimmed through the headings and the rules. There to be One Master ... there to be Five Arbitrators appointed by the Master, who could themselves never become Master ... the selection of others in case of their demise ... the supreme powers of the Master etc. Nothing about the actual contest for the Mastership.

Suddenly Andrew came to it. In the case where a new Master was required to be appointed the Arbitrators must establish a contest and select by lot five Fellows from a certain age group. When was a Master required to be appointed though? Rule X said when the Arbitrators had concern over whether the Master could continue to fulfil his office. That probably meant, thought Andrew, on the death or the physical or mental incapacity of the Master. Possibly, if the Arbitrators also doubted the ability of the Master to perform his office adequately. So, was that it? They were dispensing with the services of the Master? Andrew read on. Then he came to Rule No XIV:

> The terms of the contest shall be determined by the Arbitrators in their absolute discretion and in this matter the Master shall not be in any way involved.

Andrew's eyes skipped on down the page . . . the Duration of the Contest and, above all, the Clandestine Nature of the Contest. He was awed to think the game for the Mastership had always been played in complete and utter secrecy. Every generation a silent struggle was waged within the College while the outside world only saw the faintest of ripples on the surface as the apostolic succession passed from Master to Master. *Sic transit gloria mundi.* Now passes the light of the world. *Habemus Magistrum.* We have a Master.

Andrew skipped back a page. As he read, his awe turned to horror as his eyes alighted on Rule No. XIX. He leant back against the bookcase and sighed. There could be no doubt as to its meaning. No doubt at all.

'You're very quiet,' said the Dutchman as the chopper began its flight back to the mainland. He was finding that the return journey wasn't so bad and that the buffeting of the wind didn't affect him so much now – not after half a bottle of vodka. He looked across at Andrew, who was staring into the night, the island of Tirah far behind them. 'Well, did you get what you wanted?'

Andrew nodded. He was thinking about Rule No XIX.

> In the contest for the Mastership the present Master may also take part.

One other concern gnawed at Andrew's mind. It had been too easy to get into the College and to find the rules. Someone had wanted him to find them. Someone had been expecting him.

* * *

When the Master returned to the College from the G10 meeting in Chicago, he was told by Symes that there had been an intruder in the Lodge the previous night.

'Following your instructions I did nothing, Master.'

The Master picked up some papers from a table in his study and said casually, 'Did you determine who that person was?'

'Yes,' said Symes. It had been easy. One of the tasks of the second quantum computer was to monitor Tirah, and the interior of the College in particular. It was impossible for an intruder not to be detected by its extensive network of sensors and the helicopter had been spotted long before it had landed. That was why the College had little need of visible security measures. Symes told the Master the name of the individual.

'I see,' said the Master.

He turned back to his papers.

Later that day the Master received a phone call from one of the Arbitrators.

'Master, I have just received news that the police in Erris have closed the file on Rex Boone. They have concluded that he was killed in a car accident, though they've been unable to find out who the driver of the car was. They have decided that there was no evidence of foul play and it was a case of death by misadventure. I assume this was just as you expected.'

'It was,' said the Master. 'Thank you.'

'Master, there is one further matter. The new Fellow, Susan Corelli, has helped us check through all the documents and personal papers Rex Boone left at the Global Forum for Nuclear Research. Nothing was found about the College, nor the contest for the Mastership.'

'I see,' said the Master. 'Thank you, Arbitrator.'

The Master sat back in his chair. He thought of Tanya, Sebastien, Andrew and Ivan and how they were proceeding on their quest; he also thought of himself.

At least one of them knew the truth about Rex. About his murder, that is.

CHAPTER TEN

There are some people who are not satisfied with their nature and always attempt what is beyond it. Thus, they attempt what is impossible. They cannot succeed.

Kuo Hsiang

January. Boston.

TANYA SAT IN A BEDROOM in the five-star Bellevue Hotel in Boston. The previous three weeks, since the initial meeting in the Master's Lodge, had been very difficult for her. The death of Boone had affected her profoundly, not just because they had once been lovers, because Rex had epitomised everything about living life to the full that she could imagine. Dynamic, forceful, with a supreme confidence in himself and his abilities, he had dominated the external world in which he'd lived. Yet he had perished. The gods were truly cruel. Surely he should have become Master. And if he had, would Tanya have complained?

She watched as the porters brought her luggage into the room. It was only once a person was dead that you realised how much you missed them. She missed Rex now, so very much.

Tanya had left the College immediately after the Master had told the four Fellows the terms of the contest on New Year's Eve. She couldn't bear to talk with Sebastien. She was still furious with him for having deserted her after the initial dinner with the Master. She knew where he'd gone – off to his chalet in Switzerland. However, it would be good for him to suffer for a while.

Tanya had gone back to work at the European Computer Union (ECU) but not to her flat in Berlin. Instead, she went to stay with a female friend and had hidden herself away. She needed time to think, and to plan ahead. She had also discovered on the supernet that the Boston Newspaper and Periodicals Library had no computer link, which was why she had decided to fly to Boston, to search in the library in person.

Tanya started to unpack. Then she phoned downstairs to the hotel reception. Within a couple of minutes there was a loud knock at the door. Tanya opened it.

'Can I help you, madam?'

The hotel bellboy was in his early twenties, lanky and blond. He stared at her almost cheekily. He'd caught sight of Tanya as she came into the hotel and had made a beeline for her. He hoped his luck was as good as it had been some weeks ago with a New York exchange dealer. It was amazing what single women guests asked for sometimes, and this one was a stunner. He perused her short red skirt, black stockings and the cream-coloured jacket that failed to hide the pertness of her breasts. She must be a fund manager or someone equally high-powered. And she'd no wedding ring on.

'Yes,' said Tanya, faintly amused that his eager gaze had not yet reached her neck. Take away the sex instinct from men and there wasn't much left. 'I'll be staying here for a few days and I've brought a computer with me. I need a connecting lead.'

'No problem, madam,' said the bellboy with a grin. 'We often have similar requests. We also have executive facilities downstairs which you are most welcome to use.'

'No,' said Tanya, perhaps a little too curtly. 'I prefer to work in my room. Do you have a swimming pool?'

'Yes, madam. In the basement.' He paused and said coyly, 'My name's Tom, by the way. Just call me if you need anything.'

'Thank you.' She closed the door. Barely out of his teens and only one thing on his mind. Still he was quite dishy.

Tanya began to set up her portable computer. Her resignation as a consultant to the ECU, a body of computer manufacturers, had been both difficult and easy. Difficult in the case of her ferocious boss, Val, a middle-aged harridan who ate, breathed and only slept with computers. She was convinced that Tanya was trying to make a demand for more money, more time, more something, which of course they would reluctantly concede to her after a fight. But for one of their star employees to leave the ECU, never. Yet it was easy in the case of the head of the ECU. He listened to Val's tirade and tears. Then he simply said to the bewildered and saddened woman that Tanya should be allowed to go. Of course, Val didn't know that he was an Arbitrator. On her last day in the office Val had stood up stony-faced and angry as Tanya entered her inner sanctum to bid her farewell. Then she'd hurried from her desk to give her a bear hug before bursting into tears once more. Tanya was really touched. It was so unusual in a woman whose only passion was big chips and flat screens.

'Come back soon,' she'd said. 'Find whatever you are looking for, find yourself, Tanya. But come back soon.'

Tanya had nodded then, but she knew in the back of her mind that she never would. Something told her that part of her life was over and done with. Besides, she needed to keep well clear of the ECU. Tanya had no desire that the College keep an eye on her. Not after the death of Rex.

There was a knock at the bedroom door. Cautiously, she unlocked it. Tom, the bellboy appeared before her once more. He was trying another tack. He tried to look hip and inviting.

'Here are some of the leads which we have, madam. I hope they are suitable. Is there anything else?'

'No. Thanks.' Tanya closed the door and giggled. He could get his experience with the chambermaids. Besides, unlike Sebastien, Tanya had no real desire to play around. She began to connect up her laptop computer on the hotel bedroom table. She'd bought it new. There was too much risk that her old one at the College might be compromised.

Rex was dead. Tanya was sure he'd been murdered. But where was the proof? None, really. All she had to go on was Rex's statement that, if she was reading his computer message, 'something will have gone badly wrong.' He'd written that before he'd agreed to take part in the contest for the Mastership so he must have been concerned about something even then, but not so concerned that he'd spelt it out in his message to her. Of course, like Tanya, Rex would have known the College could gain access to even the Fellows' computers if it wanted. Tanya had done this once herself, on the instructions of the Master. But was that the position this time? Did Rex not say anything further because he was worried about the interception of his message? Or was the truth more prosaic – he was hurrying to catch the ferry to the mainland and didn't have time to put down details?

Also, what about the letter Rex had promised to write to her from Erris? Tanya had received nothing. Perhaps, he'd been going to write it the night he died. What would it have said? Was he trying to warn her of something about the game, the other contestants or the Master?

Tanya inserted a code into her laptop to access the College computer. She waited. As before, there was absolutely no reaction. The line was dead, her access denied. It was just as the Master had told them. They would receive no help from the College now. Indeed, there was no real evidence that she'd ever belonged to it. Like Rex's information, the contestants were being wiped from the records of the College, as if they had never existed. There was one more avenue to try. Tanya was one of two or three Fellows in the College who'd helped programme the second computer to which only the Master and the five Arbitrators had access. It not only monitored the island and the first computer, it also contained files on the Fellows, past and present, as well as secret data on the College itself. Quickly Tanya typed in a password. Then she began to type in an elaborate series of numerations to attempt a remote access.

'Damn!'

Nothing. Tanya closed down her machine in case the College computer might already be searching for her in return. She got up from the bedroom table, feeling depressed. She was missing

Sebastien, even though she was still angry with him. Missing not only the sex, but also the hilarious laughter with which he would have greeted her suspicions that the College might be keeping an eye on them. He'd have laughed also about her worries concerning Rex's death. Rex had stepped in front of the car because he was so bloody arrogant he'd have expected it to get out of the way, that's what Sebastien would have said. No sympathy for Rex there. It was just the way the cookie crumbled. Still, whatever Sebastien might think was not the same as a woman's intuition.

Once she'd unpacked, Tanya went down to the changing rooms in the hotel basement and put on her small bikini. She made for the pool. It was empty and she slipped into the warm water with a feeling of delight. She started to swim, a leisurely backstroke.

Rex was dead. Assuming it was no accident, the reasons for his death seemed limited. Perhaps, he'd been working on a nuclear energy project and learnt something he shouldn't. Tanya recalled there'd been the recent scandal about the leak of a US cabinet paper on foreign nuclear bases which had threatened to bring down the President. It could have been something to do with that. More ominously, perhaps Rex had betrayed the College in some way. But even if he had, would they have killed him? They had just invited him to take part in the Mastership contest. It was preposterous. The College was a foundation dedicated to peace, not some mafia. Tanya had never before had cause to worry about the integrity of the institution. Besides, Rex had left no message about nuclear secrets or personal difficulties. His message was quite specific. It was about the contest for the Mastership and that it would be more dangerous and difficult than she thought.

'Is the water warm, honey?'

Tanya eyed the elderly and large southern belle who was about to dip her toe into strange waters. Aged sixty-five if she was a day with hair dyed a purplish white she, at least, didn't look like a spy with her homely face and genuine smile.

'Yes, come on in. It's lovely.'

'Greg, honey,' she beckoned to the wafer-thin husband who followed her like her morning snack, 'let's get in.'

Tanya watched, fascinated, as a massive displacement of water was succeeded by the faintest of ripples. The pair slowly made their way across the pool, talking, their tender gestures betraying the fact that, although they were elderly, they were still very much in love. A lifelong love match. Tanya was deeply touched. That's how she'd hoped it would have been with her parents. Instead, she'd watched her father die alone of cancer. Then, six months later, her mother passed away, both irreconcilable since their divorce. How Tanya had loved them. How proud they'd have been of her achievement in getting into the European Computer Union even though they never knew who she truly worked for. Her parents had never met Sebastien. What would they have made of him? Like everyone else, they would probably have been mesmerised by his charm and nonchalance, the way in which he made everything seem so easy and made such a game of it, including life itself. Tanya watched as the elderly couple progressed about the pool, chatting all the while. Then, while she did a few lengths, she turned her mind back to more sinister matters.

If Rex's death had something to do with the Mastership Game, it was likely one of the contestants had killed him. At least she knew she hadn't. That was the one fixed point in the shifting sands. Who had killed Rex then? Sebastien was hugely ambitious but would he murder to attain his goal? Tanya knew his frailties, his womanising, his remarkable ability to turn everything to his advantage. Yet, despite his faults she couldn't believe Sebastien would have killed Rex to gain the Mastership. It was inconceivable. What about Ivan and Andrew? Just how far would they go to attain their heart's desires? Ivan in particular. These thoughts and a thousand others concerning her future continued to flow through her mind. By the end of her swim, Tanya had summarised her plan of action.

1. She'd take part in the Mastership Game, if only to find out who'd killed Rex, if anyone. Rex would have done the same for her.
2. She'd find out everything she could about the other contestants, including Sebastien. She was in a position to do that. Trawling through computer databases around the world she could probably piece together details of the background of each one of them, even without access to the College computers. In the pasts of the other contestants there could be a clue, a reason why Rex had been killed. There just had to be.

Her mind focused, Tanya climbed the steps to get out of the pool.

'Can I help you?'

She looked up into the teasing eyes of the bellboy. He was desperate. Sex was clearly a major component of his job, as he saw it. How could Tanya assist him with what he really wanted?

'Thanks.'

As he grasped her arm to help her out of the pool, Tanya pretended to slip so that her hand slammed hard into his groin. He doubled up in agony.

'Oh, I am sorry, Tom,' she said innocently. 'Did I hurt you?'

The bellboy observed her dimly, tears misting up in his eyes. 'It's no problem, madam,' he said between clenched teeth, uncertain if his testicles still inhabited their former location. Then he hobbled away like an emasculated bull. Tanya smiled at him sympathetically while she watched his undignified departure. In chatting up women, the thinking was easy, it was the performance that was difficult. He was young. He'd learn. Perhaps, Tanya would be nicer to him tonight. Give him something to dream about.

She returned to the changing room. It was time to visit Boston Newspaper and Periodicals Library. Perhaps, the answer to the Mastership Game lay there. Yet, as Tanya stood under the shower, she still didn't feel satisfied with herself. She had made a few decisions, but she'd still avoided the two big issues. She'd not yet faced the question of whether she would work with, or against, Sebastien in the contest for the Mastership. Love didn't always conquer all.

And there was one other truth about the Mastership Game she had to face but didn't want to.

Tanya wanted the Mastership. Very much.

January. Switzerland.

Sebastien made for the disco. A medley of people in colourfully knitted sweaters were grouped around the bar in the Kasteln ski centre, their faces flushed with alcohol, their lungs hoarse with shouting to compete with the music. Sebastien ordered a drink and sat down on one of the stools.

'Ice, sir?'

'No. Just a straight Scotch, and make it a double.'

No sign of Tanya. Damn her. Sebastien had left a message for her to meet him here in this small Swiss ski resort. She knew all about it, having stayed in Sebastien's chalet outside town many times. Yet she hadn't showed up. Why was she avoiding him? Because she was angry? Or perhaps she was going to compete with him after all? Him or the Mastership – which did she love more? He went to the side of the bar and picked up a phone to reception.

'Any messages for me?'

'No, sir.'

'Please keep me paged.'

'Yes, sir.'

Sebastien had not seen her since New Year's Eve. Some time after their final meeting with the Master he'd gone to her rooms to discover she'd already fled the College. However, it was important that Sebastien talk with her. Tanya must not go for the Mastership on her own. The game was much too dangerous for that. Did she already know who'd killed Rex?

'A drink on the house,' the bar girl winked.

'Thanks.'

Sebastien wondered what Ivan and Andrew were doing. They probably had already worked out how to make their twenty million dollars. Still, there was plenty of time – stay cool. Rushing into things would do no good. Besides, he deserved a bit of a holiday – some enjoyment before he got down to the serious stuff and won the game.

Sebastien looked across the dance floor. Half-dressed bodies writhed and twisted to the music, the dancers temporarily cocooned in a little web of carnality and syncopation. For a brief moment Sebastien envied them their cosy security, caught as he was in a game of power – albeit one that he had freely chosen. Yet, the dice had been rolled and he wouldn't have it otherwise. He wanted the Mastership and they'd have to kill him to stop him.

'Elsa, I don't want to dance any more.'

'You shouldn't have drunk so much, that's why you feel sick. You're such a spoilsport.'

Sebastien glanced to his right at the bar. A lovers' tiff was in progress. He watched with amusement.

'I want to go home.'

'Well, go home, Karl. I want to dance.'

With a sullen expression Karl released his grip on his partner's arm. Drunkenly, he lurched out of the disco. Elsa sat on her bar stool and watched him go. She shook her head contemptuously. What a disaster. Then she went on to the dance floor. As she swirled to the heavy throb of the music Sebastien watched the strobe lights intermittently expose her body in the darkness. A svelte figure, long blonde hair, Nordic features and a generous mouth. She wore a red sequinned dress that clung tightly to her body and knee-length leather boots. About twenty-five years old. He guessed she was a ski instructress. After a few minutes Elsa returned to the bar.

'Like a dance?'

Elsa saw a man of athletic appearance and medium height with no fat on him. He was clean-shaven, with black hair, a handsome, expressive face and a small scar to one side of his forehead. She guessed he was in his early thirties. French? French-Canadian?

'Sure,' she said.

Elsa danced not one dance with Sebastien but many. As she did so, their bodies became closely entwined. The night wore on and the music slowed. The lights dimmed further. Off the disco floor they chatted about inconsequential things and Elsa liked his relaxed and easy-going manner. Later, Sebastien breathed in the fresh scent of her hair and kissed the warm lips. She responded with caution, then eagerly. He had caught her, just as a spider knows that its prey is secure on the first twist of the silken thread. Forget Tanya, he wanted company. Forget Karl, she wanted passion and performance.

'Another drink?'

'I'm all right,' said Elsa as she rested on his shoulder. It was two in the morning. After weeks of arguing with Karl, at last she felt happy. She was finished with him and for good.

'Let's go back to my place?'

'OK,' Elsa said after only a fraction's hesitation.

She gathered her things. They left the disco and went down a side exit to the ski centre. It was full of young people necking and fondling, the air heavy with pot and perfume. They brushed through the crowd. Suddenly, an apparition appeared before them in the half-light, his face distorted into a puce grimace. Karl had resurfaced from one of the lavatories. Sebastien raised his eyebrows in a faint gesture of amusement. After he had got over the shock of seeing Elsa with another man, Karl opened his mouth one more time. On this occasion words came out.

'That's my fucking girlfriend, you bastard.'

Elsa made to step forward but Sebastien held her back with his arm and let Karl push him through the lavatory door. An elderly man was washing his hands. Nervously, he watched as a large and drunken lout stumbled in, thrusting a casually dressed man in front of him. Sebastien smiled in his direction.

'Don't mind us.'

'You stay there and I'll deal with you in a minute.' Karl lurched up to the urinal. The old man viewed the two antagonists, his exit blocked. One of them had the physique of a body builder. The other was of average build but wiry-looking. It was clear they were going to fight and a certainty who would be the winner. The old man focused on Sebastien's eyes, willing him to flee so that he could escape as well. Sebastien calmly leant against a washbasin and lit a cigarette.

'Had an enjoyable day?' he said conversationally.

The old man nodded mutely while his fingers trembled under the hot tap. He didn't have long to wait for the outcome. As Karl stepped down from the urinal, having nearly severed his over large member in his zip, a blow smashed into his solar plexus. It was so expertly delivered that he felt nothing of the additional chop to the side of his neck that completed his dream state. He was out in a second. Sebastien caught the dead weight as it collapsed into his arms. Pushing open a cubicle door, he arranged Karl on the seat. Checking his pulse, Sebastien calculated he'd be out until morning. That would be fine. He went to wash his hands in the basin.

'Everything's go around here, isn't it?'

The old fellow opened his mouth but only his dentures evidenced his astonishment. His ablutions completed, Sebastien rumpled Karl's hair affectionately and made for the door. The silent witness watched him depart, his hands still quivering under the hot tap. For all he knew Sebastien could have as easily killed Karl as knocked him out. Finally, the old man turned off the tap. Appearances were deceptive, he reflected, as he dried his hands.

He left Karl contemplating his loins.

The following evening they lay naked by the fire in Sebastien's chalet. Elsa felt the warmth of the rug under her thighs and a fine whisky stroked the back of her throat with the same deft and sensual touch her skin had experienced minutes before.

'If you had to make a lot of money how would you do it?'

At his question Elsa turned on her side. Sweat glistened in her navel.

'How much?'

'Say, twenty million dollars.'

'Marry a millionaire, of course.' Elsa kissed him and pushed her long blonde hair back from her forehead.

'Suppose you couldn't. Suppose you had to make it yourself?'

'I'd get a nice respectable job like yours, work hard and not have too many mistresses,' Elsa laughed.

'What if you had to make it fast. In a year, say?'

'That's difficult. Rob a bank, I suppose.'

Rob a bank. Sebastien had discarded that possibility long ago. Banks rarely held twenty million dollars in their vaults. Those that did were well guarded. Stealing it would require a meticulously planned operation involving many others – people who would want a share of the action. No, armed robbery was out.

'Suppose that wasn't possible. How else?'

'What, legally?'

'Yes, legally.'

'I thought you investment bankers earned a fortune?' said Elsa as she topped up their drinks.

He kissed her lightly on the nose to distract her from challenging his lies. 'Never enough. Greed is addictive.'

They spent a few moments exploring the possibilities and sipping their whiskies. There seemed to be no profession where a person, from scratch, could hope to make such a sum legally in so short a period of time. Film stars, bond dealers, money market traders – they all earned large salaries but rarely made so much in a year.

'Be a pop star.'

'Be serious.'

'Run a gambling joint. Or a brothel.'

'Take too much time to set up.'

'Write a bestseller.'

'You're joking. Writers never make any money.'

Elsa stifled a yawn, bored with the subject. 'Anyway, why so interested in all this?'

'Curiosity, nothing more.'

'Well, the least you can do is to pay me for my assistance. Like a kiss just here.' She selected a place on her thigh.

Sebastien laughed and turned his attention to more immediate matters. Later, as Elsa slept beside him, he thought of the Mastership and the contest. They had one year to make twenty million dollars. Why money and not some other task? Sebastien thought that the College had selected it to make it extremely hard to achieve in a year. Besides, it was very straightforward and not subject to dispute. As the new Master, he wondered what he would order to be done with it. A personal congratulatory cheque perhaps?

What about the other contestants? Sebastien had not the slightest doubt that Ivan and Andrew would do whatever was necessary to win, as he would himself. They were powerful opponents, particularly if they made an alliance. Not as challenging as Rex would have been, but a challenge none the less. In the world outside the College, Ivan was closely linked with the secret services, Sebastien knew that. On behalf of the College, they'd worked together on a damage-limitation exercise a while ago, arising from the near collapse of the Belgian stock market as a result of a financial scandal.

In the case of Andrew, Sebastien knew he had a military background, but nothing else. Tanya might be able to get hold of some additional info. People with these sorts of abilities would have few scruples but would they kill to attain their objective? And what about Tanya herself? He'd been wrong in believing she wouldn't take part – an important thing to remember. How deep was her love for him anyway?

Elsa stirred and Sebastien felt her warm buttocks press against his groin. Reluctantly, he decided not to wake her up, despite his desire. He'd worked out a rough plan of how to make the twenty million dollars but he needed Tanya's help since only she would have the relevant expertise. It was a scheme fraught with danger. The problem with indulging in illegal activities was the risk of getting caught. If they did, there would be no College to help them. They must also keep clear of the others, Ivan in particular. Sebastien had no doubt he'd be happy to shop them, to ensure they were out of the way and unable to return to the College in one year's time. Sebastien closed his eyes, feeling sleepy. That left two matters to solve.

One, the Chinese puzzle box.

The other, where the hell was Tanya?

A few hours later he had the answer. Sebastien smiled and crumpled the fax up in his hands. He walked into the dining room of his chalet and tossed the message into the bin. It had said 'Come immediately. Bellevue Hotel, Boston. Tanya.'

It seemed as if they were going to work together after all. Good. Sebastien didn't want to compete with his lover and they must start on the contest for the Mastership soon. Still, he'd wait for a day or two before going to Boston. No point in rushing things.

He called out, 'Let's go skiing,' as he entered the kitchen.

Elsa turned from the breakfast table. She had only a T-shirt on. 'Great, but I think Karl will be on the slopes.'

'I look forward to meeting him,' said Sebastien nonchalantly while he popped some bread in the toaster. 'It would be nice to see him other than in a lavatory. I don't like talking to strange men in lavatories. People might get the wrong idea.' He poured coffee for them both. 'I hope he's recovered from his bellyache.' He glanced at Elsa. Together they laughed.

However, Elsa was slightly concerned. If only he'd take Karl more seriously, she thought. Karl could be quite aggressive when provoked and he'd hit her many times in the past. The problem was that Sebastien had never seen Karl when he was both angry and sober. It was lucky for him that Karl had passed out the moment they'd stepped into the gents or else Sebastien could have got badly hurt.

After making love Sebastien and Elsa took a tram to Kasteln.

Elsa realised that the relationship was only a temporary one. She'd stayed with Sebastien for four nights now and had enjoyed it all – the sophisticated company, the excitement and the physicality. Certainly, there was no shortage of money. He had told her he worked as a banker in New York and that he always came to Kasteln for his winter holidays. That was all that he'd disclosed, and Elsa found this strange. Men usually wanted to talk about themselves, about their jobs and their achievements yet Sebastien had been strangely silent on these matters. Also, despite his general insouciance and the way in which he seemed to treat the world as his playground, he had on occasion a way of distancing himself from her so that she felt a complete stranger in his company. There was a depth to him she could not fathom, a drive and inner intensity that made her nervous.

'You go first.'

They got into the ski-lift and breathed in the sharp air.

'Fabulous, isn't it?' said Sebastien, as he saw the fir trees below them disappearing. 'Don't you get tired of being a ski instructress?'

'No, it's part of me – being out on the slopes, the sense of freedom,' she said wistfully. 'I could never do anything else.'

'And Karl?'

'I've no idea. You'd have to ask him. He's a very good ski instructor, you know,' said Elsa, a touch primly. 'And he does body building in his spare time.'

'Oh, I didn't notice,' said Sebastien.

'We met in Finland twelve months ago,' continued Elsa. 'When we were on an instructors' course together. He can be quite a nice person when he's not drunk.'

'I'm sure he is,' said Sebastien in a good-humoured tone. He kissed her frosted cheek. 'Will you go out with him again?'

'Oh, no,' said Elsa. 'I was wanting to end it before I met you. You just helped me make the decision.' They got out of the ski-chairs as she continued talking. 'I've decided to go back to Sweden and get work there. I think I'll go soon . . .' she hesitated. 'After you've left.'

'Sounds a good idea,' Sebastien commented. He added firmly, 'Always follow your sense of destiny.'

'And you?' asked Elsa. 'Are you going to follow your destiny?'

'Of course,' replied Sebastien. He turned to look at her, his skis on his shoulder. 'You can't help it, whether it brings good or evil. Now, let's forget the philosophy and get on to the white stuff.'

They spent the day skiing and then, in the late afternoon, sat down on one of the slopes to rest for a moment before returning home. It was not to be so. They were joined by an unwelcome third party.

'Karl. A delight to see you as always.' Sebastien extended his hand towards the approaching figure on skis. The lugubrious Finn ignored it.

'Hello, Elsa.'

'I don't want to talk with you now.' Elsa glanced at him, then quickly averted her gaze to stare out over the slopes. Karl's face went rigid. He looked at Sebastien. There was hate in his stolid heart and he stoked it generously.

'That was my fucking girlfriend,' he bawled at Sebastien.

'Yes, she *was*,' said Sebastien in a smug tone, 'and you've got the adjective right. How did you guess?' He got up and casually balanced on his ski sticks, waiting for the attack. None came. Karl eyed him for a moment, a sulphurous anger burning him up. He wasn't too keen to have another fight. He'd contemplated his navel enough.

'Do you ski?'

'A little.' Sebastien placed a modest smile on his countenance.

It took a moment for the information to sink in. When it did, like a coin in a pinball machine, it produced an appreciable result. Karl's eyes glinted and in his excitement he could scarcely get his words out. 'Well, let's ski for Elsa. If I win, she comes back to me. If you do, she's yours.'

There was a pause. Then Sebastien laughed, the tone harsh and mocking. 'Well, well, Karl, hidden behind that frail exterior is a frail interior. I'd never have thought it. A contest with Elsa as the trophy. What a great idea,' he said softly. 'I love a competition.'

Elsa, who had been looking away, now turned back to him. She pulled on Sebastien's arm and said, 'Leave him. He's not worth it. Karl, piss off. I don't want to go out with you any more. Let's go, Sebastien.'

'In fact,' Sebastien continued as he awkwardly shifted about on his skis, 'let's add a little more fun to it, Karl. How about a small bet?'

Karl eyed him suspiciously. His girlfriend was one thing, money was another.

'Nothing too large. Say, fifteen thousand dollars.' Sebastien reckoned that would clean him out for a couple of years.

Karl's neck muscles bulged as if he had difficulty breathing.

'Fifteen thousand?' he gulped.

'Yes,' said Sebastien gaily. 'I could make it more if you like. Not chicken, are you?'

The Finn's cheeks flushed deeply. Karl felt ill. Things were not turning out as he'd expected. Still, there was no going back. He couldn't let Elsa down. 'No. Fifteen thousand's enough.' My God he had to win.

Karl pointed to the ski jump. 'That's the competition.'

Sebastien nodded. 'So be it.'

Karl had chosen wisely. On the slalom Sebastien could probably have held his own. On the jump, Karl was a national champion. Elsa was beside herself. As they worked their way up the slope, she whispered to Sebastien, her tone beseeching.

'Sebastien, don't do it. Karl's a professional skier. He'll easily win.'

'Oh,' said Sebastien, 'I don't mind losing.'

'No?'

Sebastien smiled beatifically – the smile of a fallen angel.

They entered the launching shed. Both Karl and Sebastien placed their skis against the wall to check them. They prepared to put them on. As they did so, an official approached the group.

'All skiing's stopped. The wind's too strong.'

The blood flowed back into Elsa's face. Relief overwhelmed her.

'No, it's not! We're going down that fucking jump.' Karl's face was suffused with anger. A furious altercation broke out with the official as Karl ranted at the Swiss in three languages. Sebastien stayed out of the way and continued to check his skis. The official was intransigent. So was Karl. He turned to Sebastien. His face had distorted into an animal mask of pride and hate.

'Furthest wins,' he spat. 'I'll go first.'

'OK,' said Sebastien. 'I'm sure you'll impress me.'

Karl made ready. Hurriedly, he put on his skis and approached the jump. Contemplating the treacherous incline below he psyched himself up for his moment of glory. Victory was in his mouth. He was certain. Only God could stop him. With huge swings of his arms he gathered momentum and thrust himself down the ramp.

Karl hurtled out of the hut like a rocket. But, not long after he departed from the shed he discovered he had only one ski. The realisation was a novel one. By that time he had other things to think about. Hurtling head over heels, he whirled into the air like a dervish who had succumbed to the additional handicap of St Vitus' dance. It was a fascinating spectacle to behold though not quite what was anticipated.

Karl's landing on the slope, when it came, was horrible, a resounding and sickening crunch of bones that seemed to hang in the air as he continued down the incline in an inextricable tangle of ski equipment and human body. Finally, he shot off into the side of the run and disappeared into deep snow. In the shed there was complete silence as the bystanders watched the stretcher-bearers running towards the inert body. It was Elsa who spoke first, as she realised what Sebastien might have done.

'Jesus, you don't think he's dead?'

Sebastien's face was calm and impassive. Only the eyes laughed. 'Oh, I do hope so,' he said.

* * *

The following morning Sebastien drove Elsa to the hospital and waited outside. She came out half an hour later and handed him a medical report. Sebastien noted the injuries in a conversational tone. 'Broken arm, broken leg, fractured pelvis, damaged ribs, torn ligaments, bad concussion, facial bruising. And a chip to the pubic bone. Now that's unusual,' he said as he kissed her affectionately. 'You don't get that often. I wouldn't get too randy with him for a while, Elsa. Stick to mouth-to-mouth sex. Kissing shouldn't hurt him.'

Elsa sniggered in spite of herself. 'I don't think I'll be doing that any more.'

'Well, time to be going,' Sebastien said to her gently. 'Goodbye, skiing instructress. Thanks for the training.'

'Goodbye, Sebastien.'

They kissed lingeringly.

'Always follow your destiny,' Sebastien called out as he walked away. 'Remember that.'

'I will,' Elsa replied. 'Perhaps we'll meet again.'

'Perhaps,' Sebastien raised his hand in farewell. He knew they never would.

CHAPTER ELEVEN

War cannot in fact be avoided, but only postponed to the advantage of the other side.

Machiavelli, *The Prince*

January. Paris.

WHILE TANYA WAS RESEARCHING IN the Boston Newspaper and Periodicals Library and Sebastien was fooling around on the ski slopes, Ivan was in a more contemplative mood, as befitted a political thinker.

He lay back on the couch, listening to the dying strains of Wagner's *Lohengrin.* Three weeks had passed since he had left the College. He'd decided to move from his London apartment, to base himself in Paris for the duration of the contest. He'd rented a flat in one of the most exclusive *arrondissements,* taking every precaution to ensure no one knew his real identity.

Ivan cast his eyes about his new sitting room. The ornate gilt furnishings, the heavy nineteenth-century furniture, the bold coloured rugs on the floor. His nose wrinkled. Not the same décor as at the College. Still, it would do. Ivan had spent the last week consciously not thinking about the Mastership Game, to clear his mind. Instead, he had frittered away the days strolling about Paris, revisiting old haunts and generally pleasing himself as he built up his energy for the battle. Only a fool would rush in where angels feared to tread.

It was time to gather his thoughts. The various pieces of this particular puzzle needed to be fitted together. First, there was the Mastership and the contest for it. Then, there was the Chinese puzzle box. Last, there was the death of Rex Boone. How did they all interlock? Just as importantly, how would Ivan play this particular game, this game of power? Playing games of power was an art form, like any other game, and this contest, one of the greatest games of all, would require considerable care and attention. Ivan not only had to make twenty million dollars within the space of a year, he also had to defeat his rivals for the Mastership; and the competition was very great, even after the reluctant departure of Rex from the scene. Anyway, the death of Rex had underlined the seriousness of this contest and set the tone.

Ivan got up from the couch and walked across the room to the CD player. Outside, the morning was cold and bright and he observed the bustling Parisian street scene. He'd go out for a walk in the afternoon. Putting on the disc once more, Ivan reclined back on the couch and closed his eyes. The swell of the music filled the room. He lightly moved his arms to the tempo, an imaginary conductor, while his thoughts returned to the issue in hand.

First steps first. What philosophy would Ivan adopt in this contest for the Mastership? As Ivan journeyed towards the centre of the circle he needed a guide, a still, small voice of calm, to keep him on the right path; someone who had studied deeply the concept of power and how it could be used and misused. A great sage. Like Dante had when he descended into the circles of hell with the immortal Virgil as his guide.

Who was it to be? A political theorist and sometime philosopher Ivan considered them all: Hobbes, Hume, Kant and Clausewitz as well as various others. He greeted them and politely bade them adieu in his mind. What he needed was the supreme exponent in the art of power and it didn't take Ivan long to determine on him. Machiavelli. For if anyone knew how to secure the Mastership and what it stood for, it was this medieval Italian statesman and diplomat. That he had died nearly five hundred years ago was no matter, for the steps to power were the same for every age. Where should Ivan start? Well, in his work on political machinations, *The Prince*, had not this great genius commented that it was *inadvisable to fight battles before knowing the ground*. Very sensible advice. And Ivan intended to take it. The music continued to drift about the room as Ivan thought on.

Rex had appeared reluctant to take part in the contest for the Mastership. That was nonsense. In fact, he had wanted to find out whether the others knew something he did about the Mastership. And the truth was that they didn't. For that Rex had died. He had been very quick off the mark, but what he knew was of such terrible consequence that he had been killed because of it. So what exactly did Rex know? Well, whatever Rex had learned from a past Fellow, such information he would likely have had on, or near, him. Probably in his rooms in College. Access to Rex's rooms was now impossible. In any case, he would, doubtless, have made such information difficult to find. A secret that had died with him? Perhaps, but perhaps not, thought Ivan. For secrets never really die, they simply become more deeply hidden. Rex must have left some clue. Patiently, Ivan explored every avenue and finally alighted on one. The last dinner he had had with Rex in Erris was his only hope. There might be some clue there. So Ivan must revisit the scene, like a murderer reliving his act.

Ivan took a sip of water and closed his eyes again. Slowly, from the depths of his memory, as if drawing water from a well, he painstakingly recreated the scene of his final dinner with Rex in its every facet. At his prompting, Rex's massive figure, his heavy jowls and thickset visage, gradually appeared to view like Banquo's ghost. Finally, Rex raised his torpid head and the two contemplated each other. The one alive, the other the perfect creation of Ivan's extraordinary memory. Retaining Rex's image in his mind, Ivan slowly went through every aspect of their meeting, every word and every mannerism, as though meticulously inspecting each frame of a film. There must be something. There just had to be. Suddenly, his heart missed a beat.

When Rex had risen from the table he had said in a throwaway fashion, 'There's someone I have to talk to. So I'll forgo the cheese and the port.' At the time Ivan had assumed Rex had been going to meet someone, probably one of the other contestants or the Master. Ivan had foolishly overlooked one possibility. Rex had been going to phone someone.

Ivan dialled a nine-digit number. There was no sound. He dialled another two digits and waited. Finally, a voice came on the line. It was clipped and expressionless, like a machine.

'I am sorry, caller. You have the wrong number. This number is unallocated. Please dial again.'

Ivan paused and then said, 'Department Ten please.'

'I am sorry, caller, you have the wrong number.'

'Hadley.'

'Please wait a moment.'

Ivan waited, mentally raising his eyebrows in exasperation. The problem with the British secret services was that, while some parts of it had become more open, the really important parts had become ever more secretive. Which just went to show that no secret organisation ever revealed the true basis on which it was founded. Without doubt that included the College. A woman's voice suddenly came on the line, soft and attentive.

'Mr Hadley's available. I'll put you through. What is your coding, sir?'

'It's 26 25 86.'

Within a minute she'd connected them. Hadley answered somewhat nervously for Ivan never called him at work.

'Ivan. Glad to hear from you. It's been a long time since we last met.'

Ivan ignored the small talk. His voice was businesslike.

'James, I need some help. Let's meet for dinner on Friday. I'll leave the details of what I require in the usual place. You'll have to travel further than you think.'

There was a hesitant cough. 'Er, I'm afraid, Ivan, this is a little difficult. Things are very busy at the moment.'

Ivan continued as if he hadn't heard. 'Thanks, James. Please get the wheels turning.'

Ivan put the phone down. If Rex had phoned anyone that night Ivan would soon find out. As for James, what were boyfriends for if you couldn't tap them for information?

'Your turn.'

Ivan moved the chess piece and sat back to listen to Buxtehude's Prelude and Fugue in D major.

'Checkmate?'

''Fraid so.'

Hadley snorted incredulously. 'I don't know how you do it. You always win. You seem to know exactly what piece I'm going to move.'

Ivan smirked. 'Too easy to read, James, that's your problem. Whenever you play chess, you never stop to think about the person you're up against. Instead, you blunder ahead, frantically moving the pieces without considering what tactics to employ nor even analysing the psyche of the other player. That's why you lose. Simple.'

'Balls!'

'It's true,' said Ivan with a wan smile. 'James, I can read you like a book. When in doubt you exercise caution and when in difficulty you fall back on classic defences. Knowing this, the game's easy. I attack, concentrate on unorthodox moves and set traps. What happens? You don't realise what's going on, you panic and your game falls to pieces. In short, James, you're a pushover.'

Hadley raised his hands in despair. He was a lithe figure in his late twenties, smartly dressed in a dark blue suit with fine blond hair and an affable, albeit reserved, countenance noticeable for its delicate cheekbones and full lips. His rather effete look suggested an artist or a pianist rather than a spy. However, spying for the British secret service was a profession Hadley had got caught up in immediately after he'd left university and then found it difficult to get out of. He was rather like his chess moves – unambitious and lacking farsightedness.

Ivan poured them both another drink and continued, 'James, you need to anticipate how your opponent will play. If you can't do that you haven't a hope. As Machiavelli pointed out,

> *"If troubles are foreseen from afar they are easy to remedy. But if you wait until they are near at hand the medicine will be too late."'*

James laughed uneasily. 'You're just brighter than I am. That's all.'

'Not at all,' said Ivan. 'I succeed because I plan to succeed. You don't. Now, did you manage to get what I asked for?'

Hadley looked at him with a nervous glance and Ivan could see a faint rim of sweat appearing on his brow. Hadley brushed his fine hair to one side. He was the only person outside the College who knew that Ivan was a member of it and such an exclusive status impressed him enormously.

'Ivan, I did. I tapped into the phone company's records. There was only one call Boone made from that guesthouse in Erris. Please be very careful with this information, though,' Hadley pleaded. 'I'd be fired instantly if it was ever discovered. It's all quite unauthorised.'

'It won't be,' said Ivan, unconcerned. 'By the way, can you tap into the College's land and satellite lines?' Ivan was sure Rex would have made no sensitive calls from the island.

'Are you crazy?' said James. 'I doubt anyone can. The College must have every device in the world to prevent unauthorised access.' Hadley took a gulp of gin. 'Even this information I'm worried about giving to you.' His tone was plaintive. 'Why don't you approach the Director General of MI6 himself? You've got the right connections. I really am nervous about this.'

Ivan took the details from his lover and laid them to one side on the table. He reached out and patted Hadley's arm. 'James, stop panicking. I can tell you this much: it wasn't possible to get this information any other way. My colleague at the College died in strange circumstances and I'm helping the Master make some enquiries.'

Hadley appeared satisfied with the lie. A few minutes more and he rose to depart. Ivan helped him put on his cashmere coat and saw him to the door. They embraced briefly.

As they did so Ivan said, 'Please don't tell anyone else about this, James. Nor about your trip here.'

'Course not,' Hadley replied. The less said of the matter the better. He hurried away so as not to be late for his train back to London and to that boring job in the British secret services. He wished he was Ivan. Meanwhile Ivan closed the door to his Paris apartment and returned to the sitting room. Reclining on the settee in the semi-darkness he sipped his cognac and re-read the phone number Hadley had given him. It was an international call and Ivan dialled the number. Distantly, an American voice answered.

'Residence of Mrs Boone.'

Without making a sound Ivan put the phone down. Then he checked the code in a phone book. So, Boone's mother lived in the suburbs of Boston. Ivan rang Boston's phone exchange to see whether her number was ex-directory or not. It was. Boone or his mother was not anxious to disclose her whereabouts. Ivan savoured this information with his drink. Rex had phoned his mother the day he had died. Nothing strange in that, apart from one small feature: he had done so early in the morning, Boston time. A call at such an unsocial hour would not just have been to chat to his dear old mum. Rex had obviously something else on his mind.

Ivan picked up the phone again and booked a flight to Boston. It was time to meet Rex's mother, tucked away in the States. His friends there would find out her address for him. He hoped they got on well.

His sleuthing for the evening completed, Ivan poured himself another drink in celebration.

Despite being dead, Rex had talked to him after all. What a sportsman.

Ivan arrived at Logan International Airport early in the morning.

Passing through customs he hired a car and made for Boston. The traffic was heavy since it was the rush hour. Eventually he managed to get through the city and into the suburbs. The area where Rex's mother lived was more than an hour distant. As he passed through Cambridge he saw the students hurrying to their lectures at Harvard University, bespattered with rain. Ivan reflected on his own temporary lectureship there in economics some years before. His contacts among the academic community might come in useful. He felt hungry and dipped into a bag of bagels on the car seat.

In the narrow lane of a suburban quarter he finally arrived at Mrs Boone's residence. It was a large house situated in its own extensive grounds. Like most of the other buildings in the locality it was built of wooden clapboard and painted a brilliant white. It had two floors, a pillared portico and that ubiquitous symbol of patriotism, a long pole at the top of which fluttered the Stars and Stripes. Ivan got out and strolled down the drive, carefully noting everything around him. He rang the doorbell.

A rather sullen-looking woman answered it. She was in her late fifties and dressed in a nurse's uniform. She looked at him questioningly. When Ivan explained the purpose of his visit she pursed her narrow lips, then answered in a low voice.

'You'll have to ask Mrs Boone about the phone call. Please don't trouble her more than is necessary. She is elderly and the death of her only son was a terrible blow. She may also understand little of what you say. She has Alzheimer's disease.'

Ivan was guided into a bedroom. A frail, old woman lay there, her face thin and worn, the expression vacant. About her lay all the paraphernalia of dying: a disordered array of medicine bottles, a bottle of oxygen, a mask and the sickly smell of camphor. Also, a bible; to be used in case of emergency, like swotting up for an eternal exam.

Ivan sat down by the bedside and talked to Mrs Boone. She had no recollection of any phone call and it was clear that her mind was badly affected. Ivan thought for a minute and then asked permission to look through her son's papers in the house, since he was a colleague of Rex's and they'd been working on a book together. She weakly patted his hand. She probably didn't understand a word. So, Ivan left her, lost in her memories. He was sure Rex must have loved her dearly. Even the most ambitious and independent people had mothers, he reflected. Pity he had never known his own. It was tough being an orphan. But, then, there were considerable compensations. No one to argue about pocket money with, nor one's choice of partner.

The nurse escorted Ivan to Rex's room. It was on the second floor. Entering it, he discovered that it was a large and airy chamber with a pleasing view onto school fields. On the cream-coloured walls were photos of Rex's days at university. In all of them he loomed large – a figure marked out by his physique and commanding presence for great things. No one would ever know how well he had done. A Fellow of the College and a leading candidate for its Master. Great things that would never materialise now. For his destiny had caught up with him. Too bad.

Ivan began to sift through the papers. He knew what he was searching for – a clue to the Mastership Game.

Three days later and the view out of the window was becoming tedious, marred as it was by a persistent drizzle. Life could be depressing at times, Ivan thought. He had gone through all of Rex's papers and there was nothing. Much of it had been dismal reading. Endless mathematical formulae and equations, endless papers and articles on nuclear energy, all brilliant he imagined, but not the slightest use in working out the Mastership Game. Perhaps it was a good thing that Rex was dead, Ivan reflected rather cruelly – at least it had stopped him writing.

An hour more and Ivan had finished his labour of Hercules. Sitting on the floor he viewed a photo on the wall of Rex resplendent in his Chicago University football kit. Well, Ivan had truly dropped the ball on this one. He had made a false assumption. He had assumed a connection between the phone call and the contest and there was none. So, it seemed that Rex's secret had died with him after all. Ivan went in to bid farewell to Mrs Boone.

'My son,' she whispered when he mentioned Rex's name.

Ivan squeezed her gaunt fingers. 'Don't worry, Mrs Boone. I won't forget your son. He was a remarkable man. Indeed, I would dearly have liked to talk with him again.' Mentally he added that the talk would have included a renegotiation of that restaurant bill.

Ivan stepped onto the porch and breathed in the fresh air greedily. It was important he get back to Paris as soon as possible to start making his twenty million dollars. He already had the gem of an idea in his mind. He bade goodbye to the nurse and walked down the path, careful to avoid the puddles. He reached the gate.

'Excuse me,' said a voice. Then, 'Excuse me,' louder. Ivan turned to see a heavily built woman hurrying down the garden path as if in training for a heart attack. She must be the cook, a great band of white about her massy stomach. She halted just before him, her hand still clutching a dishcloth. After much panting and huffing she managed to gasp, 'I don't know whether it's of any use, sir, but one morning, shortly before he died, Mr Rex phoned. It was very early. I took the call.'

'Yes?' said Ivan.

'Well . . .' she continued breathlessly, 'Dr Boone asked me to look out some documents for him, sir. He was very abrupt, not like his usual self. Said he'd phone me again and give me the address where I could mail them to him once I'd found them. Of course, he never did, poor soul.'

'Where are the documents?'

'I'd completely forgotten about them until today when Martha mentioned you were looking for some documents.'

'Yes, but where are they?' Ivan tried to be patient.

The housekeeper retired into the house and returned. The dishcloth had been replaced by a large brown package which she gave to him. Ivan unwrapped it. He noticed that his hands trembled a fraction as he did so. When he reached a single slip of paper he felt faint.

'Are you all right, sir?'

'I'd like to sit down for a moment, if I may.'

Ivan sat in the big armchair in Rex's room once more. He eyed the photos of Rex on the wall and mentally thanked him. There would be no need to renegotiate the dinner bill after all. It was on him. He had to congratulate Rex for his exceedingly good memory. When the Master had first told them of their nomination for the Mastership on that fateful night, it had triggered something in Rex's brain. Somewhere before he had read about a previous contest for the Mastership. Ivan now held the papers that Rex had asked the cook to send him prior to his untimely death. They related to a man called Max Stanton. So who was this mysterious person and what was his connection with the Mastership Game? Ivan started to read.

Max Stanton had been a young and very ambitious chemist in his thirties at a science institute in Harvard. In the course of his work he had got to know Rex's father, a local lawyer. Ivan supposed this since, in his will, Stanton had nominated Boone senior as the executor of his estate. When Stanton had died, Rex's father had wound up the estate in the course of which he had received a number of Stanton's papers. On his father's death some years later these papers had passed to Rex. Ivan envisaged Rex hastily reading them as he cleared out his father's effects. Doubtless, he hadn't given them a second thought – save for one slip of white paper, hidden among the others.

It was handwritten by Stanton, nondescript in appearance and dated. Yet its contents were dramatic. In it Stanton openly admitted that he was a Fellow of the College. He referred to a meeting he and four other Fellows had one night with the Master, the predecessor to the present incumbent. It had taken place in the third courtyard, with no other witnesses. They were told of their nomination for the Mastership provided they were prepared to take part in a game, the nature of which would be disclosed to them only if they accepted the nomination. What the actual contest was Stanton didn't say, although he indicated that all five of them had agreed to take part.

Ivan imagined that, when Rex had come across this sliver of paper as he sifted through his father's personal effects, he wouldn't have understood it, since he was not at that time a Fellow of the College. Probably, he thought it was a fake or make-believe. However, something must have held him back from destroying it and when the Master had referred to the contest for the Mastership, Rex's brain had speedily informed him that he'd heard of this game before. So Rex had decided to do a bit of play-acting to determine if the others were also aware of it.

Needing to reread the information and investigate further about Stanton, Rex had contacted his mother's residence the following day, to get the note sent to him. Yet, Rex's play-acting had cost him his life. Someone else already knew what Rex did. Poor Rex, thought Ivan. Playing football and playing Hamlet required different skills.

Ivan sat back in his chair. It was a remarkable stroke of luck that this piece of paper had survived, since it was the custom for all material connecting them with the College to be destroyed on the death of a Fellow. Yet this sliver of information had been overlooked by the 'cleaners' of the College. Ivan had talked with Rex after all and by this simple piece of paper Rex was able to tell him some very important things. First, the Mastership Game had been played at least once before, with Stanton as a contestant. Second, given the year of the contest one of the other contestants must have been the Master. Third, Stanton had died not long after writing the note.

That left only one other matter to determine.

How did Max Stanton die?

While Ivan was finding out about Max Stanton, he would have been disturbed to know that he was not the only contestant in Massachusetts that day. Having arrived on an overnight flight from Switzerland, Sebastien unlocked the door and strolled into a darkened hotel room in downtown Boston. It was six in the morning. Tanya sat up in bed and rubbed her eyes. She reached out to give him a passionate kiss.

'How was your flight?'

Sebastien smiled and strained forward to receive her embrace. However, Tanya's display of affection was more demonstrative than he'd anticipated. She slapped him hard on the face and pushed him away from her angrily.

'You bastard. Why did you leave that night? You could have told me you were stealing out of the College. I was worried about you.'

Sebastien sat down on the bed. He nursed his cheek, an aggrieved look on his face. Not quite what he'd expected after an absence of nearly a month.

'Tanya, I'm sorry.' He watched her get out of bed. 'I had to have time to think. What the Master told us blew my mind.'

'Liar.'

Sebastien tried again. 'OK. I'm sorry. Now are you happy? Or do you want me to leave?'

'Yes, get out.'

Sebastien watched the naked figure disappear into the bathroom. Dropping his newspaper on a table he followed her in.

'Tanya, be reasonable. We need to work together.'

'No we don't.'

She pushed past him and stepped into the shower.

'Tanya.' No answer. 'Tanya, I'm sorry.' No response from the body now wrapped in a mist of hot water. 'OK,' Sebastien held up his hands in submission, 'I am a bastard. A complete and utter bastard. Now are you happy?'

No response.

'Tanya . . .' with a grin Sebastien pushed open the door and forced his way into the shower, still clothed in his suit. Tanya giggled as he pushed her hard up against the tiled wall tickling her fervently. 'You are a total bastard,' she said, straining away from him, despite her laughter. But it was no use and his persistence paid off. Eventually, she delivered up a soapy kiss and began to undo his tie, though not before soaking him with shampoo and whatever else she could lay her hands on.

Afterwards, Sebastien stood in her bedroom as he towelled himself. A brief respite. It would have done him no good bringing her expensive perfume or presents. She'd have despised him even more. He watched her while she sat naked on the bed drying her toes. Her face and breasts were tinged a soft pink from the shower and their lovemaking, her beauty all the more apparent. As she put her bra on, he stretched over the bed and kissed her on the shoulder. He waited for the obligatory lecture.

'Sebastien, this contest for the Mastership is really serious. You do realise that?'

'Yes, of course.'

Tanya took his face in her hands. 'No you don't, Sebastien. And stop being a prick and staring at me like that in a lovesick way. I still haven't forgiven you. Just listen. What I mean is this: this game is much more serious than you think. To date, we have never known the global implications of our work, nor how the College really uses this material. But this – this is a unique opportunity to be in charge of it all.'

Tanya stood as she continued dressing. Sebastien lounged back on the bed, admiring her lissom figure. He was intrigued to see her so enthused.

'It's an amazing opportunity,' Tanya continued. 'A dream come true. To see into the very heart of the system and to direct what the College has been doing for centuries, a giant spider patiently weaving a myriad threads together as it develops society for peaceful purposes. What incredible insight and power.'

'I agree.'

'Don't you want to see how it all works?'

'Of course I do,' said Sebastien. He flicked through the remains of his newspaper, careful not to appear too eager.

'Well, so do I,' said Tanya, while she clipped on one multi-coloured earring, then another. 'And,' she turned to him, 'I want you to tell me what you think this Mastership Game is about, without messing around.'

'OK.'

Sebastien threw the newspaper to one side. It was worth getting the issue out of the way at this stage and they had to discuss it sometime. For once, he dropped the banter and his tone became serious. He told her he thought the College was more influential and complex than either of them had previously supposed, even as Fellows. It was as much a puzzle as the Chinese box was, particularly in the way in which it used all the data it received. After two years at the College, Sebastien was sure that it had a policy of disseminating certain information to some countries while it withheld it from others. Also, that it deliberately damped down the power of various nations while it raised that of others – all in accordance with the will of the Master. The College was not just an advisory body. It was an organic system designed to effect change on a world scale in accordance with its own dictates.

Tanya listened to him carefully. She was sure he was right. She came to sit on the bed beside him.

'Tanya, when I joined the College the Master told me that the institution would never seek to control other countries nor misuse its power. However, that is not true, really, since the College will do everything it can to *preserve* its power. The Master's words were clever word play. You see, the College is not governed by any moral imperative, like the Catholic Church, for example. It is morally neutral or, rather, it is deeply cynical in its use of power. Anything which serves to maintain its status and temporal power is justified. The Mastership Game is the clearest evidence of it, and that was what the Master was trying to tell us. You see, the College only plays by its own rules and it has an end purpose. Gradually, it is compelling the world outside to obey its will, like a huge whirlpool sucking everything into its orbit. As governmental systems decline, the College will acquire greater and greater power and make its influence all the more visible. It will become a College of *éminence grise.* It will finally declare its true colours, and we are part of that overall purpose'.

Tanya said nothing. She got up to draw open the curtains. As she turned back to him she appeared so beautiful in the light that Sebastien almost loved her. Tanya didn't return to the bed but sat down on a chair. Sebastien noticed her subtle repositioning. He was sure he knew why and he waited.

'When I became a Fellow,' said Tanya, 'I knew there was a possibility of becoming head of the College but it was so theoretical that I dismissed it from my mind. Now, here it is. They are actually offering it to me.'

'Oh, so you've decided you want the Mastership for yourself after all?' Sebastien said slowly. He sat up on the bed on which he'd been stretched out. Just as he thought. What a minx she was. Still, he couldn't really blame her.

'Yes,' said Tanya. She tried to decipher his mood. She knew he was disappointed. 'I have as much claim to the Mastership as you.'

'True,' said Sebastien.

'That means we're in competition then?'

'I agree,' said Sebastien. 'Still, there's no reason for us not to co-operate, at least, not until the very end. In fact, there's a very good reason to work together, Tanya.' He paused. Then his voice became grim, almost menacing: 'Safety in numbers. We don't want what happened to Rex to happen to us.'

'So you think that Rex was murdered?' said Tanya, shocked. She thought that he would laugh at her. Now it made her even more uneasy.

'Certain,' said Sebastien. 'The timing was too coincidental.'

'I think so too,' said Tanya. 'This is all beginning to frighten me.' There was a pause then: 'Sebastien, do you love me?'

Tanya knew why she'd fallen in love with him. It was those deep eyes and his careless grin, that sense of ease and unconcern with which he approached absolutely everything, even though she knew he cared about things very much and about winning especially.

'I love you.' Sebastien got up and embraced her. His quests for power and for love were not wholly unrelated. He yawned from his jet lag. 'Time for breakfast, I think.'

* * *

Tanya inspected the other hotel guests while they grazed about the food carousel. Finishing off one doughnut without any hesitation, Tanya selected another. Her genes wouldn't let her down and her weight had never caused her any concern. How lucky she was. It must mean that she would have to pay for it one day, surely? She inspected her partner. Was he getting fatter about the waist? Something to tease him about. He was quite vain really.

'Sebastien, since we're working together there's something I have to tell you.'

'Me too,' said Sebastien. He had been gazing out of the window at the fast-moving traffic of Boston below. He turned back to her. 'It's confession time,' he grinned. 'Let's celebrate. Have some more tomato juice.'

Tanya waited until the serving staff had moved away from their table. 'Sebastien, I broke into Rex's computer and came across a message. Well, not really a message, more a note.'

'Oh, did you now? And what did it say?' Sebastien wondered whether Tanya had also broken into his computer. He bet she had. She was as clever as sin. He shouldn't underestimate her. She would beat him to the Mastership if she had half a chance.

Tanya hesitated. She didn't want to tell Sebastien everything. Her past relationship with Rex would remain private. Sebastien wouldn't understand, even though Rex was now dead. And something else held Tanya back, just a little. In his message Rex had warned her not to trust anyone. Yet, it was OK to tell Sebastien most of her thoughts. He was her partner, after all.

'I came across a note Rex typed into his computer the night the Master told us about the Chinese puzzle box and the game. The note was a reference to the Boston Newspaper and Periodicals Library, Room B6 and to the name Max Stanton.'

Sebastien stopped buttering his toast. 'Well, well,' he said softly, 'so Rex knew something after all when he told the Master he wouldn't take part.' He'd already come to that conclusion long ago.

'Mmm,' Tanya answered. 'And I've spent the last few days at the library, in Room B6. It contains newspapers published in the US from the year dot. Unfortunately, there's no central catalogue and Rex left no other details. I've been sifting through the major dailies for the last twenty years but I still haven't come across anything yet on Stanton.'

Sebastien pondered aloud. 'Of course, Rex's death may have nothing to do with the Mastership Game. Perhaps, it was connected with something else Rex was working on?'

'No. I think this information's important,' said Tanya, a little too sharply.

'Could be,' said Sebastien. He ladled another pancake onto his plate, noting the change in the tone of her voice. 'Let's go to the library this morning. I've an idea how we can speed up the process.'

'Well, what about your news?'

Sebastien grinned mischievously and rubbed his cheek. 'I'm not going to tell you after beating me up. In fact, I was working on the trail just as hard as you were. I'm the hero of the piece,' he adopted a mournful look, 'and what about the sacrifice I made of my suit?'

Tanya interrupted his frivolity, 'Sebastien, no chance. Either we work together and share information or we go our own ways. And we'd better get that clear right now.' Her voice was harsh and he saw a flush of anger appearing in her cheeks again.

'Yeah, OK, relax, Tanya. I was only joking.' Sebastien took a swig of coffee. 'You know the night he died Rex had been out drinking. Well, I know where. And with whom. I'll give you a clue. It's someone you know.'

Tanya's eyes widened. 'Who?'

'Yes, I thought that would impress even you. Remember the night the Master told us about the contest and Rex acted all concerned, saying he wouldn't take part until he received a full explanation about it? It was all bluff. Rex wanted to become Master more than anyone else. So why did he put on the pantomime? Because he was fishing for information. He wanted to know if we knew something he did. So I decided to keep an eye on him and that's why I left you that night. Well, the next morning Rex went to the mainland and after taking a circuitous route he ended up in Erris where he booked himself into a guesthouse. Not a place I'd normally associate with Rex. Not his style. Bit down-market. Anyway, he spent the day in his room and that evening he went to a restaurant. I followed him and he had dinner with someone.'

'Who?'

'Guess!'

'Ivan?'

'Exactly, our friend Ivan, who must have followed him to Erris. I saw them both in the hotel. It was impossible to hear what they were saying but they were obviously plotting away. Rex then left.'

'And he died shortly afterwards.'

'Exactly,' said Sebastien.

Tanya shivered. She waited for Sebastien to go on. He finished his pancake with gusto.

'And there's one other thing to add fuel to the flames. At the remembrance service I asked Ivan about Rex's death. I asked him where Rex had been. I knew, of course, since I'd seen him with Ivan. Ivan told me, "No one knows." A lie, since he'd had dinner with him that very evening. Yet, there must have been something in my look that gave me away since I'm sure Ivan now knows that I saw them together.'

'So, what does it all mean?' Tanya frowned.

'It's a puzzle,' said Sebastien, as he finished off his coffee. 'And we have some of the pieces. One Chinese puzzle box. One Mastership. Four contestants. One dead Rex. It's easy.'

'What's the answer then?'

'Work it out yourself.' He got up and went to the food carousel. 'Hey, do you want any more toast?'

Boston Newspaper and Periodicals Library, Room B6 was a large and imposing chamber with a vaulted wooden ceiling dating from the early nineteenth century. It had two floors. Both were crammed with grey metal shelves that ran along the outer walls of the room as well as down the centre. Row after row of the shelves were filled with newspapers of all shapes and sizes, most bound up in red cardboard binders. There were also some microfiche reading machines and a few Formica tables and chairs. Sebastien was surprised to see that nearly all of the seats were filled. He viewed the occupants with interest, curious as to who would want to spend their time reading old newspapers. Some were teenagers busy on school projects, a few were academics of the bearded variety, and the majority were older citizens optimistically referred to as the temporarily unemployed but who had accepted their fate and were dozing in the comforting warmth of the library until their true retirement began.

Tanya and Sebastien ascended to the second floor, up a rickety metal staircase. Hidden away at the back was a small wooden counter surrounded by shelving. It was wreathed with ancient Post-it notes and newspaper cuttings. In this hideout sat a library assistant in her early twenties. She was dressed in a lurid orange boilersuit with a multitude of nose-, lip- and earrings. Hard work was obviously not her forte since she was reading a pop magazine and chewing a great wad of gum with all the concentration of a ruminating cow. Sebastien noticed a large tub of glue beside her left elbow. She must be permanently high on it.

'Ah, someone who can help us.' Sebastien flashed a sympathetic smile. He'd chat her up.

The boilersuit announced brusquely, 'We don't have it,' and carried on reading without even glancing at him.

Sebastien stared at her. His eyes narrowed. She was in the wrong profession, he reflected. With her near-horizontal posture and ability to stay in the same position for a long period of time she'd have done well as a whore. Doubtless, she had insufficient motivation to progress to such a calling. Too much activity and being nice to people. Instead, she had sentenced herself to a life of tedium which she was clearly relieving by inhaling large amounts of newspaper glue on a regular basis and being rude to enquirers.

'I want help.' He pressed the bell on her desk.

'Lunch hour,' said the assistant, squinting at the wall clock.

It registered ten thirty, which it had done for the last two years.

'Oh, of course,' said Sebastien and stepped forward to embed her in the glue.

Tanya grinned and seized his arm. 'Not worth the effort. I've already tried.' They faced the miles of shelving. 'So, here we are,' said Tanya, as they surveyed the territory, 'two hundred years' worth of US newspapers. And most of it not on microfiche. How we'll find Max Stanton among this stuff I don't know. There are millions of pages of text.'

They sat down at a table behind some stacks.

'Do you think "Max Stanton" is an anagram or in code?' asked Sebastien. He stroked Tanya's leg under the table for want of anything better to do. An elderly man at another table viewed the sight of flesh with interest.

'No,' said Tanya, crossing her legs. 'Rex would have protected any sensitive files with almost unbreakable codes, I'm sure. I think Max Stanton is the name of a real person. From the way in which the note was written I don't think he thought it necessary to put it in code.'

'So, we need to make a few assumptions,' said Sebastien, removing his hand from her knee with some reluctance and getting down to business. 'Or else we'll be here for ever.'

'I agree,' said Tanya. 'To begin with, why should Rex refer to this library? Why not others, such as the Library of Congress? Assumption number one, therefore, is that Rex knew this library. Or, at least, he was sure he would find whatever he was looking for here. So I've switched to looking at the local newspapers.'

Sebastien thought for a minute. He nodded. 'Good idea. Assumption number two is that we should look at obituaries.'

'Why?'

'Because,' said Sebastien, 'my hunch is that Max Stanton is dead.'

It was just before five o'clock and library closing time. The orange boilersuit that comprised the library assistant had downloaded more glue and had long since disappeared.

'Wow!' The face stared out at her from the faded newsprint. Tanya whispered the opening words of the small obituary. 'Max Stanton, chemist, dies in a boating accident.'

Quickly, Tanya turned over the page. Sebastien was downstairs. A wicked thought crept into her mind. What if she never told him and simply slipped the newspaper volume back on the shelf? Sebastien wouldn't find it. It would be her secret. Perhaps the winning card to the Mastership Game. For a few moments Tanya considered this tactic. Then she turned back the page and hurriedly began to read the obituary. Stanton had drowned on a fishing trip in Cape Cod Bay not far from Boston. He had been alone. The obituary said that the most likely explanation of his death was that he'd slipped in the boat and hit his head on the side before falling overboard. Foul play had been ruled out by the Massachusetts coroner for lack of evidence, even though the precise manner of Stanton's death had remained a puzzle. A talented man, who had no reason to commit suicide, had died aged thirty-five and that was that. Nothing earth-shattering.

Had Stanton been a Fellow of the College? As expected, the obituary made no reference to it. Yet, the description of Stanton and the nature of his work as a brilliant chemist fitted in with the possibility that he could have been secretly working for the College. Also, the year he died was the year he would have played the Mastership Game against the present incumbent, assuming it had been played before. It seemed to fit.

'Tanya?'

She started. She could hear Sebastien coming up the stairs. He would turn the corner in a few seconds. What should she do? Turn the page and say nothing? Or love him and tell all? Tanya took a deep breath and made her decision. Sebastien slowly appeared to view. He had been watching her for some time. He smiled as he read the obituary. He let out a low and jubilant whistle. He'd guessed right after all.

The Mastership Game included murder.

*   *   *

Logan International Airport was crowded and it took some time for Sebastien and Tanya to reach the ticket counter and book her in on a flight to Switzerland. After that they made for the bar.

'You're sure you're all right?'

Tanya nodded. 'Yes. I'm just feeling tired. These last few weeks have been a shock. Like I'm living in two worlds. So much of me just wants to go back to where we once were.'

Sebastien smiled mirthlessly as he caressed his glass of red wine. ' Tanya, we can't go back. You know that. There's nothing to go back to. We're no longer Fellows of the College and someone killed Rex. Don't you think they won't come after us too? And even if we give up who'd believe us? Besides,' Sebastien pushed a handful of peanuts into his mouth, 'I'm really enjoying this.'

'Enjoying it!'

'Yes,' he grinned. 'I want to find out exactly what the Mastership is about. And I rather like the idea of pitting my wits against the others. Don't you?'

'Yes, I suppose I do,' said Tanya reluctantly. She thought: Sebastien, my darling, you also want to win.

'I think it's good for you to go to the chalet and have a few days' rest,' continued Sebastien. 'Get in plenty of skiing. I enjoyed myself on the slopes when I was there.' He glanced up at the screen to check the flight time. 'I'll join you in a week or so. There's some research at the Harvard University library I want to do.'

'What research?' she said puzzled.

'Tell you later.'

Tanya put down her glass sharply. 'We agreed to work together. And I told you all about Stanton.'

Sebastien hesitated and laughed. 'Tanya, don't be so suspicious. I promise I'll hide nothing from you. Honest. Just let me finish what I'm doing and I'll tell you exactly how we're going to make the twenty million dollars. I think you'll be impressed.' He put on his mock-serious expression.

Tanya thought it wasn't worth getting angry. Now was not the time. She'd get her own back. She stood up to fetch some more drinks. 'If you don't tell me I'll find out anyway, Sebastien,' she whispered as she bit his earlobe hard. 'Only make sure it's not illegal, and that we don't get killed.'

'I'll see what I can do.'

When Tanya's flight was called they walked to the departure gate and kissed a lingering goodbye.

Then Tanya said, 'Since you've already worked out your part to win the game, I'll tell you mine. Or, perhaps I'll just give you a hint.'

'Come on, Tanya, we're partners, aren't we?'

'Really?' she replied coolly. 'And who doesn't want to tell me about his research?'

'Come on. It was only a joke.'

'I've worked out how we can combine talents to make the money. You know all about banking systems and fund flows. I have computing abilities. Together, we can achieve our goal. However, we need to plan things carefully. There's still a long way to go.'

'Last passengers for flight SR 512 to Zurich and then Geneva,' blared out the announcement.

Sebastien grinned. 'Well, don't keep me in suspense.'

Tanya giggled. Sebastien needed her help and he knew it. 'Here's a hint. Start thinking about Central America.'

'Why?'

'Because their computer systems, especially their banking systems, will be easier to access without being detected.'

'But where? Mexico? Guatemala? Panama?'

Tanya waved goodbye. 'See you back at the chalet.'

'Tanya!'

Sebastien watched her depart through the security cordon. He laughed. Pretty woman. Clever woman. He'd no doubt she'd do her bit to get the money. He left the airport and caught a taxi back to Boston. He gazed out of the window, the lights of the city appearing to view. Where were Andrew and Ivan? Had they also found out about Stanton? And how far behind were they? Sebastien would give a hell of a lot to know that. The game was beginning to warm up and he and Tanya must always keep one step ahead. That was the only way to survive, now that the bloodletting had begun.

Ivan studied the orange boilersuit behind the counter in the Boston Newspaper and Periodicals Library. A diamond stud glinted when she opened her mouth. It complimented the attachments to her nose and her ears. With the metal on, or in, her it would be like talking to a cutlery drawer. Probably even her labia were pierced. He hoped she never got too near a powerful magnet.

Ivan said once more, 'Perhaps you can help me.'

With a bored sigh the boilersuited assistant said. 'I doubt it,' as she carried on reading her women's magazine.

'Wonderful,' said Ivan. His voice was still polite although the tone was a touch more menacing. 'I am looking for some information about a man called Max Stanton. In fact, I'm looking for his obituary.'

'Who's he, then?' The library assistant breathed in glue as she picked up her lunchtime sandwich situated next to the open glue pot. It was only ten o'clock in the morning but the clock had forgotten the time and she couldn't give a damn whether it was morning or afternoon.

'A dead man,' said Ivan patiently.

'Oh, yeah?'

Ivan decided to try again. Despite the fact that he was not a doctor he had a good practical knowledge of human illnesses and their cures, as did many of those who worked with him in the secret services. In the secret services a temporary cure for total stupidity or bad memory loss was money. A permanent one was death. Ivan preferred the former since it enabled repeat doses to be administered. With an expressionless face Ivan opened his wallet and placed two hundred dollars close to the glue pot. He stood back to watch the miracle. Within fifteen minutes the orange boilersuit had earned herself a lot more glue money and Ivan was reading the obituary. He nodded. Another piece of the Chinese puzzle had fallen into place. The Mastership Game was a game of power with very high stakes, just as he had assumed.

'Someone else was looking for that.'

'Who?' Ivan's wallet opened up once more.

'Well,' said the orange boilersuit, 'a woman was looking for him. She took some photocopies of that.' She pointed to the obituary notice. 'I know 'cause I watched her while they didn't turn out.' She pointed to an elderly photocopier behind the counter. Obviously, for this piece to work was memorable for its rarity and Ivan suspected the assistant was a bystander rather than a participant.

'And was she with a man?'

'Yeah.' From the description she gave it became clear it was Sebastien. Ivan's concern mounted – more so when the assistant indicated that Tanya had photocopied extracts from other newspapers and periodicals. Unfortunately, the photocopier had worked this time so that neither the boilersuit nor Ivan knew what they could be.

'Do you know when she'll be back? Did she leave an address?'

'No.' One word sufficed for both questions. The assistant was working overtime.

'You've been very helpful,' said Ivan, and he left her with enough money to finish off her glue habit and herself. He quit the building and went to sit in a nearby café. Sebastien and Tanya had done well. They were further advanced on Stanton's trail than he was, even though they hadn't visited Mrs Boone's house. Could Rex have told Tanya something about the Mastership Game? If so what? He must find out. Yet where were they?

For him to track them down personally would now be impossible. However, Ivan did not despair. The mere presence of Tanya in Boston gave him sufficient information to go on. She must have been staying somewhere in the vicinity and Ivan had a few weapons in his armoury that Tanya and Sebastien did not.

In his work for the College he monitored the secret services of many countries, acted as a consultant to some of them and was in truth registered as an employee of at least one of them. Ivan finished his cappuccino. The help of the American cousins of Hadley was required, and fast. People who kept a track on everybody and who owed him favours. Ivan left the restaurant. He reckoned he'd find out within a couple of hours.

Ivan was not to be disappointed. Within an hour, courtesy of the CIA, Ivan knew the name of the hotel where Tanya had been staying. Also, that she had flown from Boston to Geneva the night before. A call to the hotel indicated that Sebastien was still in Boston, having taken over her room. Ivan was happy. He packed and made his way to Logan International Airport.

'Cheers,' he whispered to himself, as he sat back in the first-class compartment of Swissair. Nine hours and he would be in Geneva.

Finding Tanya in Switzerland should be child's play if she continued to use her credit card – it was the simplest way in the world for the secret services to track people down. Ivan was looking forward to seeing what other information on Stanton she had garnered. Perhaps he would give Tanya some good advice in return. To get rid of her lover. While sex and power mixed, love and power did not. And this was a game of power. Helping Sebastien would be her downfall. For had not the great Machiavelli said:

> *'Anyone who helps another to power causes his own ruin'?*

The following day the orange boiler suit that constituted the librarian did not come into the Boston Newspaper and Periodicals Library. She didn't work there anyway since she was an actress. The person who paid her for her thespian skills was a 'cleaner' employed by the College.

The Master had read Rex's computer message before Tanya had ever got to it.

CHAPTER TWELVE

It is best either to treat men well or to destroy them; for men revenge themselves for small injuries, but cannot revenge themselves for great ones; so that if you injure anybody, it should be done in such a way that no vengeance is to be feared.

Machiavelli, *The Prince*

February. Switzerland.

ARRIVING IN SWITZERLAND, IVAN BOOKED into one of the best hotels in Geneva. He sipped his Earl Grey tea and looked out at Lac Léman from the window. The waters were calm and placid. That was what he liked about Switzerland – everything was in order, everything in place; a tidy society, the people and their possessions carefully arranged to secure the peace and prosperity they desired. Ivan approved of that.

He called over the *maître d'hôtel* and explained that he wanted to contact a lawyer in Geneva. He handed over the name of the individual. He knew it would be arranged *tout de suite.* So reliable, the Swiss.

There were two important things Ivan had to do before he started the Mastership Game. First, to find out where Tanya was in Switzerland, since he wanted to know everything he could about the contest before he began to play. Second, to work out the meaning of the Chinese puzzle box. Ivan began to butter his croissant and to think.

The Master had mentioned the Chinese puzzle box before

he had told them about the contest. Although this could have been a coincidence, Ivan was sure it wasn't. Therefore, the game and the puzzle box must be connected in some way. How? The Master would not have known the exact nature of the contest; he had told them this was determined by the Arbitrators and that he had no influence over it. That said, he must have had some idea what it would be about, particularly if he had once played the contest himself, which Ivan was sure of, since there was nothing to suggest the method of selecting a new Master had been a recent invention. So what did the Chinese puzzle mean?

Ivan knew at least part of the secret. He was sure the Master had been using the Chinese puzzle as an illustration. He was trying to tell them something important in general. He was saying: you may think this is a puzzle box but do not be deceived. Applying this to the Mastership Game, you may think this is a simple contest but it is much more complex than it seems. Ivan smiled to himself. Appearances were always deceptive. Had not the great Machiavelli said:

> *'Mankind in general judge more by their eyes than their hands; for all can see the appearance, but few can touch the reality. Everyone sees what you seem to be but few discover what you are.'*

Ivan must discover what the game was about; that was crucial. What clues did he have? The Chinese puzzle box, the death of Rex, the death of Max Stanton. What did Ivan make of it all? Looking at the matter on its face, and bearing in mind the death of two contestants, Rex and Max Stanton, it seemed clear that the Mastership Game really was based on Darwinian principles. The survival of the fittest. There were no 'rules' to the game. Instead, the contestants made their own rules and determined exactly how far they were prepared to go in order to win. That made the game a very dangerous one. It also depended to a great extent on the philosophy of the contestants involved.

Ivan ordered a fresh pot of tea. He wondered if the other contestants had considered one other interesting factor: the Master had never actually told them who was playing the game. True, they had been nominated. However, logician that he was, Ivan knew the fact that a person was not expressly included did not mean that they were excluded. Which meant that, despite the death of Rex, there could still be one other person who was a very great threat, a supreme exponent in the exercise of power. *The Master himself might be playing.*

The waters of Lac Léman glinted in the sun and Ivan gazed at them as he thought deeply. Was the Master playing or not? Ivan had no proof either way and he suspected it would be very difficult to find any. There was a philosophical principle, called Occam's razor, which reasoned that, when faced with multiple explanations, the simplest is usually the correct one. Therefore, Ivan should assume the Master was playing since he never said he wasn't. But why would he be playing? The Master himself had indicated that the Arbitrators established the contest and that, in this matter, he was as subject to the Arbitrators' will as the nominated Fellows were; which suggested that the Arbitrators could call for a contest in cases where they felt the powers of the Mastership were not being properly exercised or the powers of the Master were waning.

Suddenly, Ivan felt a frisson of delight run through his body. Before his gaze the vision of a large chessboard appeared. It began to increase dramatically in size. The board also assumed a height and depth in space so that the black and white squares became replicated ad infinitum above and below the original board, a hugely complex Jacob's ladder. A game Ivan would be playing against a true expert: the Master himself.

The shock of this was so great that Ivan momentarily went into a trance, his eyes glazed and the croissant remained suspended between his fingers. The waiter watched him from across the room, uncertain whether the guest was experiencing ecstasy over the bun or, as had happened before, a massive heart attack. To his relief, Ivan came to again.

The pieces were slowly beginning to fit together, like a painting emerging from a blank canvas. Or a puzzle. In reality, there had been six contestants at the start including the Master; five now with the death of Rex. Long may the depletion continue, Ivan thought.

Which brought him to another observation made by that exceptional analyst of power and the means to obtain it. The great Machiavelli had advised:

> *'The only sound, sure and lasting ways of defence are those which depend on yourself and your own process.'*

In this game, Ivan was only going to depend on himself. No deals and no co-operation with the other contestants. The *maître d'* arrived. He inspected Ivan and the half-eaten bread.

'Is the croissant all right, monsieur?'

'Yes. It's fine.'

'I am delighted, monsieur. The lawyer you asked me to contact, Herr Dr Schmidt, will see you at nine thirty this morning.'

Ivan sighed. So reliable the Swiss. He finished his breakfast.

It was nine thirty, and Ivan had a different view of Lac Léman, this time from the plush offices of one of the best-known law firms in Geneva, the practice of Heidelberg and Schmidt. He sat in a leather armchair. Opposite him was an elderly and bespectacled figure behind a large desk. Dr Schmidt stroked his goatee beard and began to speak about the firm. He spoke very slowly and precisely as if each word had been personally handed down to him as a prophecy from God. Speaking slowly was a trait of lawyers around the world, Ivan reflected. Not surprising in a profession where you got paid by the minute. They would be mute if they could get away with it.

In turn, Dr Schmidt viewed his well-dressed client: slim, darkish hair, sharp face with rounded glasses and very penetrating eyes. Obviously cultured and of good class. Dr Schmidt was content. Here was a man who could pay his bill.

'So your old friend and his wife are living in Switzerland and you would like to find where they are?'

'Precisely,' said Ivan. He tapped one of the fat law books lying on the desk. 'Dr Schmidt, I must find them at once. I have some important news for them but I don't have their address. I am sure that you can help me.'

'Of course,' said the lawyer. 'I see.' The seconds ticked by. Ivan waited. It was a pity Tanya had not used her credit cards while in Switzerland. Perhaps she had realised it made her easy to track. There had to be another way. There was always information on individuals somewhere. You just needed to dig around.

'My assistants could check the hotel registers. As you may be aware, foreign guests need to register their details.'

'That would be a good idea,' said Ivan.

'We could also check their car details if they own a car.'

'No. I imagine they'll have rented one. Anything else?'

'Do you think they own property here?'

'They may do.'

'Well, we have a land register in each of the Cantons,' said Dr Schmidt. 'It's possible to obtain details of the registered proprietors for a fee. It will take some time, of course.'

Ivan gave a wan smile. 'I think I misheard you,' he said quietly. 'What you meant to say was that it will take a very short period of time for a very large sum of money.'

The eyes of the Swiss twinkled. Such a perceptive man. Truly, he understood the legal profession. 'Ah, yes,' he said slowly. 'That's just what I meant to say.'

Two hours later, Ivan left Dr Schmidt's office with some good news. Sebastien had a chalet in Kasteln, a ski resort fifty kilometres from Geneva. Doubtless, it was built of wood with a small garden and a lovely view on to the mountains. Perhaps even a gnome. How touching. How predictable.

Sebastien really was going to have to sharpen up his game.

While Ivan went house hunting, Sebastien boarded his flight from Boston to Switzerland. He was in a pensive mood. His research in Harvard's libraries was complete and he would not return to Boston. Over the last few days he had developed a plan to make twenty million dollars within the space of a year. All he and Tanya had to do was to put it into practice; and they must start right away if they wanted to achieve it in time. It was also important that they both drop out of sight as soon as possible, before the other contestants started to track them down, since this game was a deadly one, Sebastien had no doubts about that.

'Please fasten your seat belts.'

Sebastien gazed out of the window. He felt exhilaration as the Boeing 747–400 picked up speed and then hurtled down the runway at more than three hundred kilometres an hour. Remarkable really, Sebastien reflected. One piece of defective equipment, a minor fuel leak and this great monster in which they all put their trust would tear itself into a million red-hot pieces, leaving nothing, including them, behind. Just because of one essential piece of equipment being out of place. To work, everything had to fit together and perfectly. It was the same with the Chinese puzzle and the contest for the Mastership.

The point of the Chinese puzzle was not difficult. Obviously, the Master was drawing a comparison between the box and the contest for the Mastership. The Master had also referred to the maker of the puzzle box. The secret to both, therefore, lay in understanding not only the object but also its maker. So that meant understanding both the game and the Master. Knowing how they worked and how they thought. And the Chinese connection? That was curious. Perhaps it was not significant, yet Sebastien couldn't get out of his mind a quotation, the author of which he couldn't remember:

'Know your enemy and know yourself. In that way though you fight one hundred battles you will not lose one of them.'

Still, he had plenty of time to ascertain it when he arrived in Switzerland. For the moment he could relax. Sebastien turned his attention to the young student beside him. She smiled back nervously.

'I'm sorry. I hate flying.'

They began to chat while the aluminium leviathan hurtled down the runway and took off, demonstrating that at least some of its equipment was in place. Sebastien soon discovered that his companion's name was Suzanne, that she was a model and that she lived in Geneva. By the end of the nine-hour flight Sebastien had discovered two other important things: the first was that he wanted to see much more of Suzanne physically; the second was that he recalled the author of the quotation. It was a famous military tactician born in China four hundred years before Christ. His name was Sun Tzu.

More ominously, the quotation came from a book he had written – *The Art of War.*

The road curved sharply as it wound up into the mountains. Ivan slipped the Mercedes into first gear and peered out from behind the windscreen to see past the patches of fog which hung just above ground level. Near the end of a rough track he reached the place he was looking for. Below, the lights of the small skiing resort of Kasteln glistened. He reversed the car and parked it further down the road. Cautiously, he approached Sebastien's chalet across a field at the back, using a pencil torch to guide him.

The chalet was similar to others in the area: a two storeyed affair of timber with large veranda windows that gave on to a tree-strewn mountainside. Within there was no light and no sound of human presence. Ivan was pleased. Sebastien was still in the United States, as he'd supposed. It also seemed that Tanya was out. Further, the snow would obliterate his tracks by morning. Things were going well.

Close to the chalet Ivan crouched down to contemplate his first move. It was of great importance for, just as the opening gambit of a chess player is not decisive, it tells much of his manner of play. In the case of Ivan he was playing to win. To him it was inconceivable that he not become Master. This did not derive from hubris, as in the case of Rex, a belief that he was intrinsically better than others. No. Instead, it was a personal recognition that Ivan alone had the insight and the ability to direct the College in the future.

It was clear to him as a Fellow that humanity was entering a turbulent new phase, with a gradual movement towards global dictatorship, the suppression of the individual will and the control of information by the few. This dictatorship was more subtle than in previous dark ages, since it was occurring without most people perceiving it, and with no one leader of nations having the power and the authority to challenge it directly. Ivan accepted this, human progress was cyclical. His deepest concern, however, was that the College itself should not succumb before the deluge. Even as the lights were going out elsewhere the College must remain, if necessary like a jewel in a darkened sea, its light reminding the leaders of all nations that the only future for humankind lay in peace, not in war or oppression.

The key to all this lay in the Mastership. Only it held the power and the knowledge to hold back the corrupting tide. The present Master was a great and brilliant man. However, it was also clear that he was tiring and that he did not know how to confront this new menace. Ivan also feared that he was not Machiavellian enough; he did not know the ways of power, and that, sometimes, ruthlessness must be used to defend the faith. Ivan must help the College now, in its darkest hour. It was his destiny.

He started to walk towards the house, rationalising his actions with all the casuistry of a Jesuit. Besides, to lose the game and no longer to be a Fellow of the College would be a fate worse than death. The whole of his life had been spent in a rarefied atmosphere of high intellect and dedication to an ideal. When he had joined the College five years before, its mysticism and intellectualism had filled in, like water in a hole, the human warmth that he'd never experienced as an orphan and which he had never sought as an adult. The College had become an essential part of his being and he would fight, like a crusader, to defend it to the bitter end. What, though, would Ivan do to achieve his goal? Just how far would he go in this game? He was not sure within himself as he climbed the steps to the chalet. It was one area where his sense of certitude had not hardened. Was it right to fight to secure the Mastership so that he could preserve the institution he so loved? Yes, it was. But how far that fight should be fought, just how far he should go, depended on the precise circumstances as they arose, and Ivan would deal with them as they came upon him. Besides, Machiavelli would have the answers. He perceived the nature of power and how it could be wielded without destroying its holder. Trust an Italian.

For the moment, the next step was obvious. Ivan would find out what other information Tanya and Sebastien had on Max Stanton. It was vital since it related to how others had played the game in the past. While Ivan thought he knew what the contest for the Mastership was about, he wanted to be quite sure. To break into the chalet would be one small step on his path to the Mastership and Ivan had to justify each step with regard to its end result. Otherwise, he might not reach his goal. This justification, ultimately, had nothing to do with morality. It had all to do with planning and tactics. As Machiavelli had said:

> *'Let a prince do what is necessary to win and maintain power; the means he uses will always be considered honourable, and praised by everybody.'*

Once Ivan became Master, who would worry about how he had acquired the title? No one could challenge him as the supreme authority of the College. Indeed, they would soon appreciate him as the saviour of the institution. Besides, Ivan reflected, the killing of Rex had started it all. Once that had occurred, no one could go back. Breaking into a house was in a more minor category of sin, a mere peccadillo in comparison.

Placing a Balaclava over his face Ivan approached the back

door. Stooping low beside the keyhole he cut deep into the wood near the lock with a chisel. After inserting a jemmy in the gap he brought his full weight against it. There was a muffled crunch of splintered wood. Silently, Ivan pushed open the door.

Upstairs, Tanya turned over in her sleep.

At Geneva Airport, Sebastien and Suzanne passed through the green customs barrier along with the rest of the passengers on their flight, by now a queue of weary transatlantic travellers clutching their duty free and anxious to get home.

'Where are you going to?'

'Kasteln. It's an hour from here.'

'I know it well,' replied Suzanne. 'I often go skiing there.' They stood outside the airport. It was snowing. Other passengers jostled past them as they hurried to get to the taxis. Suzanne looked at Sebastien.

'How about a drink?' she said a little nervously. Then, in a more assertive fashion. 'I mean, I want to invite you for a drink.'

Sebastien laughed. His travelling companion had been very good company. Student models invariably were. Especially one with such a lovely complexion and spectacularly good legs.

'It's late. I have to go on to Kasteln.' The words were delivered in a reluctant tone. Still, he must get back to Tanya.

They crossed over to the taxi rank.

'Where to?' said the driver to Suzanne.

Ivan stood in the kitchen of Sebastien's chalet. Where would Tanya have put the information about Stanton she'd acquired in Boston? He didn't believe she'd have hidden it already. She wouldn't have guessed another contestant would be so hot on her trail. The most logical place would be the sitting room. Ivan quit the kitchen and followed the thin beam of his pencil torch, which he directed at the floor. There was an eerie silence, broken only by the occasional crump of snow as it slithered from the roof to the ground.

The chalet followed a standard layout – sitting room, dining room, kitchen, hallway. The sitting room was tastefully furnished, with plenty of artwork on the walls and brightly decorated vases. This was surely Tanya's influence, Ivan thought. Sebastien only had good taste in women. By the faint light of his torch there now appeared before his gaze a large fireplace set into the wall. The logs were fresh. Ivan ran his finger along the mantelpiece. No dust. Either Tanya was around or they had a maid in on a regular basis. He quickly got to work. The room didn't take long to inspect. There were only a few cupboards and a sideboard with no indication of a safe or a concealed compartment anywhere. Nothing of interest. Save for one small feature: there was a travel book on Central America casually lying on a shelf. It had some annotations scribbled in Tanya's hand on the inside cover. Worth remembering. Perhaps they were going there. Knowing Sebastien, Ivan imagined he'd think of an exotic way to make his twenty million dollars.

After checking the other rooms without success Ivan started to climb the stairs. He lingered on each step to ensure there was no creak from the floorboards and to let the thick pile carpet absorb any impact. Once he was on the landing he stopped to get his bearings. He shone the torch about him, reducing its intensity by cupping it in his hands. There were four doors in front of him, all closed. Ivan approached them one by one. In each case, he slowly eased down the handle and then opened the door to peer inside. The first two were bedrooms. The third a bathroom. Ivan tried the handle of the last door. As he did so, Tanya awoke.

She had been dreaming she was back in her room at College. She was in bed and Gemma, her cat, had come in to nestle down beside her. She felt safe and warm. In her dream there appeared a faint shaft of light at the bedroom door. Gemma must have pushed it open Tanya thought to herself. Yet something was wrong with the dream and she couldn't think what it was. Suddenly, like a tired driver on the motorway who realises he is too close to a vehicle in front and is about to hit it, Tanya's consciousness screamed at her to wake up. Tanya was not in the

College; she was in Sebastien's chalet; and Gemma was not there, but the light at the bedroom door was.

Tanya sat up in bed. She watched numbly as the shaft of light widened before her gaze. Even as it did so, it took a few seconds for her brain to register that the silhouetted figure was not Sebastien. A surge of adrenalin shot through her body and her hands frantically clawed for the bedside switch. But it was too late. The masked figure had reached her and a cosh smacked against her right temple.

'Come on in.'

Suzanne led the way into her apartment, moving a bicycle to one side. 'I'm sorry about the mess. I spend so much time travelling these days, and you know what students are like.' She giggled nervously. She was only nineteen.

Sebastien glanced about him. It was a small flat filled with film posters, pictures of models and books. He contemplated the nude fashion shots of Suzanne on the wall. He liked them. They were taken under photographer's lights and showed to excellent effect her faun-like body, pert bottom and inviting loins.

'Can I get you some coffee?'

'I'm fine.'

'Wine?'

'OK.'

Suzanne went into the kitchen and took a bottle from the shelf. She turned and Sebsatien was standing beside her. It was now or never. Nervously, she reached out and pulled him to her. She kissed him softly on the lips and ran her fingers through his hair. For a moment he did not react. Then he began to caress her. She watched him undo her blouse and cup her young breasts in his hands. Quickly, she brushed aside the plates on the kitchen counter and lifted herself on to it, levering her body against his. Her skirt rode up and she felt his hardness press against her bare flesh.

The wine was forgotten.

*   *   *

Tanya was still breathing. Unhurriedly, Ivan tied her hands and feet to the bed frame and blindfolded her. He placed a gag in her mouth. Finally, he opened one of the curtains slightly so that he could watch for any approaching cars. He started to search the bedroom, taking his time and looking everywhere. Soon he returned to the bedside. There was nothing. A big problem – for them both. It was a matter of minutes before Tanya came round. She felt groggy and confused. Her mind slowly refocused itself, like a computer recovering after it had crashed. It told her that she was lying on the bed securely gagged and blindfolded. She also knew someone was sitting close beside her since she could feel a slight depression in the mattress near her legs. Who? A burglar? A rapist? One of the other contestants? Her mind began to race as her consciousness recovered. Her fear raced with it.

'What do you want?' the gag distorted her words.

Ivan sat beside her on the bed, contemplating her semi-naked body in the faint yellow light given off by a security light at the front of the house. He had nothing against Tanya. She'd always seemed to him to be a kind and loving individual – though she'd made a poor choice in Sebastien he thought. Rex would have been a more reliable man. Less the playboy and more the doting lover. However, Rex was dead and whatever happened, Tanya would support Sebastien. The two of them together would be a team capable of beating him. So how was he going to get the information about Max Stanton from her, to even the odds?

'What do you want? Who is it?'

Ivan could feel the mounting fear in her voice and it gave him a sense of satisfaction. For fear, not violence, at this stage was the key to getting what he wanted. Yet the fear must be very real. Ivan observed her, waiting for the optimal moment. For her part, while she fought against the bindings, Tanya cried out in her mind for Sebastien, although she knew no aid would come to her from that quarter. Who was this intruder? What would he do? Her sense of isolation was complete, her feeling of despair akin to the newly blind. Fear emanated from her body like fire. Ivan felt that fear and he nurtured it.

In the silence, and with her other senses gone, Tanya's sense of hearing sharpened immeasurably. She heard the noise of a body move close beside her hips, then the soft crinkle of rubber and a slight snap. The sound had an antiseptic crispness about it, as if someone was putting on surgical gloves, a pathologist about to dissect a body. What was he going to do? Her limbs convulsed, twisting against the ligatures that held her. It was useless. There was no hope of salvation.

Ivan waited until her struggling had ceased and her waves of panic receded. He heard the hoarse exhalation of her breath against the gag while he continued to sit beside her, saying nothing and doing nothing; like a priest denying the last rites. He held out no hope and only one way forward.

'What do you want? Is it money?'

Fear distorted the words already deadened by the gag. There was no answer. It seemed that time lengthened in the silence. Ivan's gloved fingers unfastened the buttons of Tanya's skimpy nightdress and exposed her naked flesh. The operation was performed slowly and methodically and after each button was undone he waited until her struggles ceased. Then a gloved hand moved across her body to gently cup each of her full breasts, feeling their soft warmth and the tremors beneath.

An anonymous index finger began to trace a meandering path away from the frightened erection of her nipples to the centre of her body. The movement was slow and deliberate, for Ivan had all the time in the world. He watched, fascinated, at each unavailing shudder, like a chemist provoking a chemical reaction. The finger encircled her belly button. It carried on, leisurely. Beneath its antiseptic touch he could sense the rigid tension of her stomach muscles, while her body contorted with fear. The finger, wet and fluid now from Tanya's sweat, continued to wend its way downwards, slowly and relentlessly. It reached soft down and traced its way through. It poised on her mons veneris, caught in the light from the window. Ivan felt like a child playing with a trapped butterfly, intrigued by its own wanton cruelty but without any intention of stopping. Before him was no longer Tanya, but just a body to play with, an experiment on a live animal with all the thrill of exercising power.

'There's a safe. It's downstairs. There's money.' The blood from Tanya's mouth began to fleck the gag as she screamed hoarsely.

The finger poised. Then, slowly, it continued its journey. The gloved finger and its companions delicately parted her legs, already drawn half open by the bindings which held her to the bed. She was too scared to resist. She could feel a finger brushing against her moist furrowed flesh with all the terrifying warmth of a snake. Suddenly, it stopped.

For one wonderful golden moment of elation Tanya thought that he would not hurt her any more. That her intruder was satisfied, satiated with his power and his control over her. She started to pray. There was silence, a perfect silence and within it she savoured her freedom. It was finally broken by the almost inaudible sound of Sebastien's cigarette packet being picked up from the side table and opened. A soft crinkle of Cellophane while a cigarette was withdrawn and a click as it was lit. Tanya felt the heat as the cigarette approached her face and slowly passed down the length of her form. Tanya knew what he would do when it reached her loins. Her body went wild.

She fought against the ligatures that bound her, caught up in her very own private hell, in which time was absent. It was no use, however, and she knew it. There was only one way out. So screaming against the gag, Tanya told the silent torturer everything he might want to know. Where the safe was, its combination number, where the documents were, where her jewellery was, where her lover was. Finally, after what seemed to be an eternity, the poised cigarette was withdrawn. Ivan continued to sit by the bed, listening to her muffled weeping. Poor Tanya. It had been necessary, of course. Justifiable in the circumstances. Had not Machiavelli remarked:

> *'Cruelties used well (if we may say "well" of what is evil in itself) are those which are necessary for self-preservation, and are carried out on a single occasion, once and for all.'*

Ivan went downstairs. Within minutes he had opened the safe and found the documents. One was the obituary of Max Stanton. The others comprised various press cuttings recording his achievements as a chemist. After reading them Ivan carefully placed them back in their original position.

He was disappointed. Tanya and Sebastien had not found out much more than he. It was time to go. In the sitting room Ivan quickly pulled books from the shelves, dislodged pictures and scored the sofa with his knife. He took some money and jewellery and tossed them into a holdall. He'd throw these away later. Tanya and Sebastien must remain uncertain whether the intruder was a burglar or not. But what should he do with Tanya? How far should he go? He extracted a knife from his pocket.

Just then the phone rang.

Where was Tanya?

Sebastien stood naked in the unfamiliar sitting room, feeling cold. He glanced at his watch. It was three-thirty in the morning. Tanya just had to be there. Unless she was with someone else. He let the phone continue to ring. Perhaps she had left him. Perhaps she wanted to compete on her own. He felt uneasy.

'Sebastien?'

'I'm here.'

'Come back to bed,' said Suzanne.

He'd leave early next morning. He would be in Kasteln by eight. Sebastien went back to bed. His hands searched for her thighs as Suzanne drew him to her. Delicately, he parted her legs with his fingers.

Ivan waited by Tanya's bedside until the ringing of the phone stopped. Dispassionately, he noticed his heartbeat had increased slightly. He dialled the phone answerback. The call was from Geneva. It had to be Sebastien. No one else would call at this hour. So Tanya had lied. She had told him that Sebastien was still in Boston. Either that or she didn't know that her errant lover had returned. In any case, Ivan must leave. Sebastien would be here shortly and Ivan had no desire to meet him on his home ground.

What about Tanya? If she remained alive she would be a formidable enemy, for she would probably guess that the intruder was either Andrew or himself and no mere burglar. It was a risk, and to have both Tanya and Sebastien after him with a vengeance would decrease his odds of winning the contest for the Mastership. What should he do? Machiavelli, that master of the use and abuse of power, had made it clear that if you have an enemy you should kill him.

Was Tanya an enemy, though? What harm had she done Ivan? Should he have pity on her or destroy her? It was a very difficult choice. If she remained alive his chances of gaining the Mastership were greatly reduced. Also, would not she and Sebastien kill him if they had the chance? Would they not feel justified? Ivan weighed all this up in the scales of his justice. Pity and compassion were such small weights.

Finally, Ivan got up. Poor Tanya. He took one of her silk scarves from a drawer. Then he sat down on the bed beside her once more. Life was a bitch. Machiavelli had always appreciated that. Carefully, he put the scarf around her neck and began to tighten it.

As the silken cord contorted against her windpipe Tanya knew that she was going to die. In the space of a millisecond her mind, ever a faithful analyst of events, informed her in a soft inner voice that her life was rapidly approaching its conclusion. It slowed down a myriad functions that it had performed since birth and it shut off the impulses that transmitted her fear. She had no need of them now. As the scarf tightened about her neck, and her consciousness began to fail, the brain started to activate its final programme. Tanya had often wondered what it was like to die. Now she was beginning to know, and she silently thanked that wonderful mind that had sustained her on her journey throughout life. For even in death it performed its final task, flooding her brain with a natural opiate, ever attentive to reducing her suffering.

Unconscious now, Tanya saw the waters of death as they approached, unhurried and all-embracing. Her mind helped her to turn towards them with a calm and inevitable acceptance. Caught in a dreamlike state, oblivious of her body, almost without form, Tanya looked into the profundity of her being for the first time. And within it she felt a love she had never known before. She began to break the invisible threads that held her back. Sebastien, the game, her memories, her hopes and fears – they all passed her by and faded as she started to enter the pool. She saw the totality that was her existence. It was impossible for her to stop the process.

When it came, the voice of her dead father was so close that it was almost beside her ear. On the very threshold of her extinction his love found her out and held her back even as she made to descend into the waters of forgetfulness. It whispered to her as to a child and in the manifold complexities of the universe it wrought its own power in the mind of others.

Ten minutes later Ivan quit the chalet and was gone.

The following morning Sebastien surveyed the scene before him in horror and disbelief. The paintings and sofa slashed, porcelain broken, the safe rifled. Grimly, he climbed the staircase to the main bedroom. It appeared like a film set for a bacchic orgy with clothing and bedclothes scattered everywhere. There had been a very violent struggle. Pieces of knotted linen dangled from one of the bedposts and there were bloody marks on them, just as there were on the bedsheets. The scene of a murder. Sebastien looked out of the window. Suddenly, he uttered a cry. He could see Tanya. He fled downstairs and hurled open the back door. Then he ran across the field to the trees, his feet floundering in the snow.

She was sitting under the firs, wrapped in a quilted jacket. Her eyes were fixed on the mountains. She didn't even glance at him as he approached. Sebastien sat down beside her, too alarmed to disturb her before she spoke. Eventually Tanya told him what had happened in a matter-of-fact, objective tone, like a news reporter. The trauma would come later. They gazed in silence at the virgin white of the landscape, their thoughts elsewhere.

'Why didn't he kill you?'

'I don't know.'

'It could have been a burglar.'

'No. It was either Ivan or Andrew.'

'Sure?' asked Sebastien

'Yes, I'm sure,' said Tanya. 'Quite sure.'

'He didn't take the documents about Stanton.'

'It wasn't necessary. He could have read them in a moment,' Tanya said tonelessly, as she scanned his face. 'Where were you last night?'

'I arrived late in Geneva. I stayed there.' Sebastien's visage became rocklike and his eyes gleamed. She could see the hate reflected in them. 'Did he rape you?'

Tanya said nothing. Sebastien repeated his question, his voice twisted with anger.

'No,' she said. 'Apart from frightening me to death, he didn't do anything.' She cast a glance at him and then away. Why did she still love him? What was it that still drew her to him, that fascinated her?

'What shall we do?' asked Sebastien.

'We carry on.' Her voice was low and determined. 'We both made a mistake. We assumed that no one else had found out about Stanton. For that Rex lost his life. We also have been too slow and too careless. We must change.'

Sebastien nodded. He felt cold and depressed, a rare occurrence.

After a few minutes he said, 'I think it's time to disappear, Tanya. We should leave today.' He paused, then continued, 'We should assume nothing about this contest. This game is for the most powerful position of all. And we should assume that Andrew and Ivan will do anything to win.'

'As will you,' she said accusingly.

'And you,' he replied.

'True,' said Tanya. 'We should assume that all of us will fight as hard as we can. And that we will do anything we can to get there.'

They continued to view the beautiful scenery. They didn't want to leave this place, once their sanctuary. Within the space of a night, however, it was no longer the same, no longer safe and, for Tanya, it now held evil memories.

'It started with the death of Rex,' said Tanya, her voice harsh and brittle. 'You'd better go and pack. I'll stay here for a while.'

Sebastien got up. 'Tanya, I am sorry. I am really sorry about what happened.'

Tanya nodded without hearing him. 'The death of Rex. That started it all,' she repeated.

She watched Sebastien depart across the snow. Pieces of the game were coming together but they had not been quick enough. A big mistake. Rex had died because of the game; because he was not quick enough to appreciate the consequences of what he knew. Tanya contemplated the natural beauty before her and her heart was full of despair. If only Rex could help her now. He would have protected her from harm.

'Chinese puzzle. Bloody Chinese puzzle.' She whispered it to the mountains. Why was she so stupid that she couldn't understand what it meant? She was lost. It all had no meaning. Like something else she had experienced last night. Another puzzle, one that caused her to question her life, its cravings and desires. When she'd thought she was going to die, her vision of the world and her place in it had suddenly changed. She had begun to appreciate who she really was. The sensation had been so fleeting that it was difficult to recall. However, in that brief moment in the cosmos she had experienced the answer to everything, to the Mastership, to her love, to her desires. Now, back in the world, it was too fragile and mystical a feeling to comprehend. Reluctantly, Tanya turned aside from it, to consider the more pressing issue of who had been at the chalet last night.

It was no intruder. It could only have been Andrew or Ivan and they had come to find out about Max Stanton. Did that mean that one, or both of them, had killed Rex? Not necessarily, for whoever had been at the chalet last night had done a very strange thing. He had taken a silk scarf and tied it around her neck to kill her. However, something had stopped him at the last moment. Instead, he had taken the scarf and gently placed it across her loins to cover her nakedness. Why had he stopped, after inducing such fear in her? Did he have second thoughts or a sense of remorse? If he had killed Rex, why didn't he kill her? And if Ivan or Andrew hadn't, who had?

Tanya looked back towards the chalet.

CHAPTER THIRTEEN

He who is skilful in winning against the enemy does not wrestle with him.

Lao Zi

March. The Congo.

'THERE'S SOMEONE TO SEE YOU, Obedi.'

Obedi stopped staring out of the window and got up from the shabby wooden desk. Thirty other schoolchildren watched him with envy. As orphans they never had any visitors. Then the female schoolteacher rapped hard on the worn blackboard with a stick and with a collective sigh they turned back to their lessons.

Meanwhile, Obedi fled down the earthen corridor. He sucked in the humid air of his freedom with deep breaths. It was not that he didn't like English lessons. It was just that he wanted to be outside, to be away from anyone else who might ever harm him.

'Obedi!'

He turned and walked back into the headmaster's study. Andrew was sitting there. The headmaster got up from his chair and put his hand on Obedi's shoulder. 'I will leave you for a while,' he said.

Obedi observed Andrew. He liked him. His face was open and friendly and he had saved them from the rebels. Obedi had never thanked him. He knew it wasn't important, though. How can you thank a person for saving your life? He knew that Andrew understood anyway. His gratitude was beyond words.

'What have you been doing?' said Obedi.

'Searching for something. In Scotland.'

'Did you find it?' asked Obedi. He wondered whether he would ever speak English well enough to talk to him in that language. It didn't really matter. They could converse in Swahili.

'Well, yes and no,' said Andrew. 'How's school?'

'OK.' Obedi sat down at the simple table. With pleasure he noted the UN man had brought something with him. A phone. Phones always gave him comfort.

'How long have you been here?'

'A few weeks.' Obedi explained to Andrew that the UN had moved them from a displaced persons' camp at Kapanga to this school for orphans in Kikwit using a convoy of trucks. It had been exciting and a change from sitting under canvas all day. Andrew noticed that the knife wound on his arm had healed.

'Is your sister here?'

'Yes. She's in another class. For older children.' Obedi would never leave her. She was the only person he had left in the world. The only person who loved him.

'I came to see you and your sister,' said Andrew after a pause.

'Yes,' replied Obedi. He was surprised the man who'd rescued them even thought about them any more. Not that he wasn't glad to see him after two months – he was.

'They tell me you will stay here for a while,' Andrew continued. 'That's good. Your schooling is important.' He frowned. 'I have to go away again but I want to give you something.' Obedi's face registered his surprise.

'It's a phone.' Andrew placed it in front of him. Obedi inspected it with fascination. It was only the size of a man's hand and its face gleamed with coloured buttons that had numbers on them. What a gift. Obedi could not imagine anything greater. He was ecstatic. God was truly thinking of him.

Andrew ignored all the explanations of how the most sophisticated of satellite phones worked. Instead, he simply showed Obedi that by pressing two coloured buttons, it would connect Obedi to Andrew wherever he was in the world. Andrew drew a similar phone out of his pocket and made Obedi phone him. Obedi laughed happily as they were linked up.

'I want you to let your sister keep the phone,' said Andrew. 'And I only want you to use it if something very important happens.'

Obedi looked at him solemnly. 'If something terrible happens?' Already Obedi had guessed the real purpose of the phone.

'Yes, if something terrible happens,' said Andrew. Not that he would be able to get back to them in time. If civil war broke out in the Congo, the gates of hell would open. 'I'll come back here when I can,' he explained, 'but I have to go to another part of the world for some time. I will come back to see you and your sister, though, I promise.'

'Yes,' said Obedi. But he was sure he wouldn't. Like his family, the UN man would never return.

Andrew got in to the Land Rover. Holding hands Obedi and his sister stood forlornly in the potholed driveway as they watched him depart. He started on the main road for Kinshasa, a two-and-a-half hour journey. Andrew knew they didn't believe he'd come back to visit them; and their own chances of survival were slim in a country that had already seen the death of hundreds of thousands. He sighed.

The Mastership Game. He had to make twenty million dollars. Why on earth did the College need such sums? He was sure they didn't. The foundation had very great wealth. Therefore, the making of the twenty million dollars was a test. How the contestants achieved something so difficult as to be almost impossible was obviously the important thing. Perhaps it was a way of showing them how difficult being Master was. Every day of one's life trying to solve the apparently unsolvable problems of mankind.

The vehicle bumped along the shattered road while Andrew swung the wheel from side to side to avoid the cavernous potholes. How would Andrew make the money? He still didn't know.

It seemed quite impossible to make it legally. And to make it illegally would appear to go against all that the College stood for. Or, at least, what it had once stood for.

As the Land Rover lurched across a river where a bridge had collapsed, Andrew turned his thoughts to the Chinese puzzle box. It was clear the Master had discussed it with reference to the Mastership Game and that they were interrelated. It was also clear that the key to the Chinese puzzle was connected to its maker just as the key to the Mastership Game was linked to the present Master. In what way? To Andrew, the only solution was to discover as much as he could about the maker of the Chinese box – the craftsman Chang. And since Chang had been dead for three centuries all Andrew would have to go on would be historical accounts and examples of his work.

When he neared the outskirts of Kinshasa, Andrew passed thousands of poorly clad refugees on the road. They walked slowly, their faces masks of dejection and despair. Coming from nowhere and going nowhere. Fleeing yet more ethnic hatreds. Andrew glanced at the tired mothers, children at their breasts and hopelessness in their hearts. He was certain the Congo would soon become the next flashpoint for a full-scale African war. He could feel the rumblings of it under this very highway along which he drove and along which a rebel army would soon appear. However, Andrew wouldn't be there. Who from the College would be? Who would fight for the cause of peace?

Andrew was sure the College was undergoing a terminal decline even while its members fought among themselves for the Mastership. The poisons of the world had finally penetrated the College and the Master, the heart of the system, was either unable to resist these encroachments or had fallen prey to their lure. Andrew remembered the recent US Presidential scandal and the claim of Paul Faucher in a suicide note that the Master had actively sought to bring down the Presidency. It had caused an uproar in Congress. There had been demands for the revocation of the College's privileged status and its being opened up. To this outcry, the College had, as always, remained silent and disaster was only averted by President Davison's declaring Faucher's allegation to be a lie and the words of a traitor. Yet, suppose it were true? Suppose the Master had been dismissed or, even though it was not permitted, he had sought to resign?

Besides, what could Andrew do even if he became Master? Preserve what had already had its day? Risk his life and those of others to achieve what was now lost in this modern world – an ideal? Why didn't he just walk away from it all? To hell with them and with their game. He didn't have to be a Fellow. He could survive without them. And yet, a world without the College, without an aspiration? James, Lord of the Isles, would have lived and died in vain.

These thoughts tormented him. Eventually, he forced his mind back to the contest. Where were Ivan, Sebastien and Tanya? He had no doubt that they were already far more advanced than he was on the path to the Mastership, and they would soon seek him out. Unless he wanted to hide himself away and partake in the game no more, he had to decide whether he wanted to be the hunter or the hunted. Kill or be killed?

As he passed through the slums of Kinshasa, Andrew reached a decision. He must determine where the others were so he could keep an eye on them while he sought to make his twenty million dollars. But how?

He reached for his satellite phone.

'Will someone get that bloody phone!'

The head of Al Johnson Investigations, one of the most famous private detective agencies in New York, tossed his cheese and pickle sandwich onto the paper plate. How many times had he told the secretaries that they shouldn't leave the office unattended during the lunch hour? Clients got pissed off when no one answered them. You had to treat clients nicely or you went broke. Al Johnson stormed through to the typing pool. His extended belly moved along with him, after a momentary time lag.

'Yes,' he bellowed down the receiver. How dare clients bother him at lunch?

Suddenly he sat down. He ran his hand across his bald pate, searching for hair.

'Oh yes, sir.' Al listened attentively to the transatlantic call. 'I understand,' he nodded. He began to jot down the details. A few minutes later he went into his partner's office and squeezed his great bulk into a tiny armchair. He fingered his fluorescent tie. It had a pickle mark on it.

'Er, PJ, listen. I've just got a client. Let's just call him Andrew. He wants two people to be tracked. Just to be tracked. Nothing else, mind you. He'll phone in once in a while to get the information. Here are the names. Money's not a problem. They're to be followed for six months. Can you coordinate it? He doesn't know where they are at present.'

PJ, a tall Afro-Caribbean with a perpetual grin and the build of a fitness fanatic, took off his earphones and turned down the tape recorder. He hadn't heard a word.

'Sounds good, baby.' He took the note from his colleague, glanced at it and carried on listening to the recorder.

Al watched him suspiciously. The noise sounded like rap music and not the client tapes PJ was meant to be working on. He decided to let it pass. PJ was good. The best in this department. In fact, the only one at the moment. Al and his stomach exited from the room while the music continued. A few minutes later the door to Al's room was hurled open and PJ stood there minus his tape recorder and with a strange expression on his face. 'Take a look at this.'

Al slowly read the fax and whistled. 'Christ,' he said, and sat down on his desk. 'What do we do?'

PJ grinned. 'Do we care?' he said. 'Look, we've got two clients. And each of them wants us to tail the other. So what do we do, huh? We do just as they say. We track 'em and we charge 'em both.'

'But,' said Al helplessly, 'then we're tracking our own clients.'

'Lovely, baby, lovely.' PJ kissed the bald pate of his partner in ecstasy. 'It's just lovely, baby. We get paid twice over and they'll never know.'

Al eyed his partner. The boy was a crook but that was why he employed him. Suddenly, he felt peckish and then hungry for money.

'Yeah.' He squeezed his bulbous nose and scratched his ear. 'Who cares? I'll look after this Andrew guy. You look after Sebastien. Provided we don't let on. Let's keep this between ourselves, PJ. We'll do just as they ask. Tell them the whereabouts of the other. Tell you what, though. I wouldn't like to be the third guy they're both after. What's his name?'

PJ glanced at the fax. 'Ivan Radic,' he said.

March. New York.

With a cough, the Head of Recruitment put down the papers on his desk. He sat in a room on the top floor of a New York skyscraper whose windows commanded a magnificent view of the urban jungle below.

'So, er . . .' he glanced at the letter, 'Sebastien, how may I assist you?'

'As I mentioned, I'd be interested in working for your organisation in Latin America.'

'Yes, I see.' The American nodded. He wore the striped shirt and thick red braces so beloved of New York bankers. This, together with his heavy gold watch, Ivy League tie and chunky cufflinks completed his Identikit picture. And on the principle of 'I like me' the clean-shaven, handsome, smooth-talking individual sitting in front of him was just what the organisation was looking for.

'Well, there are openings. Your resumé's impressive and, although you're slightly older than our usual intake, that's no great shakes. May we approach your referees?'

'Of course.'

'How soon can you start if offered the job?'

'Immediately.'

The big American beamed. He liked what he heard. Be decisive was his motto. Never say no, certainly not to the Head of Recruitment at the US Bank.

'Any other languages apart from Spanish?'

'I'm French born. I also speak Italian, German and Russian. And a smattering of one or two others,' said Sebastien. He glanced at the marbled floor and the bronze statuary. The Head of Recruitment spoke again.

'Uh huh, I think you're the type of guy we're looking for. Funnily enough your name came up a few days ago. I was talking to Georges Billoux, Chairman of the Paris Bourse. He mentioned you'd be coming to see me. He was singing your praises. Your World Bank references are excellent as well.'

Sebastien smiled. He made a mental note to call Georges and thank him.

'You seem to know what you're doing and your language skills are impressive. I'll need to confirm the position with our Latin America Department. It won't take long and I reckon you'll get a job offer. If so, there'll be a month's training here in the Big Apple. After that we'll ship you down to Central or Latin America to one of our banks there. Any particular country you're interested in?'

'Panama.'

The American raised his eyebrows quizzically. An odd choice. Most of them wanted Brazil, so they could screw girls on Copacabana beach.

'Now why would that be?'

'It has one of the largest banking centres in Latin America. And it's a financial conduit for much of the North-South trade. I also believe you intend to expand your business there.'

The American leaned back in his chair. He wasn't aware that this information had been publicly released. The Board had only agreed on the strategy yesterday. Could someone have gained unauthorised access to their files? Impossible. 'I see. Someone's been doing his homework. You're well informed, Sebastien. We'll certainly bear your wishes in mind. Well, it's been a pleasure talking with you. We'll contact you once I've discussed your case with the Director of LA Ops. He's just down the corridor.'

The handshake was warm and friendly as Sebastien was guided

to the door. The bank had a well-deserved reputation for being one of the best and most efficient in the world.

Getting into the lift Sebastien took a coin from his pocket and spun it. When the lift arrived at the ground floor an attendant stopped him and directed him to a phone.

The Head of Recruitment had some news already: 'Job's yours. Start in a week. Initial training will be in New York. After a month you'll be sent to Panama. My secretary will give you further details. Congratulations.'

Heads had won. That meant both Sebastien and Tanya would be working for the same bank, and in Panama. The first part of their scheme to make twenty million dollars was going according to plan. Tanya had already gone down there. Sebastien wondered how she was doing. He stepped outside the skyscraper onto the busy sidewalk and into the anonymous crowd. One month's training, should be a piece of cake. He cast some coins into a pan handler's hat. Oh dear, one month to kill in New York.

Well, he'd better get on with it.

New York on a Friday night was as alive as only New York could be. The city buzzed with excitement and sexual frenzy. The static lay not only in the neon lights. Sebastien had two desires that evening – a drink and a sleeping partner, and neither should be difficult to obtain. He took a cab to Skid Row and aimed for the nearest bar.

'Seat free?'

'Make yourself at home.'

Sebastien sat down on the bar stool and ordered a bourbon. The sloe-eyed dark-skinned girl considered him with interest. Her gaze was free and open. She swung her uncrossed legs towards him.

''Gon to buy us a drink?'

'Sure.'

'What's your name?'

'Sebastien. Yours?'

'I'm Dawn.'

Sebastien turned to order the drink and Dawn admired his tight buttocks and muscular physique. Soon they were chatting away like old friends, although the conversation was wholly incidental to their thoughts. Within minutes the formalities of their work and where they lived had been dispensed with. She was a young divorcée who worked in an insurance company. He was a banker who was visiting New York for a few days. Neither was interested in the details. What they said didn't matter. What they wanted, did. Both had already decided how the evening would end. However, due modesty had to be observed. Thrust, parry and counterthrust would be played out to their logical conclusion.

'Are you in a hurry to get home?'

'No, not really,' she glimmered as she sipped her Manhattan highball. He really was a charmer. She could feel him inside her already.

After the meal and after Sebastien had mentally undressed her for the third time, he casually remarked, 'Like to drop by my apartment for coffee? I'll get you a taxi back.'

She smiled at him and crushed the ice between her brilliant white teeth. 'OK, but I mustn't be too late.' She wondered whether he had a spare toothbrush. Of course he would have. He probably bought them by bulk order. Honey, she mentally told him, you'd better be ready for action. She flexed her body surreptitiously. Good job she'd worked out that morning.

In his apartment Sebastien flicked on the light switch and glanced through his mail while Dawn departed into the bathroom to check out the toothbrush position. Later, as they lay in bed, Dawn was happy. She felt him within her. She thrust her body forward in a rhythmic motion to match his own while she progressed towards orgasm. While she did so, Sebastien looked up from her soft, undulating form. He stared out of the window at the Manhattan skyline, one of the most beautiful sights in the world. He felt exhilarated to be alive. There was nothing he couldn't achieve. Nothing was impossible. Within his own being lay the world.

The body underneath him began to moan and quiver. Outside, the sun peeked over the horizon.

'Dawn's coming,' he said and smiled.

While Andrew was completing his work in the Congo and Sebastien was preparing to join Tanya in Panama, Ivan had already determined his own path to twenty million dollars. First, he must bid farewell to his boyfriend, Hadley. What better place than Paris in the spring?

CHAPTER FOURTEEN

Nothing gains a prince so much esteem as great enterprises and extraordinary achievements.

Machiavelli, *The Prince*

April. Paris.

'WHAT IS LIFE FOR? IT is to achieve goals. As Machiavelli remarked:

> *"Men pursue their goal (which is generally the acquisition of glory and wealth) by very different means; one is cautious and another impetuous, one uses violence and another cunning, one is patient and another quite the opposite; and yet all of them may succeed with their different methods."'*

Ivan considered Hadley across the Parisian restaurant table. 'Don't you agree?'

'I suppose so,' said Hadley. He hadn't a clue what Ivan was trying to tell him. However, he was pleased to see him so relaxed and contented. Theirs was a strange relationship, more like that of a disciple and a master. Hadley, clever though he was, would never be like Ivan. He had not that razor-sharp mind, that cool, almost cold, ratiocination. Yet, it didn't matter. Hadley was content to be his companion and to love him unrequited. He was quite sure that Ivan never loved him nor anyone else for that matter. He only loved ideas.

'Attaining your goal depends on the path that you take,' said Ivan. 'For the means produce the ends. I am sure of that, regardless of the approach adopted.' His eyes sparkled and he patted James on the hand. 'James, I can see you're not listening to a word I have to say. Let's talk about you.'

James smiled. 'I'm feeling rather tired, that's all.'

'How are things at the office?'

'Bloody awful.' Hadley beckoned the waiter and ordered another bottle of Chateau Lafite. 'What with the arms crisis in India and a worsening situation in the Congo we're worked off our feet. I wish I'd never joined the service. I'd happily swap jobs with you.'

'I'm sure you wouldn't. You'd be a marked man,' replied Ivan brightly.

'Why do you say that?' Hadley queried, knowing he would not get an answer. Ivan was so enigmatic, a veritable puzzle. Although Hadley knew he was a member of the College, despite their relationship Ivan never told him anything about it. Not a whisper about his secret comings and goings. Nor even why they were now having to meet so clandestinely in Paris.

'Who knows?' said Ivan. 'By the way, you mentioned nothing about your journey here.'

'No,' said Hadley wearily. 'You've asked me that before. I haven't told a soul. Not even the people at work. Ivan, what are you working on?'

Ivan thought about it. Well, just for once, he'd give his lover an insight into the world in which he lived and break the habit of a lifetime. Of course, he wouldn't tell Hadley everything. That would be much too dangerous. Perhaps just a soupçon, to widen James's horizons slightly. He put down his fork. Hadley watched. Suddenly, he felt excited. Ivan was going to tell him something after all. He stopped eating.

'Just suppose,' said Ivan in an unemotional tone of voice, 'you had to make twenty million dollars in a year. How would you do it?'

Hadley started back in astonishment. It must be a joke. Then he saw that Ivan was quite serious. He pondered while Ivan poured them another glass of wine.

'Can you make it illegally?'

'Sure,' said Ivan, 'whatever way you like.'

'Can you kill someone?'

'Yes,' said Ivan, 'if that's your philosophy. As I said, you can make it any way you like. Legally or illegally. However, I imagine you'd want to make it and live to tell the tale.'

Hadley cogitated for five minutes. 'I haven't a clue,' he said finally. 'I can't think of any way to make it legally, not in a year. And I can think of very few ways of making it illegally and staying alive and free. Why do you want to know?'

Ivan smiled. It was a terrible smile. 'Because that's exactly what I have to do,' he said. 'And there are people trying to stop me.'

Suddenly, Hadley felt the strongest fear he had ever experienced in his life. It rose up, like vomit, from the pit of his stomach to his throat. It was worse than when he'd once been surrounded by a gang of drunken hooligans on a train who had threatened to carve him up. It was the fear of a bad death – in a urine-ridden sidestreet by an unknown assassin and at night. Squalid and anonymous. The deepest fear of every secret service agent.

He had an urgent need to go to the lavatory.

Hadley viewed himself in the mirror. He knew he had the complexion of a frightened rabbit. He poured more cold water on his face. He felt very afraid. Working in a humdrum job in the British secret services, processing papers on the sexual predilections of politicians and trying to prevent them chasing little boys or girls was one thing. Having a lover who had to make twenty million dollars in a year while risking his life was quite another. He wished he had never joined the secret services. He should have listened to the advice of his history teacher. Stick to teaching medieval history, he'd said. It may be dull, but it's happened and it's safe. 'Oh God,' Hadley moaned to himself.

After he'd finished splashing himself with cold water, Hadley dried his face under the blow dryer since there were no towels. He felt terrible. He shouldn't have come to Paris. Bloody French restaurants, he thought bitterly, good food and crap lavatories. Finally, he went back to Ivan, his entire colonic region working at a velocity he would have preferred to reserve for his legs. He shouldn't have asked Ivan about what he did after all. Now he was scared to death.

'You took a long time,' said Ivan.

'Yes,' said Hadley. The window in the lavatory had been too small to get out of.

'I'll tell you how I'm going to do it,' said Ivan unperturbed as always. 'When there's something impossible to do, the important thing is to analyse exactly what skills one has to hand. And not to panic.' He looked at Hadley knowingly. 'My expertise is economic and political theory, particularly in Eastern Europe. And, shall we say, a very good knowledge of how governments really work.'

Spying, thought Hadley, but didn't say it out loud.

'So,' continued Ivan conversationally, 'twenty million dollars is a very large sum of money and the only place one can generally find it is in banks.' He sipped his wine.

Hadley looked at him, even more alarmed. Robbing banks was not his scene. He couldn't even steal sweets from his tuck shop at school.

'But banks tend to protect their money very well so I have to think of other ways of finding twenty million dollars. It's less difficult than you think.'

'It is?' asked Hadley nervously.

Ivan smiled. 'It's all a matter of history, James. I'll help you. Suppose that, until very recently, a large amount of wartime gold was held in the Bank of England on behalf of an East European country. What country would that be?'

Hadley gulped. 'Poland?'

'No,' Ivan smirked. 'You obviously studied medieval history. I will tell you a bit of modern history. During the Second World

War the Nazis invaded Albania. Among other things they stole a large quantity of Albanian gold. They hid it in some salt mines in Germany intending to make good use of it after they'd won the war. When the Nazis were defeated the Allies found the gold. They placed it in the vaults of the Bank of England for safe-keeping, intending to hand it back to the Albanians. However, things didn't turn out that way. After the war the Communists seized power in Albania with Soviet help. As a result, the Allies refused to hand the gold over to their new enemies. When the Communist regime eventually collapsed, the Allies repaid the gold, not in gold bars but its monetary equivalent. In 1996, thirty million US dollars were paid into a Swiss bank account controlled by the Albanian Government. I believe it's still there. Understand?'

'No . . .'

'Well, put simply, there's thirty million dollars in a Swiss bank account.'

Hadley nodded, still feeling queasy. Perhaps Ivan was going to rob a Swiss bank instead.

Ivan continued, 'Good. Next important point. During the Second World War, as in many other occupied countries, Albania had its fair share of collaborators and traitors who worked for the Nazis. The Allies didn't know who these people were since they couldn't break the Germans' secret service codes for Albania before the end of the war. Then, there was no point in wasting time to discover the names of these traitors. A Communist government had taken over and the Allies had little desire to help their new-found enemies behind the Iron Curtain. But today,' Ivan smiled, 'using modern computers we can easily crack the codes and find out who these Albanian traitors were.' He raised his eyebrows. 'Understand?'

Hadley wasn't sure that he did. He nodded. 'Er, thirty million dollars and some former Albanian traitors. So what?'

'Well,' said Ivan, 'there's a connection.'

'I don't see it,' said Hadley, bewildered. 'And how did you find the information?'

Ivan smiled. 'Easy. I've spent the last five weeks delving into British secret service files on Albania during World War Two. They are held in deep storage in Whitehall. Some of the files contain details of Albanian traitors but they are still in code.'

'So you used a computer to crack the code and read the names?'

'Well done,' said Ivan patronisingly. 'The CIA in Langley were kind enough to help, though they didn't know what it was for. It's amazing how quickly these high-speed computers can find the answers. Now, what's the connection between this and the money from the gold?' He watched James intently for a rapid answer.

None was forthcoming. Hadley could feel his stomach churning again.

Ivan sighed. Oh dear, James was a very poor pupil.

'Well, suppose, James, you were a very important person in Albania today and someone offered you this list of traitors? What would you do?'

'Make a deal, if the information was of use to me.'

'Exactly,' said Ivan. 'You're learning fast. And you'll be even keener if you are a very powerful and ambitious man and this information will further your ambitions.'

'Yes,' replied Hadley, 'but who is this man and what does he want? Come to think of it, what do *you* want?'

Ivan puckered his lips. 'Well now, this is the important bit, James. Do you really want to know?'

Hadley nodded unhappily.

'Well, suppose the man in question wants to be Head of State and I want twenty million dollars. So how do we both get what we want?'

Hadley became ashen-faced. 'How?' he whispered.

'We organise a coup,' said Ivan softly.

Hadley disappeared to the lavatory again.

By the end of the evening Ivan was feeling contented, that exquisite sense of pleasure only fine French cooking can bring, a contentment of the stomach and of the palate. He strolled down the length of the Paris restaurant without a care in the world. Hadley followed him, massaging his stomach. Ivan stopped at the restaurant door.

'The meal was delicious,' he said to the manager, 'and the Mousse glacée à la framboise et au champagne, so elegant. It was a masterpiece.'

The well-built Frenchman beamed and his massive proboscis twitched with pleasure. Such a delight to have clients who understood food; who not only consumed it, but who understood it. Ivan quit the restaurant.

'A pleasure, *monsieur*,' the manager called after him. His beam switched to Hadley.

'The food was just about OK but you should put towels in the lavatory. It's a disgrace,' said Hadley in a petulant tone. He made to step outside.

The Frenchman's smile congealed on his face as he considered the human cockroach in front of him. His massive proboscis pointed up into the air with disdain. 'Sir, should not use the lavatory so much,' he said grandly, and marched away.

'I'm glad you liked the meal,' said Ivan as they proceeded down the boulevard.

'Yes,' said Hadley. He had never experienced such a combination of fear and excessive bowel movement in his life.

'How are you getting back?'

'By plane.'

'Cancel it,' said Ivan. 'Do you mind taking the Eurostar? Given what I'm working on, I'm keen no one should see us together. And,' he continued, 'I don't think, James, we should meet up again for a while, for obvious reasons. No contact at all. Forget what I told you tonight and say nothing about me to anyone. Do you understand? I don't want people tracking me.'

A tremendous sense of relief began to overwhelm Hadley. 'You mean you weren't asking me to help you with the coup?'

'God, no,' laughed Ivan. 'James, you'd wet yourself just thinking about it.'

Hadley nodded. He had.

'No,' continued Ivan, 'I'll be working on my own.'

'Of course you'll have told the British about this?'

Ivan just smiled.

Hadley breathed a sigh of relief. Of course, Ivan would have told the Director General of MI6, he knew the woman personally. The College wouldn't be going this alone. There was no need for Hadley to inform anyone of Ivan's plan.

At the train station they halted at the ticket barrier. Hadley said, 'How long will you be gone?'

'About six months.'

'Oh . . .' Hadley hunched his shoulders. He would be lonely. There was something about Ivan that always gave him comfort. He knew what it was now. The presence of genius. It saw only opportunities, not difficulties. It made everything possible. In a very, very grey world it provided hope.

'I shall miss you,' he said.

'Will you?' Yes, he thought, James would. How touching, but it was not an emotion he readily understood. They bade farewell.

James watched the slim figure of Ivan on the concourse as he boarded the train. Then he settled himself down in the first-class compartment. He bought another drink, a very large one. His mind was in a daze.

Who was Ivan – the true Ivan? Hadley realised now that he had never really known him after all. It was a feeling both unsettling and sad. Was he really going to provoke a coup in Albania? If Ivan said that he would, he would. Of course, Hadley wouldn't tell a soul about the project. Even knowing about it himself made him fearful. More than that, what was happening to the College? Had it decided, at last, not only to advise world leaders but also to involve itself actively in the political affairs of countries, for money? To form a dictatorship of the elite instead of a dictatorship of the scum that were increasingly taking power? Hadley shook his head. What were things coming to? Unsteadily, he made his way to the lavatory.

Much later, as the Paris countryside rushed by, Hadley

returned to his seat. He opened his briefcase. 'Bugger,' he whispered angrily. There was Ivan's mail. He had gone to Ivan's old London residence a week ago to pick it up. He'd meant to give it to him this evening and he'd forgotten, his mind had been so preoccupied with other things. Silly old fool. The things you do for the people you love. And now he couldn't contact him. On well, Ivan wouldn't mind. It was probably just junk mail.

Hadley settled back, still feeling a residual sense of disquiet. The man opposite was one of those black men with dreadlocks and music spewing out of his ears. Hadley glanced at him nervously. He hoped the bastard wasn't going to rob him. He'd had enough for one day. He smiled, a timid smile.

PJ of Al Johnson Investigations smiled back – a big smile. The white honky with the face of a buggered rabbit had led them to Ivan Radic. They'd tracked Hadley ever since he went to pick up Ivan's mail in London. PJ continued to smile. Al would be keeping an eye on Ivan now.

CHAPTER FIFTEEN

It must needs be taken for granted that all men are wicked and that they will always give vent to the malignity that is in their minds when opportunity offers.

Machiavelli, *The Discourses*

May. Panama.

PANAMA. CENTRAL AMERICAN COUNTRY. SPANISH-SPEAKING. Population 2.5 million. Currency US dollars. Famous for the Panama Canal which runs from its capital, Panama City, situated on the Pacific coast, to the port of Colon situated on the Atlantic coast. A global banking centre with over 150 banks. Formerly part of Colombia. Declared independence in 1903. Military junta of Manuel Noriega overthrown with American assistance in 1989. Tourist attractions – the canal, white beaches, rainforest, deep sea fishing, handicrafts, friendly people. Climate tropical and humid. Three hours from Miami.

So much for the Panama Tourist Board, thought Sebastien. He tossed the booklet to one side. Now for the reality. He looked out of the aircraft window. Below, the ocean sparkled in the sharp sunlight and there was not a cloud in sight. As the plane turned to come in to land Sebastien had a good view of Panama City. Set around a wide circular bay, Panama's capital was large and sprawling, with skyscrapers and hotels encroaching right up to the water's edge – a sort of incipient Hong Kong though less flashy and less cramped. However, for Sebastien there was something much more important than Panama's hotels and casinos, its pretty women, its fiestas and carnivals, its samba and rumba. Panama had one of the largest concentrations of banks in the world and the shark had arrived.

'Please fasten your seat belts. We'll be coming in to land shortly.'

When Sebastien stepped out of the aircraft a blast of hot air hit him. The humidity was so high that, by the time he had crossed the tarmac, his starched white banker's shirt was already damp. What did he care? After the insipid climate of New York in the spring and his boring management course with US Bank this was pure joy. Sebastien made for the airport exit and the journey into town. He wondered what Tanya had made of Panama and whether she'd got herself a Latino boyfriend. He hoped not. He'd kill her if she had.

'Welcome to US Bank, Panama, Mr Singleton. It's a pleasure to have you with us.'

Sebastien returned the greeting and sat down in the manager's office in Panama City. It was colourfully decorated with the Panamanian and US flags. To prevent the other contestants following his trail both Sebastien and Tanya had decided that a change of surname for each of them was appropriate. The false passport and documentation in the name of Singleton had cost him a packet.

Sebastien inspected the bank manager. He was a broad shouldered American, about forty years of age with a tanned complexion and slightly drooping eyes. He seemed affable enough and so he was. Doug Sullivan had been in Panama for ten years now and he hoped to be there for another ten. He found it a quiet, relaxed place even though the banking system processed billions of dollars in transactions every year. People in Panama kept their lives and their private affairs to themselves and Doug liked that.

'We've heard great things about you from New York. They say you did exceptionally well on the training programme.'

Sebastien shrugged his shoulders deprecatingly.

Doug flicked on the intercom and ordered drinks. As they waited he drew Sebastien to the window. Before them lay the Bay of Panama, the water glistening in the heat haze that hung over the city for much of the year. Sebastien swept his eyes across the scene, down to the road below and to the small rock garden in the centre of which the bank was located, its name proudly etched on a great slab of marble. This bank would be ideal for his and Tanya's purposes. The drinks arrived. The manager guided him back to his chair. His voice had a slight Californian twang.

'You're going to love it here, Sebastien. Panama is a wonderful country. God's own land. It's got everything most places dream of – plenty of sun, palm tree islands, people who live to enjoy life, few political problems, no army even. What more could you desire?'

Doug sipped his tequila and continued, 'Let me give you the lowdown on it. It's a small country that's done very well for itself, especially in banking. That's why we, and all the other banks, are here. This place has one of the greatest concentrations of banks in the Western Hemisphere: it's the main conduit for fund flows from Latin America to the principal financial centres in the States and Europe, in particular London and New York. And the system's very sophisticated, all computer-driven.' He cleared his throat. 'But you may be asking yourself, why do all the banks come here rather than say, Mexico or Venezuela?'

Sebastien wasn't, since he had found out the answer long ago. He crunched on an ice cube and let the bank manager continue his flow.

'They come to Panama because taxes are low, the Canal trade is good and secrecy is paramount. We don't ask questions and we don't expect answers, Sebastien. If people want to put their money here, we're pleased to accept it. Where they've got it from is their business though, obviously, we don't encourage drug funds, money laundering and that sort of thing.' The manager waited for Sebastien to digest this information.

'Now, about the bank itself . . .' Doug Sullivan handed him

some glossy pamphlets. 'As you can see from the size of this building, we've got a big operation in Panama. We've been in this country since the fifties and we're one of the top-notch US banks with a triple A rating. We intend to keep it that way. We do everything by the book here. Please remember that. During your stay, Sebastien, we're going to put you in various departments of the bank so you can understand how it all works. Letters of Credit, Forex, Bills, the lot. Any particular choice to start with?'

'How about Fixed Deposits?'

'Sure,' said the manager, 'sounds fine. Go and set yourself up with an apartment – the people in personnel will help you – and we'll see you in the office tomorrow. You're going to love Panama, Sebastien. Everyone does.' Doug Sullivan smiled, a contented man. He mustn't talk too long since he had a game of golf that afternoon.

Sebastien stepped out of the bank and into the dazzling sunshine. He decided to take a stroll. Across the precinct were large shopping malls full of beautiful women buying the latest fashions. Glitzy boutiques were crammed with the finest creations from France and Italy while self-conscious speciality shops archly displayed delicacies designed to satiate even the most jaded of appetites. Sebastien liked what he saw. He walked along the front of the bay admiring the cars. It was an auto collector's dream: black Cadillacs, sleek Jaguars, BMWs in bubblegum colours, tinsel-town Maseratis. Panama was like Miami, without too much of the vice. Everywhere there was the feel of a happy people making money and enjoying life. Sebastien took a deep breath of sultry air. He was going to love Panama.

Not least because it was going to make him twenty million dollars.

At the College the Master had just finished a meeting with the French President. He returned to the third courtyard and to his study. Putting down some papers he stared out of the window.

The cherry trees were in full bloom and the garden had a bright green lushness to it. It was a view he never wished to give up. Symes rang.

'Jack Caldwell would like to talk with you,' he said.

The Master took the call. As he did so, he watched a solitary raven alight on a branch of the cherry tree searching for food. The Master listened intently to the caller and asked a few questions.

At the end of the conversation, Caldwell said, 'The passport, in the name of Sebastien Singleton, was issued less than two months ago. He has recently left the US.'

'Where is he now?' asked the Master.

'Panama.'

'And Tanya?'

'She's there also.'

'Please keep me informed.'

The Master put down the phone. His attention had been distracted from the raven. Perhaps it was better that it had. For a raven had a medieval significance. Death. Someone would die in the not-too-distant future. The Master had no doubt about it.

'I'll have one of the girls show you the rest of the bank, but I'll take you round the Fixed Deposits Department myself.'

'Thanks,' said Sebastien.

'Not at all,' replied Ted Baxter proudly. He was the head of Fixed Deposits at US Bank and it was his baby. 'You'll be starting off in this department, Sebastien, so it's important you get a good understanding of it.'

Sebastien waited as Ted ran his card through the security machine. The thick steel door clicked open and they passed inside. Before them were filing cabinets and a large number of desks at which teenage girls sat processing clients' instructions. They turned to stare at the newcomer. Ted strode forward and Sebastien followed him. Ted was just over two metres in height and must have been quite striking when young, thought Sebastien. Yet at fifty-five, life was not so good and with his straggly silver hair, fleshy jowls and drinker's nose it seemed clear that the ambulances, and not the girls, would soon be chasing him. In keeping with those in the managerial ranks of US Bank, Ted was dressed in an anonymous black suit, his only individuality evidenced by the lurid pink braces he sported.

'Your room's here.' Ted pointed to a small office that housed a desk, a picture of the Canal on the wall and a few succulent plants. 'And this is my office.' He proudly pointed to a large room, tastefully decorated with a map of Panama and various bond certificates encased in frames.

Sebastien noted a casting couch in the corner. He wondered whether Ted did much of his thinking lying down or whether it was just to give the secretaries a helping hand. Somewhat disappointed, Sebastien could see no cocktail cabinet. Ted must do his drinking elsewhere.

'Folks . . .' Ted clapped his hands to get their attention. He introduced Sebastien to the ten or so people in the department. His speech was brief. When it was over he guided Sebastien back towards his office, talking all the while. 'You'll find fixed deposits are easy, Sebastien. You'll know all about them from your course. Well, er,' Ted paused as he racked his memory. It was a long time since he had worked in the bank at a nuts-and-bolts level. 'Clients open a fixed deposit for a fixed period with us. It can be in any currency and for any period, though it's usually in dollars and for three to six months. How do they open it? Well, er, the client sends an instruction letter to us to open the deposit. The girls here,' he swung his arm expansively around the room, 'check the signature against our records and then process the instruction, by registering the amount in the computer. When the deposit matures we pay the client his money back with interest. There. That's about it.' He could see Sebastien was not overimpressed. Young people these days were too clever for their own good.

Sebastien nodded. 'How much do you have on deposit at the moment?'

'About one billion dollars.'

Sebastien glanced at a young secretary in a very short skirt who brushed past him. She wasn't wearing a bra, which he thoroughly approved of. Much too hot. Little point in wearing knickers either. Walk free. He whistled softly. 'That's a lot. What about numbered deposits?'

'Ah ha,' said Ted. 'You're on the ball, I see. Come into my office.'

Ted lounged back in his padded chair and put his feet on the desk. 'Numbered deposits, Sebastien, are just like fixed deposits. With a slight difference. Besides the manager and myself no one else knows who owns the deposit. You see,' he dropped his voice as if about to tell some dark secret, 'some people want extra privacy. Wealthy men who don't want to tell their wives about payments to their mistresses, important politicians, companies that don't like to reveal the extent of their financial holdings.' He winked. 'That sort of thing. Of course, at US Bank, we have to be careful for whom we open this type of deposit. We don't want the bad elements.'

'How do you check that?' asked Sebastien.

'When a new client requests us to open a numbered deposit, either I or the manager go to see them and check out the business. If it's all right, the client then signs a deposit opening form with the number on it. The manager registers these forms in a book which we keep in a safe. Thereafter, only the number of the deposit is referred to. In that way the client has a deposit with the bank but his identity is only known to the manager and myself.'

'What if he wants to move money from his numbered deposit?'

'Easy,' replied Ted. 'The client sends me a letter. He doesn't refer to the number of his deposit in the letter, he simply tells me to deal with his numbered deposit. I check his signature in the letter with his signature in the original deposit opening form. If they match we process the request.'

'I see,' said Sebastien as if he had difficulty understanding.

'Playing the devil's advocate for a moment, Ted, suppose you were dishonest. Couldn't you just forge the signature and process it?'

Ted frowned. He didn't like the idea at all. 'Oh, no, no,' he said. 'The manager also checks the signature. So we'd both have to be dishonest. Also, the client would soon find out if we'd taken money out of his account without his authorisation.' He chuckled. 'There are protections built into the system. The client doesn't want anyone else to know he has a deposit but he still wants to keep his money!'

'Yes, I see,' said Sebastien.

'Well now, let me take you to the Payments Department. It's upstairs.' Ted just had time to show the new trainee before he departed for a liquid lunch. 'You'll see how we transfer money from one bank to another. This often occurs when a client wants to cancel his deposit.'

Slowly, they climbed the stairs as they chatted about golf, of which Ted was a great aficionado, although Sebastien suspected, by the russet colour of Ted's nose, the only golf club he knew was the type he sat in.

They passed through another heavy steel door. Ted explained that, for security reasons, only he and the manager had access to all the departments in the bank.

'So I can only get into the Fixed Deposits Department?' Sebastien asked.

'Yes. For the moment, anyway,' said Ted. 'Now, who do we have here?' He beamed at the girls in front of him. 'This is Carole, Head of the Payments section. This is Maria. And this is . . .' He had forgotten her name. How could he forget the name of a woman who was so pretty?

It was Carole who remedied the lapse. 'Ted, this is Tanya. She's been working with us for a few weeks now.'

'Oh, of course. Er, hello again, Tanya.' Ted shifted on his feet with the bashfulness of a teenager on his first date, spots and sex on his mind. He turned to his new employee. 'Tanya, this is Sebastien.'

Sebastien examined his lover. He grinned.

'Hello, Tanya.'

That evening Sebastien drove out of the capital in a hired car. Old Panama City was about eight kilometres from its successor. It had been sacked by the Welsh buccaneer Henry Morgan in 1671 and not much remained of it – just the central tower of the church and a mound of crumbling stone. Morgan had never found the silver he'd been looking for after all. It had been securely buried and was reputed to be worth millions. Perhaps Sebastien would come back and look for it one day. Somehow, he doubted he'd need it by then. The Master had no need to worry about money. The College saw to that.

Beside the ruins and tucked down a side road, was one of Panama's many seafood restaurants. This was less visited. Its neon sign was slightly adrift and the yellow paint had peeled off its façade in places. It wouldn't attract a good clientele but it was quiet and out of the way. Just what Sebastien wanted. He went in.

'Hi!'

'Hi.'

Tanya's complexion was well tanned, her hair soft and glossy from the unrelenting sun. She'd obviously been spending her weekends enjoying herself on the beach. With whom? Sebastien wondered. He felt jealous. His time had been spent in less pleasant surroundings, sitting in an office in New York being bored to death with the intricacies of bank bookkeeping. Still, there was an opportunity to change all that. Time to put his bookkeeping into practice.

'How was New York?'

'OK,' said Sebastien. 'But I've been missing you.' He placed his hand on hers. They hadn't seen each other for over a month and they'd kept communication between themselves to a minimum. It was vital that neither Andrew nor Ivan knew of their whereabouts.

'Missed me?' Tanya's eyes gleamed. 'In New York? Huh, I

don't believe it. Pull the other one.' She withdrew her hand and picked up the menu. 'Well, I haven't been idle,' she continued in a casual voice, keen to pay him back for his suspected infidelity. 'I found myself a local boyfriend. The body of Apollo and the energy of a mule. We've seen the sights together. Done just about everything.' Tanya watched as Sebastien's eyes narrowed in anger, and she laughed. He was so possessive when it came to her fidelity but so neglectful of his own. Typical man. 'Only kidding.'

'How's the bank?' asked Sebastien as he sampled the local brew, Balboa.

'Fine,' said Tanya.

They chatted for a few minutes about inconsequential things. Then she raised her hand to dispense with the small talk. 'Sebastien, we must put your plan and mine together.' Her voice dropped. 'I've been busy investigating their money transfer systems. It will take time, more time than I thought, to crack the computer codes. They're immensely sophisticated. However, I've no doubt that we can transfer money without being detected.'

'By the end of the year?'

'Yes, I think so. That leaves us with the task of getting the money in the first place. That was your job,' Tanya paused. 'Why Panama, by the way? I'd been thinking of Brazil or Mexico. Their money transfer systems are less complicated than in the US or Europe, though I suppose Panama will do.'

'To make the money it's got to be Panama,' said Sebastien. He grinned, 'And I've got it all worked out.'

'Really?' Tanya smiled and swept back her hair. 'Impress me then, smart arse.'

'What do I get in return?'

Tanya licked her lips. 'Depends how much you impress me. How exactly are we going to make this money, Sebastien? It's to do with drugs, isn't it?' Her voice hardened. This was when she began to get slightly scared. The Mastership was one thing; using evil means to achieve it was another.

Sebastien noted her nervousness. 'Yes,' he said quickly. 'But not quite what you think. We need to get away with it and that requires something more clever than drug dealing. I'll tell you over dinner. By the way, how's your Spanish coming along?'

'Almost perfect,' Tanya replied. 'I can tell you to sod off when I want to.'

Sebastien grinned. 'You'd never do that, would you?'

'Oh, I don't know,' said Tanya. 'We all have sell-by dates.' There was a tang of bitterness in her words. She knew more about Sebastien and what he got up to than he thought. However, she wasn't ready to leave, yet.

Over a dinner of locally caught fish and plenty of wine Sebastien told her the plan he'd worked out to make twenty million dollars. Drug trafficking was one of the biggest industries in the world, grossing more than 300 billion US dollars a year. The top people in this industry were well paid. Drug barons often made a billion dollars or more a year individually. Even for the middle men the sums could run into the hundreds of millions of dollars. However, after his detailed research about the drug trade in the vast libraries of Harvard University, it was not the actual trafficking that Sebastien was interested in. It was too risky and those who carried the drugs, the mules, earned comparatively little. Also, they were invariably shopped by their bosses when they, or the drug routes, became too well known. So Sebastien had turned to the question of what the drug barons actually did with their ill-gotten gains.

The colossal sums these criminals earned caused them a headache since, to hide the fact that their wealth came from an illegal source, they needed to convert the drug money into clean money, and quickly. Therefore, the assistance of the international banking community was required to 'wash' the money through their payments system. This required a sophisticated operation since the police and the intelligence agencies of many countries were targeting the movement of illegal funds in an effort to cut off the flow of drug money at its most sensitive point. As a result, the drug dealers needed their people inside the banks to manipulate the payment systems and make the money transfers – people whom they could trust and who wouldn't betray them. And finding honest men was difficult these days – even for drug dealers.

'Are you saying we're going to use US Bank to launder drug money?' Tanya was horrified. 'I'm not prepared to do that.'

'Hey,' said Sebastien, 'just give me a minute before you jump to conclusions. I need to explain how the drug barons are washing drug money these days. I found out about some of this when I was working on a project for the College a while ago concerning Interpol. By the way, can you get on to all the floors at US Bank?'

'No, staff are restricted to their own floors. Apart from top management,' said Tanya.

'Um, that's a nuisance.' Sebastien tucked into his pineapple ice cream. 'In principle "washing" drug money is easy. Suppose the drug dealer's "dirty" money is with a bank here in Panama. To clean it, the drug dealer moves it to an account he opens with a bank in another country in, say, Switzerland. There's no physical transfer of cash. Instead, it's all done by electronic transfer so that the money the dealer receives in Switzerland is quite different to that in Panama . . .

'How is this done? Given that the two banks are located in different countries, the transfer is made through one of the main financial centres like New York or London, with whose central bank both the Panama and the Swiss bank will have an account. For example, the drug dealer tells the Panama bank to move a million dollars to his Swiss account. The Panama bank will simply tell the central bank in New York to debit its account for one million and credit that of the Swiss bank for the same amount. The Swiss bank then debits its account and credits that of the drug dealer. Very simple and it's all done by electronic transfer. Just moving money by accounting debits and credits. But the real magic is that the cash which the drug dealer can now take out of his account in Switzerland is different dollars, clean money. There's nothing to associate it with the money that was in Panama. It's been "washed". Within a morning, drug money becomes the most respectable of funds held with the most respectable of banks.' Sebastien grinned. 'Why use a detergent when you can use a bank? Washes whiter than snow.'

'But why should we use Panama?'

'Three reasons,' said Sebastien. He ticked them off on his fingers. Unluckily for Panama it was close to countries where drugs were produced in large quantities, namely Colombia and Bolivia. As a result, its banking system was a prime target for dealers to wash drug money through. Secondly, the main financial centres in London, New York and Tokyo were closely monitored by government authorities and their secret services. Panama was slightly less so, though they were tightening up the system all the time. Thirdly, their chances of being tracked down by Ivan and Andrew was much higher if they tried the sting in Europe or the States. And if they were discovered, there was a real risk the other contestants would betray them to the authorities, to win the Mastership Game.

Sebastien continued, 'I don't want to spend the rest of my days behind bars, do you? As a result, Panama's the perfect place. Besides,' he grinned, 'it's warm here and the beer's good.'

'OK,' said Tanya, 'I can see your logic on the transfer system and I can process the money. But you still haven't told me how we actually make it. I don't want to get involved with drugs, Sebastien, you know that.'

'Yeah, I understand. I need to tell you about numbered accounts – which are the key.' Sebastien drained his beer glass. Then he leant over and brushed away some hair that had fallen across her face. 'Before I tell you any more, there's something else on my mind that's more pressing. Much better that making money.'

'What's that?' enquired Tanya coyly. She saw the glint in his eyes.

'Sex. Let's try out your place.'

'OK.' It had been on her mind as well. She was sure the hot climate had something to do with it.

* * *

At her apartment Tanya didn't bother to turn on the light. Instead, she drew Sebastien into the darkened room and began to undress him roughly.

She felt the flicker of silk against her breasts as her slip slid down her body onto the carpet. There was nothing else to follow it and she stood naked in the moonlight. She led him to the bed. They were together again.

They started to make love – slowly at first as she accustomed herself to his body after the absence, then more passionately as she felt the violence and tension rise within him. When he was exhausted, Tanya started once again, determined to drain him as if, like two fluids, she could make them irrevocably mix. She drank Sebastien into her, knowing that, despite everything, she loved him and that she wanted him. Did he love her, though? That she could never tell.

Finally, she lay back on the pillows, and snuggled into his shoulder. Their money laundering plan was ready. At least, it was in theory. Now they just had to find someone to give them twenty million dollars.

One other thing: Tanya needed to remember that only one of them could win. Did she love him more than the Mastership? That also had to be determined. She knew what Ivan would have advised her: love and power did not mix. Still, Tanya had one or two tricks up her sleeve. She wondered where Ivan was; and Andrew. Did they know anything about Panama?

Afterwards, while they lay asleep, there was a noise at the bedroom door and the tread of feet. Tanya stirred in her dreams. The steps came closer and she felt a depression in the bed. As she did so, the nightmare returned. For a moment Tanya was back in the chalet in Switzerland, struggling against the ligatures, her mind in agony and the fear of death upon her. She started up with a terrified gasp, her eyes wide open. Then she heard the gentle sound of purring and a warm, feline body lodged against her thigh.

'Gemma – my child.'

It took a long time for her to close her eyes again.

* * *

Elsewhere, the other contestants slept: Ivan in Paris and Andrew on a jet plane, the hot sun peeking through the shutters as the aircraft flew high over the land mass of Africa on its journey back to London. For Andrew his work for the United Nations in the Congo had finally been completed and he slept soundly, his satellite phone tucked away in the hold.

Sebastien and Tanya, Ivan, Andrew. They all slept. And their dreams had a common thread – to win the Mastership Game.

CHAPTER SIXTEEN

Therefore the sage promotes all things, but does not think the effort is his own
Achieves merit, but does not claim credit for himself
And does not wish to parade his wisdom and ability

Lao Zi

May. The College.

WHILE OTHERS SLEPT NO SUCH peace was given to the manservant Symes. He was awoken by the insistent ringing of the phone. He glanced at his watch. It was very early in the morning. He got out of bed and went into a side room in the porter's lodge where he viewed a large electronic screen. It was a call using a satellite phone and it was from the depths of Africa. Symes was uncertain what to do. He decided to put it through to the Master. He was loath to do this since he'd been looking so tired recently. However, the call might be important.

'Master.'

In the Master's Lodge the Master sat up in bed, drowsy.

'There is a call on one of the satellite phones. It is from the Congo.'

'Who is it?'

'I don't know,' said Symes in a puzzled tone. 'It's a phone used by Andrew Brandon, but it's certainly not him. The voice is that of a child and he's very distressed. I don't know why Brandon gave him the phone, nor how he got through to the College. He must have pressed a default key.'

The Master peered at his watch. He'd had three hours' sleep. 'Go back to bed, Symes,' he said. 'I will deal with it.'

The Master went downstairs to his study. He flicked a button. Part of the study wall drew back to reveal a computer-generated electronic map of the world. The Master pressed another button. Within seconds a large-scale diagram of the Congo appeared on the screen. Quickly, the Master zoomed in to identify the source of the call to within a few hundred metres. He pressed a final button and the phone was connected.

'Hello,' said the Master.

At the other end of the line he could hear nothing apart from the heavy buzz of static. Then he caught the agonised screams of a young child and, more distantly, what seemed to be the crumple of rocket fire.

'Hello,' said the Master again. 'Who is it?' He waited.

After a few minutes the sound of the fighting began to fade, leaving only the sound of a child crying. Finally, there was a whisper. 'Obedi.'

The Master quietly asked, 'Tell me what has happened, Obedi.'

There was silence, a traumatised silence. The Master switched from English to French and then to Swahili as he tried to determine in what language the child would be able to speak. It was in Swahili that Obedi began to talk, sometimes incoherently, and the Master listened as the bombs began to fall again, ever closer. Often the line crackled and it became inaudible whenever the aircraft zoomed overhead, having released their deadly loads.

Weeping, Obedi told the Master that the rebels had attacked that afternoon, that his school had been destroyed and that his sister lay beside him, her lifeless and bloodied hand still entwined in his own. The Master listened while he scanned the electronic map on the screen. The rebels had broken the ceasefire agreement recently negotiated with the Government of the Congo, in which the Master had assisted. Now they had embarked on a blitzkrieg and were thundering down the main road to the capital, Kinshasa. Civil war had broken out. It would unleash a nightmare for millions. The Master listened and all the while the young child talked to him. Obedi did not want to die, but there was no one to save him.

'Please help me.'

The Master turned away from the screen to gaze out of the study window into the darkness. So much suffering, so much human need, so many demands. And one old man to hold the threads.

'I will come for you,' he said.

Seconds later there was a deafening roar as a shell exploded directly above the schoolroom in which Obedi lay. The phone spoke no more. The child had probably not heard the Master's last words. The Master continued to look from his window into the darkness. Where was Andrew? He pressed another button.

'Symes, I must go to the Congo, immediately.'

'But you have a full schedule tomorrow. The Canadian Premier will be here and there are a large number of conference calls.'

'I know, Symes,' said the Master patiently. 'However, I must go. Civil war has broken out in the Congo. And please get the UN Secretary General on the line.'

One hour later the first news of the Congo disaster began to filter around the world. Andrew heard it at six o'clock in the morning, the moment he stepped out of his plane at Heathrow Airport. He hurried to the ticket desks. The airlines serving the Congo all told the same story: it was impossible to return there. All flights to the country had been suspended, the international airports there had been overrun and contact with air traffic control lost.

Andrew sat in the airport lounge using his satellite phone, trying number after number. The only reports from the networks on television were brief and told a tale of unparalleled slaughter. The rumblings that Andrew had felt under the road on his last journey to the capital had proved to be true. Finally, after a long time, Andrew got through to the UN compound in Kinshasa, using a rerouted call. After a considerable delay a UN liaison officer, Paul Hanlon, came on the line. In the background the air was rent with screams and shouts as people fled the place in fear of their lives all desperate to get on that last convoy, or perish.

'Andrew,' the voice of Paul rang out above the din, 'it's complete chaos. The Government's left Kinshasa. The rebels are only fifty kilometres down the road and they'll be here in less than an hour. We're moving to the coast. The UN is sending in planes to try to get us out tonight. The power and most phone lines have been cut.' He stopped to shout an order to someone in the background, then continued, his voice quickening, 'It is a bloodbath. The rebels are slaughtering everything they meet, people and animals.'

'I saw it on the news this morning.'

'Where are you?'

'In Europe. I've been preparing for a trip to the Far East.'

'Right, well stay there, Andrew,' the liaison officer said. 'I'm telling you, stay there. There are no planes into the country and there's nothing you can do. Umbote's men have overrun the south, coming up the main Kananga road overnight. The place is just a sea of bodies. Even the hospitals have been attacked. There's nothing you or anyone can do now. The situation's completely out of control.'

'What about the children, Obedi and his sister? I can't get through to them on my satellite phone.'

The voice went silent. Andrew knew then. He had failed them.

'Andrew, I'm very sorry. The orphanage at Kikwit was wiped out. One of the UN people drove past it on the road this morning. There were no known survivors. They bombed it to a pulp.' Hanlon hesitated. There was nothing more to say. 'Keep phoning me once in a while so that we can stay in touch. I'm sorry. I must go now.'

Andrew slowly put down the phone. Tears welled in his eyes. For the sake of the Mastership Game two people he might have been able to save had died and their lives were on his conscience. So were those of many others. If he had been in the Congo, he might have been able to do something to stop the war or, at least, to mitigate the slaughter. Yet he had deserted them in his own quest for power.

Grimly, Andrew gathered his things and left the airport. There was no way back now. He would see the contest through to the end. Whatever the cost.

One of the few buildings that had not been ransacked in Kinshasa over the last few weeks was the football stadium. The rebel leader, Christian Umbote, had decided not to destroy it since, as a child, he had once seen a Manchester United scratch team play the local boys. So the stadium was saved by the quixotic memory of a madman, an understandable thing in a nation of the mad and the afflicted. Now it was the place for an alternative fixture, one that Umbote liked since he was the captain in this game. Or almost.

The Conference leaders blinked under the flashlights as they sat out under the large makeshift awning erected in the centre of the football pitch. Cameramen from around the world had flown in earlier that day. Already they were wilting in the strong sun as they took just one more picture for the global networks. After the cameras, the journalists would start, followed by the media commentators. The supermedia would get to the truth in their own way. Yet, by the end of it, the truth would be the least important part of the story.

'Could you smile once more, gentlemen?'

Christian Umbote tried not to scowl as he signed the new agreement, bending the nib of the foreign pen while he scrawled a mark. The corpulent figure of the President of the Congo sat beside him. Then they shook hands and both of them grinned like wolves. The President was also behaving himself. He had remembered to discard his leopardskin shawl. Someone had told him the US and European public were trying to save endangered species so it wouldn't look good. Killing people was less problematic since there were more of them. They weren't endangered.

'Smile!'

They both smiled again with all the panache of dental adverts as the cameras whirred, clicked and hummed. Their huge grins explained their message more eloquently than words. A grin that last week had said 'I am a murderer' this week said 'I'm your friend, really. You misunderstand me'. This week the President and his Christian brother needed the huge sums of money the Western governments were going to give them, to rebuild the shattered country and to satisfy their personal needs, in inverse order. Of course they could resolve their differences – provided they got a big enough slice of the cake. More than half each. That was fair.

'Smile!'

Christian Umbote smiled once more and stared around the stadium. It was great to see the Secretary General of the United Nations there. What a picture to show his wives and any of his illegitimate children that might still be alive. But where was that other man? The clever one who solved everything? Didn't he want to get his picture taken? Didn't he want to be famous? Silly idiot, he wouldn't get anywhere if he didn't get into the headlines. Take it from Christian. Any publicity was good publicity – even if you had to kill a million people to get it.

Meanwhile, in a makeshift hospital one hundred kilometres away, the hospital nurse escorted a man down a bullet scarred corridor. She admired his courage. Travelling to this part of the country was a deadly risk since all law and order had broken down. Yet he seemed unhurried and attentive.

'They brought him in two days ago. His sister is dead. I'm afraid we have no facilities here to save his sight. He came from Kikwit. We're not sure he'll last.'

The man sat down by the hospital bed and took the small child's hand in his own. Obedi stirred from his drugged sleep while his other hand clutched the twisted plastic of the phone. Obedi said nothing for a long time. Then he murmured in Swahili.

'Are you the man at the end of the phone?'

'Yes,' said the man.

'Have you come to take me away?'

'Yes,' said the Master.

Obedi settled back. His mind was at peace. The man at the end of the telephone had arrived. He would not fail him.

Three weeks later, after a number of operations, Obedi awoke once more from his drugged sleep. He knew he was no longer in the Congo though he didn't know where he was. He smelt the sweet smell of antiseptic and the bedsheets felt soft. He ran them between his fingers, the bandages still covering his eyes and much of his body. From the silence of his room Obedi could hear sounds distantly – the calling out of a name, the clang of a door.

'How are you today?'

Obedi liked it when the nurse spoke. He pictured her as an angel. His sister had told him that they existed although she'd never actually seen one. He had heard the voice for some days now. It came in the morning to feed him, and twice more during the day. The remainder of the time he was not conscious of it, as he recovered from the operations to remove shrapnel from his body and legs. Obedi knew that he had been very close to death since his sister had visited him in his sleep. She'd told him it was not yet time for him to die.

The nurse sat down on the chair by his bed and said to him very slowly in English, 'There's a man coming to see you. A very important man.'

She straightened the bed and left him. Obedi waited. Outside the Washington General Hospital, President Davison of the United States made a speech about his new health care programme and the national scheme for awards to outstanding hospitals. Eventually, amid all the plaudits and the fanfares, he went inside to say a word or two to the staff before moving on to his next appointment.

Obedi heard none of this. He sighed and turned over in bed. His body still ached and his head ached, not because of his eyes and the bandages covering them, but because, try as he might not to, he thought of his sister. Of her last agonised gasps and her hand tightening around his. He knew she would have done anything in the world to stay with him. She had promised her parents that, yet God hadn't let her. How strange the merciful God was.

A door opened.

'And this is the young man they have brought in from the Congo, Mr President.'

'Thank you.'

President Davison entered the room. He closed the door and went to sit beside Obedi. They were alone, which Obedi thought strange since he'd been told by his father that important people always had hundreds of people around them to show how important they were. Perhaps this man was so important that he didn't need anybody. Like the man on the telephone. He felt a slight thrill.

'Hello, Obedi. I've come to see you.' The voice was confident and powerful. Obedi warmed to it. A hand clasped his. The grip was firm.

'I just want to tell you that you're going to be fine. And you're going to be staying in the United States for a while.' The President spoke very slowly, so that Obedi might understand him. As he did so, Davison looked out of the window. In his mind's eye he was on an island, by the side of a pond and it was snowing.

'We have something in common,' he said.

Obedi turned his head slightly. What could an orphan with poor English and no eyesight have in common with such an important man?

'You see,' continued the President slowly, 'once I had a big problem, and someone helped me. And I know he has also helped you. Which means that we have something in common. And that's good.' He paused. 'Now he has asked me to help you, and I will.'

Davison considered the blinded child. He thought of his own

daughters and how he would feel if this had happened to them. 'Everything's going to be all right, Obedi. Just wait.'

Then Davison patted Obedi on the arm and he left. Obedi hadn't spoken a word yet this man was going to help him. A very powerful man. The most powerful man in the world, the nurse later told him.

All because of the man on the telephone.

CHAPTER SEVENTEEN

One able to make the enemy come of his own accord does so by offering him some advantage.

Sun Tzu, *The Art of War*

June. Panama.

'IS THE PLAN STILL ON?'

They sat on the floor of Sebastien's spacious apartment in an exclusive area of Panama City. Tanya had come to visit him secretly by night since no one must know of their relationship. She kissed him. He hardly noticed.

'There's a big problem,' he said.

'What?' she replied anxiously. 'Is it solvable?'

'I'm not sure.' Sebastien scowled. 'In fact there's two relatively small problems, but together they make it one big problem. We may have to think of something else.'

Tanya sipped a tequila. 'Perhaps, we should give up?' she said a little nervously. It was June – half a year in the Mastership Game was almost gone – and it was the first time she'd ever seen Sebastien at a loss. Or so angry.

He raised his eyes to the ceiling. A stupid comment like that did not even merit a reply. Give up the Mastership? When hell froze over. He continued, 'The plan will go ahead. However, we're going to have to make some changes. Getting twenty million dollars from a bank is more complicated than I thought.'

'Why?'

'It doesn't matter.'

'Sebastien, tell me. I may be able to help. Don't be so proud. We have to work together.'

Eventually Sebastien explained that, if they were going to extract money, it would have to be from a numbered account, since only Ted Baxter, the Head of Fixed Deposits, and the manager worked with these and there were no other people who knew about them. Less chance, then, of someone else in the bank discovering about the removal of the money at an early stage. Numbered accounts also invariably contained much larger sums that the general fixed deposits. But therein lay the problems. US Bank had more safeguards than Sebastien's preliminary analysis had led him to believe.

'Details of the numbered accounts are recorded in a register kept in a safe. Only the manager knows the combination. Ted won't even tell me where the safe is. That means I don't know the identities of any people with numbered deposits – far less those with deposits of more than twenty million dollars. And there's no real chance of breaking into the safe. It will be wired up with alarms.'

'What's problem two?' Tanya stroked his thick, black hair. She was glad he was in Panama with her. It hadn't been much fun without him. She'd felt as lonely as a virgin.

'Problem number two is that, when money is moved from a numbered account, both Ted and the Manager check the signature on the letter of instruction against the signature card filled in by the holder when he or she first opened the account. Ted let on to me one night, when he was half drunk, that, in case of even the slightest discrepancy, they reconfirm it with the client. Therefore, simply copying or forging a letter of instruction is too risky.'

Tanya thought about this for a few minutes. 'I can think of only one solution,' she said.

'What's that?'

'If we can't get to the account or forge letters of instruction, once it has been opened, we must open the account.'

Sebastien stared at her. Then he pulled her to him and

grudgingly kissed her. 'That's for being so clever,' he said. 'That's my conclusion as well, but it took me a bit longer to work it out. What I need to do is to get in a completely new client for the bank and a very rich one at that. I need to get access to a numbered account at the very start of the process, when they set it up. Once the account's opened, the system's tamperproof. I'm going to start working on it right away.' He stretched out on the floor. 'What about you?'

'I'm fine,' said Tanya. 'Working in the Payments Department I now know how they send payment instructions on the inter-bank network as well as most of the secret code. That is, the code the sending bank puts on the payment instruction so the recipient bank can check it to make sure the message's authentic.'

'What do you mean, most of the code?'

'Well,' said Tanya, 'the secret code is made up of two parts. One part is computer-generated by me whenever a payment instruction is sent out from the bank. That's fine since that's my current job, and I can handle that. The other part of the code is computer-generated by Carole, my supervisor. It authorises the payment. However, there's no way Carole would tell me her part of the code.'

'So what do we do?'

'We have to crack it.'

'God, how long will that take?' said Sebastien.

'Not long,' said Tanya.

'You're joking,' said Sebastien. 'It will take centuries.'

Tanya laughed. 'Hey, Sebastien, you do your job and I'll do mine. You see, I've linked in my computer to two Cray computers. One is in the United States and the other is in Germany. I'm borrowing a bit of their time.'

Sebastien looked at her admiringly. 'Now I know why you're a Fellow of the College,' he said. 'Does that mean that you can break into any computer in the world?'

'Uh, huh,' said Tanya. She smiled sweetly. 'You see, I can find out much more about people than you think.' She kissed her finger and put it to his lips.

'That's what I am worried about,' said Sebastien with a chuckle, his bad humour forgotten.

Tanya had already started to investigate the backgrounds of the contestants. The last few weeks she'd trawled the computer network to find out about Andrew. She'd come up with two interesting pieces of information. After leaving university he'd worked in the military, in a Euro-American surveillance unit that tracked arms shipments on a global basis. Then he'd joined the UN as a consultant where his work had taken him to many global hot spots. Tanya's guess was that Andrew monitored military organisations and mercenaries worldwide on behalf of the College. With a background like that he could easily have killed Rex if he'd wanted to.

But had he? Tanya had only talked with Andrew a couple of times. He'd always seemed kind, almost shy. Yet how a person appeared and how they were within could be quite different.

Tanya would start researching Ivan next. Then Sebastien. She watched her lover playing with the cat. Would that not be betraying him in some way? Suppose she found out dark secrets about her boyfriend? Of course, she wouldn't tell Sebastien about her investigations. That would be her insurance policy. She turned on her side and gave him a lingering French kiss. Kisses of deep affection and of betrayal were not so dissimilar she thought. Only the former was tongue in cheek.

'Have you managed to persuade Ted to help you with anything?' she asked.

'Yes. Ted's been very helpful.' Sebastien grinned, 'Wait for tomorrow. Who knows what good tidings the Lord bringeth.'

'Sebastien? Is that you? It's Doug Sullivan, manager of US Bank, here. Sorry to bother you on a Sunday. Can we talk? Not busy or anything?'

Sebastien sat up in bed and motioned Tanya to be quiet. 'No. Fire away.'

'Bad news, I'm afraid.' Doug Sullivan hesitated. 'Ted's in

hospital. Poor fellow's been mugged. He was coming back from the golf club last night and they waylaid him.'

'Who?'

'Oh, I don't know. You know what these Panamanian gangsters are like. He says four men jumped him. Beat him about the head badly and gashed his leg. So I've given him a couple of weeks off to recover.'

'He'll need a month at least,' said Sebastien equitably. 'These things take time. I knew a ski instructor once who went off a ski jump on the wrong foot. He was badly shaken up. I got him to hospital and he was very grateful. With luck he'll be walking by now.'

'Er, yes,' said the manager. 'A month may be required.' Tactfully, he didn't mention Ted would also be spending some time in an alcohol rehabilitation clinic. That was none of Sebastien's business.

'Well, poor old Ted. I'm sorry to hear that,' said Sebastien, caressing the nipple of his bedmate with the tip of his finger. Tanya put her tongue out at him.

'So am I,' said the manager. 'Ted was a key man. I don't know how we're going to cope with the extra workload. Anyway, in respect of the Fixed Deposits Department, I've decided you should take over Ted's job temporarily. That means you'll be working with me on the numbered deposits. Can you do it? Course, we'll pay you a bit more.'

'Thanks a million,' said Sebastien.

'No, no. I've no doubt you'll do your best and you'll soon get the hang of it.'

'No doubt at all.'

Sebastien put down the phone. Good old Ted. Prone to exaggeration as always. So there were four gangsters? Rubbish. He'd only paid for two.

'What was that?' Tanya asked.

'Oh, it's just about Ted. An accident at the golf club. Ted was off on his usual swing. Tripped over a bar stool.' Tanya didn't need to know any more. Sebastien kissed her on the cheek.

* * *

One week later Sebastien walked into the worst bar in the red-light district of downtown Panama. It throbbed to the deep tones of rumba and salsa. Through a pall of tobacco smoke the customers could barely be seen as they sat at the coarse wooden tables littered with cigarette ash and toppled beer bottles. The clientele were mostly foreign sailors and the low life of the city. Drunken and rowdy, they fondled the bodies of the teenage prostitutes and bawled out cheap words of endearment. The gloom in the place was Stygian from low-wattage light bulbs in metal shades. In a far corner a strobe light flickered. Ignoring the stares, Sebastien ordered a double rum and went to sit at a table with his back to the wall.

'Hey, this bar's for regulars only.'

Sebastien glanced at the bouncer who stood before him, his arm muscles flexing in the tight leather jacket he wore. Then he looked down at his drink again.

'Hey, you,' said the bouncer. 'I'm talking to you, *amigo.*' A finger stabbed in the air. Soon it would be a knife.

'I'm waiting for Juan,' Sebastien replied, unfazed.

'Oh.' The violent expression was replaced by one of nervous concern and a weak smile. 'OK, OK,' said the bouncer as he departed to look for trouble elsewhere. Pissing off Juan could only result in death and at twenty-one he didn't want to die.

'Can I sit down?'

'Sure,' said Sebastien. He regarded the young girl encased in a crumpled red dress that had only been put back on a few minutes before. She was needle-thin with a worn and hollow complexion despite being no more than a teenager. Sebastien felt a twinge of sadness for her. She wouldn't last a year. An overdose or despair would see to that. Some people were born to lose. 'What will you have to drink?'

'Rum, please.'

'What's your name?'

'Clarita.'

'Local?'

'Colombian.'

'Been in Panama long?'

'Nearly five months.'

'I see you have company,' a rough voice came from the gloom.

Juan sat down heavily beside Sebastien. He was a thickset man in his late thirties with a deep knife scar down one side of his forehead. He smoked small Havana cigars continuously. Like the bouncer he was dressed in black leather, though his clothes were better tailored. A silver medallion of the Madonna hung round his neck and he had a large gold Rolex watch on his wrist. He kissed Sebastien warmly on both cheeks and then he grinned at Clarita. He'd had her before, in many places. He bent over the table and squeezed her breast as though feeling fruit on a market stall. Her mouth twisting in disgust, she got up and walked off.

'So, how do you like the bar?'

'Not bad. I thought you were more upmarket,' said Sebastien.

Juan laughed. 'I am, but it's never a good thing to be seen in the best hotels all the time. One needs to remember one's roots.'

Sebastien nodded. Juan carried his roots around with him. There was no mistaking the slime. Sebastien was assiduously cultivating contacts with the underworld. Invariably they were dealers engaged in smuggling in some form or another – arms to the Far East, coke to the States, women to Amsterdam and Eastern Europe. However, they were small-time crooks and Juan was likely to be the same. Sebastien knew he had to be patient.

'So how are things going?'

'So-so,' said Sebastien. 'I'm rather short of funds at the moment. Since we're friends I hoped you could lend me a bit more.'

Juan tut-tutted like an affectionate uncle. Sebastien wondered how many people he had killed.

'No. I can't lend you any more, Sebastien. You're the one who works in the bank, not me. By the way, you owe me three thousand now and pay time's coming up soon.'

Sebastien shrugged unconcernedly. 'I'll find the money.'

Juan laughed heartily and ordered more rum. There was no

reason for him to be worried. He would get his money. He always did. Corpses always paid up. Sebastien was a good drinking companion, Juan thought – harmless, with an obvious failing for the drink and for money. Someone to prey on. The shark had started to circle its victim. However, Juan was unaware that it was circling its own kind.

It was a long night. By the early hours they were both very drunk and Juan's head was nodding dreamily at a phalanx of bottles in front of him while he talked to Sebastien. It was then he remembered what he wanted to say. The words were a long time in coming, his tongue unable to get in between the narrow space between the beer bottle and his mouth.

'There's a big party on next weekend,' he slurred. 'A big party.' Juan raised his hands expansively. 'It's in my home town, Cali, the best place in the world. I want you to come, Sebastien. To enjoy yourself. And I promise you, my best friend, a wonderful time. Cali has the most beautiful women in Latin America.' He brought his fingers up to his sodden lips, kissing them clumsily. 'Beautiful, like coconuts. Open them up and the milk never stops flowing.'

'I can't. I've got another party next weekend.'

'Hey, don't let me down.' Juan reached forward and grasped Sebastien's shirt collar. 'Don't let your friend down.' His tone was melancholy and menacing.

'Well, maybe, Juan. Let's drink to your party.'

Sebastien turned his bleary eyes away. At the bar a fight had broken out. A massive stevedore with a grizzled beard was arguing over payment with a whore. He had her by the throat and was slowly strangling her. She was desperately fighting back, clawing at him with her fingers. They couldn't reach his face and the stevedore's grip tightened implacably. The bystanders watched the spectacle with casual interest. It was a common occurrence in this place and they had no intention of getting involved. They could as easily serve you death as a beer in this place. Humankind and its suffering was all part of life. Sebastien glanced across at the commotion.

'I'll get another drink.'

He tottered over to the bar. The girl's agonised thrashings had brought slightly greater attention among the clientele when they realised the stevedore would probably choke her to death. Sebastien saw that it was Clarita, the young prostitute who had sat with him some hours before. He turned his head back towards Juan. The mobster was spread-eagled over the table, his head resting on the wood. Sebastien shrugged his shoulders. He glanced again at the face of the victim, the white of her eyes showing unnaturally and her visage turning a deep purple. It could have been Tanya – in the chalet. Still, it wasn't, and it wasn't his business. That was the way of the world. Don't get involved in the problems of others and don't be surprised when they don't help you.

'A bottle of beer.'

The barman served it to him. It was too light. 'No, make it a bottle of whisky.'

It was handed over. Sebastien took it and began to turn away. Suddenly, he inverted the whisky bottle so that its neck was in the palm of his hand. Rising up on the balls of his feet to get the maximum power, Sebastien brought it smashing down on the back of the stevedore's head. A roar of delight went up from the crowd at this unexpected development. The stevedore fell to the floor like a stone, his skull caked with blood, whisky and shards of glass. Death had moved on elsewhere. After a momentary lapse conversation among the bystanders started again, the stevedore forgotten in a collective fit of memory loss. Sebastien stepped over the body and ordered another bottle of whisky. Meanwhile Clarita looked at him, her hand at her neck, gasping and choking as she sought to get her breath back. He had saved her life. Sebastien ignored her and staggered back to the table, just making it. Meanwhile, the bouncers dragged the stevedore outside with the empties.

'What did you do that for?' Juan uttered the words with great difficulty.

'He stood on my foot.'

Juan nodded sagely. He could understood that. That was reasonable. He could kill a man for less.

Juan met Sebastien at Bogotá Airport the following Saturday. As he appeared from behind the customs barrier, Juan shoved people aside and clasped Sebastien to him, happily kissing him on both cheeks.

'I knew you would come, *amigo.* Have I got some fun for you!'

They drove from the airport into Bogotá, through dusty backstreets and to the centre of the huge conurbation. Sebastien noticed the absence of traffic even though it was early evening. The reason was simple. Between them the military, the guerrillas and the drug dealers had turned Bogotá into the most murderous city in the world. Sebastien mentioned this to Juan, who spat out of the window.

'No balls. Fucking faggots and cowards. That's why people hide in their homes.'

Puffing away on his short cigar, Juan expounded his philosophy of life while the car hurtled recklessly down the alleyways. Violence made you respected. It was a commodity that could be bought and sold. Morality didn't. It didn't make money. Therefore, it was worthless. So, the more violent you were, the more wealthy you became, and the more respected. It was so obvious, *hombre.* Even an idiot could understand that. Which is why Juan was surprised more people were not like him. Fucking stupid, they must be. Sebastien nodded. It was true, morality was a poor protection.

After many twists and turns in the street and after almost running down an old woman, the car arrived at the best hotel in town. Juan burst through the doors, like Freddie Mercury arriving at a church bazaar.

'*Chicas, chicas,* time to party.'

They had entered what was more like a high-class bordello than a hotel since it was decked out with an opulence so excessive as to be gaudy. Huge gilded mirrors, tables of the finest Italian marble, crystal chandeliers, Spanish religious paintings, copies of erotic Roman mosaics, all married together in a quixotic pastiche. It was as if a lapsed religious artist had copulated with a schizophrenic car salesman.

Juan grasped Sebastien's arm and led him through the throng. The downstairs restaurant was crammed with both sexes, cavorting about in various states of intoxication as they put on party costumes of the time of the conquistadors. Juan's arrival was greeted with delight and raucous calls. He made the rounds kissing and feeling whatever part of the anatomy was proffered, while he introduced Sebastien to the other guests and snorted large doses of cocaine. His *sotto voce* comments to Sebastien reflected his true sentiments.

'Sebastien, come and meet Don Manuel. *One of the biggest dealers in town. Rich, stupid and a complete fucking bastard.*'

'Sebastien. I want to introduce you to the fragrant Donna Carla Lopez. *A whore of the worst sort. Would frighten off a donkey. Don't even touch her.*'

'Sebastien, say hello to my oldest and best friend Señor Santiago Ceballos. *Son of a bitch owes me twenty thousand dollars. If he doesn't pay by Monday I'll slit the throats of his children.*'

It was a night to be remembered. At the sound of a bell all those not already wholly incapacitated descended into the dining room. There, every form of delicacy imaginable was presented by beautiful serving girls who removed a layer of their already skimpy clothing each time they served a repast. Most of the guests followed suit and the orgy began. It had all the makings of a Roman bacchanalia save that the audience was more international and the lark's tongues had been replaced by piles of a white substance.

Juan noticed Sebastien's attention was fixed on one of the nubile waitresses who was smearing her roseate nipples with cream.

'Save yourself,' he chortled. 'They're bringing in schoolgirls from the countryside.'

Eventually, in the early hours of the morning Sebastien left Juan recumbent on a table and made his way back to his bedroom, climbing over inert and twitching bodies. It was a palatial apartment with a four-poster bed. On it, patiently waiting for him, was a young Indian girl, naked and very frightened.

'Do you like these people?'

She darted Sebastien a fearful look and shook her head. Her hands covered her virginity.

'Nor do I,' he said. 'Put your clothes on.'

Sebastien lay beside her as she slept – plotting his next move. Juan was beginning to irritate him, just a little.

One of those to whom Sebastien had been introduced at the party was a Señor Gonzalez. He was an affable, well-preserved man in his fifties, full of bonhomie and seemingly cultured. Sometime during the party he had invited Sebastien and Juan to visit his hacienda next day. It was not until late in the morning that Juan stirred from his drug-induced sleep and they finally departed from the city. Sebastien drove.

As they left the dreary backstreets, the urban sprawl suddenly gave way to a lush cultivated countryside. The air was warm and the sky cloudless. It was rather like Panama, though not quite so humid. Sebastien felt contented within himself, like anyone who has a mission in life and is proceeding to fulfil it. He glanced into the back of the Jeep.

'Hey, Juan, any problems with guerrillas on this road?'

The sprawling figure muttered under his sombrero, 'No problem. Señor Gonzalez takes care of them.'

About an hour later they turned off the highway. Some miles further down the side road narrowed into a single Tarmacked lane, which led through a plantation of coffee trees. At the end of it, in the distance, was a magnificent house just like a French château, its whiteness gleaming against the backdrop of the mountains behind. They passed down the lane, watched by horseriders in the fields who stopped and stared.

'This the place?'

'Yeah,' Juan raised his dopey head, 'that's it.'

After being searched by guards at the entrance to the château they passed through a large hall and into an expanse of garden at the back. The building and its decor, Sebastien noticed, was in surprisingly good taste. He wondered who the architect was. Señor Gonzalez was by a huge pool, his small children screaming and splashing about in the water. He welcomed them with a slight nod and settled back in his sun lounger leaving Sebastien to swim with his children and his raven-haired wife. Juan disappeared off to the bar inside the house, to resurrect his limited mental faculties.

The sun glinted on the water. Sebastien sipped his wine and watched a solitary cloud scuttle across the sky. After a long while, Gonzalez stirred.

'Want to see a bit of the ranch?'

Horses were brought for Gonzalez and Sebastien and they saddled up. Gonzalez proudly showed off his possessions, like a middle-aged businessman who'd made good and had retired early to enjoy life. Unlike Juan, his boss was elegantly attired and knew the value of money. Sebastien was impressed. Gonzalez had learnt quickly. The tattoos on his hands were more difficult to erase. Yet, unlike so many of his other attributes, they were at least skin-deep.

'See the land over there? Over by the mountains? It's all mine. My father used to have a smallholding here and I extended it. I own the coffee plantations as well and a lot of property in Palmira.' Gonzalez took out a cigar and started to smoke it as he let his horse meander. 'Juan said you were in banking. Good profession?'

'Yes. I work for US Bank.'

'Yeah?' said Gonzalez unimpressed. 'Well, I've been in business all my life. Just like my father. I've got the farm here; with my associates, I also do a lot in the import-export business. Sugar, machinery parts, paper and that sort of thing. It's usually profitable but, like everyone else, we have good years and bad years.' He led his horse down a narrow gully, picking his way among the cacti. 'We've been thinking of expanding, perhaps to the US or Europe. We're looking for a good banker. Juan says you're trustworthy.'

Sebastien sounded uninterested. 'I'm sure US Bank would be happy to lend you money if you have the collateral.'

Señor Gonzalez grunted and they rode further into the plantations. 'It's not loans we're after. We want to send money out of the country to invest elsewhere. But you know how it is. There's exchange problems, nosy customs men, government officials. This country is going to the dogs. They all want to rob us blind. It hardly seems worth doing anything. What I want is privacy. Someone who can help us without asking too many questions.'

Sebastien appeared to reflect on it, struggling with his conscience as a reputable banker. 'Well, perhaps I could help you. I work with numbered accounts. That said, we only deal with large amounts and the costs are high.'

'Yeah,' Gonzalez spat in the dirt. 'These banks always rip you off.' He drew his horse close to Sebastien's and touched him affectionately on the arm. 'I know your problem. It's just like everyone else. Too many desires and not enough money.' He laughed grittily. 'I'm the same. Perhaps we can help each other.'

Sebastien watched the evil bask in his eyes, like a bright flame flickering across the surface of an oil slick. He grinned.

'Don't worry, Señor Gonzalez,' he said with the sincerity of an estate agent selling his own house. 'I'll treat your money just like my own.'

'Er, yeah,' said Gonzalez after a moment, patting his horse. 'I think we understand each other. So what do me and my associates do to move some money on a regular basis?'

'Open a numbered account in Panama. All I need is a signature on some forms. When you want to move money to the US or Europe send a standard letter of instruction to the bank. No one will know who the money belongs to apart from the bank manager, his deputy and me.'

'Yeah. They'll want to know who I am?'

'Of course,' said Sebastien. 'And one of them will come down here to look over your businesses. There shouldn't be any problem. You and I can arrange that.'

'I don't want any difficulties,' said Gonzalez.

'We need to open an account for you in Switzerland as well,' continued Sebastien, smiling. 'Again numbered. That will be easy since US Bank will vouch for you to the Swiss bank on the basis of your account with them.'

Gonzalez inspected the coffee trees. 'And how much commission do you want?'

'One hundred thousand dollars. Up front. And fifty thousand each time you move money.'

Gonzalez exclaimed in disgust. 'Too much.'

'That's my price. I have to take a bigger risk than you, Señor Gonzalez, and to trust you. Of course, if you can't afford it . . .'

Gonzalez dug his spurs into his horse. 'No,' he snarled, the friendly mask slipping. 'We'll pay, but I want no problems. Get me?'

'Perfectly.'

They rode back to the château and round to the swimming pool. Gonzalez pointed to the girl Sebastien had been playing with earlier in the pool. 'What do you think of her?'

'You have a lovely wife.'

Señor Gonzalez threw back his head and roared with laughter, the light dancing on his gold-capped teeth. 'She's not my wife. She's the waitress Juan saw you staring at last night. Have a good evening, my friend. Come back to me next week with the forms. And,' he looked at Sebastien closely, 'one piece of good advice: never let me down.'

Gonzalez watched Sebastien and Juan depart in the Jeep with the waitress. Small time crook, he thought.

At dusk Juan drove back to Cali. They dropped the girl off at the hotel.

Juan looked at Sebastien.

'There's something Señor Gonzalez wants you to help me with,' he said.

They drove to a car park overlooking a side road. It was almost empty and Juan slewed the vehicle into a bay. He told Sebastien to get into the driving seat while he jumped out, the ever-present cigar between his lips.

'I'll be back in a few minutes. I want you to look over there and watch out for a motor scooter.'

Sebastien waited, his eyes fixed on the road, which was no more than twenty metres away. There were few passers-by and twilight was approaching.

A scooter soon appeared to view. Two men were on it, one driving, the other on the pillion. It went slowly, idling along the road. Then it sped up slightly. It seemed to be following a man who was hurrying along the pavement, eager to get home. From the style of his dress and his slightly shabby overcoat Sebastien imagined him to be an office worker, perhaps a bank clerk or an insurance agent. One of life's quiet people, with a wife and a couple of kids. A man trying to hold on to a respectable life in difficult circumstances, a good man in an evil world.

When the passer-by crossed in front of Sebastien's line of vision, not fifteen metres from him, the scooter began rapidly to increase its speed and the pillion rider extracted a piece of tubing from inside his coat. With an icy shock it suddenly dawned on Sebastien what was going to happen. He hurled open the car door and got out to shout a warning. However, it was too late. The pedestrian, hearing the noise of a motor very close to him, turned to look behind. As he did so, Juan levelled the shotgun at him and discharged both barrels into his chest. The scooter veered off the road and accelerated over the pavement within a few inches of the still twitching corpse. It drove at full speed towards Sebastien and stopped. Juan and his companion casually got off. They dumped the scooter against a fence and got back into the car.

'Get out of here,' said Juan. He started to giggle.

'What did you do that for?' Sebastien's eyes narrowed.

Juan glared at him and pushed a finger against his chest. His voice was low and threatening. 'It's a lesson, Sebastien. Just for you. Señor Gonzalez wanted to show you what happens to people if they give him problems. There are no second chances. Remember that.'

'What did the man do?' asked Sebastien.

'Him?' said Juan, the incident already forgotten. He tossed his head to one side and got out a new cigar. 'Er, nothing. He was just there.'

Doug Sullivan, the manager of US Bank, was delighted that another numbered account was going to be opened and by a major Colombian businessman. Sebastien had done well. They still had to be sure drug money was not involved. Ted Baxter had now recovered from his mugging and had come out of hospital. More importantly, he had almost completed his Alcoholics Anonymous course. So the manager sent Ted and Sebastien to Colombia to have the relevant papers signed. Sebastien told Juan of this development and what he wanted done.

'Don't worry,' Juan laughed delightedly. 'We'll put Ted on cloud ten. It will be showtime!'

The moment Ted arrived in Cali he was plied with drink. True, he saw Gonzalez sign the forms to open a numbered account. True also that Ted received balance sheets of the companies controlled by Gonzalez and his partners and that he was pleased with them. So he should have been since Gonzalez's accountant was more creative than Walt Disney on LSD. However, it was not true that Ted visited the businesses himself. After a heavy night's drinking and the attention of not one but two attractive playmates who resurrected his every muscle and joint, Ted was unable to rise the next morning to get to the shower, far less inspect Gonzalez's companies. Which was just as well, since they never existed. Thoughtfully, though, Gonzalez provided him with photos of other people's buildings. Photos of Ted's sexual indiscretions Gonzalez retained for future use. It was amazing what bankers got up to, he thought. He'd given them less credit than they deserved. What a portfolio.

There was one other matter that Ted failed to witness, and it would have troubled him considerably had he done so, as it would have Gonzalez too. It was on the return flight to Panama.

'Back in a minute,' said Ted as he lurched off to the rear of the plane wondering whether it was the tequila or the women that had finished him off.

'OK,' said Sebastien.

While Ted reflected on the possible spontaneous combustion of his digestive tract in the aircraft's lavatory, Sebastien opened Ted's briefcase. Within seconds he had substituted the forms signed by Gonzalez for identical forms on which Sebastien had forged Gonzalez's signature.

'That's better,' said Ted as he got back to his seat. 'It was that bloody greasy food that upset me.'

'Me too,' said Sebastien. He imagined that Ted would be the star turn at his next Alcoholics Anonymous meeting. He would have a lot of explaining to do. The aircraft came in to land.

'Oh, yes,' Ted twisted the hairs on his small moustache nervously, 'just one small thing, Sebastien. I don't think we need bore the manager with all the details of our business trip. Just keep to the important stuff, eh? He's a busy man.'

Sebastien glanced at him. 'Don't worry, Ted. If everything was known, we'd both be dead.'

'Er, quite,' said Ted.

US Bank opened a numbered account for Señor Gonzalez with an initial investment of five million dollars. They also opened a numbered account for him with the top-class bank, Banque Lex in Geneva. Since the request came from the Panama branch of a well-known American bank, Banque Lex did not require an independent check on Gonzalez. Sebastien simply faxed them the completed application forms for the Panama numbered account, containing his own forgery of Gonzalez's signature.

By the end of July the Panama account held over ten million dollars, of which Gonzalez ordered half to be moved to Switzerland. Sebastien received Gonzalez's transfer instruction, a standard bank form which the drug dealer had signed. Sebastien binned it and prepared an identical letter of instruction, forging Gonzalez's signature. This he passed to Ted who, with the manager, checked the signature against the original account opening forms. Since Sebastien had forged both of them they corresponded. The money was transferred and Gonzalez received a confirmation note. As a result, everyone was happy including Ted.

'I reckon you're getting the hang of this, Sebastien,' he said delightedly while he calculated the commission Gonzalez would be paying the bank.

'Yes, I think I am, Ted,' said Sebastien, thinking of his personal commission from Gonzalez which he would use to pay off his debt to Juan. 'It's a funny old world, isn't it. Moving people's money from one pocket to another and you get paid for it. It's a laugh.'

'Do you really think we're going to get away with it?' asked Tanya.

They lay sunbathing on the pristine white sand, watching the waves glide against the shore.

'I don't see why not,' said Sebastien, 'and if anything goes wrong they'll never suspect you were involved. I'll be the one that takes the rap.'

'I'll visit you in prison.' Tanya kissed him on the shoulder. They had not been together for some time. So they'd decided to meet on this deserted beach on an island off the coast of Panama, to relax and catch up on the news without being seen. Tanya had missed him greatly during the last few weeks while Sebastien was out hooking a drug dealer, much more than she thought. Gemma the cat was insufficient company. Tanya turned over, to let her buttocks get well tanned. She wanted him to make love to her again. She was getting the hang of making love in the sand.

'Have you worked out how we're going to get out of here when we make the sting?' Sebastien asked as he sipped a beer. He didn't want to be around when Gonzalez found out they'd permanently borrowed some of his money. He hadn't told Tanya all the details of his trip to Cali since he didn't want to alarm her. However, he knew that Gonzalez was not a forgiving man. He'd yet to forgive his mother for giving birth to him.

'Yes,' said Tanya. 'The fastest route's by plane. So as not to draw too much attention to ourselves we should drive down to the other end of the Canal, to Colon, and then take a private jet to Miami. I've arranged the flights.' She giggled. 'I've booked you down as Mr Master.'

Sebastien laughed and passed her a beer. 'Fine. The target date is October. That gives us three months. So we should just sit back and relax.'

'What about the others? There's still Ivan and Andrew to consider. Do you think they'll have tracked us down?'

'No,' said Sebastien. 'Don't worry, we'll turn our attention to them soon. First, though, we need to finish things here and make the money.'

'Is it right to take this money from Gonzalez? I'm beginning to have qualms about it.'

'What, taking money from a drug dealer?' Sebastien sat upright. 'Come on, why not, Tanya? He'd use it just to buy even more drugs. I've no moral qualms about it, I assure you. Gonzalez will get what he deserves. Just think of the lives he's destroyed to get this money.'

There was silence. Sebastien frowned. Tanya had not been herself lately. More withdrawn. More distant from him. Their paths were beginning to diverge. It was as if something had happened to her that night in the chalet. Had she been raped after all? Or was she getting ready to part company? Sebastien reflected that it was a sad feature of the world that you could never really trust anyone. Not even those closest to you.

'Do you think that Andrew and Ivan are doing something similar to us to get their money?'

'I'm quite sure,' said Sebastien. Then in a quizzical voice, 'Is there something you know about them you haven't told me? Remember, we promised to work together.'

Tanya hesitated. It was the moment of decision. Would she compete with him or not for the Mastership? There would not be enough money in Gonzalez's account for both of them. So, what should she do about Sebastien? She knew that, for all his faults, she loved him very deeply. Why? He made her happy, he made life fun, he had style and panache – it was as simple as that. Tanya lay back in the sand and looked up at the sky. That was the problem. She knew Sebastien desperately wanted to be Master and, if it came to it, he would compete against her. Tanya thought she'd win such a contest. However, there was something more. She loved him, and when you love someone you sometimes put aside personal desires that had so gripped you before. She had reached a moment of decision. Well? Tanya decided that she'd help Sebastien to become Master. When he fulfilled himself, he would love her all the more.

'Sebastien . . .' Yet a small voice told her not to tell him everything yet. Not her past relationship with Rex. He wouldn't understand. 'Sebastien, I want to tell you something. I've been doing some research about Andrew through computer databases.'

'Oh?' he said. 'Tell me what you've discovered.' He started to dig in the food hamper.

Tanya told him she had found out that Andrew had been in the military and that, as well as being a UN consultant, he monitored military and terrorist organisations on a worldwide basis for the College. Which meant he could be a very dangerous man, someone who would have had few qualms about killing Rex, if required. Andrew was also someone who could easily have broken into the chalet that night in Switzerland.

Sebastien listened to it all. Then he chuckled. 'So you've decided to trust me after all. I was waiting for that vote of confidence. You've obviously decided I didn't kill Rex. Cheers!' He swigged back another beer and put his hands behind his head. 'I agree with you about Andrew, that's why I'm keeping well away from him and I always have. Try to see what you can find out about Ivan.' He continued in a casual voice, 'Have you checked me out yet as well?'

Tanya looked at him, her eyes unwaveringly fixed on his. 'No. There's no need. I love you and I trust you.'

'Likewise,' said Sebastien though he didn't believe her. 'Well, since you've been honest with me, I'm going to tell you what the secret of the Chinese puzzle box is.' He kissed her firmly on the lips and settled back on the sand to gaze out at the waves breaking on the shore, at the clear blue sky, at the brilliant sun. You couldn't get much better than this, he thought. They were almost in paradise. The Mastership would be the final touch.

'I think, Tanya,' he said slowly, 'that the whole point of the Chinese box was to warn us that appearances are deceptive. This is not an ordinary game we are involved in. It is a contest. And a contest is a form of war. The Master did not refer to the Chinese puzzle box lightly. He was trying to tell us something and I'm sure I know what it was.'

'What?'

'That this is not some Machiavellian game of power with a philosophical angle where the ends justify the means. It is much more simple. It is war and there can only be one winner. Never mind how you or I, or even the Master, got into the war. Here we are and we must do everything we can to win. There's no moral dimension to this Game, just as in life. In reality, people use moral arguments as a tactic to help them win the war. It looks good to be pious when you are the Pope or the Master because it inhibits others from attacking you. It causes any potential adversaries to have moral qualms. However, although you pretend that you have them, actually you don't! The perfect way to weaken the enemy.'

Tanya nodded. She half agreed with him. Her view of the College had also undergone a dramatic reappraisal over the last few months.

Sebastien continued, 'The other interesting thing is that the craftsman Chang, who made the puzzle box, lived in the reign of the Chinese emperor Kangxi – probably China's greatest and most powerful emperor. I've been doing some reading up about him. Who was he? A non-Chinese, a Manchurian who used his innate cleverness and military might to get what he wanted – control of China. And to do that he used a guide, a little book of military tactics, which helped him to win.'

'*The Art of War* by Sun Tzu,' said Tanya.

Sebastien laughed happily; she always surprised him. 'Yes,' he said. 'Now how did you know that?'

'Because, Sebastien,' Tanya flicked his private parts with her finger, 'some people are just as clever as you, you show-off. I've also been reading my Chinese history.'

'Well, then,' said Sebastien as he moved out of range and crunched on an apple, 'you know what Sun Tzu said:

> *"War is a matter of vital importance to the State; the province of life and death, the road to survival or ruin. It is mandatory that it be thoroughly studied."*'

Tanya nodded. 'He also said,

> "*All warfare is based on deception.*"'

'Exactly,' replied Sebastien. 'We are in a war and the Chinese puzzle box is a deception, a clever trick. It couldn't be otherwise. How could any man make for the Emperor the most difficult puzzle box of all? It is impossible. There's nothing in the box. That's the belief of the Master and I agree with him.'

'So what are you getting at?'

'What I am getting at is this,' said Sebastien. 'I've been thinking a lot about the College and its true nature. It only survives because it can play off countries and political leaders against each other. In that way it keeps its power and maintains its central position. And it does this with consummate skill and deception.' Sebastien's voice was eager. 'Don't you see that's what they've been doing for hundreds of years, Tanya? The College holds all the threads and it subtly pulls them to direct things as it wishes. Of course, the complexity of the overall global system is so great that not even the College can dominate it nor manipulate the outcome of every event. Still, it *can* direct it so that the College always retains its privileged position. It's like those old astrological charts you see in medieval books, the great concentric circles of heaven and earth and, on an earthly plane, the figure who stands in the centre and controls it all. It is the only means of exercising power over very long periods of time, whatever changes there may be in the political and economic systems of individual countries. The Master really is a master, a master of manipulation and deception.'

'And?'

'And that's what he is trying to teach us. Don't you see? We are like the sorcerer's apprentices, practising to assume power, seeing what it would be like to stand in the centre and to direct it all. And we are being forced to learn the ropes the hard way. How to achieve what is almost impossible with only our wits to guide us.'

'If that's so, why did the Master offer us the Mastership?' said Tanya, puzzled. 'If it's all about power, he'd do everything to keep power.'

'Exactly,' said Sebastien triumphantly. 'He didn't offer us the Mastership. He told us that the Arbitrators control the Mastership Game. That means, I'm sure, that the Master will do everything he can to retain power. He didn't say that he would give it up.' He paused. Then: 'You see, Tanya, I believe there are only two basic things that hold together any system and enable it to adapt and to survive. And that applies whether that system is cosmic or terrestrial.'

'And what are those?'

'War and Peace. War because it divides and forces change. Peace because it binds. And it is on these simple concepts that so many of the great political and philosophical thinkers have pondered.'

'Which of the two is the more powerful?'

Sebastien kissed her on the cheek. 'Both you and I know in our heart of hearts, otherwise we wouldn't be playing this game.' He tossed aside the apple. 'It is war.'

And, by God, he would win it.

CHAPTER EIGHTEEN

For, whenever there is no need for men to fight, they fight for ambition's sake; and so powerful is the sway that ambition exercises over the human heart that it never relinquishes them, no matter how high they have arisen.

Machiavelli, *The Discourses*

July. Albania.

ALBANIA WAS A REMARKABLE COUNTRY, Ivan reflected as he stood outside the airport in Tirana, its capital, waiting for a car. The poorest in Europe and the most mysterious. A mountainous place on the Adriatic, wedged between Greece on one side and the former Yugoslavia on the other with a population of only four million. It was also a country with a troubled history. For centuries its people of Illyrian stock had been under the domination of the Turkish Empire and it wasn't until 1912 that Albania became an independent State. In the Second World War the country was invaded by the Italians and, later, the Nazis. After the War the communists took over under a home-grown dictator, Enver Hoxha. Not a very happy history, Ivan thought. Like a succession of prison sentences.

'Taxi?'

Ivan waved the driver away with his hand. He was waiting for someone else. Enver Hoxha had been an interesting piece of work. For forty years he had ruled over this Land of the Eagles with a fist of steel. He had been an old-fashioned dictator, a psychopath, not like the current half-breeds who pandered to the people with bread and circuses and fled at the first sign of a riot. No, for Hoxha it was the concentration camp for dissenters, with torture if you were lucky and extermination if not. Hoxha had obviously taken to heart the advice of Machiavelli that to get a firm grip on a State you should destroy the family of the previous ruler. The only problem was that Hoxha had been too enthusiastic and destroyed almost everyone's family. Except his own, of course. You need someone to do the cooking, a problem that the great political theorists sometimes overlooked. So, from the Second World War until he died in 1985, Hoxha had presided over a toytown dictatorship of the worst sort. Free speech was ruthlessly crushed, hard-line communism the order of the day. Apart from Hoxha and his cronies who led the good life, Albanians had no cars, no private property, no taxes, no political opposition, no mortgages, no classes, no crime, no banks, no foreign travel, not much of anything in fact. The Land of Eagles was the land of the nihilist, an interesting experiment in negative social engineering. However, there was one, albeit minor, fly in the ointment that Hoxha missed. The country had no future either.

'Mr Ivan Radic?'

Ivan nodded at the military guard and followed him outside the small airport. Poor Albania. For forty years the largest concentration camp in the world with the possible exception of North Korea. When Hoxha died and the Soviet Empire collapsed so did Albania. From the 1990s it had been declared a democracy. This was a polite fiction. In reality, and even more so after the war in Kosovo, it was controlled by the army, the secret services and various local factions. Ivan knew all about it from his detailed investigations; and a lot more besides.

'Mr Ivan Radic?'

Ivan examined the man standing by the government car. Of average height, with dark hair and a swarthy complexion, he had a pock-marked skin with crow's feet around his eyes. A rather cruel face, Ivan thought.

'My name is Lef.'

'Ivan.'

'Jump in. There is no need for your bags to be checked. You are the guest of General Durres.'

They shook hands and Ivan got in the vehicle. As he did so he glanced at the epaulettes of his companion. Four red pips indicated that he was a major. However, this was no mere army man. He belonged to the Albanian secret service, Ivan was quite sure. One of Durres' boys. A good start. Good to be with the same team even though it belonged to another country. The car hurtled off.

'Do you smoke?'

'No.'

They sped through the countryside. It was a hot summer's day and Ivan felt drowsy. The journey from the capital to Saranda in the south of Albania should take about four hours. He sat back to relax. Before him, on the poor quality road, the startling beauty of the country flashed by. Olive groves perched on the rugged mountainsides, chestnut trees, sunflower crops and, from time to time, glimpses of the startling blue of the Adriatic. In the fields Ivan could see men and women gathering in the harvest while donkeys and ox carts stood patiently by. The twentieth century, far less the twenty-first, hardly existed in Albania. No planes, very few cars – just people working in the fields who stopped every few minutes to stare at the world in a languid, unhurried sort of way. And everywhere concrete pillboxes. For one of Hoxha's many obsessions had been that someone would invade Albania. So he had concrete pillboxes built everywhere, a greater number than the entire population of the country. Another aspect of toytown, the country of concrete mushrooms.

Lef spoke. 'General Durres invites you to his house. We have booked you into a hotel in Saranda. It's a small town on the coast.'

'Really?' said Ivan naively.

'Yes,' replied Lef. He started to tell him about the sights in

Albania and its history. Ivan ignored him. If only Lef knew. For Ivan had been to Albania a number of times before and he was well acquainted with its ugly secrets and tortured past – all that British and American secret service files had to reveal. Also, and much more interesting, Ivan had read information about Albania held on the computer at College not long before the Mastership Game had begun, in preparation for another secret trip to update files. Still, ignorance was bliss. Ivan settled back. In the heat of the afternoon, alternating between light and shade as they passed along the tree-lined highway, drowsiness overcame him. Now and again, disturbed from his slumber he caught a glimpse of farm buildings or a flock of goats being herded along the roadside. The Master and the game were temporarily forgotten as Ivan slept in a lazy, fitful sort of way.

When he awoke, he was thinking of twenty million dollars.

Saranda was a small town in the very south of Albania which nestled close to the Greek border. From time immemorial it had been a place beloved by those who had sought the quiet life: beautiful, clear waters, a rugged coastline with sheltered inlets, warm Mediterranean weather. Both the Greeks and the Romans had sought solace and quietude in this idyllic setting. Little had changed over the centuries. Although wars had ravaged Europe as nations and peoples rose and fell, Saranda and the natural tranquillity of its surroundings had remained largely undisturbed.

After a swim Ivan settled down on the veranda of his small hotel. Not five kilometres across the water was the Greek island of Corfu. During Hoxha's reign many Albanians had tried to escape across this narrow strait. They had been gunned down by their own people even as they struggled to swim. Staring at the crystal-clear blue sea, it seemed unbelievable to Ivan. Such a thin sliver of water, such an enormous divide in cultural and political beliefs.

Lef came to collect him in the evening. He pointed out their destination. Around the bay from Saranda and high up on a cliff top was a large tract of land that local people were forbidden access to on the basis that it was a restricted military zone. It was, of sorts, for located within a large olive grove was the magnificent house in which Durres lived. As they drove up the winding pathway, Lef turned to Ivan. He was clearly nervous.

'Perhaps, I ought to tell you a little more about the General. He is an important man in our country even though it is now a democracy.'

Ivan nodded. Lef was being more than economical with the truth. General Durres had been a very important man in Albania long before democracy had come. The present head of the Albanian secret service, the General had retained a similar position during the Hoxha years, for the General was one of those cultured and ruthless men who survive whatever the change in weather. He knew all the dark secrets of his country, since he had personally dispatched and buried many of the bodies. And like the former General Pinochet in Chile, people were loath to take on such a man even when the winds had changed, for experience had taught them that the wind could as easily blow back again, in one's own face.

They reached the olive grove and passed through large wrought-iron gates, then down a beautifully manicured drive, the sun glinting through the poplar trees on either side. Five minutes later a mansion loomed up before them. The General came out to greet Ivan. He walked down the steps, ignoring Lef and two soldiers who stood to attention at the front of the mansion.

'It's kind of you to visit an old soldier who will only bore you with his war tales.' He squeezed Ivan's hand tightly. His voice was deep and sonorous and his command of English was good.

'Come on in.' Durres guided Ivan in front of him. His was a bull-like figure with the musculature of a miner, even though he was in his seventies. Despite his physique there was no coarseness or stolidity about him, and this was reflected in his large leonine face with alert features and penetrating eyes. They seemed kindly and reassuring. However, Ivan had little doubt that the General was a master of deceit and a shrewd exponent of the use of power. He would have had to have been to have survived under a pathological maniac like Hoxha. He wondered whether General Durres knew the Master. Possibly.

The house itself was spacious and magnificently decorated like the residence of a rich Italian magnate. Roman works of art, Etruscan pottery, Greek colonnades, marble floors – everything exuded good taste. In fact, Ivan thought that the General's artistic tastes were similar to his own. He hoped the General also appreciated the works of Machiavelli.

'You like ancient art?'

'Very much.'

'Good.' The General called to a servant. 'He'll show you around. Afterwards, we'll have drinks. Please take your time. It's one thing we have plenty of in Albania.' Half an hour later Ivan returned and went out on to the balcony. Durres was sitting on a rattan chair gazing across the narrow strip of water to Corfu whose white buildings gleamed in the distance.

'Your collection is magnificent.'

'It's not bad,' the General said in a tone betraying his false modesty. 'I have a particular interest in Greek sculpture, as you'll have noticed. I've picked the pieces up here and there. Do you like classical art?'

'Very much.' They talked for twenty minutes and the General soon realised that he was talking with a fellow expert.

'Which piece do you like best?'

'It's hard to say. In the hallway I noticed a second-century figurine of a Greek youth about to hurl a javelin. It's a very lifelike piece, with a wonderful agility and tautness to it.'

'Yes, I like that one,' said Durres. 'I rescued it from a Nazi art collection at the end of the war. I don't know who owned it before. It has given me endless pleasure since I acquired it all those years ago.' He made a magnanimous gesture with his hand. 'I give it to you.'

Durres' words took Ivan's breath away.

'I couldn't possibly take it.'

Durres pursed his lips in a tight smile. He knew that he had pierced to the heart of the collector. And whatever Durres gave he expected it to be returned, in spades. 'Please, it's yours. As a token of our future friendship and our mutual love of culture. Don't say anything more. I want you to consider the view.'

In silence they watched as twilight approached. To their right was the town of Saranda, to their left the jagged Albanian coastline. Before them the sea stretched out, the glint on its waters slowly dissipating. On the island of Corfu the lights had been turned on and they produced a brilliant glow. It was an enchanting sight. Like a vision that would shiver and dissolve even as you reached out to touch it. A jewel in a box.

'Let's have dinner.'

The General escorted Ivan to the dining room. It was classical in its simplicity: a long marble table, wooden chairs, white walls, two life-size Roman statues. On the wall directly in front of the door was part of a magnificent Roman frieze, of troops quashing some Eastern rebellion.

'Third century AD, from Butrint,' said the General.

Ivan raised his eyebrows a fraction. Doubtless, the good General had not stolen it from the nearby Roman town but was preserving it for the Albanian people, thoughtful man that he was. Ivan noticed that one of the statues was of Julius Caesar, a good sign. Megalomania would play an important part in his discussions.

Dinner took more than two hours yet it seemed to pass so quickly. Ivan had little opportunity to appreciate the good meat and wine, nor the goats' cheese and strong coffee that completed it, since the evening was spent in conversation. Pleasantries dispensed with, they talked long and deep of Albania and its politics, and the General soon discovered that his dinner guest had a profound knowledge of his country, its leaders and its current parlous economic and political state. It was a knowledge that the good General knew could only have come from a detailed inspection of the secret service files of a number of countries. Perhaps, research even deeper than that. For unless he was badly mistaken, the man sitting before him was a Fellow of the College and probably the very man who specialised in his country. That intrigued and impressed even Durres.

'Why haven't we met before?' he asked. 'You must have visited Albania a number of times, you know so much about it.'

'I have,' said Ivan. Then he told him of clandestine visits he'd made in the past to Albania's Head of State on behalf of the Master, visits that not even General Durres, as head of the secret services, had known about. They talked on. Durres was even more impressed. Here was a man who truly understood the real basis on which states survived; the furtive workings that went on below the political surface; the secret decisions of cynical men who bound the whole together; realpolitikers who understood power and the ends that it sought to attain. They talked like old friends and political philosophers, about power, its use and misuse and about the need for power to be in the hands of strong men. When Ivan spoke his honeyed words, the General saw himself once more a young man, but with the insight and knowledge of old age; and it burnt and inflamed his heart as power, and the craving for power, always does.

Finally, they sat out on the balcony again. The lights of Saranda and of Corfu shimmered in the darkness. All they could see in the black void were those lights. Yet Ivan knew that the lights were not just lights, they represented a town. And in similar fashion, so the Chinese puzzle box represented the mystery of power and its deepest meaning. For power, like the beauty of the box, entrances and bewitches the beholder. Its fatal attraction, once grasped, cannot be given up voluntarily. Like an addiction, there is only one real cure. More. The Master, General Durres and he were all the same: they all had power and they all knew how to wield it – skilfully, like a rapier in the hands of a fencing master, elusively like an *éminence grise.* However, they also knew that power had become an essential part of them, like ivy attached to a tree, and that after a long period of use it could not be detached without destroying its host.

The General stood up and poured some raki. 'I found your

letter of great interest,' he said. 'And I wanted to meet you in person. Of course, it's always a pleasure to meet a member of the prestigious Institute of Foreign Affairs as well as someone who works for British Intelligence. But beyond this, I found your letter tantalising, so tell me more.'

Ivan smiled. 'I didn't think it appropriate to put everything down in writing,' he said. 'Just sufficient to prove who I am.'

'Quite,' agreed the General. Ivan now felt a subtle change in tone as the Head of the Albanian secret service took over from the ebullient host. Ivan had anticipated it and the approach he should adopt.

'General, I would like your advice on a matter,' Ivan said in a slightly hesitant tone. 'It's rather difficult.' He stopped to frown, as if thinking deeply. 'Suppose I have recently been undertaking research on Albania during the Second World War – let's say, among British secret service archives – and those archives contained captured Nazi intelligence documents which included a list in code of Albanian double agents . . .'

Ivan stopped. The General beckoned him to go on with a slight incline of his head.

'Suppose this material only came into the hands of the Allies after the war when they had no interest in deciphering the list since they had no desire to help Hoxha. However, using modern computers, suppose the list were deciphered, would that not be interesting?'

Durres contemplated the stars, but his mind was elsewhere. 'Yes. Very interesting,' he said finally. He put down his glass on a sidetable and poured another drink. 'Is it a detailed list?'

'Oh, yes,' Ivan answered. 'And suppose, for argument's sake, I had deciphered that list and I was the only person alive who knew who these Albanian traitors were . . .'

'For argument's sake,' said the General. He smiled, a philosophical smile. It was all theoretical, of course.

Ivan continued, 'Most of the people on the list are now dead. However, suppose one or two are in positions of great power in the present Government. In fact, if their previous activities were to be disclosed publicly, there would probably be a constitutional crisis since wartime betrayal is still such a traumatic issue in Albania, what with the massacres of Albanian people by the Nazis and other atrocities. In that kind of situation, I imagine, the present Government might collapse and the military would have to step in.'

'That is possible,' said the General, 'if this were really true.'

Ivan went on, 'I would like to make one final supposition. Suppose there is thirty million dollars in a Swiss bank account, the proceeds of Albanian gold that the Allies paid back a few years ago. And suppose that money can be accessed on the signature of the acting Head of Government. If there were a constitutional crisis someone important – perhaps even yourself,' he shrugged, 'would have to take control of the country for a while. Then you would be the guardian of your country's finances.'

The General considered him, his expression giving nothing away. 'What about the West? What would they say if the Albanian Government collapsed? Wouldn't they do everything they could to support it?'

'Yes. But what could they do if this list proved to be authentic? To authenticate it they would get expert advice from the international institute best equipped to advise on such matters, the Institute of Foreign Affairs, who would ask their expert on Albania to analyse it . . . me.'

'Ah,' said General Durres. 'And the College?'

Ivan grimaced slightly. 'Oh yes, I think they would also ask the College to give its opinion. Secretly, of course. And the College would consult the person most qualified.' He stopped and looked at Durres with a gleam in his eye.

'Ah, now I see,' said the General. He was silent for some minutes. He looked at the stars again. He could feel the sweet scent of power coming closer, and even to an old man, its scent was glorious. Like the deep, rich, smell of mother earth. Invigorating and full of promise. 'Do you read Machiavelli, Mr Radic?'

'Yes,' said Ivan.

'I thought so.' Durres sipped his raki and mused. 'As I understand it, what might happen could be this. Some Second World War documents on Albania are released, who knows by whom? The world press gets hold of them. They are authenticated by the prestigious Institute of Foreign Affairs. The College also secretly advises Western Governments that they are genuine. There is nothing the Western Governments can do. There is a constitutional crisis in Albania, the Government falls. I reluctantly step in and you are paid for your excellent services in exposing traitors.'

'Correct,' said Ivan, 'apart from two things. There's no need to acknowledge my contribution. I am a modest man. And my fee is only twenty million dollars, which leaves a goodly sum for other requirements.'

'I see.' General Durres had always wanted to be Head of State. But it was probably an expensive post, a very expensive one. If not, he'd make it so. 'Of course, the timing would be crucial. To step in at the right moment, when no one else was prepared.'

'Yes,' Ivan agreed.

'And when would I be able to see these documents?' The General finished his raki in one swig.

'Copies of the documents within three weeks,' said Ivan. 'Originals on payment of the twenty million dollars, which I imagine will be the same time as when the coup occurs.' He coughed and carried on sympathetically. 'General Durres, I could understand it if you wanted to be Head of State. Under the old system you most certainly would have been.'

The General laughed. He had always heard that Fellows of the College were clever and knew what motivated men. 'You haven't told me who these double agents are. Name me one name. Impress me.'

'The President.'

General Durres stared in his direction in utter amazement. Suddenly, he grinned, a mighty grin that declared, 'I smell another's death, and my glory.' 'Why are you doing this?' he asked.

Ivan had not the slightest intention of telling the General the truth, of the Mastership Game and his own quest to preserve the College. However, there was something about Durres that he admired, something that was also an ingredient of Ivan. Perhaps it was his detached cynicism, perhaps the ruthlessness of purpose that pricked below the surface of him. Ivan thought: I will be like this when I am Master, but far greater. I will be able to manipulate even this man. The thought did not displease him.

'Let's say I'm a philanthropist, so I need the money. Do we have a deal?'

The General pretended to ponder on the matter, but the decision was already made. Power. You always want more. Julius Caesar had understood the problem as well as the solution. Take more. Life was just a big game anyway. Durres liked games. He smashed his empty raki glass against the balcony wall.

'Done,' he said.

Two days after Ivan had returned to Paris from Albania, Sebastien received a phone call as he was about to go into US Bank in Panama to start his day's work. He listened intently to a man's voice. There was a strange noise in the background. It sounded like rap music.

'Ivan is in Paris did you say? OK, thanks very much. Please keep trying to track down Andrew Brandon.'

Sebastien put down the receiver. So, they'd found Ivan. Al Johnsons Investigations had done a good job. They'd tracked him down through his boyfriend. Oh dear. Ivan really was going to have to improve his game. Sebastien would tell Tanya later.

In their office, Al waited until PJ had completed his phone conversation. Then he phoned his client, Andrew Brandon. Afterwards, PJ wondered what would happen if their clients arrived in Paris at the same time. They would have an interesting get-together with the man they were both looking for. Why were they looking for him? What the hell did PJ care? He got paid just the same. He turned up the rap music really loud.

Heavy money, heavy music.

CHAPTER NINETEEN

Without going out of the door, one can know things under heaven
Without looking through the window, one can see the Way
Lao Zi

August. Taiwan.

ANDREW CHOSE TAIWAN TO MAKE his twenty million dollars.

Taiwan, or Treasure Island, lay only ninety miles off the coast of mainland China. It was a truly remarkable place. Separated politically from its mighty communist neighbour since 1949, this small province of fewer than twenty-five million people had soon become a bastion of capitalism in the Far East where its people developed an economy that was one of the most dynamic and buccaneer in the world. On its small island, Taiwan had many features similar to Hong Kong – a crowded capital packed full of skyscrapers, endless traffic snarls, a population addicted to making money as well as to gambling, casinos and the good life. In short, an entrepreneur's paradise. Andrew decided on Taiwan since it was familiar to him. He had lived there with his parents when young. Also, from Taiwan he could visit China and its capital, Beijing, the place where the craftsman Chang had presented the Chinese puzzle box to the Emperor Kangxi.

There was another reason for Andrew to come to Taiwan, more important than the others. It was one founded on a supreme irony. Taiwan, with all its hustle and bustle, its assertion of self and human cravings, would have been the last place the mastercraftsman Chang would have lived or visited. However, when the communists had come to power in mainland China in 1949, and the former political ruler, Chiang Kaishek, fled to Taiwan, he took with him five thousand cases of the rarest treasures from the Imperial Palace in Beijing.

Among them were three of Chang's puzzle boxes.

'Andrew, what brings you here?' The plump Chinese-born banker greeted him enthusiastically. 'You should have told us you were coming. I'd have organised a dinner for you.'

David Chen directed Andrew to a sofa in the executive suite of the Grand Hotel in Taiwan. They'd known each other for years and had been at university together. Their paths had then diverged as Chen went on to become a successful corporate financier with one of Taiwan's top banks while Andrew had become a special consultant to the UN.

'How are things?' asked Andrew. His friend had become slightly grey-haired since he had last seen him, more than two years ago. There was no change though to his immaculate dress sense, nor to the youthful face and enthusiastic smile.

'Well. Very well. Business is booming. I couldn't wish for better, despite the volatility in the East Asian markets.'

'And the family?'

'Monica is well and the kids are shooting up. The little one's taking after me and concentrating on maths. We'll make a financier of him yet. Anyway, why are you here? Dealing with China-Taiwan relations, pre-handover?'

'No. I've resigned from the UN.'

'Resigned?'

'Yes.'

'Oh . . .' Chen waited for Andrew to go on, but no explanation was forthcoming. Chen was puzzled. Was it that Andrew simply wanted time off? Or had his consultancy with the UN taken a disastrous turn?

A waiter arrived and served them drinks. Chen tried to sound positive. 'Well, needless to say, Andrew, if you want any help, just ask. I've got masses of contacts here. What line of business were you thinking of getting into? They'll be queuing up to give you a job, with your qualifications and languages. Fluent Mandarin and Taiwanese is no mean feat.'

'I wasn't planning to start another career at the moment,' said Andrew. 'There are some other things I want to do while I'm here. I'm looking for an apartment. I thought in the area near the Museum of Chinese Art.'

'Don't worry about renting one,' Chen said with a pleased expression, happy to help. 'I've been doing some property speculation. I've a big flat in a block not far from there. It's free at the moment. You can stay there for a few months. No charge.'

'No thanks. I prefer to rent it from you.'

They talked about Chen's work and his family for another ten minutes. Suddenly, David caught sight of the hour. He groaned. 'Andrew, you must forgive me. I'm afraid I have to go. I've a business reception I just can't get out of. The head of the bank will be there. You know how it is, climbing up the greasy pole.'

'I know.'

'Let's meet up for dinner one night. Monica and the kids would love to see you again. You won't recognise them.'

'Good idea.'

Chen stood up. He had to ask. Andrew was his friend after all. 'Andrew, forgive me for being rude, but you don't seem your normal self. Are you sure everything's all right? No crisis?'

'I'm fine.' His eyes looked back at the questioner calmly. Yet to Chen's gaze they had seemed more melancholy, more troubled, than before.

'David, I'd be grateful if you could keep my presence here in Taiwan confidential. Just you and your wife.'

'Yes, er, sure . . .' Chen said rather hesitantly.

Chen departed. What was going on? When he'd last seen Andrew, he appeared to be fine and very busy with the UN. Of course, it had taken him a long while to get over the death of his wife, Amy, almost a year previously. She was a Taiwanese, a pretty and vivacious girl, a TV presenter with a cheerful personality and a wonderful future. Then she'd died and the child she was bearing had died with her. It had been a terrible blow. However, Andrew had seemed to take it philosophically. Could it be that the trauma of this had now come back to haunt him? Or was it something quite different? Something to do with his work and the UN?

Chen stepped into the lift in a reflective mood. How dreadful to lose your wife and child. What would he do if that happened to him? He couldn't bear to think of it.

The Taiwan Museum of Chinese Art was a large concrete building, modern and functional. Andrew went up its wide steps and through the glass-fronted entrance, past throngs of primary schoolchildren who milled around the counters as their teachers handed out tickets to them. It was a day's outing and the children were waiting to see a special exhibition on Chinese art which the colourful posters in the foyer declared was especially designed for the young. Smartly dressed in miniature uniforms with little shoulder bags, they chattered incessantly, some twirling about on the parquet flooring while others stood still, their hands clasped together and their faces comically wide-eyed as they whispered childhood secrets to one another, locked in a mysterious inner world from which adults were excluded.

'It's upstairs to the right, sir. On the second floor.'

Set well apart from the wide and spacious chambers on Qing and Ming furniture was a relatively small room. The lighting was subdued and the walls were painted a deep seagreen with splashes of white, providing a sense of tranquillity and introspection. This room contained the Chinese puzzle boxes made by the craftsman Chang. Presently, it was empty of people. Silent. Contemplative. Remote. In the centre of the room was a case of toughened glass. Andrew went towards it.

They lay on a bed of green velvet, three in number, stunningly beautiful, with the same black lacquer and filigree that Andrew had seen on the Chinese puzzle box the Master had shown them. Chang had etched in gold an exquisite picture on the lacquer face of each. One was a hunting scene, another was of the city, the third, a temple in a garden. The combinations of these puzzles boxes had been worked out long ago and now they lay open, to reveal the exquisite lattice work inside. In the centre of each box lay a precious stone – a ruby, a sapphire and an emerald. Despite their extraordinary beauty, in some way Andrew felt disappointed. For none of these boxes had the same perfection of detail and haunting attraction as the puzzle box the Master had shown the contestants that fateful night. It had been so much rarer, more elusive, in its approach.

So what was inside the most difficult puzzle box of all? A jewel? Or nothing, as the Master supposed? If there was nothing, what was the craftsman Chang trying to say – the intimate secret he wished to reveal? Andrew inspected the puzzle boxes for some time. Try as he might, their true answer eluded him. He could look and look but still not see. Finally, he made to go. It was sad that so little of Chang's work remained. He had been a craftsman of true genius yet, over the centuries, the wonderful work he had wrought had been steadily lost or destroyed, in wars, by accident or through human folly.

'Are you searching for other things by Chang?' the elderly curator in a red museum coat emerged from a side door to ask him. He had noticed Andrew staring at the puzzle boxes. Andrew glanced at his wrinkled and bent frame.

'Yes, I am.'

'Well, apart from the boxes in the case which you have seen we only have two vases. Other museums around the world have some more of his things, but these vases are the most magnificent.'

He led the way into another room, even smaller than the previous one but painted the same colour. In its centre, behind toughened glass, were two extraordinary vases, their texture given an additional clarity by the natural light that filtered through a ceiling shaft to fall directly on them. They were freestanding, about half a metre in height; their small bases blossoming out into a melon shape that narrowed again at the top to finish in a wide open lip. Cobalt blue and white in colour, they comprised the finest porcelain of the Ching dynasty. The only features to distinguish the two vases were the different pictures painted on one side of each. On the other side, in the case of both vases, there was painted a delicate spray of cherry blossom. Its colours, a clear ruby red and a translucent white, remained as pure and vibrant as the day on which the scene had first been painted.

'Sit down and look at them,' said the old man as he pointed to a padded seat. He sat down beside Andrew. They contemplated the vases.

The first vase depicted Chinese children dancing round a mulberry tree in a pastoral setting. Village elders sat in the foreground and there were high mountains at the back. Chang had excelled himself in his painting; not only by the consummate skill in which he had depicted the spontaneity of the children's play but also the careless ease of their dance. With their heads thrown back and slightly bowed gait, they moved in a fluid motion, faces alive with excitement. Youthful joy and vitality radiated from the vase and one could almost hear their childish laughter. However, the extraordinary thing was that the painting carried over from one vase to another. For one of the children, even as he danced with his companions, had glanced over his shoulder as though he was staring directly at the scene on the other vase. Unlike the others his look was pensive, almost sad.

The other vase depicted a man, an artisan, crossing an arched bridge as he made towards a backdrop of high mountains, as though about to start on a long and hazardous journey. The man's hand was raised in farewell. It seemed clear that this man was the boy's father. The scene was deeply poignant. For even as he crossed the bridge the father had glanced back, drawn by an irresistible impulse to gaze on his son for the last time.

Andrew stared at the two vases spellbound. The person who had fashioned the Chinese puzzle box had also made these incredible works of art; and Andrew had no doubt that the artisan who stood on the bridge in the painting, his face one of untrammelled calm, was Chang himself. It was an amazing artistic sleight of hand. Even though each of the vases individually contained a picture that had meaning, it was only when the two vases were placed side by side that the true focus and overall intent of the vision became apparent.

'What do you know of these vases?' Andrew asked the curator.

'There is a story told about them,' he replied. 'A rich and powerful Chinese merchant once asked Chang to paint a scene on two beautiful vases he had and he insisted that Chang include himself in the painting. In that way he thought the vases would be worth even more. So Chang painted the two vases. But when the merchant saw them he was appalled. For they depicted Chang leaving his son. In China to have a son is the most important thing to do, to carry on the family line. To paint a father leaving his son, therefore, is to paint an act of tragedy. No one would want the vases. Furious, the rich man demanded an explanation.'

'What did Chang tell him?'

'That he had painted two beautiful vases but that the rich man was too attached to worldly things to see this. That even the most important possessions in the world must be given up in order to transcend them and to comprehend their true value. It is also said that Chang quoted the words of a Chinese taoist to the merchant:

> *"Whoever gives weight to what is outside of him is inwardly clumsy."*

You see, for the merchant, his possessions and wealth were the most important things in the world and he thought that by attaching Chang's name to the vase he would gain even more. To the artist Chang his son was the most important thing in the world. To others it might be something else. Yet Chang was seeking to help the merchant understand that to crave these things is actually to lose them. For you no longer appreciate their worth. Detach yourself from such things, however, and you will be able to see their true worth. Craving will be replaced by insight.'

'Do you believe the story?'

'I don't know,' said the old man. 'I only know these are indescribably beautiful vases and I look at them every day.'

There was silence. Then the old man continued his reminiscing. 'It is strange how these vases attract and hold you, do they not? There is a man who comes here once a year. He sits and looks at these vases all day and then he departs. He has come here ever since I have been curator, for more than twenty years now.'

'Who is this man?'

'I don't know,' said the curator. 'He never talks.'

Andrew continued to stare at the vases. In a flash of insight the truth of the Chinese puzzle box began to dawn upon him. For the puzzle box and the Mastership were one and the same. The first illustrated the nature of the second. It contained nothing. Yet, at the same time, it contained all.

And the man who came to gaze on these vases could only be the Master.

CHAPTER TWENTY

Pope Alexander VI never did or thought of doing anything but deceive others; and he always found someone to trust him. There never was a man who gave more convincing assurances or backed them up with greater oaths; and never a man who kept his word less. And yet he could always deceive people whenever he liked, being a great master in that art.

Machiavelli, *The Prince*

September. Panama.

'It's time to start the sting.'

Tanya came from the kitchen of her small apartment carrying two rum and Cokes. She placed them on the coffee table. Then she sat in an armchair opposite Sebastien, who reclined on her sofa with a hand over his eyes. It was two in the morning and he'd only just arrived. Tanya wondered where he'd been. Probably out with his drug dealer friend, Juan, whom she'd never met but whom she'd heard a lot about from Sebastien. She was worried about Sebastien's mixing with that kind of person. Not just the danger – his behaviour towards her had begun to change, he seemed to be more unfeeling and he hadn't touched her for days. She wondered whether he had been down to the brothels with his friends. They were drawing apart. It had to come. Gemma jumped on her lap. At least there was someone who still needed her.

'Are you sure?' she said.

'Sure. We're running out of time – only four months left and we still have to find Andrew and Ivan.' Sebastien yawned and sat up. The heavy partying with Juan was beginning to take its toll. 'Is there a problem?'

'No. I'm going to miss Panama.' She would be sorry to leave, she reflected. Tanya liked the climate of the country and the people. She'd come back one day. That is, if she survived. For whoever had killed Rex and had attacked her was still out there. 'How much is in the account?'

'In Panama, just under twenty million dollars. In Switzerland, two.'

'We need either twenty million dollars for one or forty million for both of us.'

'We don't have enough time to wait until there's forty million,' said Sebastien brusquely. 'Besides, I don't think Gonzalez will ever put that much into one account. Now's the time to act. I'm going to clear out whatever's in there. The less money Gonzalez has, the less chance he'll be able to come after us. Besides, he's going to have a lot of explaining to do to his Colombian partners.' He chuckled.

Sebastien also had a good idea what might happen to Juan when Gonzalez discovered his money was missing. Gonzalez was not the sort of magnanimous man to overlook a small accounting error. That gave Sebastien pleasure rather than pain. Juan would deserve all that he got.

'What are you going to do?' Tanya asked.

Sebastien explained, his eyes closed with tiredness. He was going to Switzerland for a few days. He'd told Ted Baxter, the head of Fixed Deposits, he was taking some holiday. He would appear at Banque Lex and instruct them to move all the money that lay in Gonzalez's Swiss account on a certain day to an account in New York. From there it would pass round the interbank network, to accounts Sebastien had opened in Tokyo and Bermuda. Finally, the money would end up in a joint account which Sebastien had opened in their names in the Caymans. Banque Lex would have no problem in transferring the money since they'd think Sebastien's forged signature was that of Gonzalez. However, Sebastien wanted to appear in person to make it even more convincing. There could be no hiccups. Their lives were on the line.

Tanya nodded and sipped her drink. 'Yes, but whose money is this, Sebastien, for the purposes of the Mastership Game? Yours or mine?'

Sebastien hesitated. This was going to be the trickiest part and would require some careful manoeuvring. Only one of them could win and he was determined that it would be him. Tanya would get over it in time, he was sure. He'd make it up to her somehow. However, it was vital they didn't part company yet since it required both of them to effect the sting. The Chinese tactical genius Sun Tzu had said that nothing was more difficult in war than the art of manoeuvre. What was difficult about it was to make the devious route the most direct. Tanya must want the Mastership just as much as he did, so deception was the key – even between lovers.

'I don't think we should discuss this now, Tanya. Let's just keep the money in the joint account. There's no rush, provided the twenty million dollars goes to the College by the end of the year. There's no point in squabbling over this at the moment. We should concentrate on getting the money first, then decide who goes for the Mastership. Besides, there's still Ivan and Andrew to consider. Possibly, the Master as well since we both agree he'll not give up power unless he has to.'

Tanya adjusted her red silk gown and made an affirmative gesture. It wasn't worth arguing with him at this stage. Patience was the key. 'I agree. What next?'

'After I return from Switzerland,' continued Sebastien, 'I hand in my resignation to US Bank. Three weeks later, I depart. The day before I leave the bank we transfer all the money. Next day I fly to Miami. You also take a few days off on holiday and come to Miami, on a separate flight. We celebrate. You return to the bank and resign, let's say, a month later, just to make sure that no connection is drawn between us both. By the time this has happened, it will be November and I'll have tracked down the others. We meet up in Europe and work out how to deal with them.'

'OK.' Tanya put down her drink. Sebastien could see that she was unhappy with something.

'Is there a problem?'

'No. Well, yes. I'm frightened about what will occur if Gonzalez or US Bank finds out. If it's Gonzalez, he'll kill us. If US Bank, we're looking at a long prison sentence.'

Sebastien laughed. 'That adds spice to it all. Don't worry, Tanya, nothing will go wrong. I swear. Trust me.'

But he could see that she was unconvinced and worried about the consequences of their actions. 'Look, Tanya, we have to go through with this. We have no option. If we don't win, we are no longer Fellows of the College. We also stand the risk of being wiped out. But if either of us wins the Mastership, we hit the jackpot.'

'Suppose we refuse to go on?'

'Yeah,' said Sebastien sarcastically, 'great idea. Then we risk the others killing us for nothing. Do you think they'll just accept we are no longer playing? What about Rex? And suppose we were to break our oath of secrecy and tell the world about the game – who would ever believe us? The College would deny everything, we have no proof and we have no influence. For all we know, that's exactly what Max Stanton tried to do and look what happened to him. I think we should stick to winning, don't you? We elected to take part in this game and we have to suffer the consequences. I'm not stopping now. Nothing will go wrong, I promise. Don't chicken out on me now.'

Tanya felt very tired and she wanted to go to bed. Even if the sting was successful, there were other loose threads to tie up. She switched tack.

'Do you really think the Master is involved in this contest?'

Sebastien closed his eyes again. 'Tanya, that's the really big question. The answer is that I still don't know. It's so difficult to find out who and what the Master is. What information do we have about him? We know he was a Fellow of the College thirty years ago, and that he once was a contestant for the Mastership in a game which I assume was similar to our own. We've also been told that the Arbitrators, and not the Master, control this contest. But is he playing? I'm not sure. If he is, he'll be a formidable opponent. The most formidable of all. This guy has been Master for years. He'll know all the tricks about the use and abuse of power and he has huge resources at his command.'

'Do you think he's evil?'

Sebastien slicked back his hair. 'What's good and evil when applied to someone in the position of the Master? It's like asking whether the Pope is good or evil. Do you mean the man or his office? As the representative of God on earth, technically, he can do no evil. However, the medieval popes, especially the Borgias, construed their role somewhat liberally. Fornication before faith, murder before mass. Must have been great. What I believe is that the Master is one of the most brilliant people of our time and he has influence beyond our ken. Therefore, he should never be underestimated.'

'Will he turn to evil?'

'Oh yes, I think so,' said Sebastien, 'if necessary, to preserve his power. Look, as Master, you wield enormous power in terms of the advice that you give and the information you pass on to leaders of countries. And in wielding it you have to make ruthless decisions sometimes. The greater the power, the more ruthless the decision may have to be. That's just the way it is. Besides, there can only ever be one winner in this contest.'

'And wielding power includes killing people?'

'Yes,' said Sebastien, 'in the final analysis it may include killing people. Don't tell me you don't know that, Tanya.'

They contemplated each other in silence. Sebastien poured another drink. Now they both knew where they stood.

The path to the Mastership was a murky one.

October. Switzerland.

'The general manager will be with you shortly.'

The entrance hall to Banque Lex bore no indication that it was part of a bank. Rather, it seemed like a nineteenth-century country house in a superior part of Geneva. It was from an era of customer service that had almost disappeared – one of due deference and studied formality. Sebastien liked that. It amused him. He gazed at the painting of the cherubs on the ceiling, their fleshy colours given an added sheen by the huge crystal chandelier. Sebastien was pleased to think he had chosen this bank for Gonzalez – it showed real taste. That would, at least, ascribe one positive feature to the drug dealer.

'Señor Gonzalez!'

The general manager approached along the red carpet, walking like a crab, his back bent in an almost perpetual statement of obeisance. He fingered Sebastien's hand as if it were a religious object. It was, for mammon was his god.

'I am charmed to meet you, charmed.'

Sebastien smiled in reply and soon they were chatting together like childhood friends. A few million dollars soon made anyone a childhood friend, bank managers especially.

'I have come about my account.'

'Of course, sir.' The general manager beckoned Sebastien into a side room. Immediately a flunkey appeared with a full tea service and a wonderful arrangement of bonbons. Sebastien took one.

'I have decided to move some of my money to another account I have.'

'That will not be a problem at all, sir. Simply tell us when you want to do so.' The general manager could see from the very fine cut of Señor Gonzalez's clothes that he was discerning. Further, his English was quite impeccable, no trace of a Spanish accent. And, of course, the reference from US Bank was excellent; he looked even more distinguished than his photo. Just the kind of client they wanted.

'You will receive a large amount of additional funds from

Panama in three weeks time. When you do, I want to move twenty-two million dollars from my account with you,' said Sebastien. 'I'll tell you why.' He leant forward, waiting until the elderly man had placed his proboscis as close to his own as possible, like two conspirators. 'My wife's found out that I have money here and in Panama.'

The elderly man's eyes opened wide in shocked sympathy. He knew exactly the problem. There was no need to say more. He took a bonbon to calm himself as well.

'Here are the instructions,' said Sebastien. 'And here is the account to which the money is to be moved. Please transfer the balance of the funds immediately. Of course, I don't want to close my account with Banque Lex.' Sebastien smiled graciously. 'I will be placing more money in it, but perhaps not quite so much this time, a smaller sum for my wife to use.' He winked.

'I understand totally,' said the general manager. Ah, the problems of being a multimillionaire and having a rapacious wife to support. So difficult for the plebs to appreciate.

The vulgar business of money having been dispensed with, over tea, they had a long and polite conversation about the political situation in Switzerland. It hadn't really changed for the last two hundred years.

Sebastien departed. From the window the general manager watched while the flunkey held up an umbrella for the client as he got into his hired Rolls Royce. Sebastien waved him goodbye and the flunkey traipsed back inside. Such a gentleman, thought the general manager. And with such a good knowledge of Switzerland. You'd have thought he lived here. A pleasure to deal with. He would long remember him.

One week after returning from his holiday in Switzerland to Panama, Sebastien submitted his resignation to US Bank. The manager took it philosophically, but Ted, the head of Fixed Deposits, was heartbroken. Sebastien had become his boon drinking companion, and they got on so well together. With great sadness, Ted pencilled in his diary the date of Sebastien's departure – 25 October. Of course, they'd go out for farewell drinks. He could fit it in just after his Alcoholics Anonymous meeting. Despondently, Ted sat on the bar stool in the golf club watching the manicured grass disappear under water. The rainy season had not yet finished in Panama. Bloody weather.

What the hell did Sebastien want to join another bank for? And in Australia? What was wrong with Panama? Ah well, the spirit moved in mysterious ways.

Ted ordered another.

Wednesday, 25th October.

On his last day at US Bank, Sebastien arrived at Tanya's apartment very early in the morning to confirm that all was in place. It only took a few minutes of hurried conversation. Tanya followed him to the door.

'Sebastien, are you sure you know what you're doing?' Tanya dreaded this day. The reality of what they were about to do was striking her ever more forcefully. All for the Mastership.

'Relax.' He gave a careless grin. 'Are you sure you've worked out the supervisor's part of the code to put on the payment instruction?'

'Yes,' said Tanya. 'Carole handles hundreds of payment instructions a day. When she does a reconciliation of them next week, there'll be absolutely nothing to distinguish the fact that I, rather than she, put down her part of the secret code. I've worked it all out. Trust me.'

That was just it. The moment of truth. Did they really trust each other? One error now and it would be total disaster. What if Tanya made the transfer and then left him in the lurch? What if Sebastien was unable to fool the manager or Ted with the instruction letter?

They kissed each other on the cheek.

'Bye, Sebastien.' She could not determine his thoughts. Would he betray her?

'Bye.'

When Sebastien reached US Bank, Ted was already there, reclining on the couch in his office and looking much the worse for wear. Hastily, he got up and told Sebastien that he'd been preparing for the rigours of the day. Sebastien grinned. It was more a matter of recovering from the excesses of the previous night since they'd both been at the golf club until the early hours. It had been worth it for it was vital that Ted should not be too alert on this special occasion. Sebastien kept a close watch on the clock throughout that long morning, when the time seemed to drag just to annoy him. Eventually, the fatal hour dawned and Sebastien got to work.

Just before lunch he submitted to Ted a number of instruction forms completed by clients. In the middle of the pile was one that he had forged with Gonzalez's signature, to transfer twenty million dollars to his Swiss account. Ted tottered off with them to the manager's office to confirm the signatures. He soon arrived back again. Sebastien felt an iron grip on his shoulder.

'Could you come into my office?'

Sebastien's heart lurched. He scanned Ted's face. It was deadly serious. As in a dream he got up and followed him in. Something had gone badly wrong. They must have phoned Gonzalez. Or had Tanya betrayed him? Sebastien eyed the door. He could get out of the department, but could he get out of the bank itself? They would surely activate the security alarms too quickly for him.

'You can guess what it is, can't you?' said Ted closing the door so no one else could hear. His voice had a nervous ring to it.

'I'd rather not,' said Sebastien.

'Well, you're not getting away lightly,' said Ted. 'I have it all planned.'

'Planned?'

'Your last night. I'm taking you out to Las Cumbres. Striptease will set you up nicely for your new job. Don't say no.' Ted's leathery face was wreathed in a grin as he raised his hands in protestation. 'My little thank you for helping out with the numbered deposits when I was in hospital.'

It took a full minute for the icy expression on Sebastien's face to be replaced with an uncertain smile. 'Ted,' he murmured, 'you just blow me away!'

'Thought you'd like it,' said Ted, rubbing his hands in expectation of another liquid evening and the refreshment of parts that other women, such as his wife, preferred not to touch. 'Here's all the rubbish, by the way.' He passed the forms to Sebastien. 'Have them sent up to the Payments Department.' He nursed his somewhat fragile head. 'And let's get out of the office early.'

'I agree with that.' Sebastien had just taken twenty-two million dollars off Señor Gonzalez so he was happy to call it a day. One mustn't be too greedy. Moderation in all things.

Meanwhile, up in the Payments Department, Tanya was processing the instructions of a myriad clients for the transfer of their money around the world. When she came to one, she typed her own code into the computer. Then, she slipped a disk into the computer's memory. Within a few seconds, the computer had revealed the secret code that Carole, her supervisor, used to authorise the making of payments via the interbank network. Memorising it, Tanya typed in that code as well, just to make sure that Carole had no opportunity to question the transfer. Gonzalez's money began its journey.

Easy money, easy flight.

Sebastien would remember Las Cumbres for the rest of his life. He reclined on a leather couch in the private club while he watched beautiful Venezuelan girls stripping off their meagre clothing as they danced to samba music. It was rather like the party in Colombia, Sebastien thought, but without the whipped cream. He would miss South America. It had been remunerative in so many ways. He watched as Ted lurched across the floor with another drink. Poor fellow, he'd be dead within a few years. He knew Ted had no intention of changing his lifestyle, drinking himself into a liquid grave. It was also clear that Ted had blotted out from his mind the inevitable result. Sebastien thought how strange it was that, when people embarked on a path of self-destruction, they went about it so fast. The direction of people's lives could rarely be changed and once they had set themselves on a course of action it was almost impossible to deviate from it. The Mastership Game was no exception.

'Cheers, Ted. Another one for the long and winding road.'

They bid farewell at the club door. It seemed fitting.

'Goodbye, Sebastien. And all the best of luck.'

'Thanks.' Sebastien shook the trembling hand. He was keen to get away.

'Oh, there's just one thing. Now what was it? No, it's slipped my mind.'

'Not to worry.' Sebastien started down the stairs.

'No. Oh yes. That's it,' said Ted, 'something very strange. I was walking down the corridor this afternoon and just as I was about to leave,' he burped loudly, 'one of the bank messengers stopped me. You know, the one that carries the fixed deposit forms upstairs, Fernando something or other. Anyway, he was most upset. Something about a money transfer in respect of one of the numbered deposits. The one for Gonzalez. Wanted me to check it with Gonzalez.' He burped again. 'Sorry about that, a bit of wind. Anyway, I didn't know what the devil he was talking about. Told him it was none of his business.'

'And did he check it with Gonzalez?' asked Sebastien. His voice had become a little dry. Probably the Scotch.

'Don't know,' said Ted. 'I doubt it. That's not his job,' he said indignantly.

Sebastien gave a rather false laugh. 'Oh, I wouldn't worry,' he said. 'In any case, I sent Gonzalez the payment confirmation this afternoon. It's on file. He was just moving some dollars to his Swiss account. Nothing to be concerned about.'

'Oh good. That's what I thought. Well, goodbye, Sebastien. And the best of luck.' Ted raised his empty glass and turned back to the dancers. Sebastien would never see him again.

Sebastien got into his car. He noticed his hands, almost imperceptibly, were shaking.

* * *

Señor Gonzalez had not become a rich man through ruthlessness alone. He had less appealing qualities. He ascribed to his fellow man the same base instincts that he himself possessed. As a result, he automatically assumed that everyone would cheat on him given half a chance. In the case of Sebastien, Gonzalez had been a little more charitable. He thought that Sebastien would be content with his 'commission' providing he had no other opportunity to get his hands on Gonzalez's money. And Gonzalez couldn't see how he possibly could, since US Bank was a highly respectable institution and everything was done by the book. Also, the money could only be moved on Gonzalez's written instructions, so the system seemed foolproof. However, because Gonzalez was habitually cautious, he had inserted one additional safeguard. A small bribe was paid to one of the messenger boys at US Bank. His task was simple. When carrying money transfer instructions from the Fixed Deposits to the Payments Department he was to note any relating to Gonzalez's numbered account and to phone Gonzalez. In that way Gonzalez could check that his instructions were being carried out. And, of course, since they always were, the phone calls soon became a matter of routine.

Gonzalez stretched out in bed. The work of a major drug dealer had its problems. Nothing in life was ever perfect, even though there were some compensations in his occupation. As with all businesses, providing one could cope with the stress and make some tough decisions, it was a living. Still, one had to keep an eye on the ball. There was no social security if things didn't work out, and things could go up in your face as well as your nose.

'Hey, *guapa*, come to bed.'

He was on holiday in Medellin. With his favourite mistress. What more could he want?

'Come on!'

'In a minute. I'm busy combing my hair.'

Bloody women, thought Gonzalez. Why did they comb their hair to get into bed? He watched her.

Sex. One of the great pleasures of life but not the greatest, thought Gonzalez. Sex was fun. However, eventually, it lost a little of its spice and piquancy, however inventive a man like him was, making due allowance for his bad back and touch of sciatica. In the end even a sybarite got bored of his harem. Then there was money. Make a hundred dollars and people sneer at you in the street, make a million and they become polite, make ten million and they are so firmly embedded up your backside you can't pass wind in the morning. However, in the end money also palled a little. There was a limit to the food and the possessions one could stuff down one's greedy maw.

'Be with you in a minute, darling.'

But power. Ah, that was different. Girls you could play with, money you could spend, but power you could wallow in for ever. It had no depth. It was endless in its pleasures and its scope. Regardless of one's profession, it was the same. The village priest dreamt of becoming Pope, the small-time crook dreamt of becoming Mr Big and the employee at the bottom of the corporate heap dreamt of crowing on top of it. It was the same the world over.

'Almost there.'

Gonzalez was no different to anyone else. Sure, he'd always been wicked, yet the career path was really just the same. With his money, he was now buddies with the Colombian President. Give him a few more years and he'd take his place. Then? Well, Presidential trips abroad, fingers in the treasury, any woman he wanted, every pleasure satisfied. That was the way of the world. Power. Little fish wanted to be big fish, big fish wanted to be whales. Heaven would be the same. Get as much power as you can and hold on to it. God knew the answer. He gave humanity the Bible and a few words of encouragement but he made sure not to give up His own position. Sensible fellow. The meek would only inherit the world in their dreams. Silly buggers.

'Ready.'

Gonzalez turned away from his profound philosophy. Stick to the practicalities. He could teach the wise a thing or two. Soon he was happy. He had his hands full. He liked girls with big breasts and big thighs. The Latin American dream. The bigger the better.

'Let me get on top.'

'No, it's my turn.'

The bed began to quiver, the springs squeaked, the table lamp juddered and Gonzalez was content. Who said there was no peace for the wicked? It was while Gonzalez was concentrating on the most intelligent part of his being that the phone rang. He swore violently and picked up the receiver.

'Who the hell is it?' he bawled. 'I have my hands full.'

'Fernando Lambada, Señor. Your account in Switzerland has been credited.'

'Yeah, piss off.'

Gonzalez grunted and put down the phone. He continued with the task in hand. It was about two minutes later – no one was counting the time – when the air was racked by an agonised cry.

'Honey, I wasn't ready,' his mistress complained.

Another cry followed. In front of Gonzalez's glazed eyes the ground was approaching, and very rapidly.

His mistress clasped him in consternation. Gonzalez's face was engorged with blood that had rapidly transferred from one part of his body to another. His mistress felt him slip out of her, then the full weight of his body. My God, was he having a heart attack? What would they tell his wife? More to the point, would she get to keep the diamond necklace?

'Someone's stolen my money.' Gonzalez gasped out the words like a death rattle.

Thrusting her aside, he hurled himself at the phone.

Sebastien expertly spun the wheel of the Jaguar and swung it down Avenida Balboa. There was a screech of tyres. He turned in to Avenida Nacional.

'How did Gonzalez find out?' Tanya's face was drained of colour.

Sebastien quickly explained.

'What are we going to do, Sebastien? What will this man do to us?'

Sebastien continued to drive very fast. He wanted to get out of Panama City. Gonzalez would doubtless have henchmen there. As the Chinese tactician Sun Tzu said,

'Where he is strong, avoid him.'

If they were going to fight it should be on ground less favourable to Gonzalez.

He turned to Tanya. 'Airports and ports are out. Gonzalez will put people there as soon as possible. That leaves the Pan-American highway. Either south to Colombia or north to Costa Rica. Would you like to go to Colombia? We could visit Gonzalez's ranch?' He laughed good-humouredly.

'Sebastien, stop joking,' said Tanya, angry and frightened. 'You will get both of us killed.'

'OK,' said Sebastien reluctantly. 'Colombia's out. Let's go to Costa Rica.'

'And after that?'

'A change to your holiday plan. Come to Costa Rica instead of Miami and stay with me for a few days, then return to Panama City. I don't think you should be around while Gonzalez is here in Panama.'

'How can we get him off our trail?'

'Don't worry, Tanya,' said Sebastien, his tone becoming more serious as they crossed the bridge of Panama and sped on to the Pan-American highway. 'I'll deal with Gonzalez, and soon.'

'What if Gonzalez finds us?'

Tanya caught sight of his eyes against the flickering green of the dashboard. She didn't say any more for she knew exactly what would happen.

'I would try and get some sleep if I were you,' said Sebastien. 'It will take us eight hours or so to get to the Costa Rican border.'

He glanced at his watch. It was nearly midnight. Gonzalez would not be able to get into Panama until 8.00 a.m. tomorrow, when the airport opened. All hell would be let loose after that. Sebastien put his foot down and the Jaguar shot forward. The Pan-American highway stretched out before them.

Life was going to be interesting. They had a few hours to get out of Panama. Or become food for the dogs.

The private jet went very fast but not fast enough for Gonzalez. He would have shot the pilot if it would have helped but it would only have delayed things and bloodied the sheepskin-covered furniture. The flight from Colombia to Panama took two hours and Gonzalez spent every second of it making phone calls and plotting his revenge. Every imaginable cruelty and torture tantalised his fevered brain and he endlessly refined them down to the smallest detail. As soon as the plane landed at Panama International Airport, the drug dealer and his entourage scrambled out, Gonzalez leading the pack. It was just after eight o'clock on a Saturday morning. Gonzalez pointed to his massive bodyguards.

'Juan, take these two. Go to Sebastien's house. I want him alive, just. Bring him to the plane and kill anyone else there. You lot, come with me.'

He commandeered a taxi and headed for US Bank. Death was on his mind. They got out and hurried up the steps, past the large marble sign.

The doorman listened to Gonzalez, then politely replied, 'I'm afraid the bank's only open for depositing money, sir. If you want to talk to the manager you'll have to return on Monday.'

Viciously Gonzalez thrust him inside the bank and clubbed him to the ground. 'If he moves, kill him,' he instructed one of his henchmen. Then he made for the elevator and the manager's office.

Saturday mornings. They were so good that God must have

invented them. Doug Sullivan sat back in his chair. Nothing important was in the post and his wife had gone shopping. A perfect Saturday.

He flicked on the intercom and spoke to his secretary. 'Suzanne, tell Ted I'll meet him in the golf club in twenty minutes. I expect him to be sober.'

Going to a cupboard Doug Sullivan extracted his clubs. A round of golf – what better way to enjoy life? He made towards the door of his office, whistling 'Dixie'. He opened it, but he got no further. It took a scintilla of a moment for his brain to register that a small group of people had mysteriously appeared from nowhere. More precisely, a raving lunatic and two thugs. Doug Sullivan recognised in the depths of his mind that golfing was out for today.

Gonzalez hurled him back into his office. 'Where's my fucking money, you *hijo de puta*?' he screamed, as he pushed details of his account into the manager's chest.

Stunned, Doug Sullivan eyed the figure before him. Gonzalez was now in a state of apoplexy. Flecks of foam had gathered at the side of his mouth and his eyes gleamed with a maniacal hatred. Still, Doug kept calm. Clients could be so difficult at times. He gathered up the fallen papers and sat down at his desk. As he did so, he touched a small button hidden to one side of his chair. He flicked the intercom as he tried to stop himself shaking.

'Oh, Suzanne, please bring me the file of numbered account 116202339 and the signature cards.' He motioned to his unwelcome guests. 'Do sit down.'

Within a minute the manager had Gonzalez's file before him.

'What's the problem, Señor . . . er?'

'Gonzalez. Someone has taken money from my account.'

'Yes,' said the manager. 'Twenty million dollars were moved yesterday from your Panama account to your account in Switzerland.'

'I never told them to do it.'

'You must have forgotten,' said the manager in a kindly tone.

'Here's the instruction letter on file.' He extracted a sheet of paper from the folder.

Gonzalez snatched the letter from him and stared at it. 'That's not my signature,' he screamed, his head shaking like an alarm clock.

The manager observed this activity, flabbergasted. It was clear the man was mentally ill. 'What do you mean, it's not your signature, Señor Gonzalez? It is the same signature as on all the other instruction letters. And,' he flicked open some pages in the file, 'on the numbered deposit opening forms.'

Any self-restraint Gonzalez had left completely evaporated. Pulling an automatic from inside his shirt he pointed it at the manager's forehead. The air in the room froze. Gonzalez slowly licked his lips, like a wolf about to devour its prey.

'Give me the file.' He thumbed through the pages and then hurled them onto the floor. 'None of them is my signature. Give me my money.'

The manager gulped. He was used to dealing with stupid clients. There was a limit, however. Even when someone held a gun at your head. He was frightened but determined to resolve the matter. Surely, Señor Gonzalez would understand, he was meant to be a businessman.

'Señor Gonzalez, this is your account, yes?'

'Yes.'

'And in the past you've ordered us to move money from this account to your Swiss account. Yes?'

'Yes.'

'And you've had no complaint in the past when we've carried out your instructions.'

'No.'

'I see,' said the manager, though he didn't. 'Señor Gonzalez, you agree we have always carried out your instructions correctly to date. Yes? Fine. You now say that you didn't give this ultimate instruction to move money to your Swiss account. Even if this is so, you haven't lost the money. Simply instruct Banque Lex to transfer it back.'

'I can't!' Gonzalez screamed hysterically. 'The money's gone. Banque Lex say they moved it according to my instructions.'

The manager smiled despite himself. 'If so, Señor Gonzalez, you must raise the matter with Banque Lex. We can't possibly help. However, I have to tell you I am now in real doubt whether you own this numbered account. I must ask you to sign your name, to see if it matches our records.'

The manager took out a pen and placed it on the desk. There was an expectant silence. Gonzalez knew that he had lost.

Doug Sullivan continued, his voice recovering some of its authority. 'Señor Gonzalez, if you have any complaint against US Bank, please return on Monday. The Panamanian legal authorities will investigate your allegations and, of course, you will have to prove the ownership of these funds as well as their source.'

One of Gonzalez's henchman whispered in his ear. The bank had raised the alarm. Armed Panamanian police would soon arrive. With a look of hatred that would have shamed Lucifer, Gonzalez stormed out of Doug Sullivan's office. At the airport, boarding a plane for Switzerland, he turned to his henchmen. By now, events had conspired to drive Gonzalez far down the evolutionary chain. His face had assumed a neolithic quality of beauty and intelligence.

'Find Sebastien,' he snarled, 'and kill him. I want him put through a meat slicer. Slowly.'

Sebastien leant over and stroked Tanya's face. He kissed her on the forehead. She was so beautiful.

'I think we have a small problem.'

They had arrived at the Panamanian border town of Paso Canoa. Before them a long queue of cars and lorries waited to pass through the border checkpoint to cross into Costa Rica. Sebastien had got out to stretch his legs, leaving Tanya to sleep. After a few minutes he had come back to awaken her.

'Bad news, I'm afraid. The border police are searching every car looking for a man who matches my description. Looks as if our friend Gonzalez has contacts in high places.'

'What are we going to do?' Tanya started up, fear beginning to flicker within her once again.

Sebastien pulled out a map. Apart from the border crossing of Paso Canoa on the Pan-American highway there were no other roads which crossed from Panama into Costa Rica. Flying was also out; Gonzalez would already have people monitoring the airports. That left only the possibility of traversing scarcely penetrable mountains on foot. He surveyed Tanya in her thin cotton dress. She would never make it.

'Tanya, there's a hotel not far from here. It's up in the mountains. We should go there for a while. We need to talk about various things.' He got back into the car.

The Hotel Cerro Punto was a small luxury hotel much frequented during the summer months by visitors who came to enjoy the cool mountain air, trout fishing and wonderful scenery. It was also close to the Costa Rican border, which lay not thirty kilometres distant as a crow flew, across mountainous terrain. They approached the hotel up a winding road. Sebastien stopped the car.

'Tanya, I don't want them to think we're together. Gonzalez doesn't know anything about you yet. So I'll drive in and book a single room. You follow on foot. Go into the bar and order a drink. I'll pass by with my room number. We'll meet up in my bedroom in ten minutes after that.'

Some time later Sebastien entered the hotel. He explained at the reception that he wanted to book a room for a couple of nights, to get in some trout fishing. Sebastien watched as the desk clerk recorded the false details he gave him.

The man seemed nervous and on edge and Sebastien noticed that he kept glancing at the Jaguar outside. Gonzalez's henchmen must have already contacted the hotel. Sebastien could feel the crisp thud of a nail being driven into his coffin, slowly.

Tanya entered the bedroom. Sebastien cast an eye in her direction as he finished making up a kit. Her expression told him everything. It was clear she didn't think he'd make it. Her look was one of farewell, as if she was trying to record their final moments together. Sebastien moved to embrace her. He knew they had reached a watershed and that he was trapped. However, panic was not his style.

'Tanya, you should leave now. Go to the village down the road and catch the local bus to Paso Canoa. A coach will pass through there to Costa Rica at three o'clock this afternoon. Take it and cross the border. Gonzalez is not looking for you so you'll be safe. Don't use the car, just in case.'

'What about you?'

'I'll start out over the mountains in a few minutes. I need to deal with Gonzalez first.' Sebastien extracted some papers from his suitcase. 'We'll meet at the agreed venue in San Jose in two days' time.'

'And if you don't come?'

Sebastien sat down on the bed. Time to face reality. 'If I don't, I won't be in the land of the living any longer,' he said. 'And what will you do?'

'I don't know.' Her visage was ashen. 'I haven't thought about it.'

'Well, you need to think now, Tanya,' said Sebastien in a businesslike manner. 'Life will go on even after I'm dead. I think you should complete your holiday and then return to the bank. In a few weeks' time hand in your resignation. After that, you need to start tracing the others.' Sebastien tied up the rest of his kit leaving his suitcase open on the bed. He tried to be matter-of-fact though he could hear his voice breaking ever so slightly.

Tanya stood watching him. She gripped the doorframe for support, the tears silently coursing down her cheeks. 'I don't know whether I want to continue with the Mastership Game,' she said quietly.

'Tanya . . .' Sebastien rose from the bed. He hugged her tightly not wanting to let go. Tenderly, he stroked her hair as she sobbed. The soft and elusive scent of her perfume penetrated his senses, making him feel even more wretched. He buried his face in her mane of hair and they stood together for a while, conscious that their parting might be for ever. Deep within himself, Sebastien began to experience a tiny seed of doubt – to wonder whether he was going to fail after all, that the Mastership, which he'd striven for so fiercely, was beginning to slip from his grasp. Brutally, he suppressed the thought. At last, he said, 'Tanya, you must continue. We have completed the first part of the contest, the most difficult part. Now you simply have to appear before the Master.'

'What about Andrew and Ivan?'

His face suffused with a deep anger. 'Andrew must never become Master. He has already killed Rex. He must be stopped.'

Tanya stood back. 'So you think Andrew killed him? I knew you were holding something back from me.'

'No, I wasn't,' said Sebastien. 'I was going to tell you anyway.'

He sat down on the bed, weary. Sebastien explained to her that he had come to the belief that Rex had been killed because he had foolishly told one of the other contestants about Max Stanton and that the game was a killing game. That seemed to be the only reasonable explanation. The killer had decided to take Rex out early on in the contest to prevent him from getting a head start and to keep the knowledge to himself. The killer could only have been Andrew or Ivan, and Sebastien personally did not think that Ivan was capable of killing people. Ruthless yes, a member of the secret services yes, a murderer no. It had to be Andrew. It was also Andrew who had attacked Tanya in the chalet. He was going to tell Tanya this when he'd gathered together further evidence. Tanya listened in silence.

'Couldn't someone else have killed Rex?' she asked.

'Tanya, who? Rex's death was not an accident and I don't believe the Master killed him. He wouldn't have shown his hand so early on, even if he is playing this game. That leaves only you and me.' Sebastien looked at her directly in the eyes. 'Do you think it was me?'

'No,' she said after a moment. She turned her head aside, wiping the tears away with her fingers. 'I don't want to go on.'

Sebastien sat with her and waited for her to calm down even though he knew every minute that passed reduced his chances of staying alive. 'Tanya, you must. For me. If you really love me. Do you love me?'

'I do,' she said, 'and I always have. If it was between you and the Mastership, I would have chosen you.'

Sebastien eyed her in disbelief. 'Would you?'

She nodded, her cheeks still fresh with tears. 'Of course, I want the Mastership. However, I also love you, and I know that you love me. Sometimes you have to choose what you love more.'

Sebastien nodded slowly. Then he continued, his voice low and determined: 'Tanya, I want you to promise me you'll find Andrew and kill him. It would be disastrous for the College and the world outside if he were to become Master. I have never asked anything of you before, but I ask now. This is a matter of far greater importance than your destiny and mine. If Andrew becomes Master, he will destroy the whole institution. You know that. Promise me.'

She backed away, horrified. Sebastien went on: 'Not only for the Mastership, but to save your own life, Tanya. For once the killing starts, it's impossible to stop. Andrew will come after you, mark my words. He will not stop.'

Tanya stared at him. She knew she would not see him again. Sebastien continued, his face pale but resolute, as he gathered together his things. 'Al Johnsons will help. They already know where Ivan is in Paris. And I'm sure they'll have tracked down Andrew by now. There's plenty of money in the Caymans. You must promise me, Tanya, to find Andrew and to kill him. It's not only to avenge Rex. It is for the very survival of the College.'

'You'll get out. I know you will,' said Tanya. 'We'll meet in Costa Rica in a couple of days.'

'Of course,' Sebastien replied in a defeated tone. 'The last cards have yet to be played. But in case I don't make it you must promise me. If you love me, that is.'

At last, through her love for him and with her spirit broken, Tanya promised. She would track down Andrew, then Ivan and kill whoever had killed Rex. They embraced once more. A few minutes later Tanya rose to go, her body racked with tiredness and despair. At the bedroom door she turned to look at Sebastien. Desperately, she tried to preserve a picture of him in her mind – a snapshot for her memory. The lithe figure with the handsome face, sensuous lips and deep, unfathomable eyes. She departed, her farewell complete.

When she reached the bottom of the slip road to the hotel, Gonzalez's henchmen, Juan and two others roared past her. Tanya didn't notice them. She was deep in thought.

Tanya had never told Sebastien about the intruder who'd entered Rex's room at the College the day she had discovered his message on the computer. Someone who would have had a vested interest in stopping Rex from disclosing what he knew about the Mastership Game at an early stage.

The Master.

Switzerland.

'The general manager will be along in a minute.'

'I want to fucking see him now. Now!'

André, the rather effeminate flunkey at Banque Lex, regarded Gonzalez with complete astonishment. Never had a client spoken to a member of staff in that manner. He flounced off, his long blue tails between his legs. He was nearly in tears.

After a while the general manager appeared at the end of the corridor and traversed it in his almost prone position of subserviency as usual. He held out his hand

'Mr, er . . .'

'Gonzalez. I want my money, *mi plata*!' bawled Gonzalez, ignoring the proffered digits.

The general manager noticed the tattoos on his fingers. 'Oh dear, oh dear,' he murmured to himself. One could always tell a gentleman before he opened his mouth. Gonzalez was living proof of that. 'Of course, sir. Would you like to come this way?' He led him into a side room. 'How exactly can we help you?'

'I want my money,' said Gonzalez, smashing his fist down onto the antique table as he emphasised each word. He threw his bank statements onto its now scratched surface. 'I want my twenty-two million dollars.'

'No problem, sir,' said the manager. 'I'll be back in just one moment.'

Gonzalez marched up and down the conference room while the general manager scuttled away. On the manager's return three gentlemen appeared with him. They all smiled pleasantly and sat down as if they had assembled for a business meeting. Outside, a Swiss clock chimed. There was silence. Gonzalez wondered whether he'd overreacted. It all seemed so civilised. Perhaps it was just a clerical error?

The general manager glanced at his colleagues. His craven manner had now been replaced by a tight smile. 'I'm afraid there's a small difficulty. The money has been moved to an account outside this bank. You see, we had written instructions to do so. Señor Gonzalez personally came to the bank last month and talked to me, a delightful gentleman.' He carefully emphasised the ultimate word.

When this information had penetrated his cranium at last, Gonzalez stood up and revealed his true feelings. Quivering with fury, incapable of words, Gonzalez gave an impressive performance of a neolithic man who suddenly finds himself caught up in a New York traffic jam. The general manager and his companions viewed his novel acting début with polite interest. After some time the general manager gave a slight cough by way of a dénouement.

'If I may show this to you, Señor Gonzalez . . . It's a fax I have just received from Panama. It contains very full and detailed allegations about you and your assets in Colombia. Also, about drug trafficking.'

Gonzalez stepped back as the awful truth began to hit him. The general manager smiled at him again. The same placid smile he gave when clients had overdrawn their accounts. 'There are some people who would like to discuss this matter further with you.' He turned to his companions.

'May I introduce Chief Inspector Drucker of the Swiss Drug Squad and his colleagues.' He frowned apologetically, 'I'm so sorry I can't offer you tea and bonbons.'

CHAPTER TWENTY-ONE

He leads the enemy deep into hostile territory and there releases the trigger.

Sun Tzu, *The Art of War*

Panama.

SEBASTIEN SAT IN THE WOODS above the hotel. He watched Juan and his two companions get out of the truck. The situation was worse than he'd anticipated. Gonzalez must have guessed he'd make for the Costa Rican border and sent Juan and his thugs up to Paso Canoa by plane earlier that morning.

In the courtyard below things were hotting up. 'Pedro Gordo,' Juan jumped down from the truck and shouted to one of his passengers, 'you stay here and get the guns out the back. Pedro Flaco, you come with me.' They entered the hotel.

Sebastien passed into the woods. He had to put himself in the mind of his enemy if he wanted to stay alive. Sun Tzu had observed:

> *'Invincibility depends on one's self; the enemy's vulnerability on him.'*

Well, his enemy was formidable. Juan would stop at nothing to kill him, and he couldn't really blame him. Gonzalez would have him exterminated if he didn't bring back a corpse. Juan had also chosen his companions well: two of the most unpleasant people in Gonzalez's little troop of warped personalities and psychopathic killers. Pedro Gordo, fat Pedro, made a speciality of torturing people even after they told him what they knew. Being conscientious and service oriented, he was anxious to provide too much service rather than too little. Also, it was rumoured, he had a collection of human body parts in his freezer at home. Thin Pedro, Pedro Flaco, was a former trapper who had turned animal hunter to man hunter.

Not much vulnerability there. Meanwhile, Sebastien was alone and he had nothing apart from a small sheath knife to fight with. He could only think of two things in his favour. The terrain would be unfamiliar to all of them. Also, Juan would be in such desperation to get hold of him that he might make an error. It was a faint hope. However, it was important to have something to focus on.

Juan appeared outside the hotel. 'He's gone,' he said to Pedro Gordo. He pointed towards the rocky terrain at the back of the hotel leading in to the woods 'Time for some hunting.' Juan laughed, a wolf-like cry. Dissecting Sebastien would be a change from motorbike killings. Besides, fresh air was good for his health. He and Sebastien had a lot to talk about.

Unfinished business.

The border region between Panama and Costa Rica is diverse. Near Paso Canoa it is rocky and thickly wooded in most places. In others the farmers have started to cut down much of the woodland to make way for cattle ranches. Further north, as a person travels from the region of Chiriqui into that of Bocas del Toro, the woodland degenerates into very dense and mountainous jungle. Overall, the region is sparsely populated, with a few native Indian tribes scattered over a wide area. Given the thick canopy of trees, it is also impenetrable by road or by air. One of the last wildernesses in Central America. Sebastien made for it as fast as he could.

Sebastien decided that Juan would likely assume he'd try to cross into Costa Rica as soon as possible and make for its capital, to lose himself in the crowds. As a result, Juan would probably have already told Gonzalez's henchmen in Costa Rica to go to the border. So, if Sebastien wanted to stay alive, he should do the opposite. As Sun Tzu had said,

'Do not let your enemies get together.'

Sebastien quickened his pace. He wanted to get to the river Changuinola by lunchtime. It was an interesting river he'd once read up about in a tour guide. Worth a visit.

Three hours into the jungle and the going was getting tough for everyone.

'Come on, you fat, fucking pansy,' Juan screamed at Pedro Gordo, 'or we'll leave you behind.'

Pedro Gordo was not a contented man. Lugging twenty stone of flesh around a Panamanian jungle was not an enjoyable task where the ground temperature exceeded a hundred degrees Fahrenheit. He looked up at the sky. There was none. The jungle trees which towered above him completely obscured the light from penetrating through their foliage. As a result, it was not only intensely hot, it was dank and gloomy. Pedro Gordo slashed away at the creepers and vines hoping there were no snakes. For a man whose only experience of jungles was watching videos (he liked the killing scenes) the reality of nature was an unpleasant surprise. Already the gnats and the leeches were beginning to plague him and he peered around fearfully at any moment expecting to see the presence of a lion or a tiger, unaware that Panama had none. A considerable distance ahead Pedro Flaco and Juan were progressing fast and talking excitedly. Flaco reckoned that Sebastien was less than half an hour in front of them and tiring rapidly. They were discussing what they would do to him.

Pedro Gordo sighed as he lumbered on. He was beginning to think about alternative employment. Torturing humans was a skilled occupation and one met interesting people. However, he wasn't sure one could make a lifetime career out of it or whether it was another dead end, like all the previous work he'd had – butcher, drug courier, assassin. He pushed branches aside, moodily reflecting on this. What he would really like in life was to get into the food business. A small restaurant in Bogotá would be fine. Nothing lavish. After all, he liked his food and he was a customer-friendly person at heart. These thoughts continued to provide him with a crumb of comfort as he continued plodding his slow way to hell. Soon his companions were lost to sight.

By lunchtime, Pedro Gordo had reached the banks of the river Changuinola. It was murky and slow-flowing. Huge trees overhung its banks, festooned with creepers. The atmosphere was foetid and there was something deeply unsettling about it. Pedro Gordo felt frightened. He was lost. He'd tried shouting out to that bastard Juan and to Pedro Flaco but whenever he followed the direction of their return calls he seemed to lose his way even more as the jungle distorted the sounds. How would he cross the river?

Just then Pedro Gordo saw a faint movement on the opposite bank, not twenty metres away. Extracting his binoculars he focused on it. Suddenly, a huge sense of pleasure rippled through his corpulent body. He couldn't believe his eyes. On the opposite bank Sebastien lay, half naked. He was crawling feebly in the mud. It dawned on Pedro Gordo what had happened. In his flight from them, Sebastien had clearly injured, or broken, his leg. Exhausted, he'd swum the river and then collapsed on the opposite bank, unable to go further. Oh what joy.

Pedro Gordo, who was an intermittent Catholic, thanked God, here was his moment of salvation. If he found Sebastien, his reward from Gonzalez would be great. Gonzalez would probably even let Gordo exact his sweet revenge on Juan for leaving him. Of course, Pedro Gordo would need some token to show Gonzalez that he'd found Sebastien. His head would do. Perhaps even just an ear. No point in carrying too much around. As he witnessed the continued agony of Sebastien on the further bank, Gordo salivated both with delight and frustration. How could he get to his prey before it escaped? It was too difficult a shot across the river. Inspiration came. He'd creep up on him. Hurriedly, Pedro pulled off his clothes apart from his Levis. Wrapping his pistol in a waterproof bag Pedro Gordo slipped into the river and began to float towards his unsuspecting victim, borne aloft on the waters like the carcass of some bloated sheep. Who said that God never helped people? It was a lie. God was helping him. He had his eye on Pedro.

'Pedro! Where are you?' The cry came from further down the bank.

Pedro ignored it. 'Fuck them.'

It was as Pedro reached mid-stream that Sebastien squirmed around in the mud and slipped back into the river. He made towards the floating windbag. While he swam, to take his mind off things, Pedro thought of his restaurant and the food he would serve. Pizza, fried chicken, battered fish. Pedro had all the right ideas. It was just a pity Pedro had not dedicated more of his busy life to a study of the latter, for as he swam he was not alone. *Serrasalmus nattereri* swam with him by way of company. Suddenly, Pedro felt his ankle being grasped and a stab of pain. He turned to see Sebastien frantically swimming away. He'd slashed him in the leg.

'*Puta!*'

Pedro stopped in the water for a moment. It was only a scratch. He sniggered. Sebastien had nothing more than a knife on him. All the better. Leisurely, he made for the bank. As he was doing so *Serrasalmus nattereri*, the red-bellied piranha, attacked.

'Fucking hell,' said Juan.

They watched the spectacle further down the river. The piranha when isolated is a nervous and timid fish. When in shoals, however, the twelve-inch freshwater carnivore is the most ferocious creature in the world and unstoppable once it has tasted blood. Its powerful jaws and razor-sharp interlocking triangular teeth will strip a large animal like a calf within two minutes. In the case of Pedro with all his adipose it took them a little longer and they started from his ankle. Juan and Pedro Flaco watched with horror as the fat one disappeared into a boiling thrashing caldron of water only to shoot up into the air again like a tossed pizza.

Sebastien watched Pedro while he dressed on the other side

of the bank. He turned away from the aquatic display. Shame on Pedro. Everyone was into the environment these days. Piranhas are found only in Brazil save for one other river, the Rio Changuinola in Panama. Sebastien disappeared into the jungle. Five minutes later all was calm in the water. The piranhas left the carcass and the Levis, still attached to it, to be finished off by the alligators. Pedro Gordo should have been pleased. God had had his eye on him after all. Pedro had discovered his true vocation.

Lunch had been served.

Hours passed. It was late afternoon. Sebastien had quit the jungle and made towards the Costa Rican border once more, Gonzalez's men still hot in pursuit. The landscape had changed. they were back into rocky terrain and scrubland with intermittent deciduous forest. It seemed clear that Sebastien would try to cross the border into Costa Rica by nightfall.

'He's slowing down,' said Pedro Flaco delightedly.

'You said that before, you cretin,' Juan reminded him.

Yet half an hour later God was to help Juan. He tapped his companion on the shoulder. They peered through the telescopic sights of his rifle. Silhouetted against the darkening sky, Sebastien had crossed a rocky outcrop and was stealthily making for some trees. Juan chuckled. With great care he lined up the shot. As Sebastien reached the ridge, he squeezed the trigger. The air rang with the noise of the retort. The body swayed and then toppled over.

'Come on, he's ours.' They got to their feet and ran forward.

The bullet had nicked Sebastien in his left arm, near the shoulder blade, hurling him off balance to the ground. Blood spurted out. He grimaced with the pain.

'Shit.'

Not what he had expected. He lay on the ground for a moment, badly stunned. Sebastien had made an error. He had been too clever after all. He should have guessed that they would have telescopic sights with them. Probably night sights as well.

As he lay there in agony, he experienced fear. He had made a mistake by allowing them to get too close. Now the tables were turned. They were going to get him after all. His plan to lure them on until they got to the mountains would have to be dropped. Gritting his teeth with the pain, Sebastien clamped a handkerchief over the wound and forced himself to his feet. He could hear them clattering over the rocks below. Sebastien made for the forest. This would be the killing ground, though it was not the ground of his choosing. He disappeared into the dense tree line.

The killers entered the forest warily. Juan motioned with his hand to Pedro Flaco to swing round to the right while he made for the left. The sun was beginning to set and they needed to find Sebastien in daylight. The wood was dense with trees but there were no vines or creepers so their progress was relatively unimpeded. They would soon have him. Then they could chat about Pedro Gordo and share the joke.

Pedro Flaco took his time. A natural hunter he knew the dangers of rushing ahead, especially in the case of wounded prey. He soon found splashes of blood on the leaves. Then they stopped. Slowly Flaco raised his gun. To his right, behind him, he heard a muffled cry. 'Pedro.' It was Juan. He turned towards it. However, in the very moment of turning Pedro Flaco suddenly realised something was wrong. The call was to his right when it should have been to his left.

This moment of inattention cost him dearly for Sebastien, who was actually behind him, released the thick branch. He had bent it back as far as possible like a bow. In the gloom there was a swish and the knife, tied to it, arched across the path with all the force and tautness of an arrow. It embedded itself in Pedro, the narrow tip penetrating his spine at the sixth thoracic vertebra. There was a savage hiss of air from his lungs on the impact. Then Pedro Flaco began to scream, the tone shrill and agonised.

It was not difficult for Juan to locate his erstwhile companion even in the absence of the noise. Through the sights he espied him transfixed, his back to a tree. He waited to see whether there was any movement from Sebastien. Finally, he went down to him. Pedro watched as Juan picked up his rifle, extracted the ammunition and threw the gun away. He took the handgun from Pedro's holster and did the same. Juan was careful not to disturb the knife, which would kill the thin one if removed. Best left where it was. Pedro tried to focus on him, his eyes glazed, the blood dribbling from his mouth.

'Help me. Please. For the love of God.'

Juan said tersely 'You fucked up. You're no further use to me.' He left him. Pedro Flaco needed to be taught a lesson. Don't piss around when there's serious work to be done. As he walked off, Pedro began to weep and this annoyed Juan. It was not the wretched sight he found unsettling, it was the whine like that of a dying animal. Juan didn't like whining. It reminded him of weakness and since childhood he had never shown that. Any thought of a mercy killing was now out of the question. Besides, Juan had to get away from the place. Darkness was falling and he wanted to find a secure spot before nightfall. Tomorrow Sebastien would be much weaker and Juan's telescopic rifle would be of use again. Juan aimed for the place he knew Sebastien would go to find shelter during the cold of the night: the mountains ahead and the ravine between them.

Pedro was to cry out to an inattentive God until the wild animals found him. Sebastien heard his final despairing scream as he passed into the mountains.

That night Sebastien was busy. The first thing was to keep moving. With his shoulder wound bleeding badly and the intense rain and cold he knew he'd die if he stopped. Tomorrow would be the last day. Yet, now, he had no weapon at all. He gazed across the ravine. On the other side a thin light burned in the darkness, high up among the rocks and precipices.

Meanwhile Juan sat by a small fire in a cave. He ate Pedro Flaco's rations. His own he would keep until tomorrow. From his secure position he looked out. It was pitch-black and the monsoon rain hurtled down, drowning out any sound. Juan was disappointed by the poor showing of his companions. The two Pedros had been a fat lot of good. Besides, Juan didn't feel well. The absence of cocaine was beginning to have an effect on his physical functions. He started to shiver. Still, Sebastien was in even worse shape than he, and that gave him comfort. Tomorrow, he would deal with Sebastien. God had his eye on him. Juan settled down to an uneasy sleep.

At three in the morning, Juan awoke, disturbed by the faintest of noises. Slowly, he stretched out his hand and felt for his rifle. Then he picked up a torch and flicked it on. The apparition before him was rather pitiful.

Sebastien stood there. He had been bending down to look for food. Now he straightened up. His clothes were torn, his hair matted and his left shoulder was badly hunched, marked by a raw chunk of flesh from which blood oozed. Despite the ragged exterior Juan could see that Sebastien had lost nothing of his courage. The face that stared back was calm and proud, the eyes gazing intently at him, the expression one of controlled anger. Juan smiled as he levelled the rifle at his heart. This man had not been what he seemed. He had fooled Gonzalez and he had fooled Juan; and Juan respected that.

'I congratulate you,' he said. '*Señor, tu eres un hombre.*'

For here was a man, a man with real courage. Juan had seen so many men die. He knew the brave from the cowardly. And it took a brave man to accept his fate calmly.

'*Adios, amigo mio,*' said Juan triumphantly. He squeezed the trigger.

Outside the cave, the sound of a bullet made no impact. It was not heard by the wild animals as they feasted on Pedro Flaco. It made no impression on the alligators as they enjoyed the remnants of Pedro Gordo. It was not even heard by the howler monkeys as they chattered under the branches in the ravine below.

The death of a man was nothing to the jungle. The rain beat down.

CHAPTER TWENTY-TWO

The enemy must not know where I intend to give battle.
Sun Tzu, *The Art of War*

October. The College.

AN EARLY SNOW WAS FALLING on Tirah. The Master sat at the table in his breakfast room. On the walls, pictures of the first holders of his office gazed down at him. A large and bulky document, cataloguing human rights violations around the world, lay before him. The Master glanced at it and then turned away. Nothing changed really, he reflected. War, murder, torture, rape, violence, neglect . . . the litany of cruelty remained depressingly the same down the centuries. For power corrupted people so insidiously that it stripped them of their humanity as quickly as taking off their clothes.

Symes entered the room. 'Master, I have the Permanent Secretary to the British Foreign Office on the phone. Shall I put him through?'

'Yes.'

The Master went into his study. The voice of one of the Fellows came on the line. 'Master, I am sorry to disturb you but I thought to inform you of some important news.'

'Thank you.'

'We have just had a call from the British Embassy in Panama. A body was discovered in a ravine near the Costa Rican border a few days ago. There was very little left, since it had been out in the open for some time and wild animals had got to it.

They say there was enough clothing and materials though to identify the corpse. A local pathologist also performed a full autopsy.'

'What was the cause of death?'

'A fall. It looks as if the man had been on a climbing expedition and had fallen from a precipice into a ravine. Naturally, one can't be sure since a lot of contraband is smuggled over the border in that area of Panama and he may have surprised bandits and been attacked.'

'And his identity?'

'You asked us to keep an eye on him. It is Sebastien Defrage. His identification was in the name of Sebastien Singleton. However, there's no doubt the body is his. He'd been working with a bank in Panama City and had resigned recently. They assume he went on a climbing holiday before leaving the country for good. He booked into a local hotel and went missing. The British Embassy in Panama contacted me. The cremation will be held in Panama City today. I am very sorry to pass on the sad news.'

'Thank you, Sir Douglas. The Panamanians are clear about the identification?'

'The pathologist's report says there is absolutely no doubt. I've checked with Symes, and the blood type matches what the College has on file. There were also documents on the body and a signet ring which people at the bank identified as being the one he habitually wore. Sebastien Defrage is dead, Master. A short obituary will be published in the local Panamanian newspaper tomorrow. Of course, no mention of the College will be made.'

'Thank you.' The Master put down the phone. He drew another piece of paper to him and jotted down two names.

'Symes, please phone these two people. I'd like them to contact me this evening. I have some news for them.' The Arbitrators needed to be informed, to confirm the position.

'Very well, Master.'

The Master returned to the breakfast table. He ate no more. He was eating less and less these days. Instead, he stared out of the window. Snowflakes were softly falling in the garden. October already – and soon it would be Christmas again. Soon there would be another Fellows' Banquet. Who would wear his mantle at that feast? Who would take the robe from his shoulders?

'Tanya!'

She turned, her black dress rustling in the warm still air. Carole, the supervisor in the Payments Department of US Bank, slipped her arm through hers. 'Such a tragedy, isn't it? What a terrible waste of life. And to die in the mountains so alone.'

'Yes,' said Tanya sadly. 'Of course, I never really knew him. I only met him once in the bank.'

They left the crematorium together. Ted Baxter and some of the other bank staff followed behind. Ted had been particularly upset at the funeral and had wept for Sebastien. People said that it may have been a premonition of his own death a year later from cirrhosis of the liver.

That night Tanya sat out on the balcony of her apartment. Below, the busy traffic of Panama City hummed. Above, the disinterested stars looked down. Tanya gazed at them, the tears glistening on her cheeks.

'Sebastien,' she whispered over and over in her mind. It was impossible to believe he was no longer with her. Impossible to believe that one so clever and talented could have failed after all. What terrible evil the contest for the Mastership had wrought on them in their pursuit of power – contestants brought down by their own ambition and hubris. She wept.

Tanya had waited for Sebastien in Costa Rica for a week, sitting by the phone all day, her holiday forgotten. It was on the Thursday that she received the first piece of news, a small extract on page six of the *New York Times.* Gonzalez had been gunned down while he was being driven from a Swiss prison to court, to be tried for various alleged offences relating to drug trafficking. Doubtless, his Colombian partners had wondered where their ill-gotten gains had disappeared. Tanya felt no sorrow for him. Gonzalez had received what he had so often dealt out to others and his death had probably been more merciful.

The second item of news Tanya read on the Friday. A small paragraph in *La Prensa,* Panama's national newspaper. It was tucked away on the back page next to an advert on car finance and an announcement of a visit by the Bolivian Trade Minister to Panama City. A mutilated body had been found near the Costa Rican border. Briefly, it gave details of Sebastien's assumed identity and his personal effects together with a statement that an autopsy had been performed and forensic tests undertaken. Tanya had read it with horror. She had immediately flown back to Panama and obtained a copy of the autopsy report from the local pathologist's office.

In this report, the life and death of the man Tanya loved so had been neatly summarised in smart black type. White male, about thirty-five found in a ravine at the base of Mount Fabrega. Severe degradation of the body as a result of wild animals, exposure to the elements and immersion in water. Estimated time of death 5–7 days previously. Fatal injuries consistent with a fall off the mountainside of over a hundred metres. Severe crushing of bones and damage to all vital organs. Blood type, personal effects, individual characteristics etc, etc. Tanya read no more, agonised by the vision of Sebastien in that bleak landscape as he was cornered by Juan and his companions. He would not have stood a chance.

She sat out on her balcony for hours, revisiting memories of their time spent together and her love for him. She had so wanted Sebastien to win, not least because he had such a will to achieve his goal. Yet, with the death of Rex a terrible thought had started to gnaw and waste away her love for him: the thought that Sebastien might have killed Rex, that he was the murderer in this killing game. However, her heart had told her it could not be so. Her heart told her that, although Sebastien may have wanted the Mastership, his ambition and desire for power were not so great that he'd have killed for it. So Tanya's mind and her heart had waged war against each other and she had suffered the buffets of each. Now she would never know.

She felt a slight movement brush against her legs and a purr.

'Gemma . . .'

Tanya continued to weep, but she had made up her mind. In one month she would resign from the bank and return to Europe, to track down the others. Andrew first. Tanya would carry on with the contest for the Mastership, and she would fulfil her promise to Sebastien.

Nothing would stop her.

CHAPTER TWENTY-THREE

The farther one goes, the less one knows. Therefore, the sage knows without going through.

Lao Zi

October. Beijing, China.

POWER. THE GAINING AND THE holding of power.

In the Far East, for hundreds of years, all roads invariably led to Beijing. In the thirteenth century the great Kublai Khan founded his capital there, having entered China from Mongolia across the Great Wall to displace the ruling Sung dynasty. It was also in Beijing that the Emperor sat on this dragon throne to rule the Middle Kingdom – a kingdom that for centuries comprised the largest concentration of people on earth under the rule of one man. Finally, it was in Beijing in 1654 in the imperial palace, the so-called Forbidden City, that the greatest of China's emperors was born into an imperial structure of Government already two thousand years old when he uttered his first cry.

Kangxi was a mighty emperor, one of the most remarkable in the annals of human history. Of medium height, his face was pock-marked, his voice deep and he had very bright eyes set within a countenance that was agreeable and affectionate. In the sixty years that he reigned in China he administered the empire with extraordinary diligence, though no dissent to his rule was ever tolerated. For Kangxi, the ideal was peace for the empire and prosperity for his people and to that end he strove until his dying day. Books and literature were one of his passions and in his reign the great imperial dictionary as well as many other works were written under his personal supervision. He himself translated the history of China into the Tartar language. When he died, Kangxi left in his will the statement 'I leave the empire peaceful and happy.'

There was one other feature of Kangxi's reign that was of interest to Andrew: during that period the craftsman Chang had also lived.

In the centre of Beijing, Andrew passed into the Forbidden City, through Tiananmen, the gate of Heavenly Peace. Before him lay the imperial palace, with its nine great halls carefully aligned to central and subsidiary north-south lines, all in accordance with Chinese ideas of cosmology. The halls led up to the very heart of the imperial sanctum, the Hall of Supreme Harmony, the Taihedian, where the mighty emperor used to sit and hold sway over his subject peoples as he exercised his truly awesome power – a power that even the modern day Oval Office was but a pale shadow of in terms of its scope and its absoluteness.

Andrew absorbed the scenery about him. The yellow tiles of the buildings gleamed in the bleak winter sunlight and the air was still. So little had changed in the imperial city. Time itself seemed to have slowed down in homage to a place where probably the greatest exercise of individual control in the history of the world had once existed.

Slowly, Andrew progressed into the body of the palace, passing through its courtyards. It reminded him of somewhere else, of other courtyards where enormous power still resided. He sat down beside a marble bridge. It was across this bridge that the great Kangxi had progressed each time he entered and left the imperial city. In his mind's eye Andrew could see the proud countenance of the Emperor as his retainers bore him aloft in a palanquin so that the Son of Heaven should never have to place his foot on the ground.

Andrew reflected that it was on this same day, in October

1682, that an elderly man had passed over this bridge. Perhaps, the craftsman Chang had also stood here for a moment, to gaze at the goldfish so beloved of the Chinese, as they slowly drifted among the reeds. And to contemplate the vanity of human wishes before he was summoned to present the most beautiful and the most difficult Chinese puzzle box of all. To the most powerful man of all.

What would the craftsman Chang have said to Andrew as he gazed into these same waters and across the centuries?

In one of the warrens of streets behind the business district of Beijing, Andrew had the pedicab driver turn down a narrow lane and stop. He got out and continued on foot past the multitudes of Chinese people and their bikes. They scarcely noticed him as they hurried off to work.

The Historical Faculty itself was a nondescript concrete building located in a small compound. It appeared dusty and unused. Andrew walked up the steps and into the entrance hall. Proceeding down a passageway, he knocked on the glass pane of a door. In Chinese a voice bade him enter.

'Professor Wang?'

'Yes.'

Andrew shook his hand. 'Thank you for agreeing to see me.' Professor Wang was a small, elderly man with a stoop, a head of white hair and watery grey eyes. He examined Andrew with interest. He had been a professor of history and philosophy at Beijing University until the Cultural Revolution when he had barely escaped with his life after daring to criticise Mao Tse Tung. Instead, he had been exiled to a remote province for many years. Andrew estimated that he was nearly eighty. He contemplated the heavily lined face of the professor, marked with deep furrows like a tractor through soil. The lines, Andrew realised, were of suffering.

'Shall we sit in the garden?' Professor Wang led him into a small courtyard. 'I call it a garden,' he smiled, 'even if, as you can see, it is scarcely so.' He pointed to the few potted plants located on a dusty patch of compacted earth. 'In my eyes, it is my garden.' They sat down.

'I wanted to talk to you about the Emperor Kangxi and the craftsman Chang.'

'I see.' The professor waited for him to continue.

'The imperial records in the Royal Historical Archives indicate that in October 1682, the craftsman Chang was summoned by the Emperor Kangxi to the imperial palace. The records also say that Chang was commanded to bring to the palace a puzzle box the Emperor had previously ordered him to make. The Emperor had expressly indicated in his mandate that the box must be the most beautiful and the most difficult puzzle box of all.'

The professor nodded.

'Have you ever seen this puzzle box?'

'No,' said the professor. 'It is believed to have been destroyed over two hundred years ago. I have no doubt that it was a box of surpassing beauty. Chang was the greatest craftsman in Chinese history.'

Andrew paused. Then he said, 'What do you think the Emperor Kangxi said to Chang when he received the box?'

The old professor sat back and raised his eyes quizzically. 'I do not know. You see, there is no record of what actually passed between them. This is extremely unusual, as was the meeting.'

'In what way?'

The old man reflected for a moment, then replied, 'All meetings with the Emperor, whether public or private, were always attended by a multitude of court officials and guards – for the Emperor's protection as well as for show. However, the official record simply indicates that Kangxi talked privately with Chang in his imperial quarters that day and that they talked alone for many hours. This was quite extraordinary, if not unique in Chinese history; and what was said was known only to both of them since no record was kept of their discussion.'

'Why was that?' said Andrew. 'What would the greatest ruler

of all at the very height of his powers have wanted to talk to a simple craftsman about? What do you think?'

The professor went inside. He came back with a small pot of Chinese chrysanthemum tea and poured out two cups of the yellow liquid. They waited for the tea leaves to settle.

'What do I think?' said Professor Wang. 'What I think does not really matter. I am just a humble ex-professor of history and philosophy.'

'I would like to hear your thoughts. Please.'

'Well,' said the professor, 'I think that they talked about the puzzle box that Chang had crafted, and its meaning. I also think that whatever Chang said to the great Kangxi was quite remarkable.'

'Why?'

'Because,' continued Professor Wang, 'we have a faint idea of what might have been said at that meeting. You see, Kangxi himself wrote something in vermilion ink at the bottom of the imperial record. It can only have been the Emperor since he was the only one in the empire permitted to write in vermilion ink. And the Chinese characters are without doubt the handwriting of Kangxi.'

'What did he write? '

'He wrote a quite unique thing,' said the professor. 'And I have no doubt that his officials would have done everything they could to have expunged it from the record. That was impossible though, since it was written by the Emperor and to change even a character meant certain death. Therefore, the record was preserved until the Cultural Revolution when, to my knowledge, it disappeared. Doubtless it was destroyed by the hooligans that obliterated so much of China's heritage. However, I and one or two other people in China, have seen the original. There are also copies. I have no doubt it was Kangxi who wrote what he did.'

'What did he write?'

'The Emperor wrote that he had talked with the craftsman Chang who had brought him a box of surpassing beauty. He also wrote that, at the end of the audience, he ordered a yellow scarf to be brought to him. On this scarf the emperor stamped the great seal of the empire and he ordered Chang to take it. He also wrote that Chang took the scarf and that he left the Hall of Supreme Harmony at the end of the audience.'

'And?'

'That as Chang was leaving the imperial palace he crossed a marble bridge. At that bridge he bowed to the Emperor and he left the scarf on the top of the bridge. The scarf was then returned to the emperor. This was all written by Kangxi in his own writing. There is no reason to disbelieve it.'

Andrew pondered on the words. 'What does this mean?' he asked eventually.

'The meaning is clear,' said the professor. 'What Chang told the Emperor was so profound that the emperor offered him his empire.'

'And Chang refused it?'

'Yes,' said the professor.

After a pause, Andrew asked, 'Who was Chang?'

'He was a simple craftsman who created things of exceptional beauty. He was born in obscurity. It is not known where he died.'

'What was he like as a person?'

'Very little is known about him as an individual,' said Professor Wang. 'Though it is known that he believed in the philosophy of Taoism.'

'Is anything else known about the maker of puzzle boxes?'

'Not much,' Wang replied. 'He is remembered for his humility and for his kindness. As an artist and a craftsman he was one of the very greatest. And yet, though he could have secured huge riches and fame, he wanted nothing of it. His was a natural ability unclouded by material wants and cravings. I like to think that the craftsman Chang was, as the Tao says,

"the emptied man who strolled as he pleased."

That is, he sought to live life according to his own true nature, free of human deceptions, lies and cravings.'

'What of the Emperor Kangxi. What was he like as a person?' Andrew asked. 'More must be known about him.'

'Oh, yes,' said the professor. 'He was a very famous individual and meticulous records were kept on him. He took up the reins of government at the age of fifteen and immediately broke the authority of the ministers who had assumed control when he was young. He fought many battles to ensure peace within the borders of China. He was an enlightened ruler, a soldier and a statesman, a great wielder of power.'

'What doctrine or religion did he follow?' said Andrew. He still did not understand what the Emperor and the artist could have had in common.

'It is unlikely the Emperor followed any from personal inclination,' said the old man. 'We do know that he was greatly interested in the writings of Sun Tzu. In particular, on war as an instrument of statecraft. Have you read *The Art of War*?'

'Yes, but I fail to see how the doctrines of Sun Tzu and Taoism can be reconciled.'

'I'm not sure they can. Both have observations on the State and on the nature of power. However, Taoism approaches these matters from a universal perspective rather than in analysing short-term expedients to win or to defend a kingdom. It also concentrates on the essential nature of human beings since, regardless of whether a person is the ruler of a mighty empire or is a simple peasant, he is subject to the same basic cravings and desires. Only the scale is different. Taoism also considers the end purpose which human beings are aiming for, as well as the means to attain that goal.'

The professor paused. They drank the tea.

Andrew asked, 'Do you think at their meeting Kangxi and the craftsman Chang talked about the nature and use of power?'

'I think so,' said the professor, 'but I am just a simple man. One thing is curious. In Taoism the essential thing is to be free from outside burdens, since they blind you to your true self and your own happiness. Power is a burden. A story is told of one of the founders of Taoism, Chuang Tzu. He lived a hermit's life and was famous for his sayings and his philosophy. A Chinese king was once so impressed by him that he sent him very expensive gifts promising to make him chief minister. Chuang Tzu merely replied that he preferred the enjoyment of his own free will. You see, he understood that the gift was not a gift, it was a burden.'

At last Andrew began to connect. 'And you think that the great Kangxi offered the craftsman Chang his empire because he realised that the person who should be invested with the greatest power is the one who wants it least?'

Professor Wang placed his hands together. 'I think,' he said, 'that Kangxi, despite being the greatest ruler in Chinese history, realised that the man before him was much greater than he. That this simple craftsman was unaffected by human cravings and desires and thus he was able to realise his true self. You see, Kangxi had asked Chang to provide him with the most difficult puzzle of all. And Chang did that. For the most difficult puzzle of all for Kangxi as a human being was to understand himself. Chang sought to show him that, to understand himself and his place in the universe, all his outward riches and power would not help him but that if he looked within his own being, there he would discover what he truly sought. Only there would he find real happiness and fulfilment that would not pass away, like his empire.'

'So when Kangxi offered him his empire it was as nothing to Chang?'

'Yes. But when Chang offered him a puzzle box that contained nothing, he offered him an understanding of the universe and an insight into his own being as a human soul. I believe, you see,' said the professor quietly, 'that the artist Chang, by wanting nothing, had already gained all.'

By wanting nothing to gain all.

Andrew took a trip out to the Summer Palace, the holiday residence built by a successor to Kangxi just outside Beijing. Sitting on the hillside he looked across the lake. On the opposite side were two beautiful wooden pagodas. They were located on islands connected by a delicately arched bridge made of marble. The beauty of the view reminded Andrew of the lacquer painting on the face of the Chinese puzzle box. Much had changed since the death of the craftsman; but these works of natural and human beauty had not and the insight of Chang was as relevant today as it was then.

Andrew sat on the hillside throughout the day – alone and deep in thought. The craftsman Chang – had he really obtained insight into the human condition with the unclouded clarity of a mirror? Had he really just pursued the dictates of his inner being? More importantly, had he followed one of the great principles of the Tao, to find yourself and then you have the solution?

Andrew reflected on this and he came to some conclusions. He would reveal where he was to the other contestants and wait for them to come to him although it was incomparably dangerous. He'd also put into action his own plan to gain the twenty million dollars. After that, he must resolve the position of the Master.

The air became very cold. He shivered as he left the Summer Palace. Andrew now began to comprehend the meaning of the Mastership and of the Chinese puzzle box.

Nothing and everything.

CHAPTER TWENTY-FOUR

When you are ignorant of the enemy but know yourself, your chances of winning or losing are equal.

Sun Tzu, *The Art of War*

November. Panama.

ONE MORE WEEK AND IT was time to bid farewell. *Adios Panama.* Tanya stood against the railings of her balcony. Further down the cobbled street, she could hear the raucous shouts of drunken youths as they made their unsteady way home. In the apartment block opposite the lights were turned off one by one as their inhabitants went to bed, the washing hung out to dry across poles, the carpets slung over the metal railings. The sights and sounds of Panama. It had all seemed so strange to Tanya when she'd first arrived here. Now she was going to miss it so much and she didn't want to go. To leave would be to leave behind many memories of Sebastien. The bars and restaurants where they had met, their lovemaking on the beach, his secret visits to her at night. No future now, not for him, but for Tanya the Mastership Game went on. She went back inside to her sitting room. Gemma sat contentedly on the sofa, her soft purr giving no indication whether she knew of Sebastien's fate.

'Time to get to work, Gemma.'

In her last weeks at US Bank, Tanya had been very busy, but not on the bank's business. Instead, every night, she came home to snatch a quick supper and, afterwards, to turn on her computer. Before she confronted Andrew and Ivan, she wanted to know all she could about them – their backgrounds, their pasts, their secrets, anything that might give some clue as to why Rex had been killed when he was. In the end insight and knowledge would be her only protection against them, she was certain of that. She already knew from her previous investigations, about Andrew and his military connections. Ivan would be more complex, as befitted a spy. But a spy for whom?

Basic information on Ivan she knew. He was a senior faculty member of the prestigious Institute of Foreign Affairs, and highly thought of for the brilliance of his economic and political analysis. Over the last few weeks Tanya had investigated all that she could about the Institute and trawled through its vast range of data and publications. There had been nothing of interest. After that she had accessed the networks of the many academic institutions with which Ivan was connected. Again a blank, save for one helpful item of data, Ivan's national insurance number.

That night and the following nights, sitting alone in her small flat in Panama, Tanya delved long and deep into the global computer networks, Ivan's national insurance number a ticket to roam. For it gave her access to the computerised Inland Revenue files on him. Through them she linked into the British Government's mainframe computers on tax, social benefits, health, births and deaths, passports, customs, defence and many more, an endless databank of information. On and deeper, as she searched police and Special Branch files. Secret services files were more difficult to penetrate. However, the codes and passwords were relatively simple for a woman who had spent her adult life to date trawling the computer systems and networks of the world on behalf of the College. There was always a way in and a way out. This was an essential premise on which all computers were built and in many cases the College had ensured, via its Fellows working in the computer manufacturing industry, that a secret trapdoor be inserted, to permit entry should the College need it. The College had its contacts and its threads everywhere. Where necessary, Tanya secretly used the contacts and passwords of her colleagues at her former place of work, the European Computer Union.

Delve as she might she could find nothing. The College had done a very good job. Throughout the entire system, Ivan appeared as nothing other than a very talented economist working for a well respected institute. No suspicious record, not a whisper of secrets. However, Tanya simply didn't believe it. What to do? Carry on. She had no alternative.

A few nights later the mystery began to unfold. This time Tanya searched the personal records of other faculty members at the Institute. Not the learned academics with the lengthy lists of initials and impressive titles after their names, but rather the plodders, those nearer the bottom of the lists. For she had a hunch. At last, she struck pay dirt. Three of the faculty members had a curiously similar past. Having left university they went into the British civil service. Then, after two or three years in the civil service, they moved into the Institute. Nothing suspicious about that, save for one small detail. While their civil service records contained no further information on these people, their tax coding indicated that some part of the civil service was still paying them. Now why would the civil service still continue to pay them if they were working for the Institute? The answer was soon forthcoming. Despite their salary payments being routed through various shell companies the trail led back to the civil service and then to the secret services. Which suggested that the Institute was a front for the British secret services. More investigations revealed that Ivan not only had a British tax code; he also had a US one. After yet more digging Tanya was sure that, unlike his staid British counterparts, Ivan was also working for the US secret services and, in both cases, he was being paid through dummy intermediary companies.

'Gemma,' Tanya took the purring bundle in her arms and cuddled her, 'our friend Ivan is more clever than he looks. I think he's on the books of more than one secret service. With them, but not for them. I think he's monitoring them for the College.'

To be able to do that Ivan must have some powerful friends in powerful places, which made him a formidable enemy.

That night Tanya couldn't sleep. True, she had found out what she half suspected: among his other roles, Ivan was a spy. How did that link in with the death of Rex though? She still had no idea. Although she was clear in her own mind that Rex was murdered because of something to do with the game, she still didn't know the precise reason. Perhaps Rex had discovered about Max Stanton and was about to reveal that the Mastership Game included murder?

Tanya toyed with the idea. If this was correct, who was the murderer? Was Rex killed by the College on the orders of the Master so that the secret would never get out? Or was he killed by another contestant – who had already discovered this terrible secret and was determined to dispatch Rex first, knowing that Rex might do the same as soon as he had the opportunity?

The Master, Ivan, Andrew or Sebastien. Which one did it? The question kept thundering in her mind. Sebastien didn't think it was the Master. He was sure it was Andrew, though he had no proof. Well, for her part, Tanya didn't think it was the Master, she wasn't even sure he was playing this game. True, she had seen him enter Rex's room. However, it may have been to try to find out how Rex had died.

Tanya thought it was Ivan or Andrew. Yet, all her researches on them had disclosed nothing that suggested they would kill to win the game. Talented, ambitious but then, for God's sake, so was she. Tanya needed something more concrete to go on, something that could clearly exclude one of them. And she had nothing.

These, and a myriad other possibilities, tormented her brain. And despite analysing each one they always led her to a dead end. There was no evidence to prove it one way or the other. Tanya swore at herself. She was thinking in a straight line, not laterally. Her thoughts were a muddle and, therefore, what she perceived appeared muddled, all shifting sands and flux. There had to be some clue, some key.

'Gemma!' It was two o'clock in the morning and Tanya sat up in bed. The cat started up as well and it took a minute for Tanya to calm her. Tanya threw on a nightdress and hurried to her computer. Now she was thinking laterally. On another track.

Whoever had been in the chalet the night she'd been attacked had gone there to find out what information she or Sebastien had on Stanton. How did the intruder know the information would be there? One possibility was that he could have traced Tanya or Sebastien to Boston. Ivan could have done that with relative ease, using his contacts.

But how did the intruder know that Tanya had returned to Sebastien's chalet? That was the big question.

Within minutes Tanya had produced on her computer screen the passenger lists of the flight she'd taken from Boston to Switzerland. There was no record of the names of Andrew or Ivan on it, though they could possibly have given false names and she would never know. Another blank. But suppose Andrew or Ivan hadn't followed her on the flight, but they'd found out she was making such a flight. How would they, or their henchmen, have tracked her after she had got off the plane in Geneva? Someone could have been watching her when she came out of the airport and tailed her when she took a car to Kasteln. It would have been difficult to do, but not impossible.

What, though, if her attacker had traced her in Switzerland through Sebastien? But how? Sebastien hadn't gone to the chalet until after Tanya had been attacked there. What did Sebastien have in Switzerland that could be tracked? Tanya started to think very rapidly. Ten minutes later she reached for a phone.

'Yes, madam, we try to be helpful,' said the young girl at the Swiss Land Registry. 'I'll look up the information now. Please don't worry. I'm sure you paid the bill. Please wait a moment. I'll just look at the screen.'

Tanya patted Gemma and waited. The Swiss girl's voice came on the line again. 'Yes, you paid, madam. The enquiry to the Geneva Canton Land Registry office was made on 13 February. It related to the property of Mr Sebastien Defrage, as you said.

The inspection fee was two hundred Swiss francs, which meant it was an urgent enquiry. And I'm pleased to say the bill was paid.'

'I've got no record of it.' Tanya sounded anguished.

'Because, madam, payment was made by your lawyers, Heidelberg and Schmidt. By direct debit. Dr Schmidt himself made the enquiry. And their address is . . .'

Fifteen minutes later, in Geneva, Dr Schmidt's secretary's voice came through to his office. 'I have a call for you, sir.'

Dr Schmidt took the call and gazed out at Lac Léman, the waters so placid and calm. The female voice was soft and attentive and he was delighted to help as always. Could he get away with charging a fee? he thought to himself. Alas, no. The request was too minor, even in his book. This time the client would escape.

'Yes, the bill was paid. In cash. I remember it well. And by Mr Radic. Yes, he was trying to track you and your husband down. He did succeed? Oh, I'm so glad. If I can be of any further assistance please don't hesitate.'

Tanya put down the phone. So reliable the Swiss. Now she knew who'd attacked her that night in the chalet, but who had not killed her.

Ivan.

CHAPTER TWENTY-FIVE

For men resemble certain little birds of prey in whom so strong is the desire to catch the prey which nature incites them to pursue, that they do not notice another and a greater bird of prey which hovers over them ready to pounce and kill.

Machiavelli, *The Discourses*

November. Albania.

THE NEWS IN ALBANIA HAD not been good for the last fifty years. Even so, the past few days had been particularly depressing. Riots in Tirana and Elbasan, a lynch mob in Gjirokaster, the destruction of police posts in Korça and Vlora. General Durres put down the military report.

'Terrible.'

'It's terrible and it may get worse,' said General Lleshi, Albania's military Chief of Staff. He was a skinny man with grey bags under his eyes and a tremor in his nicotine-stained fingers. 'Do you think I should come to the capital?'

Durres sat with his guest on the veranda and contemplated the town of Saranda, basking in the morning sunlight. 'I think so,' said General Lleshi. 'The military need you there, General. You know how to command respect. This country is beginning to fall apart.'

'And the politicians?' Durres played the good Samaritan and offered the Chief of Staff another cigarette. Anything to help death.

General Lleshi raised his eyes to the heavens and took a long drag to get some smoke into his lungs. 'Chaos. No one trusts anyone else. I've sounded them out. Only that bloody democrat Peza would object to any intervention. The rest will fall into line.'

'Really?' said Durres, pleased. Then, reluctantly: 'Well, I don't know if we should intervene. Are we not overreacting?'

'No,' replied Lleshi in a harsh voice. He brushed aside the cigarette ash from the coffee table and slapped a creased folder onto it. 'It is much worse than you think. Copies of this list of World War Two collaborators,' he opened the folder with nervous energy, 'have been circulating everywhere. The Government is losing control. Although most of the traitors themselves are dead, their families and those of the victims' are at war with each other now that the truth's come out. And look at the names . . .'

'Yes,' said Durres in a sympathetic tone. 'Dreadful what rumours can do.' He gave a concerned facial expression, as if someone had run over his child. He loved play-acting. Julius Caesar had been his favourite part in school plays, apart from the end bit. Now he played for real.

'General,' said Lleshi desperately, 'it's more than rumours. An original of the document has been authenticated by the Institute of Foreign Affairs in London. By their top man, Ivan Radic.'

'I know,' said Durres. It was time to play the moral integrity card to put the good general off the scent. 'But I despise rumours,' he spluttered. 'What we need is proof. I won't damn a man on rumours.' True, in Hoxha's time, they'd killed people without a whisper. Ah, the good old days, the late nights and the bodies . . .

'Of course,' said Lleshi, even more worried. He'd never seen the general so worked up. Things were really bad.

'Well,' Durres idly wondered what he would have for lunch, 'well, General, I am loath to get the secret services involved, particularly in our new democratic society, which I strongly support. However,' a long pause, 'I think you may be right. Perhaps I have underestimated the situation. We need to work together to contain this tragedy. The problem is that the question of traitors in Albania is such an emotive one. Even if the traitors themselves are no longer alive, the burden passes to their children. There could be a complete meltdown of law and order in Albania.'

'Yes,' said the Chief of Staff.

'I think that we need to put the army on full alert and move troops into Tirana,' said General Durres. 'I'll do the same with our secret service personnel.' He winced. 'And I'm afraid I have some more difficult news.' He felt a sudden urge to grin at Lleshi's facial expression.

'This is absolutely top secret,' said Durres. He leant forward, knowing that it would be common knowledge as soon as Lleshi got back to the capital. 'I've obtained details of a second list. In fact, I have asked the expert from the Institute of Foreign Affairs to fly to Albania today to authenticate it. If it's true, we are in for a crisis. The President is on this list.'

General Lleshi gave a good impression of a man swallowing his cigarette. Durres offered him the rest of the packet. Perhaps, after all, he would try that imported Australian wine for lunch, with some olives.

'If that is correct, the military will have to take over,' Lleshi stammered, his face a deadly hue.

'I'm afraid so,' said Durres. He waited expectantly. People were so pleasantly predictable.

'You must take charge,' said Lleshi, 'I won't. I can't. I'm not in good health.' He was pained and fearful. 'Besides, it wouldn't be acceptable. At least you hold a civilian portfolio as well.'

'Oh no, I couldn't possibly,' said Durres. 'To be Head of State would be a terrible burden. I've no desire for power. I am a simple man, you know. A man of the people.'

'You must.'

'Perhaps,' he sighed.

Durres walked to the door with the Chief of Staff. As he got into his battered limousine, the latter turned. 'General Durres, I order you as Commander in Chief of the Army to take over as acting President. You will be the saviour of our nation.'

General Durres smiled. 'Oh, surely not,' he murmured.

'I leaked the second list this morning.'

General Durres nodded, 'No problems?'

'None at all,' said Ivan. 'On the basis of my advice the British and American secret services have advised their political masters that these lists are authentic and that some intervention by the military in Albania is inevitable, at least on a temporary basis. They assume General Lleshi will take control.'

'I'm not so sure,' murmured General Durres. 'The good general is looking a touch unwell these days. He fears he could even be assassinated by a traitor. Dear me, what terrible times we live in. Now, how will we agree payment? In person?'

'No,' said Ivan with the hint of a smile. 'Unfortunately, General, I won't be present in Tirana tomorrow to celebrate your appointment. I'm sure you'll appreciate why. The payment should be made in Switzerland. Here are the account details. Payment against originals of the lists. And here is the name of the lawyer who will handle it.'

'Fine,' said General Durres. They strolled out to the car. 'You remembered to add the other names I requested to the list? Best to make a clean sweep all at once.'

'Yes.' Ivan shook his hand. 'Congratulations, General. I'm sure you'll be a great success as acting President. The beginning is always the most difficult bit. What was it that Machiavelli said?

> *"When a man seizes power in a State, he should decide what cruelties are necessary, and carry them all out at once, so that he will not have to renew them every day."*

Perhaps, you should remember that.'

General Durres laughed. 'I will. Goodbye, Ivan. It's been a pleasure doing business with you.'

General Durres watched the car depart into the distance. He called to Major Lef, who had first driven Ivan to Saranda. 'We have a busy week, my son,' he said. 'Get yourself another uniform. You are promoted to colonel. There's going to be a coup in Albania on Friday.'

Lef grinned. 'Is that all, sir?'

'No,' said the General. 'On Friday you're going to Switzerland to hand over some money.'

'Yes, sir.'

Durres continued, 'Oh, and two days after the payment, I want you to track down Ivan and to kill him.'

Best to leave no traces. Ivan must have forgotten that Machiavelli had also said:

'Destroy all those who have the will or power to harm you.'

30 November. Geneva.

Dr Schmidt got up from his desk and looked out of the window as he waited for the client. The sun flickered across the waters of Lac Léman, tranquil and placid as always. It was a view Dr Schmidt could never tire of, since it was so reliable. He turned to the matter in hand. His instructions were very simple and he couldn't think how he could draw them out in any way, to earn a greater fee. Pity really. Not that the payment in this case was ungenerous: two thousand dollars to hand over some documents. Mr Ivan Radic had insisted that they agree the sum in advance and he had been most generous. Such a pleasure to deal with a good client.

There was a knock on the door and his secretary peered around the door with a slightly bewildered face.

'A gentleman to see you, sir. He won't give his name.'

'Ah yes, please show him in.'

Dr Schmidt shook hands with the dark-haired man and tried to enter into polite conversation. Despite his civil efforts, Colonel Lef was not disposed to talk, so Dr Schmidt got on with it.

'Can you provide me with evidence that you have paid twenty million dollars into our law firm's account with the Swiss Bank?'

Lef handed over a receipt. Schmidt checked its contents and, in turn, handed over a sealed envelope. 'Please open it and confirm that the documents are in order.'

Lef opened the envelope. The originals of the lists of Albanian traitors were there, culled from British secret service files, together with the decrypts. He nodded. Dr Schmidt then phoned his law firm's bank, which confirmed the account had been credited. 'It is a pleasure to do business with you,' said Dr Schmidt. The man appeared Russian, but one never could tell. Lef said nothing and departed.

Dr Schmidt phoned his law firm's bank again. 'Please now send on the money in accordance with the client's instructions.'

While twenty million dollars went to the College, Dr Schmidt settled back in his chair. An easy way to earn two thousand dollars. He picked up a newspaper and began to read the front page. Big rise in the stock market in the US . . . collapse of major car manufacturer in France . . . Portuguese dock workers on strike . . . coup in Albania.

After watching Lef depart from the lawyer's office in Geneva and having checked with the law firm's bank that the twenty million dollars had been paid to the College account, Ivan made a number of short journeys within Switzerland to throw off his trail anyone who might be following him. Finally, he took the train back to Paris. It was a pleasant trip and he consumed a very good bottle of champagne on the journey. He would write to congratulate General Durres in due course. No doubt they would meet in the future, when Ivan was Master. That would impress even the acting President of Albania.

It was late afternoon when Ivan got out of the train and took the Paris metro. Humanity streamed past him. Men on their way home to their families, to get nagged. Students on their way to the discos, to get laid. Little old ladies with poodles on their way shopping, to get mugged. Finally, old men shambling along with their dreams. Ivan saw none of humanity, his thoughts, like those of everyone else, fixed on other things.

He was thinking of Hadley and what he would say when Ivan became Master. How even more impressed James would be. Dear James, they lived in different worlds. Despite that, he was very useful, and somewhere in his heart Ivan had some affection for him. Ivan walked up the metro steps to the street above, oblivious of the undulating crowd that brushed past him on their way down.

Abruptly, Ivan swivelled round, motivated by an unconscious prompting. A person in the subway below . . . unrecognisable and yet . . . For a moment he thought he had seen a familiar face. It couldn't be. It was impossible. Impossible for anyone to have tracked him. He'd covered every trace. Ivan anxiously scanned the crowd. There was no one. And yet. And yet.

He began to run. Glimpsing back, he caught sight of the face again, secreted in the crowd.

Forcing people aside, Ivan hurried along the crowded streets, convinced that someone was pursuing him. He must get back to his apartment. He could protect himself there. As he ran, gasping for breath, his mind worked overtime. Like in a chess game it went through every permutation. Had he made any mistake? Any slip? And on every occasion the answer came back. He'd made no mistake. It was impossible.

He turned into a quiet side street and stopped. He was imagining things. There was silence. He waited. Then his worst fears were realised. In the distance he heard the clatter of feet over the cobblestones.

Ivan turned and fled down the river bank to the Seine. His only hope was the apartment.

As he ran, Ivan felt a great sickness in his soul as he realised he had made an error after all. He had failed to assume one tiny thing. Fate. It had happened too, to the greatest gamesplayer of them all. Machiavelli had based his work, *The Prince,* on his hero, Cesare Borgia, one of the most ruthless of medieval princes, who had set out to become the ruler of Italy, using whatever means were necessary – assassination, deception, cruelty, torture. He had nearly succeeded save for one fatal flaw: that, as fate would have it, at the very moment when he was ready to seize power he would be dying. And now Ivan realised with great sadness that he had made a similar, fatal, error. He had considered every possibility. Bar one. An almost inconceivable slip of fate. That Hadley would unintentionally betray him. For they must have tracked him down through his lover. Poor, stupid, Hadley. He should never have joined the secret services. He should have been a medieval historian after all.

Ivan ran, for every man kills the thing he loves.

Five minutes later Ivan hurled open the glass door to his apartment block. Then he threw himself at the stairs, his lungs bursting, great wheezing noises escaping from his throat. His eyes went bleary. He frantically grasped the banisters as if he'd forgotten how to climb. For once in his life Ivan considered the Almighty and he prayed. Please God, help me. As he ascended the stairs he counted each flight knowing there would be no mercy from his pursuer. Below, a door was forced open and footsteps thundered on the steps. Then, mysteriously, they stopped. Ivan no longer cared. He'd make it after all. Ivan ran across the landing to his apartment. Inside was security and a gun. He'd make it after all. The error could be corrected. As in a chess game, the King could be saved.

As he grasped the door handle, Ivan thought of Tanya. Now he knew what it felt like to be trapped and pinned down like a butterfly, and how hateful it was. Despite everything, he was glad that he had not killed her that night in the chalet, for theory and practice were quite different, whatever Machiavelli said. Many things could be justified by Ivan in his quest for power. But to kill one who had never harmed him? No. That was not the path. It was a sin that not all the power in the world could expunge.

When Ivan opened the door the bomb went off, a massive explosion that took out the whole landing. Ivan was killed instantaneously, as were two diplomats living on the same floor. Minutes later the street was filled with smoke, the wail of ambulances and the high-pitched screams of a dying child. Firemen fought to contain the inferno. All eyes were on those trapped in their apartments. In the chaos, Ivan's killer slipped quietly away.

As to who planted the bomb no one ever knew. Middle Eastern terrorists, drug cartels, Italian mafia – the international press fanned the speculation for a few days, concentrating on the Italian diplomats. The story died away, with no leads and no motive. The death of a very talented economist on the same occasion was also reported and short obituaries appeared in the international newspapers and various learned journals. There was even less to be said about the cause of his death. Ivan Radic just seemed to have been a bystander in the wrong place at the wrong time.

The Master was privately informed of Ivan's death within minutes of its occurrence. The other contestants read about it when the story broke in the world news. There was one other person who was informed.

'Father?'

'Yes, Lef,' answered President Durres.

'I regret to say that Ivan Radic died in a bomb explosion. The French papers have the full story.'

Durres reflected on this as he sat in the Presidential chair. Behind him draped the flag of Albania. He was a very busy man but he could spare a moment to contemplate the death of a friend. An old friend.

'How sad. Your handiwork?'

'I regret to say no. Someone got to him before I did.'

'It will have been the British or American secret services. They must have found out about his part in the coup.' Durres smiled. 'How very sporting of them. You can come home now, Lef. Things are looking up here.' It was going to be a very costly Presidency after all.

The death of Ivan left only two contestants – Tanya and Andrew. Or was it three?

CHAPTER TWENTY-SIX

Therefore the good man is the teacher of the bad and the bad man is the material from which the good man learns.

Lao Zi

November. Taiwan.

'ANDREW, YOU'RE WORKING TOO MUCH,' said David Chen. 'We never see you. This is only the second time since you arrived in Taiwan, and you've been avoiding us like the plague. It's not good enough. Why are you being so secretive?'

They were sitting in the lounge of Chen's spacious penthouse overlooking the river. His two children had been put to bed and his wife had gone next door to chat to their neighbours about a forthcoming gala event. Chen relaxed on the plush sofa, a large glass of whisky in his hand. Andrew gave a faint smile.

'I don't think it would be a good idea if I told you, David. However, I have a couple of requests for you.'

'Fire away,' said Chen good-naturedly.

'The first is that I'd like to open an account with your bank. A large sum of money will pass through it, in transit. I'll give you the number of the account to which the money should be sent on.'

'No problem. Delighted.'

'The second is this: there's a person in Taiwan I'd like to meet but I don't know how to get in touch with him. You or your contacts may know.'

'I'm sure. I know just about everyone of importance in Taiwan,' said Chen modestly.

'Hew Li.'

Chen choked heavily on his whisky. He pulled out a handkerchief and spluttered into it. When his face emerged, it was red and considerably alarmed. 'What the hell are you getting yourself into, Andrew?' he hissed. 'You're playing with fire.'

'Who is Hew Li?'

'I don't know,' Chen scowled. 'And I don't care to know. These are very dangerous waters. Search in Taiwan's police files if you really want to,' he said, his voice rising in anger. 'I imagine someone like you could get access to them.'

'I have,' said Andrew, not saying how, 'and there's precious little on him. When I stayed here years ago, he was talked of as a legend. A sort of mythological demon.'

Chen turned his head towards the door to make sure that his wife had not returned. He wondered what had happened to his friend. Something had gone terribly wrong. He was getting into bad company.

'That's exactly what he is. Andrew. An evil man. A man who anyone in his right mind keeps well away from.'

'Why?'

Chen swallowed hard, yet he knew Andrew wouldn't be put off. He felt hot and bothered. If Andrew's wife had still been alive, she would have prevented this. His friend was losing himself. He had never really got over her death after all. It had badly affected his judgment. He was obviously trying to make some quick money by very dangerous means.

'Look, I'll tell you what I know and after that I don't want to talk about him again, OK? Hew Li's the most powerful Triad leader in Taiwan, and that's saying something. He's certainly the most dangerous. The stories about him and his cruelty are legion.'

'Where did he come from?'

Chen lowered his voice until it was almost a murmur.

'He operated in South China before the Communists took

over in 1949. People say that he was head of the underworld in Canton and that he and his brother were into every criminal activity you can think of: drugs, prostitution, slavery, gambling, the lot. They virtually ran the place.'

'I can't imagine him getting on with Chairman Mao,' Andrew said drily.

'He didn't. Mao went after his sort when the Revolution came. Hew Li escaped and slipped away to Taiwan. His brother wasn't so lucky, though.' Chen poured more Scotch. 'The Communists captured him and for all I know he's still in prison in China. Anyway, within a short time, Hew Li had built up a powerful Triad movement in Taiwan, based on casinos and prostitution. He also moved into smuggling goods and drugs into China. However, unlike the others of his sort who soon finished themselves off, rumour has it that Hew Li was very wise.'

'In what way?'

'Because,' said Chen, 'most of the other Triad leaders just wanted money and sex. Not Hew Li. He wanted not only them but political power as well. Everyone he couldn't intimidate he corrupted. That's why the police were soon unable to do anything about him in Taiwan. There were too many politicians and judges protecting him. All the time he's been one step ahead of the authorities, an untouchable. Even today. The moment the police link him to something it falls apart. Witnesses die, jurors are suborned, the evidence disappears and Hew Li himself is never to be seen. Every so often you can feel his presence, like a crocodile, lurking in the shadows and the filth. I'm not exaggerating.' Chen winced. 'This man's real evil. In the bank we got a whiff of him in a huge property development deal a few years ago and everyone was scared stiff. Yet no one wanted to pull out in case something nasty might happen if they did.'

'And?'

'The banks went ahead with the transaction and lost every cent.'

'If he's so clever, why doesn't he get his brother out of China? Doesn't he want to?' asked Andrew.

'Of course he does. It's said this has been a source of shame to him ever since. You know how the Chinese value family and blood relationships. Despite all his wealth and influence he can't get his brother free. The Chinese leaders aren't interested in a deal. His brother may even be dead for all I know.'

They both heard a faint click of the outside door as David's wife returned and went into the kitchen. Chen spoke *sotto voce.* 'I'm telling you as an old friend, Andrew, don't go looking for Hew Li. Anyone who gets close to him ends up in the foundations of buildings like this one. So leave well alone.'

'Just one more question: where do his Triads hang out?'

Chen sighed slowly. 'You have a death wish, my friend.'

'Just tell me.'

'Try the so-called Forbidden Quarter,' Chen muttered, anxiously looking up as his wife came in.

'Good conversation? Catching up on old times?' she said.

'Yes,' Chen replied, his voice too definitive. Shortly, afterwards, Andrew got up to depart. Chen's wife, a Taiwanese, embraced him. 'Please come and visit us again soon.'

Chen bade him farewell on the landing. He was very unhappy. 'Andrew,' he said, 'we have been friends for a long time but I don't think we should see each other for a while if you are going to get mixed up with Hew Li.' He grimaced. 'I have a family, you see. Well, you know what I mean.'

'I know, Chen. I'll get in touch with you when it's all over.'

Chen grasped him by the hand and held it for a moment. 'Goodbye, Andrew. Tread carefully, tread very carefully.'

I will show you sorrow and the ending of sorrow. So said Buddha.

Andrew wondered whether Buddha would have been so optimistic had he visited the Forbidden Quarter. Situated in the poorest section of Taiwan, it had a frightening reputation even among a local people hardened to iniquity. It was an area that had been wholly given over to crime and to vice, and its fame was such that few honest men ever ventured down its narrow and twisting backstreets where the light itself scarcely penetrated.

Had they done so they would eventually have arrived at a huge walled ghetto crumbling with decay and neglect. Like a collection of evil spirits, Hew Li's Triads had long made this locality their own. Here, they had developed a society that had not progressed beyond slavery. Girls and boys born to satisfy the appetites of others, men and women whose only purpose in life was to be used as disposable pawns. Beggars, cripples, pimps, gangsters, hit men, petty thieves, night-club owners, casino operators, all carefully directed by a will about which they knew little, just as across the river, many bankers, lawyers, shipowners, commodity dealers and traders were also controlled by a malign power whose threats they felt and obeyed even though they had never met its ultimate source.

The whereabouts of their overlord was not truly known even to his henchmen. Beyond the flicker of neon, beyond the cheap karaoke bars and brothels, deep within the very heart of the Forbidden Quarter, Hew Li had founded his lair where he lived in unbelievable luxury. Not for him the dirt and the filth, not for him the squalor and the despair, but opulence on the grandest scale.

For him the operatic scale living rooms, the Olympic-sized swimming pool, the private cinema, the indoor gardens, the pornographic library, the museum filled with the greatest private collection of jade in the Far East, all underground, all for him to cosset as his own. This excessive personal indulgence, built on the skulls and deprivation of others, reflected one aspect of Hew Li's twisted being, just as a diet of ginseng, bears' paws and lions' penises all sought to ward off a gnawing fear of the one uninvited visitor that Hew Li knew, try as he might, he would be unable to suborn or to corrupt. Death. So Hew Li lived, like an old crocodile, growing older and more evil.

There were few in the world that could match power against his. Save perhaps a Master.

Having found out all that he could, Andrew returned to Beijing and to Professor Wang. They sat again in the small courtyard.

Andrew mentioned Hew Li and the professor's face registered his distaste.

'I have heard of him and the atrocities he committed in China. He is evil and very influential, and it is far beyond my limited means to deal with such a person. I don't even know whether his brother is still alive. Hew Li is still talked about with fear and loathing in this country.'

'How can I find out more about his brother?'

Wang looked at Andrew and sipped his tea. 'As you may be aware, I had a difficult time during the Cultural Revolution. But even in the case of such bad things there are compensations. Many of those who suffered with me now hold powerful positions in this country. They, if anyone, will know.'

Wang got up and went to his writing table. Taking a piece of paper he wrote some characters on it and gave it to Andrew. 'Years ago, I rendered a service to a man when he was in great difficulties. He may not recall it but I can try. He might be able to help you.' He gave the note to Andrew.

At the door, Andrew made ready to depart. Wang said, 'Andrew. Since we were talking of the artist Chang, it may be worth recording these simple words of the Tao:

"Let your ability stop at what you cannot do."'

The professor stood at the doorway of the forgotten Faculty and bid farewell. He watched Andrew depart. There was one question Andrew had not asked him. Even if he had, he would not have secured a reply.

The elderly professor went to ring the Master.

The following day Andrew was taken in a large black sedan to Zhongnanhai, that part of Beijing where China's leaders reside. The car swept through the massive red-studded gates and past a quotation of Chairman Mao which said, 'Serve the People.' It stopped at a simple guesthouse. Not ten minutes later Andrew was face to face with the man who guided the destiny of China's millions. They talked for some time, though no record was kept of what was said. Andrew then flew back to Taiwan.

The following morning he visited a well-known politician. He was greeted at the door of the campaign office by the man himself, who exuded an oily servility for which he was famous.

'Hello. How are we today? Are we well?'

'Please give this to Hew Li.'

On reading the addressee the politician's plastic smile was quickly replaced by a scowl. 'I don't know who you're talking about.' He coldly thrust the missive back into Andrew's hands.

'Just give it to Hew Li.'

Three days later, when Andrew returned to his apartment late in the evening, an elderly, well-dressed Chinese man of medium height and grandfatherly disposition rose from Andrew's settee to greet him.

'I am Hew Li,' he said.

'I asked myself, why would you want to talk with a frail old man like me?' said Hew Li, extending his slender hands expressively. 'However, as requested in your letter, I came, your humble servant.' With a slight gesture, he motioned Andrew to sit down in his own house. Like a poltergeist he had already assumed possession.

'Most kind of you,' said Andrew. 'Can I offer you a drink?'

'No.'

'Perhaps something to eat?'

'No.'

Andrew was not sure how he'd previously envisaged Hew Li. There was no doubt that the physical appearance and the behaviour of the man were quite at variance. Physically, he could have been mistaken for a high-ranking diplomat or a mandarin, with his finely chiselled face and an attitude of exaggerated courtesy, but his eyes scarcely moved. In fact, they almost seemed incapable of movement. They focused on an object and they transfixed it, as a cobra does with its prey.

When Hew Li spoke, it was in a coarse, guttural Chinese. He had an aura about him too, an ability to project a deeply unsettling feeling in others, a sort of visceral fear that came from the stomach. Chen had spoken of Hew Li as being a person of very great evil and Andrew now knew what he meant. He sensed this man fished in the lakes of human darkness. Worse, he cast his net into it with glee.

'So,' said Hew Li, after the pleasantries had finished, 'you know where my brother is?'

'Yes. He's been moved to a labour camp in Pu'er, in Yunnan province.'

'And his condition?'

'Satisfactory, considering he's nearly eighty.'

'How did you get this information?' said Hew Li. 'How much did you pay for it?'

'I didn't pay anything,' replied Andrew. 'It came from the superintendent of the camp. Here is his report.'

Hew Li took it from his hand and scanned it quickly. 'If you didn't pay for this material or steal it, you must have very good connections. Very good guanxi,' commented Hew Li slyly.

'Yes,' said Andrew. 'This is the man who ordered the report.'

When Hew Li saw the strokes of calligraphy, he gasped. His narrow eyes darted to Andrew's face. A possibility he had yearned for might come true. 'You move in the very highest circles,' he said suspiciously.

Andrew watched him. He was like a cobra working its way down into an animal's burrow, the soft form rasping against the earth.

'Well,' Hew Li continued, 'even though I am an old man, I can still open many doors. However, there are some which I still cannot. I have heard no news of my brother for more than a year and I believed that he was dead. I am glad that he is in good health. It comforts me.' There was silence. Hew Li looked at Andrew. His eyelids drooped slightly over his eyes as if they were hooded. The cobra within him began to raise its head with interest, sensing there was something in the lair.

'What do you want?' said Hew Li sarcastically. 'Why have you brought me this information? Is it to mock me?'

'I'd heard that you would like your brother freed.'

Hew Li viewed him with scorn. 'That's impossible. The Communists will never free him. Don't you think I've tried for years?'

'Maybe you have,' said Andrew. 'However, I am prepared to make a deal with you. I'll deliver your brother to you in Taiwan.'

Hew Li's eyes glinted. 'How?'

'A trade. For twenty million dollars.'

Hew Li waved his hand dismissively in the air. 'Hah! I've offered such sums, and much more, to the Chinese Government in the past,' he sneered. 'They've always refused. Only one man could give permission and he hates both my brother and me. Not even the glib tongue of a former Fellow of the College will persuade him otherwise. You are wasting my time.'

Andrew drew in his breath slightly. It was very remarkable indeed that Hew Li knew he'd been a Fellow. Even more remarkable that he knew Andrew was no longer one. He must have a very well placed contact within the College. Andrew watched the human cobra gently swaying from side to side. Hew Li would do him no harm for the moment, he would toy with his prey.

'That may be so. My price is twenty million dollars. Here is a photograph of your brother.'

Hew Li took it. There was no doubt of the identity. He stared at the face for a long time. For once he was anguished. He had still failed to fulfil a vow he had made to his parents more than a quarter of a century before – a vow to free his brother whatever the cost. Could this man, an ex-member of that exclusive institute really achieve these things? Perhaps Andrew had stolen this information from the College. Was that why he was no longer a Fellow? His eyes fixed unwaveringly on him.

'Mr Brandon, you must either be very influential. Or very foolish.'

'Neither. The offer is on my terms. Are you interested?'

Hew Li was intrigued. Andrew had correctly indicated the place where Hew Li knew his brother was being held and he had obtained a report reserved only for the eyes of the most powerful man in China. Finally, he had a photo. Clearly, Andrew had the highest connections. Was China's leader now proposing a secret trade?

'What are your terms? Tell me all of them.'

'I will deliver your brother to you in Taiwan,' said Andrew.

'Alive? And free?'

'Yes. For twenty million dollars.'

'Very well. Hand him over in this very apartment,' said Hew Li.

'No,' said Andrew. 'If I delivered him here, there'd be no safety for me. You could easily break your part of the bargain and have me killed.'

Hew Li's face bore a resentful look while a flicker of amusement registered in his eyes. 'I'll keep my word. What's twenty million dollars for the life of my brother? I have wealth beyond count.'

'Still,' said Andrew, 'I will choose the place.'

'It has to be Taiwan,' insisted Hew Li.

'So be it. Not on land. On water. I will hand him over to you on a junk inside Taiwanese territorial waters. You must come alone.'

'No,' whined Hew Li. 'I am an old man. My health is poor and I have enemies. I need some protection.'

'Very well. No more than two bodyguards, and one person to operate your junk.'

'You want me to bring the money with me?' asked Hew Li.

'Twenty million dollars is too large a sum to carry around. It could get lost,' replied Andrew succinctly. 'Open an account with this bank'. He handed him details of the bank where his friend Chen worked. 'Issue instructions that twenty million dollars is to be transferred from your account to this account once you have given a password.'

'And?'

'When I hand over the man and you're satisfied he's your brother you give the password to the bank over a mobile phone. The bank will have someone standing by to process the transfer; and I will check it has been made.'

'Ingenious.'

Andrew ignored the mock compliment. 'You must provide me with evidence that you have opened the account. I have contacts in the bank. They will check it for me.'

'And afterwards?

'Someone will come and pick me up from the junk. Your brother will then be free to go. That's the deal.'

Hew Li nodded. 'When will you hand over my brother?'

'It will take a couple of weeks to make the arrangements. I will be ready by mid-December and I will contact you to inform you of the exact time. Oh, there's just one other matter to discuss, Mr Li.' Andew waited so that the message would sink in. 'It concerns the case where I produce your brother and despite this you fail to keep your part of the bargain and try to have me killed.'

'Impossible,' said Hew Li, shocked. It was clear that he couldn't conceive of such an occurrence. The long fingernails of his hand rasped slightly against his silk garment.

'I will set out the terms of our bargain,' continued Andrew, 'and place them in a sealed envelope. It will be given to the head of the Taiwan police in the event of my untimely death.'

Hew Li pondered on all this for some minutes. 'Very well,' he said very deliberately. 'Twenty million dollars for my brother, alive and free, in Taiwanese waters. But please note, Mr Brandon, that I never make bargains lightly. Fail me and I won't answer for the consequences. You are obviously in need of a very great deal of money; be careful your greed doesn't lead to your downfall. Contact me soon.'

Hew Li descended the stairs in a meditative mood. A retinue of bodyguards magically appeared. So, Hew Li thought, it seemed that the Chinese were prepared to trade his elderly brother after all. Better the money now than a corpse and no money later. Who would get the twenty million? The Chinese leadership? Hew Li thought so. Why was Brandon involved? Probably as a go-between so that the Chinese didn't have need to reveal their hand and Andrew could take the blame if things went wrong. Hew Li passed out of the door into the street, his decision made. The young man was so stupid he was hardly worth bothering about. The Chief of Police was a personal friend of Hew Li's anyway.

Hew Li thought that Fellows of the College were meant to be clever. He smiled to himself and returned to his lair, to cast his net once more into the darkness, this fisher of lost souls.

Al Johnson of Al Johnson Investigations in New York picked up the phone. It was lunchtime and, as usual, Al was being bothered by clients. Didn't they know that even people in investigation agencies ate? He reached over his desk and picked up the phone, draping his florid tie into his mayonnaise and gherkin salad.

'Yes!' he bellowed.

Al listened to the soft voice at the end of the line. It was sexy and gentle. Within a few seconds his view had changed completely. Of course clients could phone him at lunchtime. In fact, at any time if they had voices like that. He bet that she was as pretty as a picture as well. Why did he never see his clients in the flesh?

'Yes, madam.' Al looked at his schedule. 'Er, he's in Taiwan.'

'Are you sure?' asked Tanya. It was remarkable how they'd managed to track down both Ivan and Andrew even accepting that she and Sebastien had paid them a fortune for their work.

'Yes, madam. We're quite sure. We think that you will find him at this address. No, no. No bother at all. Please phone me whenever you like. And I'll give you my home phone number as well, just in case.'

Al put down the phone. That was the problem. He was a pussy-cat really. The clients always walked over him. He tucked into his sandwich as he watched his Afro-Caribbean partner roller-skate past him, narrowly avoiding a fallen gherkin. While he ate it, Al had a twinge of conscience. Should he have told Tanya that Andrew had said they could release his name to her, and to the other bloke – what was his name? He looked at the schedule – Sebastien?

Al Johnson thought about it as he continued eating. Nah, she'd find out anyway.

CHAPTER TWENTY-SEVEN

Therefore the sage seeks for self-knowledge, not for self-parade.
For self-love, not for self-importance.

Lao Zi

Mid-December. Taiwan.

'This seat is reserved. I'm afraid you'll have to move to another table.' The place was always booked for Mr Andrew Brandon in the evenings. He was a regular client of the Taipei Star Restaurant. The head waiter turned and his heart sank. The client had arrived.

'I'm sorry, sir . . .'

'That's all right.' Andrew regarded the woman sitting in his chair. 'Hello, Tanya.'

Tanya smiled. 'Hi. Since I've taken your table, please join me.'

'I'd be delighted.' Andrew sat down beside her. The waiter brought them menus.

Tanya watched him. His behaviour was not what she'd expected. Indeed, he didn't seem in the least surprised to see her. That worried her. She'd expected him to be astonished and uneasy at the sudden arrival of another contestant out of the blue and on his own ground. Either he had nerves of steel or she was walking into a trap. She started to turn it over in her mind. Had someone warned him she might come? Al Johnson?

'What would you like to drink?'

'Vodka on the rocks.'

Andrew ordered for Tanya and a whisky for himself. He studied her. She was a beautiful woman with her slim figure, long dark hair and a face whose soft contours and full lips still gave her a certain innocence and vulnerability, even as an adult. Yet the appearance was deceptive. Despite her innocent look, Andrew knew that Tanya was very clever and that her calculating mind was not just restricted to computers. Andrew had always thought that in the end, while others might depart from the scene, Tanya would remain. He liked her a lot. Sebastien was a lucky man.

'You'll be wondering why I decided to come and see you,' said Tanya, after they had indulged in a few minutes of small talk. She cradled her glass in her hands. Providing she stayed in the restaurant she'd be safe. It was crowded. He wouldn't do anything here, she thought.

'I imagine you want to discuss the contest for the Mastership.'

'Yes. Ivan is dead, he was killed in a bomb explosion in Paris.'

'I know.'

'We're the only ones left. Sebastien is also dead.'

Andrew said sharply in disbelief, 'Sebastien dead? How did he die?'

Tanya told him about their exploits in Panama and Sebastien's fall from a mountainside. She carefully monitored his expression as she did so. Andrew didn't seem to know about any of this. He should have been delighted at the news since it left them as the only remaining contestants, yet his face remained impassive. What was going on in his mind? Tanya began to feel increasingly unsettled. Had she been set up? A terrible thought came to her. Could Andrew and the Master be working together?

When she had finally completed her story, Andrew said almost as an aside, 'Have you made the twenty million dollars?'

'Not yet.'

Andrew observed her for a moment but Tanya didn't think he'd detected her lie. Still, she shouldn't have come. The conversation was not going as she'd imagined even though it had been her decision to talk to him. Like Sebastien she was sure that he was responsible for Rex's death just as she was sure it had been Ivan who had attacked her in the chalet in Switzerland. Despite this, and despite her promise to Sebastien, before she killed him Tanya wanted to be certain of the truth. That was very difficult.

She couldn't prove that Andrew had killed Rex or Ivan, just as she couldn't prove that Ivan had been in the chalet. Whoever had killed Rex and Ivan had covered his traces very well, so perhaps it had been foolish to have expected that something in Andrew's demeanour might give her a clue. In fact, his casualness and apparent lack of concern was luring her into a false sense of security. Just as he intended, she thought. He would have done the same with Rex. All her instincts told her that she should leave now, but she stayed.

'What about you? Have you made twenty million dollars?'

'No,' said Andrew, 'not yet.'

'Are you still trying?'

'Yes,' he said, 'and there's something I want to tell you.'

He ordered more drinks. Then, to her utter surprise, over dinner, Andrew began to tell Tanya about his own progress in the game. He told her about the work he had been doing in the Congo and about Obedi and his sister. He told her about his return to the College and his finding the rules of the Mastership. He told her about Hew Li and his plan to make twenty million dollars. The only things he didn't tell her about were his conversation with Professor Wang and his own understanding of the Chinese puzzle box. All the while Tanya sat and listened. She was intrigued. Why was he telling her all this? It was the last thing she had expected. Was he playing games with her?

'If the rules say that the Master can take part, does that mean he is taking part?'

'Your guess is as good as mine.'

'Tell me what you think,' said Tanya, curious at this unexpected new clue. Was Andrew going to suggest an alliance against the Master?

'I don't think he is,' said Andrew, 'though I still don't fully understand why.' Then he pushed aside his coffee and eyed his watch. He said reluctantly, 'Tanya, I am sorry but I must go now. I have to make a call to the Congo. If you want, we could meet up later this evening and talk more. I'd like that.'

In the light of all that he had said Tanya felt so confused. It was as if she was playing a game with someone who seemed to know how the game should be played when she didn't. A game in which there could only be one winner. She felt frightened. She had to get out. She needed to think things over. His sweet reasonableness was getting to her, just as he planned. 'No, not this evening.'

Andrew nodded.

'We could meet up tomorrow,' she suggested.

'OK. I'll drive you back to your hotel,' said Andrew.

'It's all right. I can find my own way back.'

'It's not a problem.'

'Thank you.' She'd change hotels tomorrow.

They stepped out of the restaurant and Tanya waited until he brought his car round to the door. A couple of men wolf-whistled her. She ignored them. She thought about Andrew. At College she'd only met him a couple of times, always in the company of others. She'd been impressed then by his modest bearing and self-effacing stance. He was a likeable person, even if he was a killer. Pity things weren't different.

'Hop in.'

The car slowly wound its way through the narrow alleyways. All around them there was the hustle and bustle of street vendors, the flashing neon of the casinos and the shouts and catcalls of the drunks as they staggered out of bars and sideshows. Despite the crowds Tanya felt lonely and despondent. They arrived outside her hotel.

'Won't you come in?'

Andrew paused, his hands resting on the steering wheel. 'Not tonight,' he said, hesitating a second. 'Let me invite you to my place. Say, tomorrow for dinner.'

'I'd like that. Good night, Andrew.' She made no effort to kiss him or shake his hand.

Tanya entered her hotel apartment and sat down on the sofa in the darkness. Her mind screamed to her – think, think! Andrew had to be the killer. That was what Sebastien believed and so did she. Yet, despite their meeting, she had no further clue. If it wasn't Andrew, who could it be? The Master? She doubted it. Could Sebastien have killed them? If so, why hadn't he killed her? He'd had plenty of opportunity. In any case he was dead. Could Rex's death really have been an accident after all? And Ivan? Could he have been killed by others, not the contestants? Tanya went to bed. She couldn't sleep. By two in the morning she realised that she was torturing herself. The simple answer was the answer. Andrew was responsible. Tomorrow she would kill him. Somewhere isolated and when he was at his most vulnerable. She would fulfil her promise. Tanya settled back to sleep, for once content. Her mind was made up.

Besides, Andrew was in the way of her path to the Mastership and was it not the Mastership that she desired above all else?

Meanwhile, Andrew went back to his own apartment in another part of the city. He also was puzzled. Tanya had been very surprised when he had told her about the rules of the Mastership. Further, it was clear from her body language that she didn't trust him. Why had she come to meet him alone? Was Sebastien really dead or was she tricking him? More importantly, when would she make her move? All his senses told him that he was now in great danger and that evil was rapidly approaching. Now was the time to strike, surely.

Andrew picked up the phone and put a call through to Paul Hanlon, the UN liaison officer in Kinshasa, who'd left an urgent message for him to call. They'd kept in touch over the months. Paul had been posted back to the Congo only recently since it had been too dangerous to return to the war zone before, even for UN personnel. The country remained on a knife edge with the recent assassination of the rebel leader, Christian Umbote, by one of his lieutenants, Musawena, who had decided that he also wanted half of the cake that was the Congo. On a different level it was the same in the Mastership Game. Everyone wanted power and in their pursuit of it they would destroy anything in their path.

Hanlon talked with Andrew for a while on the rebuilding of the UN operations in the Congo. Paul wanted to prepare him for what was coming. It was only at the very end of the conversation that Hanlon mentioned the children.

'I've some more news for you, Andrew. The girl Shisvannah is dead. I'm sorry. There's no doubt about it now. Over two hundred thousand people were slaughtered in that region alone, and we have details of those who survived the massacre at the school. Only four, I'm afraid: one teacher and three children. They bombed the place even though they knew it was a school. What animals.'

Andrew sat down on a chair, the memories flooding back to him. He thought of the malnourished child in a red dress. His last vision of Shisvannah was of her standing in a potholed road waving farewell to him as he drove away, her hand clutching that of her small brother. And he had failed her.

'But Andrew, we think the boy Obedi is still alive.'

Andrew said nothing, so stunned was he by this news.

Hanlon continued, 'Well, at least, we think so. We're still not certain, so don't get your hopes up too much. We think he was one of five children airlifted out of Kikwit on a special flight and sent to Washington General Hospital in the US. Our information is he had very bad shrapnel wounds. Anyway, that's all I have. I suggest you contact the hospital. Andrew, are you still there?'

'Yes.'

'Well, good luck,' said Hanlon. There was a pause. 'And Andrew, you didn't fail them, you know. It's just the way things turned out.'

Andrew said nothing for a moment. Then he softly replied, 'Thanks, Paul. Let's keep in touch.'

Andrew contacted the Washington State hospital. Eventually

he was transferred to a ward sister and Andrew explained who he was. She confirmed that they had Obedi with them.

'I'll put him through, Mr Brandon, but I'm afraid there's something you should prepare yourself for. He's been in and out of the hospital many times. Although he's recovered well from the shrapnel wounds to his body despite two operations, he'll always have difficulty with his sight. He's partly blind.'

'Blind?'

'Yes. There will be some improvement over time but he'll never be able to see clearly again. He's taken the news badly. He won't talk to anyone even though we've brought in a nurse who speaks Swahili. He sits in his room all day.'

'Obedi?'

Obedi said nothing. Suddenly, at the sound of the voice, a terrible black curtain of sorrow and despair lifted. For a moment he was able to feel happiness as if someone had returned from the dead. Then the curtain swiftly descended again.

'Obedi,' Andrew continued to talk, saying he had heard about his injuries and his treatment in America, while the small child listened. After a long time, Obedi began to speak, very slowly in Swahili – his language, Andrew's language. Finally, he burst into tears, tears from the depths of his being. He had one friend still alive. One person who knew him as he once was, a simple child born into a maladjusted world. It was not his fault that his sister had died and that his family had perished. Not his fault that he had been born into a country that was a living hell, not his fault that he suffered. He had one friend, someone who had returned to him. Perhaps, life could go on after all. If this man and others could help him, he owed it to them to help himself. It's what his sister would have wanted, even though it would have been better if he had died with her.

They talked for a long time. Near the end of their conversation Andrew asked Obedi who had brought him to the United States. Obedi told him he didn't know. They had simply put him on board a plane.

'A man came to the hospital in Kinshasa.'

'Who?'

'I don't know,' said Obedi. 'I couldn't see him. But I phoned him and I asked him to come. He came.'

'Who?'

'The man at the end of the telephone.'

After the call, Andrew reflected on the Mastership and the man at the end of the telephone. The answer had been before their eyes all the time and they had failed to see it. Through the imperfection of their own sight.

Just as the Master had said.

At twilight Andrew left his apartment and took a short drive to the banks of the Tanshui river which flowed through Taiwan's capital. He got out and walked. Soon, he stood by the side of a nondescript road, the commuter traffic hurtling past him. He looked across at a lamppost on the far side. It was at that spot that his wife, Amy, had died, together with their unborn child.

Amy had been hurrying to meet him at a nearby hotel that balmy summer evening five years ago, full of joy at the news from the hospital that the ultrasound had indicated she was bearing a son.

As she walked along, she was hit by a car. It had swerved violently onto the pavement, driven by a drunk driver returning from a losing streak at the casino. Later, the driver couldn't remember a thing. A young girl, a passer-by just like Amy, had also been killed. It was another traffic accident, another statistic. Yet, for Andrew, there had been no chance to say goodbye to his young wife, to say the million and one things he would have wanted to say, to tell her how much he adored her, how her life was an essential part of his. But he couldn't. She had died because she was in the wrong place at the wrong time. Not because of her fault or his. Because another human being had exercised his power so selfishly.

Andrew stood there while the disinterested traffic passed and the twilight became darkness. He had not returned to this spot since the night of her death. He had loved Amy so much and he had buried so much of himself with her – his emotions, his capacity to forgive, his faith in humankind. In that way he and Obedi were the same, tortured by an unforgiving past. Perhaps, with Obedi and his sister, Andrew had tried to efface something of the tragedy that was indelibly imprinted on his mind. And by failing to save them, he had recreated his own anguish in failing to save others who had been so much closer to him.

Andrew stood by the roadside for a long time. He reflected on the Mastership and on the vases painted by the artist Chang as he had bidden farewell to his own child. Andrew had come here to do the same. To bid farewell to those whom you most love, but not to lose them. To turn anguish into insight.

If life had any meaning at all, and if the Mastership Game had any meaning at all, from out of the evil there had to come good. If Obedi could recognise that and continue with his life while accepting the past, so could he. Andrew stood by the roadside and wept – for Obedi and his family, for his wife and child, for himself.

For his blindness.

When Tanya stepped through the door to his apartment, Andrew knew she would kill him that night.

'Hi.'

She kissed him on the cheek, trying to avert her eyes from his gaze. She was dressed to murder. A small, tight-fitting affair in crimson silk that showed off every inch of her sensuous body to its best effect.

'Come and sit down. I've almost finished. Hope you like Chinese cooking.'

'Yes.' Tanya sat on a sofa, keeping her shoulder bag close beside her.

The apartment was large and spacious. Besides the standard décor to be found in furnished apartments, in the sitting room Andrew had put up on the walls some watercolours of the Australian outback and the sidetables contained a few ornaments.

Everywhere there were books, maps and CDs. An upright piano stood in a corner. She liked the room. It was unassuming. Andrew put his head round the kitchen door.

'Drink?'

'Red wine, please.' What did blood look like when it came pouring out of a man? Like red wine? Would it splash her?

'Sure.'

'You play the piano?' said Tanya. She wished she'd asked Sebastien more questions about how to do it. When you shot someone did it take long before they collapsed? Would he shout out?

'Yes. And you?'

'Yes. My mother taught me when I was young.' Should she go into the kitchen and get it over with now?

'Feel free to play.'

Tanya went over and played a few notes. She inspected the score on the music stand. Mozart's Piano Concerto No 21. Her mother had said she could die listening to that music. Suddenly she was back in a small sitting room in Rome, her mother at the piano and her father relaxing in an armchair. Back in the world of her childhood. What would her parents have thought of her now? How much her desire for power had corrupted her.

'Dinner will be ready in a few minutes.'

'You lived in Australia for long?' she called out, looking at the watercolours. She already knew his past. She wanted to know whether he lied.

'I was born there,' Andrew replied from the kitchen. 'My parents moved to Taiwan when I was a teenager. After university I went into the military and did a lot of travelling before I got married.'

'Are you still married?'

Andrew came through into the lounge. 'No,' he said softly. 'My wife died in a car accident a few years ago. Here in Taiwan.'

'Oh, I'm sorry.' Tanya already knew the details. Hit by a drunk driver on a pavement not far from here. Died aged twenty-six.

Woman pregnant with a son that died with her. Driver given three years. And Andrew not there. If she killed him, would anyone come to his funeral? Did he have a current girlfriend? Would anyone buy him a headstone?

'Food's ready. More wine?'

'Please,' said Tanya.

Tanya got through dinner. In fact, she thoroughly enjoyed it. Unlike Sebastien, who always dominated events with his intensity and drive, Andrew let her talk and seemed genuinely interested in what she said. Tanya appreciated his unpretentious and reflective style. Not that that changed anything, of course. They talked about the College and their work for it over the years. He told her about his time in the military and some of the projects he'd been tasked with.

'It's strange that we never worked on a project together,' she said. 'Do you think that was the reason why we were chosen for this contest?'

'No. I don't think so,' said Andrew. 'The rules said that the contestants were to be chosen by random selection. Besides, I worked with Ivan and with Rex in the past.'

'But never with Sebastien?'

'No. I knew, of course, he worked for the World Bank, but our paths never crossed. The College is involved in so many things, it isn't really surprising.'

True, Tanya reflected, it wasn't that surprising. What could be though was that both Rex and Ivan had worked with Andrew and both were now dead. Did they know something about him and his past? Why had her computer investigations not turned anything up?

Dinner finished, Andrew took the dishes into the kitchen. She could see from his gaze that he liked her company.

'Like to go outside, down to the riverside? I wouldn't mind a breath of fresh air.'

Tanya nodded. She was sure he didn't suspect she'd do anything to him tonight. He was obviously going to fish for more information. 'Just give me a minute.' She made for the bathroom. A breath of fresh air would be fine. She wanted to put off the evil hour, even though she knew it would come.

They stood at the riverside. About them a myriad lights sparkled. Behind them lay Taipei, one of the most crowded cities in the world, with more than three million people. And before them across the water lay mainland China, one billion three hundred million people. So many people within such easy reach. All living life in similar ways. Crying, laughing, hating, loving, living, dying. Why did she feel so horribly alone despite their presence? Was it the absence of Sebastien? Or was it more, the lack of something in her own psyche to make her fulfilled? Was she seeking to fulfil a dream or was it just a hollow ambition that would not make her happy even if she achieved it? Part of her nature, or just a vain title?

'When the Master told you about the contest, were you surprised?'

'Of course,' said Andrew, 'and angry. I could accept that there would be a competition for the Mastership and that it would be in secret. That fitted in with the ethos of the College. However, the nature of the contest I found almost unbelievable. I was sure then that the College had become corrupted and that it was failing.'

Tanya watched him closely as they stood side by side. 'You never asked me whether I thought the Master was involved in this contest.'

'No. I didn't,' said Andrew. 'Well, what do you think?' He turned away from the scenery to look at her.

'I think he is playing,' said Tanya. 'For a long time I was unsure. But now I think that he is, and that he's far more gifted than all of us. He is the perfect gamesplayer. He has tied us all up with doubts and uncertainties. You see, he wants all the other contestants to destroy themselves before he steps into the ring.'

'Do you really believe that?' His tone was curious – or was it suspicious?

Tanya turned to face him. She was so close she could almost kiss him. Did she want to? She moved away, confused.

'Why do you think the Master referred to the Chinese puzzle box?' Andrew asked.

'I think he was trying to tell us something, and that he was using the box as an illustration. Both the box and the Mastership are a form of contest. In both, I think the Master was saying, "Look carefully. Things are not as they seem. You think the Master is not playing but he could be. Assume nothing, trust no one. Solve the puzzle yourself." '

'I agree,' said Andrew, 'that the puzzle box is an illustration of the Mastership. Solve the puzzle and you solve the Mastership. I also agree that each person must solve the puzzle for him- or herself. In the end the contest, and the Mastership, relate to the acquisition and use of very great power, in particular the approach people will adopt to gain it. Is the Mastership a great prize to be battled for, to be seized as booty, like in war? Or is there something more, something deeper? That is one of the fundamental questions.'

Tanya nodded, seduced into agreeing with him by the reasonableness of his argument. Suddenly, she gasped, shaken out of her reverie. An iron grip seized her heart. Where was her shoulder bag? She was alone with Andrew, near water, with no witnesses and she had lost her bag. A great void opened in her consciousness. Andrew had taken it, had found the gun. She knew what he was going to do.

'Are you all right?'

Andrew came slowly towards her. His facial expression was strange and his movements seemed tense. Tanya backed away, frightened.

'I've lost my shoulder bag,' she stammered.

Andrew was next to her now. He had only to reach out and seize her, to force her to tell him what he wanted to know. Had Tanya been involved in the killing of Rex and Ivan, or had it just been Sebastien? That was the only question he had left. Andrew felt so sad, for if she had been involved, it meant that she would kill him if she could, perhaps even here, close to where his wife had died. How might he find out? Tanya would never tell him voluntarily. He would have to put it to the test.

'Didn't you leave it over by the wall?' said Andrew. He watched her as she went to pick the bag up. Could he ever kill Tanya even if she had killed others? Could he kill her for the Mastership?

Andrew would find out that night.

They returned to Andrew's apartment. Tanya felt cold, and shivered slightly as they stepped back into the warmth. She kept her bag close beside her.

'Like a liqueur? And coffee?'

'Mmm. I'll put some music on.' Tanya grasped a CD disc at random. The opening notes of Mozart's Piano Concerto No 21 filled the room. She wanted to weep. Over coffee, she told him of her own work and the computer programming and analysis she had undertaken both for the European Computer Union and the College. Tanya wanted to keep him talking until late. She needed to stay the night.

'How does the College have the ability to link into so many computers worldwide?' he asked.

'Easy,' Tanya smiled. 'Two of the Fellows work for computer manufacturers. When the computers are designed a special gateway is secretly built into their memories to enable the College to access information. In others we can access them by using the passwords used by the technicians to service and operate them.'

'Do you also programme and monitor the College's computers?'

'Yes.'

'Can you still do that?' said Andrew in a low voice.

'Possibly. Why do you ask?'

'Because I want to know how powerful the quantum computer used by the Master and the Arbitrators is and what sort of information it holds.' Andrew frowned. 'After I entered the Master's Lodge I became sure they'd actually allowed me to break in. Do you think that's possible? Would they have been able to detect me?'

Tanya pursed her lips. 'No doubt. They monitor the whole island. No one can get onto Tirah without the Master knowing. That's why I discarded that possibility. What's the point of your question?'

'That means the Master is aware I found out about the rules. Also, that I know he might be playing.'

'And?'

'The fact that the Master might be playing is a sort of clue, isn't it?' continued Andrew. 'Rather like a clue to solve the Chinese puzzle. An indication of where a specific pin should be placed in the side of the box.'

'Yes,' said Tanya. She'd already reached the same conclusion.

'I wonder whether there are any other clues?'

'I haven't come across any,' lied Tanya. Of course she had: Max Stanton. He was a clue, a very big one. Andrew's clue and hers put together meant, for her, that the Master was playing and that Stanton had died at his hands in a previous contest. However, she had no intention of telling Andrew. These clues would likely save her own life. Let him work it out. Everyone for himself.

'Yet, if the Chinese puzzle box was not a puzzle box, any clue wouldn't matter, would it?' continued Andrew. 'It would be a false clue, a false trail. Nothing would matter apart from what the Master actually told us.'

From her puzzled look it was clear Tanya didn't understand what he was saying. Andrew was sure she'd no intention of helping him, by telling him of any clue that she and Sebastien may have discovered.

Tanya changed the subject. 'Andrew, it's very late. Do you mind if I stay the night? It saves me going back to the hotel.' He still suspected nothing, she was sure, still fishing for information. He was probably intending to deal with her later. How? Like he'd done with Ivan?

'Yes, that's OK. There's a spare bedroom. I have to get up early tomorrow and so I won't see you. Just close the door behind you.'

'Fine.' There would be no tomorrow for him.

'Good night then.' Tanya got up.

He rose to his feet. 'I suppose we'll next meet just before the Fellows' Banquet.'

'Perhaps,' she said. 'Though we've still both got to make the twenty million.'

'Of course,' he replied, with a bleak smile. 'Well, good night.'

Tanya looked at him awkwardly. She should kiss him good night. But could a murderer do that to their victim? Slightly embarrassed she turned and retired to the spare room. She locked it. It was past two o'clock. She would give him two hours until he was sound asleep and there was no prospect of resistance. Then she would leave, go back to her hotel and check out. She'd be out of Taiwan within an hour on a flight to Thailand for a few days' rest to kick over the traces. Then, Tanya would decide what should be done about the Master. They probably wouldn't discover Andrew's body for a week. She'd leave nothing to connect her to it.

At four Tanya got up. Noiselessly, she opened her shoulder bag and took out the gun with its silencer. It contained three bullets. Point it at the heart and just press the trigger, then it's all over. So simple. She went to her bedroom door and noiselessly turned the key. Andrew's room was not ten feet away, and the door was ajar. Tanya paused, but she could hear nothing. She approached it. In the faint light from the corridor she saw his sleeping form and heard the faint sound of breathing. She raised the gun and her finger tightened on the trigger.

Tanya did not know how long she stood there – probably five minutes. Yet it seemed so much longer. For thinking about killing a person and actually doing it were completely different things. The one was easy, the brain could plan the functions with a ruthless and efficient logic. Point the gun, fire and flee. So very simple. However, in the act of squeezing the trigger and its discharge lay an agonising dilemma of moral and emotional choice. As if she was about to cross a barren and waterless landscape, every human instinct told her she should not do it, told Tanya that once she had passed over that threshold she would enter a moral hinterland from which she would never return. Rationalise it, justify it, yes, her intellect would easily provide an excuse, and would continue to manufacture them without fail for the rest of her life. However, her soul would never forgive her, it would remind her that she had transgressed the most basic tenet of humanity and that, try as she might, the evil she had done could not be washed away.

Tanya waited and took a deep breath. She psyched herself up again. Andrew was the killer. In due course he would kill her. Killing a killer was justifiable. She had promised Sebastien she would kill him. She wanted the Mastership. All these intellectual justifications surged through her mind, angrily informing her that she should just squeeze the trigger and have done with it. Forget the moral consequences, for God's sake, just do it. Here was her moment of triumph.

Still she could not. Why not? His soft breathing was his only defence and its shallow sound relentlessly pressed upon her conscience. It told her – if you kill him, you are no better than he is. You have descended to his level and abased yourself. That is a truth from whose moral meshes you will never escape. Kill him even if he is a murderer and you kill your own soul. In your quest for justice you substitute your own tyranny. For is it justice you seek, or is it power? Finally, Tanya lowered the gun. She went back to her room and closed the door.

Sitting on her bed, she wept long and silently. The capacity to kill was not in her and she was no closer to the truth that she sought. Who would, who could, help her with that?

Andrew lay in bed, awake. He heard Tanya depart. That was the problem for both of them: the use of power to fulfil one's own wishes. The power of the gun, the power of decision – there was little difference. They were just facets of the same hard diamond on which people would break themselves to attain their goal. And what was their goal, Tanya and Andrew's goal?

The Mastership. The greatest of powers which, if they could only attain it, they were convinced they could use for the greatest good. And yet, the very way they sought to attain it would defeat all their rosy promises of how they would use it, once it was in their hands. If they used evil means to secure it, what chance was there they would forgo evil even as they wielded it?

Andrew closed his eyes. He thought once more of the Chinese vases he had seen. Like the humble artist Chang he stood on a bridge, the bridge of decision, and he surveyed the vast power that might be his with the Mastership. Yet on that same bridge he perceived the humility of the artist Chang. Wherein lay the true greatness? To acquire by domination or by insight? It was time for Andrew to make his decision.

Andrew opened his eyes once more. Then he started to dress. He knew one answer now. Tanya herself would not kill him to attain the Mastership. Whether she would kill him because of her love for Sebastien was another matter, for Andrew had only her word that her lover was dead. Tanya was one thing, Sebastien quite another. Andrew did not know what he could do in the face of very great evil and how its force could be counteracted. Perhaps the Master alone knew.

Yet there was one small way in which Andrew could help Tanya in her own quest. By giving her an insight into his own being. By showing her the true killer.

It was first light when Tanya awoke. In her exhaustion she had lapsed into a disturbed sleep. She started up. She was in Andrew's flat stretched out on the bed, the gun by her side. What should she do? She must leave. She should get out of Taiwan immediately and go to the Senior Arbitrator. She should tell him that she thought that Rex and Ivan may have been killed by Andrew and that the Master might be playing the game. She should tell him everything. Above all, she should tell him the one thing in all this horrible puzzle that she did know – that she had killed no one and that she had no intention of killing anyone. She was not prepared to do that – not even for the Mastership. Perhaps she would also return to the College at the end of the year? Who knows – Andrew might not have made his twenty million and the Mastership might still be hers.

Would she also tell the Senior Arbitrator that she had intended, indeed she had tried, to kill Andrew? It would be difficult for her to confess her moment of great weakness. Of course, it would never happen again. Not even if Andrew was a killer. Leave others to deal with him. Tanya sat up on the bed. Time to go. She opened the breach of her gun.

Suddenly, a shaft of absolute fear ran down the full length of her spine. The three bullets were missing.

Fighting back the panic, Tanya quickly checked the bedroom door. It was still locked, so Andrew could not have come in while she was sleeping. He must have taken the bullets from the gun when they were down at the riverside, which meant he would have known then she'd come to kill him. So, why had he not harmed her?

Tanya got up and opened the door. The apartment was silent. Hurriedly, she glimpsed into Andrew's bedroom. He was not there. She checked the other rooms. Finally, she entered the kitchen. There was a note on the table. She read it.

Andrew asked Tanya to meet him in two days' time at three o'clock in the morning in a speedboat off Matsu island, one of Taiwan's islands a few kilometres from the coast of China. Tanya frowned. Two days' time. That was the day before the Fellows' Banquet.

There was something else on the table.

Tanya's three bullets.

CHAPTER TWENTY-EIGHT

Determine the enemy's plans and you will know which strategy will be successful and which will not.

Sun Tzu, *The Art of War*

21 December. Beijing, China.

ANDREW BOARDED THE FLIGHT TO Beijing and sat back in his seat.

To want nothing and yet to have all. How simple the nature of the Taoist philosophy was and how difficult to live. What a remarkable man the craftsman Chang must have been, for the works of art he had fashioned had reflected his true nature and the spontaneity of his inner being. They had not been created to secure power or praise. Rather, they were an expression of his love for the universe, an innate recognition of the mystery of it all without an assertion of self. Without human cravings. Without endless contradiction. Without alternatives. Without these forms of human illness. As the Tao said:

'The sage is free from the illness
Because he recognises the illness as an illness
He can prevent the illness thereby.'

The plane took off.

When possibly the most powerful ruler in recorded history, Kangxi, had commanded the craftsman to make the most difficult puzzle of all, the simple carpenter had obeyed. However, instead of a clever jewel box, Chang had used it to illustrate the distinction between illusion and reality, to help Kangxi understand what for him was still the most difficult puzzle of all: the purpose of his own being. For despite his power and control over the external world, Kangxi had been no nearer to finding himself and the nature of his existence as an individual soul within the universe. And that reality, the craftsman was telling him, could only be found by contemplating the universe – the internal world where a man could be richer beyond imagination. As the Taoist, Chuang Tzu had said:

> *'A boat may be hidden in a creek; a net may be hidden in a lake; these may be said to be safe enough. But at midnight a strong man may come and carry them away on his back. The ignorant do not see that no matter how well you conceal things, smaller ones in larger ones, there will also be a chance for them to escape. But if you conceal the universe in the universe, there will be no room left for it to escape. That is the great truth of things.'*

For this, Kangxi had been prepared to give up his throne, since he realised that the simple craftsman had shown him that there was no puzzle at all. The imperfection lay in his own sight. Being an emperor was as important as it was unimportant. That wasn't the point. Being was the point and he could be without having to be an emperor. For humanity the real mystery to it all lay within each individual, and each had an equal opportunity to discover it. Which is why Chang refused his offer of the empire. He was freer and wealthier without these things than with them. Identifying himself with the universe he could never be lost. He had found the Way just as Kangxi could not see it. He was a master of his fate. A true master with an empire more powerful than all Kangxi's armies. An empire of insight. Without power he could see the truth. With it, he was blind.

So both Chang and the Master were teachers and if the answer to the Chinese puzzle box lay in Chang's own personality, then the answer to the Mastership lay in the being of this Master.

Further, if Chang and the Master had the same insight, this meant two things: that the Master never wanted power, and that the Master had told them the truth.

Illusion and reality.

The plane flew on.

Tanya sat back in the taxi to her hotel and watched the world gliding by as in a dream. It was irrelevant what was happening outside. Her thoughts were elsewhere. With Andrew. She felt a deep sense of warmth and happiness grow and expand inside her. With the death of Sebastien, her world had been shattered and she thought she'd never recover. The last promise she'd made to him had also haunted her. Now it need no longer be fulfilled. Andrew had not killed Rex or Ivan and, last night, he'd realised that she was not a murderer either. So neither of them was a killer and they both knew it.

What of the Mastership? She would wait and see whether Andrew made the twenty million dollars before deciding. Perhaps she didn't want the Mastership after all. Sebastien had been wrong on one point. He had said that all systems, including the College, in order to survive, involved a struggle between the great principles of war and peace and that war was the greatest of the two. This was not so. In the end and above it all, there was only peace. The rest was an emptiness of self-glorification and she never wanted to hold the Mastership on those terms. Tanya got out of the cab and entered the hotel.

The doorman noticed her face was vibrant with health and happiness. Lucky woman, he reflected ruefully. She has it all. Tanya smiled at him and he felt the warmth of her love radiate from her, like the ripple of water. Tanya stepped into the lift. She was thinking of Andrew. She would be there to meet him at Matsu island when he came back. She liked him. She was attracted to him. How she wished she could fall in love again.

Her hotel bedroom was full of fresh flowers. Where had they come from? Tanya ran to draw in their sweet smell. She perceived their beauty and she laughed, her life seemed so fresh and new to her. This time she understood what it was. When she thought that she was dying at the chalet, she had experienced a similar sense of detachment and peace – that all was well in the universe. Now she must cultivate it from within herself, and forget the past. True, she had adored Sebastien to the depths of her soul and she would have done anything for him, even given up her own life. But, brilliant and far-sighted though he was, even Sebastien could be mistaken, and he was mistaken about Andrew. He was a gentle human being, not a murderer. She knew it, she felt it, just as she experienced the beauty of the flowers. There was no possibility of her being mistaken over this – it was an insight that had welled up within her. She was experiencing a new part of herself she'd never known before.

'Hello, Tanya.'

With a cry Tanya turned and fainted. The flowers tumbled from her hands.

Sebastien took her into the bedroom in his arms. He hugged and caressed her until she had recovered consciousness.

'It's all right, Tanya,' he whispered. 'It's all right. There's no doubt about it.' Sebastien sat beside her as she wept and clung to him.

'Sebastien, it cannot be . . .'

He laughed, that same careless laugh of invincibility which she knew so well. 'I told you I'd be back. It just took me longer than I'd expected.'

'But you were dead.'

'Just about. In fact, it was a little too close for comfort.'

They lay back on the bed, Sebastien told her of his adventures with all the enthusiasm of a raconteur, embellishing bits here and there, apparently without a care in the world. Tanya listened to his tale in silence. Even as he described what had happened to him her face began to register her despair.

'How did you get away from Juan?' she asked tersely.

Sebastien explained about his journey into the mountains and the demise of the two Pedros, avoiding some of the gorier details;

he didn't want to spoil her breakfast. 'Their problem was that they were so sure they'd get me they began to make mistakes. Then, I knew I'd win.'

'How?' said Tanya.

'In the end it was a question of tactics. They thought I was fleeing when, in fact, it was the opposite. As Sun Tzu advised

"Pretend inferiority and encourage his arrogance."

Simple tactics. I wasn't fleeing at all. I was luring them on, to choose the right moment to attack. When they got separated and divided their strength, I moved in and picked them off. Fat Pedro first, then his brother. The rest of the jungle lent a hand. For Juan, it was different. I changed my approach. I was waiting.'

'What for?'

'Nightfall.' He said it with such quiet menace that she shivered.

'That was something my friend Juan had not thought about in his stupid little head,' Sebastien continued, his voice cold and distant as he relived the experience. 'At night you can often achieve by stealth what only guns can achieve during the day. Juan thought there was no possibility I would attack him in his cave since he was so heavily armed. That was exactly the thing to do. As Sun Tzu advised,

"Attack where he is unprepared."'

'What happened?'

'I went into the cave very early in the morning when I thought he'd be catnapping. I knew Juan was so used to snorting coke he'd get withdrawal symptoms – disorientation, lethargy, sleep. Do you want me to go on?' Sebastien looked at her face. It was ashen. She inclined her head.

'Juan made an error. In a jungle if you want to avoid someone attacking you at night, you put out any fires. That's obvious. Yet Juan kept a small one going. I think because he was more scared of the jungle than of me. That was his downfall because I was able to get very close to him. I took his rifle and removed the bullet. Then I took his pistol.'

'You killed him?'

Sebastien watched her expression. 'Juan woke up and saw me, not realising I'd intentionally disturbed him. He was so pleased with himself because he thought he was going to kill me. But when Juan pulled the trigger nothing happened.'

Tanya gripped Sebastien's arm in horror. He continued, 'That give him a bit of a shock. Then I told him it was my turn. I pulled the trigger and I blew out his brains.'

Tanya shuddered. Sebastien did not tell her of his parting words to Juan before he killed him. Nor that he had calmly finished off Juan's rations afterwards. There was no need to distress her further.

'What about the pathologist's report?'

'Easy,' scoffed Sebastien. 'It was time to disappear, not just to put Gonzalez's henchmen off the scent, but so that the other contestants would also think I was dead. I changed clothes with Juan and then pushed his corpse off the mountainside into a ravine. I threw away his rifle and went to the nearest farmstead. A *campesino* bound up my wounds. After resting for a day I went back to the body. There was not much left of Juan. The local wildlife had tucked in. They probably got high on him. After checking to make sure everything was OK, I went back to the hotel in Cerro Punto at night and took Juan's truck. Then, I returned to Panama City.'

'Why didn't you contact me?' Tanya asked.

'Too dangerous for both of us. Juan was dealt with but for all I knew Gonzalez's partners and sidekicks could still be around. I found out the name of the local police pathologist in Panama City and went to see him. He patched me up and we had a talk.'

'And the pathologist faked the report?'

'Of course. A *campesino* saw a body in a ravine and contacted the police who notified him. They all went there. Juan was nearly all gone, poor fellow, just a few bones. Anyway, the pathologist, Senor Lopez, was kind enough to bag him up and take the remains back to Panama City. For the sum of $100,000 he misidentified the corpse as me. I provided him with a modest amount of assistance, blood samples, the lot.' Sebastien grinned. He didn't tell Tanya he had also threatened to kill Senor Lopez, which had resulted in a Pauline conversion on the part of the avaricious Panamanian.

'Did you go to your funeral?'

'Oh yes,' laughed Sebastien. 'I couldn't miss a cameo role. I was the grave digger in the far corner of the graveyard, with my shoulder bound up like the hunchback of Notre-Dame. I almost thought you recognised me. You were very good, by the way.' Sebastien stroked her cheek with his finger. 'Very good indeed. In fact, I couldn't see a tear on your beautiful complexion.'

Tanya pushed him away from her. 'If you knew how much I wept for you, you bastard. It broke my heart.'

'Well, at least I saw Ted weeping copiously,' said Sebastien. 'So much so you would have thought it had been his mother, until I saw a bottle peeking out the back of his trousers. I bet he consumed more than the crematorium.' Sebastien laughed heartily. He lay back on the bed. Life was just too delicious.

'What did you do afterwards?'

'I'll come to that in a minute,' said Sebastien. 'Now you must tell me about your adventures. Did you find Andrew?'

'Yes. He's here in Taiwan. Al Johnson located him.'

A flicker of interest seemed to cross Sebastien's face, although he already knew from Al Johnson Investigations that Andrew was in Taiwan. 'Do you know where he lives?'

'Yes. It's not far from here.'

'Did you talk with him last night?'

'Yes.'

Sebastien was silent for a while. 'You came home early this morning,' he said. 'Has he screwed you?' The words were soft and with a tang of bitterness.

'No, of course not.' She was frightened.

Sebastien examined her closely with his eyes. Then he laughed again. There was a brutal edge to it this time. 'I bet he wanted to though. I bet he lusted to get inside your pretty little knickers.'

Tanya turned away, almost guiltily. 'I don't know, Sebastien, but I do know that he didn't kill Rex and Ivan.'

'Why do you say that?' He stroked her hair. She tensed.

'I just feel that he didn't,' she said eagerly. 'He doesn't seem to be capable of such a thing. We must be wrong. We should leave him alone. Too many people have died already in this game.'

'Tanya.' Sebastien shook his head sadly, his tone gentle and caring again. Slipping off her dress strap he kissed her naked shoulder. 'You're a lamb among wolves. Did Andrew say anything about the contest?'

'Yes.' She got up. 'I'll tell you in a minute. It's a long story. First, I'm going to have a shower and make some coffee.'

Sebastien watched her undress and leave the bedroom. He leant over the bed and picked up the thin white slip she had worn that morning and the night before. A lingering perfume emanated from it. Also Tanya's body scent, a faint musk, sexual and arousing. Sebastien clasped the garment to him. Then he let it fall to the ground by the bed. Had she been with Andrew the previous night and was she now bound to him with ties deeper than friendship? Agonised, he stared out of the window. Had she been covered by his nemesis, like a bitch in heat? She'd never admit it, even if it was so. Why had she betrayed him? He'd have ensured she would have been all right. Sebastien would never have let her down once he had the Mastership. Tanya or the Mastership, what did he care for more?

Tanya returned with the coffee and a towel wrapped round her.

'Andrew told me about the contest. He also told me about Rule No. XIX.'

'Oh, what rule?' Sebastien's eyes narrowed. He put the coffee down untasted.

Tanya explained.

'So,' said Sebastien, 'Andrew went into the Master's Lodge. How very enterprising of him.' He sank back into the pillows. 'Let me think.' He closed his eyes for a while.

'Does Andrew believe that the Master is taking part in this contest?' he asked eventually.

'No,' said Tanya.

'I see. Tell me about Andrew's plans to make twenty million dollars.'

Tanya told him about Hew Li and Andrew's attempt to get his brother released.

Sebastien listened, fascinated. Then he said, 'What does Andrew want you to do?'

'To meet him off Matsu island in a speedboat in two days' time.'

'Will you go?'

'I must, though I don't know why he wants me to go there.'

'Oh, but I do, Tanya,' said Sebastien grimly. He sat up. 'To kill you. Once Andrew has made his twenty million, you are the only person alive he thinks can stop him becoming Master.'

'No.'

'Yes, Tanya. Don't be a fool. He is tricking you just as he did Rex. You are being fooled because he seems so honest and reasonable. We have to stop Andrew. We have to stop him dead in his tracks.'

'Sebastien. I can't kill him,' Tanya said forcefully, 'I won't. Not even for the Mastership.'

Sebastien shook his head sadly and kissed her. 'Tanya, darling, I can still see you're worried and unsure of who killed Rex and Ivan and you suspect me. I know. Don't lie. I can see it in your eyes.' He spread out his hands defensively. 'I can assure you I didn't kill them. But you don't believe me. Go on to the rendezvous with Andrew. I will help you. But go with a gun for I swear one of you will be killed and, at the moment, my money's on it being you. You want the truth? Fine. Go and find it. Kill or be killed, Tanya, it's your choice. That's what this game is all about – choice.'

'What will you do?' asked Tanya.

'I intend to visit the Master,' Sebastien replied, 'to warn him.' He got up from the bed and gently unwound the towel from her naked body. 'I love you,' he whispered. 'Let's make love.'

'Later,' she replied. Not now.

CHAPTER TWENTY-NINE

Those who are able to understand me are very few
And those who are able to follow me are very hard to meet
Therefore the sage (who is not understood) looks like he is wearing coarse garb, but he has a precious jade in his heart
Lao Zi

23 December. Taiwanese waters.

THE WATERS LAPPED AGAINST THE sides of the junk. All was peaceful as the vessel bobbed up and down. It was pitch-black apart from the stars, whose faint gleam was further obscured by mist rising from the sea. In such a location all sense of time and space was lost. Andrew felt as if he was in a sealed capsule from which nothing escaped. So it remained for an hour until another junk glided alongside his. Both vessels lay just within Taiwanese territorial waters not far from Matsu island. Andrew got up and stretched, his muscles rigid from the sea breeze. He stepped forward to the side of his vessel to greet Hew Li.

The elderly gangster came onto the deck of his junk assisted by two huge bodyguards. He whispered to them, 'Do nothing until I tell you.'

Standing by the side of the junk he regarded Andrew. The gap between the two vessels was less than three metres. Hew Li adjusted his exquisite silk jacket without any sense of haste. The guards stood behind their overlord. Finally, Hew Li clasped his hands together. His expression was thoughtful.

'Good evening, Mr Brandon. I hope for your sake you've not brought me here for nothing.'

Andrew met his gaze. 'Your brother is on board. He is resting from his long journey. Now, I would like you to make the payment of twenty million dollars.'

'Show me my brother first,' snapped Hew Li.

Andrew nodded and went below deck. In a few minutes he had brought out a frail, elderly figure who leant heavily on his arm. They walked to the side of the junk. The old man, wheezing from the effort, clung to the rail. Slowly, he raised his worn eyes and stared into Hew Li's face.

For many moments neither spoke. Hew Li gazed at his own flesh and blood whom he had not seen for so many years.

'Are you well, my brother?' he asked finally.

'I am well but tired.'

Haltingly, they began to talk in a local dialect. Andrew left them to it as he drew down the sail of the junk.

After fifteen minutes, Hew Li called out to Andrew, 'You have done very well, Mr Brandon. I am impressed. Only the leader of China could have ordered my brother's release.'

'Which he did,' said Andrew.

'How very thoughtful of him. He is obviously a considerate man,' said Hew Li. 'My brother must rest. Let him pass over to my junk. The bargain was that you deliver him to me alive and free.'

'Agreed,' said Andrew. He placed a metal gangplank between the two vessels. 'You must also keep your part of the bargain, Hew Li. Order the payment to be made to my account.'

Hew Li hesitated. If he attacked now, his brother would suffer injury. Just a few minutes more. From his pocket he took out a mobile phone and gave an instruction and a secret codeword. Within a minute the sum of twenty million dollars had been moved from an account opened by Hew Li at the bank at which David Chen worked to an account opened by Andrew at the same bank. Hew Li announced to Andrew that this had been done. Then he observed him closely, a sardonic smile upon his face. Andrew made a phone call and spoke to David Chen.

'Has my account been credited?'

'Yes,' said Chen, 'and I'll send on the money immediately to the account you told me to.' It was to the College account, though he knew nothing of this.

Andrew clicked his mobile shut. 'The transfer is complete.'

'Of course.' The gangster knew Andrew would soon countermand the order. 'Now give me my brother.'

Hew Li's brother passed over from one junk to another. As he did so, the gangplank was withdrawn by Andrew. At the same time Tanya appeared on the scene in a speedboat. She had arrived early and had been waiting a slight distance behind the junk.

Hew Li exclaimed bitterly, 'Yes, I was wondering, Mr Brandon, how you planned to make your escape. I can tell you now, you have no chance. I want my twenty million dollars back.'

Andrew stepped into the speedboat and stood beside Tanya. 'We made a bargain,' he stated. 'I have kept my part of it. I have delivered your brother to you, alive and free. Now you must keep yours.'

Suddenly Hew Li's eyes flared in fury. 'No,' he spat. 'Keeping bargains is for fools. Did you really think I would pay you twenty million dollars? Now my brother is old and no further indignity can be heaped on him, you and the Communists want to profit from his carcass.'

'Your brother committed terrible crimes. He has served his sentence. We made an agreement and you must keep your word.' Andrew looked at Hew Li dispassionately.

'Must?' Hew Li was apoplectic with anger. 'Must? Who are you, you insignificant wretch, to tell me what I must do? I will have my money and my brother. You do not know who I am and the influence I have.'

Andrew sighed. 'Hew Li, how rightly the Chinese judged you. They told me you would never change. Listen to me very carefully. You have received what you have paid for. Don't cheat me for you can only lose.'

Hew Li threw back his head and cackled with delight as if watching a child telling off its own father. 'You will repay me, you wretch. In money and in blood.' He examined Tanya, devouring her with his lidded eyes. 'And I shall enjoy the girl, every bit of her, piece by piece.' Suddenly, he made a sign. In the distance they heard the noise of engines being revved. Then five speedboats raced towards them from out of the mist and the darkness. At their prows stood Hew Li's men, dressed in black with machine guns unleashed. Hew Li cackled exultantly. 'See if Taiwan's Chief of Police can help you now! These are his boats.'

Andrew took the wheel from Tanya and quickly spun the speedboat away from his attackers. He opened up the throttle and they shot off. Hurriedly, one of the other speedboats stopped to pick up Hew Li, then they proceeded after Andrew. Already, the gap between them was lessening.

Tanya seized Andrew by the arm. 'Don't go back to Taiwan. Make for China, it's our only chance.'

Andrew shook his head. Hew Li would have made certain they would never reach the Chinese coast under any circumstances. Andrew shouted something to Tanya, but she couldn't hear what he said above the roar of the engines and the spray. She glanced back. Even with full throttle the other speedboats were easily gaining on them and started to enclose them in a pincer move. They would have no chance in Taiwanese waters. She made to seize the wheel. However, Andrew resisted and pointed ahead as they raced into a dense blanket of fog. Within a couple of minutes they had passed through. Now Tanya saw why he had taken this direction. For, hidden by the fog, an entire flotilla of the Chinese Navy lay before them – twenty gunboats and a destroyer. Andrew quickly passed between their ranks and cut back the throttle.

'We'll return to Taiwan in a few minutes.'

'What will happen to Hew Li?' asked Tanya.

'He has committed terrible crimes,' replied Andrew. 'The Chinese agreed to free his brother since his sentence had been served, on one condition. If Hew Li sought to renege on his bargain and tried to kill me, they would take him.'

'They knew he would cheat.'

'Of course and so did I,' said Andrew. 'Great evil begets its own downfall in the end, even though it may be a long time coming. You see, one thing that Hew Li did not consider was that Chinese vessels would come into Taiwanese waters. It was inconceivable since it would amount to a declaration of war between the two countries, unless . . .'

'Unless?'

'The leaders of Taiwan and China reached an agreement to get rid of Hew Li. One thing he never anticipated.'

They watched as Hew Li's vessels shot out of the fog into the hands of Chinese justice.

It took them forty-five minutes to reach a Taiwanese harbour. Tanya operated the speedboat. Andrew sat in the stern with his back to her looking out over the water.

As they neared land, Tanya asked, 'Did you get the twenty million dollars?'

'Yes.'

'I see.' Tanya's voice was flat and unemotional. She cut the engines and the boat slowly drifted towards the jetty. There was silence. Sensing a noise behind him, Andrew turned round in his seat to look at her.

'Tanya, if you're going to kill me, do it now.'

Andrew regarded the gun in her hand and her. Her face was drawn and the eyes fearful. Andrew said softly, 'Is Sebastien still alive?'

Tanya nodded.

'I thought so. I also imagine Sebastien will have told you that I killed Rex and Ivan.'

Again she nodded.

Andrew gazed at her with a steady expression. 'There's nothing I can say to prove otherwise, and no reason to prefer my word to Sebastien's, whom you clearly love.'

Averting his gaze, Andrew fixed his eyes on the harbour scene. The sun had appeared over the horizon, lighting up the sky, just as it had done on the first morning of all life. Andrew did not look at her – not through fear but because he could not bear to gaze into lovely, and yet so troubled, eyes for the last time.

'If that is what you really believe, Tanya, kill me now.'

Tanya kept the gun levelled at his heart. Her mind and her soul were in turmoil and the profound depths of her sadness and indecision clearly registered in her face. Was it possible to care for two men at the same time, for different reasons? Even if one of them was a murderer who desired your own death to fulfil his destiny? Love, desire, death and betrayal, the most powerful emotions of humankind swirled within her being, inextricably mixed and Tanya could not see a solution. Would that she had the vision of the Master to solve this puzzle. Would that she could see.

'Why do you think the Master is not taking part in this?' she said.

Andrew raised his hands wearily. 'Because of what the Master said that night he told us of the Chinese puzzle box. He said, "All problems have a solution. When people declare that there is no solution it simply means that they cannot see one. The solution is neither confused nor complex. It is the beholder who brings confusion to the object beheld and, by their failing to discard their desires and prejudices, the search is usually in vain." Our quest for the Mastership is our problem. The Master also told us the solution.'

'What?'

'"People who wish to find the solution must first consider themselves and analyse their own thoughts. In that way they can reflect on the situation with the unclouded clarity of a mirror." When talking of the puzzle, he also said to us, "It is we who assume that the box is a Chinese puzzle box. This supposition arises from our preconceived notions. **The answer lies not in the box but in ourselves.**"'

'Yes, but what does it mean?' stammered Tanya.

'It means,' said Andrew, 'that the Master told us the answer to the contest at the very beginning but we could not understand it. He told us the truth. Just as there is no puzzle to the Chinese box, there is no puzzle to the Mastership. The Master was saying to us. "Look into your own hearts. Within yourselves is the answer. If you crave the Mastership, it is not for you. For the Mastership is not a prize. It is a terrible burden. It is a gift of power. And just as power corrupts, so does the quest for it. For power makes you progressively blind to the truth. Like an illness, it maims you so that you can no longer see the reality of things." '

He looked at Tanya. Tears streaked her cheeks.

'Yet we, like fools, rushed ahead,' continued Andrew. 'Ever anxious to win the game, we searched for clues, just as in trying to solve the puzzle box we searched for clues in the painting on the face of the box. But these clues are irrelevant. The words of the Master were all we needed to know.'

'So the Master is not playing?'

'Exactly. Whatever the rules say is irrelevant. The Master himself told us the answer. He said that there were five people nominated for the Mastership. The five of us. Not him – however it may appear otherwise.'

'Is this true?' said Tanya. 'How can you prove it?'

'I can't. That is the test,' said Andrew. 'Like the Chinese puzzle box it is not possible to prove the truth of it without destroying it. Like smashing the box to look inside. A perception of the Mastership is an inner perception, an insight into the nature of power which is personal to each of us. The Mastership cannot be seized, nor bought, nor deceived. It simply lies within or it does not. The Master is as he seems. Like the Chinese box there is nothing more. Yet, in that nothingness there is everything.' He continued sadly, 'It also means one more thing I have failed to understand.'

'What?'

'Just as there is no puzzle, there is no game.'

*   *   *

Tanya's hand trembled on the trigger of the gun.

Now she knew the truth. If she had really understood the Master's words, she would have realised from the start that the Mastership could never be attained by evil or illegal means. Since the position comprised a burden and not a prize, the person ultimately selected for the Mastership would be the one who desired it least. It could only be comprehended by those who had put aside their own selfishness. By seeing what they would do to attain great power the Master could determine who was truly worthy.

'Tanya . . .'

'Stop,' she shouted at him as the flow of her thoughts continued. And the terrible consequences. 'Is Sebastien evil? Is he the murderer?'

'That is for you to decide,' said Andrew. 'I didn't kill Rex or Ivan; and I'm sure that you didn't either. I believe that Sebastien killed them – because he wants the Mastership above everything else. He sees it as the greatest prize of all which justifies the taking of any action to possess it. In the pursuit of power people will do the most terrible things – we see that every day. For the greatest power all the more so. It is frighteningly corrosive in its nature. And the only protection the College has against this is insight which enables it to see the evil that craves it, even as it approaches in the most deceptive and seductive of guises.'

'So, why didn't Sebastien kill me if this is true?'

'I don't know, Tanya. Perhaps, because he loves you, perhaps because he needed you to help him win the Mastership. But what I do know is this: I will have no part in harming the Master. He is a most remarkable human being and one who is truly capable of exercising his office without causing harm. So the decision is yours. To kill me or not. That is your exercise of power, and your choice, just as Sebastien's is his.'

Tanya pondered. Their desire for the Mastership had produced small acts of evil, then correspondingly greater ones as she and Sebastien thought they were nearing their goal. Yet all the time it had become more distant. She had been ready to kill another. For what reason? For power and her craving for it. She knew now that she was trapped in an illusion. It tempted and deceived her even as it led her down the path to perdition. Ivan understood that. He had spared her life, because killing her was a bridge he would not cross to attain the Mastership. When Ivan had tied the scarf about her neck, he had shown her both his power over her and his choice. He had also sought to warn her that one whom she loved may have already crossed that bridge and passed far beyond.

Now Tanya stood as if on a bridge. She could still see the Mastership but it lay far ahead in the distance, elusive as always. She realised that it was not for her; she didn't have the insight to wield it. It would bring about her destruction even as she sought it.

It belonged to another.

With the gun she motioned Andrew to step out of the vessel onto the jetty. He did so.

'Where are you going?'

'To see Sebastien.'

'Tanya, you mustn't. It's not safe. I'll come with you,' Andrew said in alarm and made to descend again. However, Tanya revved up the engines and moved the speedboat slightly away from the jetty. If she took a flight from Taiwan, she'd get back to Tirah in time to appear before the Arbitrators. First, she'd phone Sebastien as she'd promised. The news would be different from what he wanted to hear. She would tell him Andrew was still alive and that she wouldn't kill him after all. She would also tell him what she now knew.

'Where is he?' shouted Andrew from the jetty, above the noise of the motor.

'He left last night,' said Tanya, 'to see the Master. He'll be at Tirah now.' One thing was certain: she would make Sebastien see that the Mastership was not for him, and that it could not be seized. Sebastien would listen to her. However evil he was, he would not harm her. He loved her. She would make him, force him, to understand.

Andrew began to gesticulate wildly, 'Tanya, stop the boat. Get off the speedboat,' but she didn't hear him for the roar of the engines now at full throttle. As she turned the vessel round, Tanya phoned Sebastien on her mobile phone.

His opening words were gentle and affectionate, as always. Then he said in a more distant tone, 'Is Andrew dead?'

'No.'

'So Andrew is with you now?'

'Yes.'

Suddenly, in an almost suicidal leap, Andrew flung himself from the jetty into the speedboat. He landed in the bow. Tanya turned from the wheel to see him rushing towards her. She turned to face her attacker, the phone falling from her grasp as she grabbed for her gun. But her resistance was in vain. Andrew seized her and hurled them both over the side into the murky waters. Even as they sank, Sebastien pressed a button on his mobile.

Tanya and Andrew descended into the watery depths, Andrew pulling her down as far as he could, ignoring her desperate struggles. Above them, the boat mushroomed into a massive fireball as the bomb went off, activated by the mobile. Tanya peered up. Bright blue and orange flames seared across the water and then plunged down into the darkness to seek her out, to touch and caress her with their warmth, even as Andrew frantically drew her lower into the murk to save her from a certain death.

At that precise moment something died within Tanya. The Master had told them, with clear sight, there were no puzzles. While she gasped for air, she realised it was profoundly true. She had loved Sebastien but he had never loved her – not when love came into conflict with what he really craved: the Mastership. The solution to the death of Rex had also been before her all the time, but she had refused to see it, refused to contemplate her part in that terrible event. For the secret to the death of

Rex lay in the past, their past. Rex had been killed because of his love for her.

Tanya did not know that Sebastien had found in Rex's room in Erris a half-finished letter in which Rex had written to Tanya of his undying love and his wish to work with her to win the Mastership Game, a letter in which he also referred to his fears about Max Stanton. What she did know now was that Sebastien had killed Rex – not only to win the Mastership Game, but because losing her to Rex was beyond comprehension. Jealousy had been the simple seed for evil to grow and she hadn't seen it, hadn't wanted to see it.

Tanya closed her eyes. Sebastien was right. War was the strongest thing of all in the universe. For her love was irrevocably destroyed. Tanya opened her mouth and let the water flow in to her lungs. Death would be her only lover now.

Gasping with exhaustion, Andrew dragged her unconscious body from the filthy waters to the jetty. Summoning help, he watched as the ambulance began its frantic journey to the hospital, the sirens blaring. Tanya might live but another would die. He began to run. He must contact the Master. However, even as he ran, he knew it was too late.

The Mastership was broken.

CHAPTER THIRTY

To serve one's own spirit so as to permit neither joy nor sorrow within, but to consider the inevitable as the appointment of destiny and to be at ease, there is the perfection of virtue.

Confucius

23 December. The College.

IT WAS LATE EVENING. THE Master went into the third courtyard and sat on one of the benches located in the simple maze. He looked up at the stars. The night was a clear one and they streamed on into the Milky Way. How many of his predecessors, the Master wondered, had sat here gazing at the universe as they grappled with the intractable problems of mankind?

Tomorrow was the Fellows' Banquet. The Master felt some sadness, for he was coming to the end of a long journey. Like a helmsman he welcomed the port, though there was also melancholy, knowing that this voyage would never be repeated. For all his genius he felt the poignancy of human destruction. Yet he was fixed on his course, and sadness and joy could scarce find their way in. He yearned for nothing. For a long time the Master watched the sky, letting thoughts and impressions flow freely in his being while he absorbed the emptiness about him. In it he found peace.

What had he achieved? The Mastership was a burden which he had never wished to bear, but which had been imposed on him. For it, he had sacrificed marriage, children, the hopes and fears of a normal life. As the long years passed that burden had become all the heavier. For the Master knew a great truth. Power corroded human beings like acid. It bit into their souls. It whispered false promises. It created wonderful illusions. It promised an easy victory even as it spurred on its prey to defeat. It made people evil and, like an illness, it progressively blinded them to the truth. The Master had seen it so clearly in others that he knew that the immense power of the Mastership would eventually destroy him.

So wherein lay the answer to his own and humanity's salvation? For him it lay not in books, not in learning, not in the human story. It lay out there. Beyond all the evil and the terrible things, beyond the dark and the misery, it lay out there. A universe perfect and entire, untouched by man. Such a belief had sustained him on his lonely voyage throughout the years and if wishing enough could make it true, it was true.

In this existence he had been like a teacher, though himself the pupil of others with greater insight and wisdom than he. He thought of the Chinese puzzle box and the magnificent vases that he would not see again. He thought of the College and its future direction. He thought of the brief span of his own existence. He no longer thought of the Mastership for, like all names and titles, it was a limitation. As the Taoist said, names and titles were only the shadow of real gain. How much the Master would have liked to have talked with the simple craftsman Chang, and the Taoist who said of the perfect man:

> *'The mind of the perfect man is like a mirror. It does not move with things, nor does it anticipate them. It responds to things, but does not retain them. Therefore, he is able to deal successfully with things, but is not affected.'*

How easy to say. How difficult to live.

The Master rose and went back inside the Lodge to his study. Tomorrow was the Fellows' Banquet, yet his work was not complete even at this late hour. The final test was to come and there was a small boy to help. The Master had sent Symes to the mainland. He would be back tomorrow. With a sigh the Master started on a document; the Mastership did not cease even with the death of a Master.

A while later the clock chimed midnight. The Master went to his library to collect some papers. He returned. The fire had burnt low so he placed some logs on it. As he did so he heard a step behind him. He looked round. Sebastien was standing quietly in the gloom.

'I apologise for intruding into your domain,' said Sebastien. 'There is something important we should discuss.'

They went to one of the reception rooms in the Lodge and sat at a table.

'Perhaps you thought I was dead,' Sebastien remarked to begin the conversation. 'I'm sorry if I alarmed you. Personally, I never believe newspapers. Nor pathologists' reports.'

'Nor do I,' said the Master succinctly.

Sebastien laughed. 'No. I thought not. With such a wide experience of human nature you know that all people have their price, including pathologists. I can assure you, though, that Rex and Ivan won't be reappearing. They're dead, I'm afraid.'

'You killed them?'

'Yes.'

There was silence. They sat opposite each other, the one youthful and strong with a forceful expression and an acute stare, the other older, but with an appearance no less commanding. A young lion and an old lion. Yet, there was a difference. In Sebastien's face there was a dynamic and restless fluidity, an activeness, while the face of the Master was as immobile and serene as glass.

'Death is always unfortunate,' said Sebastien. 'In this case, it was necessary. A small evil to attain the desired end about which you, Master, know so much.' He shrugged. 'What person has not attained high office without some act of evil? It is the only way to acquire power. The greater the power, the greater the evil. We see it daily in this world around us. And for the Mastership, probably the greatest prize of all, it could not be otherwise. I enjoyed the contest, Master, and it has taught me much of power and the true means of its exercise, a wonderful experience for things to come. In the end the College and the world are the same, they only differ in degree.'

'What have you learnt?' asked the Master.

'That the great tacticians were right. That Sun Tzu was right. War is the road to the survival or ruin of a state, and the College is a state like any other, that can only survive by playing off its neighbours against each other.

'That Machiavelli was right. To rule, destroy those who have the will or the power to harm you, for it is safer to be feared than to be loved. And one of his sayings which you will appreciate, Master, since both of us have trodden that same path:

> *"Princes who have cared little about good faith, and have used cunning to confuse the minds of men, have achieved great things; so that in the end they have outstripped those who founded themselves on honesty."*

'This, Master, is our world, yours and mine, and these writers recognise it for what it is. All else is pretence and delusion. Your analysis of the Chinese puzzle was quite correct. Behind the gilt and the trappings there is nothing. The reality of power is power, not insight.'

Sebastien recounted his path to the Mastership. Rex was the only one whom he'd intended to destroy.

'Rex would have killed me first if he'd had the opportunity. He wanted to win just as much as I did and he knew what the real nature of the Mastership Game was. Besides, when Rex turned and saw me before the car hit him I can assure you that the look on his face was one of hate. Hate that he was destined to die and not me. I've no regrets. Rex's luck ran out, that's all. He forgot the rule of all tacticians: strike early, strike hard.'

The Master watched him keenly, 'There was something else.'

'Something else?'

'Yes. You didn't kill Rex just because he knew more than you about the contest for the Mastership.'

'Why do you say that?' Sebastien asked in a strange tone.

'Because power corrupts what is already within. Your reason for killing Rex would have been prompted by something other than just a desire for power.'

Sebastien answered. 'How very perceptive of you, Master,' he said grimly. 'How well you understand human nature. I suppose there's no harm in telling you now. That night you told us about the contest, Rex went to the town of Erris to talk with Ivan but not to make a deal with him. You see, Rex wanted to make a deal with someone else.'

'Tanya?'

'Yes. Rex left in his room in Erris an unfinished letter, to Tanya. It was clear he loved her and that he once had a physical relationship with her, about which Tanya never told me. Rex also wrote that he would take part in the contest and that he wanted to work with her. So Tanya must choose between him and me. Of course, there was no choice. Not for me.'

'But you never gave Tanya the choice,' said the Master. 'She may have chosen you above Rex and the Mastership. She may have loved you more.'

Sebastien said nothing for many moments. He turned away from the eyes of the Master. Finally, he went to the sideboard to pour them both a drink. He continued, 'The other deaths were unfortunate, albeit understandable. Ivan attacked Tanya in my chalet in Switzerland, to get information from her. In that way he brought his doom upon himself. Besides, he was sure I had killed Rex. At the funeral service for Rex he told me he didn't know where Rex had been the night he died. This was untrue since I'd seen the two of them at dinner. Ivan said it to test me and there must have been something in my look which gave me away. So, I had to deal with him. No witnesses.'

'And Andrew and Tanya?' asked the Master

Sebastien smiled grimly. 'I sent Tanya to kill him and she failed me. She betrayed me. In the end I could no longer trust her because she had become his bed mate. Like Ivan, I killed them with a bomb, this time on a speedboat. Besides, the path to the Mastership must leave no trace, just as the perfect crime must leave no trace. No footprints in the sand. Was it not so with Max Stanton as well, Master? In the end, Tanya was an expendable agent. One of those whom Sun Tzu called a spy, a person who is deliberately given fabricated information to confuse the enemy and is expendable. Tanya helped me but she would not, could not, have made that final ascent. I had to go on alone. No one can connect me to any deaths and no one can connect me to the twenty million dollars. Further, no one can prevent me from winning the contest for the Mastership. Apart from one person.'

'Who?'

'You, Master.'

The Master said nothing.

Sebastien continued, as he walked about the room, 'I confess that one matter troubled me throughout this contest. Were you really prepared to lay aside the greatest of power, for nothing?' Sebastien wisely shook his head. 'If history tells us one thing, it is that no one willingly gives up power. And the more power the less willing. You would never give up the Mastership without a struggle. Isn't that so?'

At that moment a phone rang. The Master rose from the table. 'If you'll excuse me . . .'

'Of course, but do come back.'

The Master went to his study and picked up the receiver. As he did so, Sebastien approached the door to listen. At the end of the brief discourse the Master simply said, 'I understand,' and put down the phone.

He pressed a button to ensure no further calls would be put through that night and returned to the reception room.

Sebastien sipped his cognac. 'As I was saying, I knew you would never willingly renounce the Mastership. And two pieces of information confirmed it.'

'What were they?' asked the Master

'The first was information Rex had. In your own contest for the Mastership, Max Stanton died in a mysterious accident during the competition. This proved what I already suspected: there could only be one winner and that death was on the cards. Not that I object to it,' said Sebastien apologetically. 'It is consistent with our world.'

'And the other information?'

Sebastien said in a withering tone. 'That I obtained through good luck, though I had already had my suspicions. Andrew told Tanya about the rules of the Mastership, rules he had discovered in this very Lodge. So that leaves me and you, Master.' Sebastien raised his glass. 'Your good health,' he said. They drank.

The Master studied Sebastien reflectively. His voice was filled with dismay.

'Sebastien, you think this contest's a deadly one. You are wrong. You have chosen to interpret it so. It's true that Stanton died in a contest for the Mastership, a competition which I was also involved in. However, no one killed him and certainly not I.'

'And Rule No. XIX?'

'The rules say the incumbent may elect to take part in the contest for the Mastership. It says "*may*", not "*must*".'

'And, doubtless, you have decided not to.'

'That is so.'

Sebastien stared at him for a moment. Then he threw back his head and laughed. 'Bravo, Master. A magnificent performance.' He clapped slowly. 'Bravissimo. One I'd have expected from a man of your genius. But not quite good enough.' He leant forward. 'You lie,' he sneered, his voice thick and ugly.

'No.'

'You lie, Master,' repeated Sebastien, 'though I must congratulate you. You have consummately played your part and I have enjoyed every minute of it. Your description of the Chinese puzzle was a *tour de force* and it threw me off the scent at first. A brilliant ruse. But the reality remains. There is no puzzle to this contest. No moral dimension. This contest is an act of war.'

He tapped his finger on the table. 'A war in which you and I remain. A war in which there can only be one victor.'

'What do you intend to do?' the Master asked.

Sebastien sat down. He drew his hands together as if in prayer. The new Master.

'That problem is solved, Master, and in the only way possible, for you have taught us much of the meaning and the use of power, perhaps too much. It is only fitting, therefore, that your departure from this world should be a Socratic one. Your drink was drugged and you have only minutes to live before your heart is paralysed. Given your age everyone will assume you have succumbed to natural causes. And tomorrow evening, at the Fellows' Banquet, I will assume the Mastership.' He spoke with elation. 'You see, I've outwitted even you. I will be Master. To be otherwise would be to fail.'

'No. To do something against your true nature is to fail,' said the Master firmly.

Sebastien contemplated him. A crimson hue had already started to appear in the Master's cheeks as the poison began its deadly work. It was not this which surprised Sebastien, rather it was the look of serenity, the face of a man at peace with himself and wholly unafraid. A man uncowed by evil.

Sebastien watched him closely for signs of weakness. 'Are you not sad to have lost?'

The Master sighed, an agonising pain in his chest. In his mind he could see the vessel was ending its long voyage.

'Sebastien, you still fail to comprehend. The Mastership cannot be seized.'

There was silence. A dying silence. The old man scrutinised Sebastien, his eyes dim. His breathing became laboured. Haltingly, he said, 'Sebastien, you must not become Master. What you believe about this contest is not so. The contest involves neither good nor evil. You are the one who has chosen. The means you've used to reach your goal are the wrong means. You have let your ambition and desire for power dominate all else. The Mastership does not contain these things. The path you should have followed has eluded you. You can't take by force what is not yours by right.'

'You lie, you lie,' sneered Sebastien. 'You lie because you have lost.'

'It is not so.' The Master's voice was tremulous. His sight began to fail him, yet his will remained supreme. 'Sebastien, I implore you, reflect on my words. Don't compound your error.'

'You lie. The Mastership is mine. I have fought and I have won.'

'War is like fire,' gasped the Master. 'Those who will not put aside weapons are consumed by them. You can't seize the truth. I beg of you, think on this. The Mastership itself holds only insight, not war. That alone can control great power.'

Sebastien watched him. He knew the Master was lying. He got up and left the room, leaving his victim alone.

The Master felt the excruciating pain as the poison began to finish its fell work. Now, as he reached the very portals of death, doubt momentarily came upon him. Was Sebastien right after all? Is the universe itself subject only to iron laws – that those with power and unafraid to use evil always win? And that the greatest of power is held by those who crave it most? An eternity of oppression? Had he and the artist Chang been wrong? Had they spent their lives in a dream, like children, desperately believing in something that never was? The dark night of the human soul was upon him as he passed across its barren and polluted waters.

Suddenly, the Master sat back. In his inner self, he was as a small vessel reaching the safety of the harbour. He threw away the oars and gave himself up to the universe. Yet, the universe did not fail him. For the Master lost nothing and gained all. Willingly, he surrendered to the process of living and dying. What he had always believed was true, was true. The light from the beacon before him was so strong that its sanctity eclipsed his face. His being surged outwards, beyond the farthest reaches of human experience. He had found the Way. Now he knew it in his innermost being. In the empty puzzle box of one simple carpenter, as in the tomb of another, there lay no deception. In that nothingness there was everything. The mystery of it all.

The greatest of power was held by one who would never abuse it, and it could never be seized.

Sebastien waited. After a while he re-entered the study. The Master lay slumped in his chair. The figure that only minutes before had sat so stern was shrinking, almost vanishing, into thin air. However, his expression, with its supreme sense of peace and certainty, remained. It radiated the power of wisdom. Momentarily, Sebastien felt afraid. He placed the poisoned glass in his pocket.

In front of the Master lay some papers. Sebastien noticed that the Master had written a message on one of them. It must have been written before Sebastien arrived. It was a quotation from Sun Tzu:

'I can forecast which side will be victorious and which defeated.'

In fury, Sebastien seized it and thrust it into his pocket. Then he hurried from the chamber, upstairs to the sitting room where, on that fateful night, the Master had first discussed the Chinese puzzle with the five Fellows.

Hurling open the door, Sebastien looked about him wildly. On a small table lay the Chinese puzzle box. Sebastien snatched it up. It was truly spectacular, the final and greatest achievement of the simple craftsman. For a moment Sebastien marvelled at its beauty and its genius. Then, casting it to the ground, he smashed it open with the heel of his shoe. . .

A low animal groan escaped from his lips. The shattered box was empty.

Now he knew the truth.

CHAPTER THIRTY-ONE

He who wants to lead the people should place himself behind them.
In this way, the sage is above the people, but the people do not feel him as a burden;
He is in front of the people (leading them), but the people do not feel him as a hindrance.
Therefore all the people under Heaven revere him and do not tire of him.
Just because he does not compete with others,
Nobody under heaven can compete with him

Lao Zi

Christmas Eve.

THE DAY OF THE FELLOWS' Banquet was cold and bleak. The snow wafted about the third courtyard in great gusts and lay thick on the branches of the cherry trees. Outside, there was chaos and turmoil. Within, all was tranquil. The only noise to permeate the confines of the study was the sound of a clock and, more rarely, the creak of the oak floorboards as they eased in the heat from the burnt-out fire. Otherwise, all remained silent in the Master's Lodge. On this occasion, however, the silence reflected an even deeper absence, a loss that cast its pall over all. The College was in mourning.

It was Symes who found him. He arrived at the Lodge just after dawn and walked down the snow-covered path to the entrance. Closing the door, he ascended the marble staircase and passed into the various rooms to open the curtains as he had done every day for more than a generation. At first he thought that the Master was asleep. When he touched the reclining figure, he realised that the Master was no longer in this world.

Symes continued with his normal duties, his mind unable to comprehend this shattering event. He passed into each room like a ghost – through the dining room with its gallery of pictures and its long table, into the salon where the Master was often to be found working on summer evenings, then to the library with its myriad books. These and all the other chambers. Afterwards Symes went down to the kitchen and made tea which he took upstairs to the Master's bedroom. It was only when there was no reply to his voice that the actuality of the Master's death hit him.

Symes slowly put down the tray and entered the room. He sat on the unused bed and looked out of the mullioned window. Suddenly, he was overwhelmed with grief. Had he not been sent to the mainland by the Master, he would have been here at the end. How sad, after so many years, that he had been unable to say farewell to him, in some small way to add his thanks to the millions of others. For he knew that the Master had done all that he could during his life to bring peace. Symes was a simple man and there were others far greater than he, yet in his soul he understood the unique humility of the individual whom he had cared for. He knew of things they never would.

He surveyed the bedroom, that of a man whose words the great and the mighty had listened to, whose insight had helped many to see when they themselves could not. Here was his room, the room of a man of true power. It contained virtually nothing. A simple bed and a chair.

Symes went to the window. He pressed his face to the glass and he wept.

In another part of the world, far from the College, Jack Caldwell stepped into the Oval Office. President Davison put down the phone and smiled. Things were going well, the economy was good and his problems of a year before were long forgotten. Then, with concern he saw that Caldwell looked worn, almost ill.

'Jack, are you feeling all right? I thought you were going on holiday to Europe today, for a well-earned rest.'

Caldwell said, 'I am going. However,' he continued, his voice breaking with emotion, 'Mr President, I have some very sad news to convey to you. The College has contacted me. The Master passed away this morning.'

Davison felt tears start up in his eyes. 'I see,' he said quietly.

Caldwell continued, 'Mr President, yesterday I received a letter from the Master. I was to give it to you.'

Davison observed him. He didn't ask why the letter had been delivered to Jack. He was sure now that the man before him was a Fellow of the College. But it didn't matter. The secret would be safe with him. What mattered was that Jack and the Master had once rendered him great assistance. Everyone needed guardians sometimes and he could not wish for better. President Davison took the letter and said gently, 'Thanks, Jack. I think you should take that holiday.'

Caldwell nodded and walked towards the door.

'Jack.'

Caldwell turned.

'He was a very great man,' said the President.

'The greatest I had the privilege to meet,' replied Caldwell.

Davison nodded. The President of the United States opened the letter and read it. Then he got up from his desk to look out onto the White House lawn. Had the Master known that he was about to die? President Davison thought not. For it is not given to men to know of the precise time of their coming or going in this world. Of course, the Master's request would be fulfilled. He couldn't do otherwise for one for whom he had unbounded admiration. President Davison picked up the phone and gave the necessary orders.

One day Obedi would know that the Master's last thoughts were for him, for it was the Master's wish that he come and live at the College to help Symes and the new Master. At last, Obedi would find peace in a world which had shown him none and be with people who would ensure that he was safe.

The man at the end of the telephone had not failed Obedi just as he had not failed others. Like James, the founder of the College, the Master knew that peace and compassion, not power, led to the heart of the universe and into the mind of God.

That morning Sebastien declared his candidacy to four of the Arbitrators when they attended the College for the Fellows' Banquet. The fifth Arbitrator was expected to arrive later that day. The Arbitrators acknowledged that Sebastien had fulfilled the first part of the contest in making twenty million dollars. However, he had to fulfil the second requirement, which was to appear before the Arbitrators at eight o'clock that evening prior to the Fellows' Banquet. This seemed to be no more than a formality. Rex and Ivan were dead and the Arbitrators had heard nothing from Tanya and Andrew, though they were investigating reports that they had died in a terrible speedboat accident in Taiwan.

In the Master's Lodge the Senior Arbitrator required Sebastien to read aloud the oath the Master elect was required to give:

> 'Candidate for the Mastership, if you know of any reason why you should not become Master bearing in mind the great burdens and responsibilities of this office, for the benefit of the College as well as the world beyond, you must renounce your candidacy so that the person most fitted for this office may be elected. Swear that you know of no such impediment.'

Hesitating only a fraction, Sebastien said, 'I swear.'

After the oath, the other Arbitrators departed leaving Sebastien alone with the Senior Arbitrator.

He said to Sebastien, 'It is customary for the Senior Arbitrator to give the funeral oration for a deceased Master. I have prepared my speech. However, you must read it.'

'I would like to defer to you,' said Sebastien.

'No,' said the Senior Arbitrator. 'It was the Master's wish. He told me recently that the funeral oration for him should be given by his presumptive successor.'

Sebastien was startled. 'Why should the Master have contemplated his own funeral?'

The Senior Arbitrator looked at him shrewdly. 'Because the Master was dying,' he said. 'From cancer. He knew of this more than a year ago.'

The Fellows of the College gathered in the small, granite-built, chapel where, a year before, they had held the service of remembrance for Rex. It was here the funeral of every Master was held prior to his burial within the confines of the College. Outside, the snow fell thickly. Across the landscape there was only whiteness. Within, the candlelight did nothing to dispel the all-pervading gloom. Sebastien stood before the simple coffin. Then he went to the lectern to give the funeral oration. Outwardly, he was in control. Within, the murderer was already passing a terrible sentence on himself.

As he walked down the narrow aisle, Sebastien felt as if he was in a dream. It all seemed so long ago. In his mind's eye he could see them. Rex striding down to the loch, the oars suspended over his great shoulders; Ivan, as he glanced up from an artefact, cool and self-possessed; Andrew disappearing into the African distance; and the Master, far ahead, effortlessly walking a path that for Sebastien was irretrievably lost. Finally, there was Tanya. She stood at the water's edge. Her gaze was sad and forlorn. Sebastien turned away from the image in his mind. He could not bear to look on her.

Sebastien stood at the lectern and read the funeral oration written by one who was wiser than he. He told the audience of the Master. Of a remarkable human being who had placed the concerns of the College and the duties of his Mastership above himself. Of an individual who had faithfully discharged his office and yet remained uncorrupted by the enormous power and authority with which it was endowed. A moral and spiritual beacon in society's wasteland.

While he read these words, Sebastien realised that what he had spoken of the Master out of duty was profoundly true in reality. This unconscious knowledge permeated to the core of his self, and try as he might, he could not stop its admittance. For the Master really had been as he seemed and Sebastien had committed the most terrible wrong. A desire to attain the Mastership and its power had become a craving, and one act of evil had in fact led to correspondingly greater acts of evil. By his own hubris, he had damned himself. Like a blind man he could no longer see what he had most sought. Tears began to form in his eyes, tears from his soul.

He came to a passage that applied to Sebastien even as it had to the Senior Arbitrator. He read to the gathering: 'Once a Master showed me a Chinese puzzle box by the famous craftsman Chang. A Chinese emperor had asked Chang to make for him the most beautiful and the most difficult puzzle of all. What, then, is the most difficult puzzle for us as human beings? Is it not to understand the purpose of our own existence? For it is this we endlessly try to solve during our short lives, as we blindly stumble through a sense of failure and success, not really knowing which is which? Yet few men desire to look within, to contemplate that their acts and their cravings may get them no closer to the goals which they truly seek. So how do we solve the puzzle? For Chang the means was not through outward achievements or force. It lay within. A man who truly follows his inner nature will yearn for nothing. He will wander free from illusion to see, in himself, the universe unfold.'

Sebastien glanced towards the coffin. 'For the Master, I believe, it was the same. Detached from possessiveness, he remained unaffected by possessions. Uninterested in power, he was truly suited to exercise it. With the unclouded clarity of a mirror he alone had the insight to help others solve the problems they could not. As an emptied man, one without cravings, he strolled as he pleased.'

Sebastien stopped. He looked at the people assembled before him. Then he continued, his voice heavy with despair.

'For the Master, what was the answer to his puzzle, the purpose of his own life? It was to live according to his own true nature.' He stumbled over the final words:

'And, by wanting nothing, he gained all.'

At the end of the service Sebastien stayed on in the chapel, alone with his crippling guilt and the ghosts of those whom he had once known. The other Fellows returned to the College to prepare for the Fellows' Banquet. Sebastien watched the patches of light flicker on the columns of the chapel. The Master had won after all. He had prevailed by giving up his own life to show Sebastien that he was profoundly mistaken as to the nature of the Mastership. It was not a prize to be won but a millstone to be borne, as the Master sought to negotiate a perilous path in helping society without abusing his own power. All to achieve peace. For peace was not only an absence of war. **It was a state of enlightenment**.

He raised his head. The Senior Arbitrator stood some distance from him.

Sebastien said: 'I have only one question. How did Max Stanton die?'

'We believe he committed suicide,' replied the Senior Arbitrator. 'He killed a fellow contestant in the hope that he might secure the Mastership. But the path to the Mastership does not lie that way.' He paused. 'I think you now understand its real nature, Sebastien, and the consequences of your acts. I will leave you alone with your thoughts.'

Sebastien listened as his departing footsteps echoed on the stone.

Sebastien left the chapel and began to walk down to the seashore. He strode along the beach, the memories of Tanya and the others pursuing him like avenging furies. In his selfishness he had destroyed what he had most loved. He knew now that the path of evil could only lead to greater evil, never to good. He saw other forms before him on that dark path, the dictators of this world, as they walked towards the pit, ever convinced that they wielded power for the good of others whereas, in truth, it was only to satisfy their own cravings to dominate and to control. Sebastien sought to turn away from the nightmare. What of those political theorists whose thoughts he had closely followed, as doubtless had millions of others in their time, to plot their path to power? Despite analysing all the tricks and feints of battle, had not Sun Tzu concluded:

> *'For to win one hundred victories in one hundred battles is not the height of skill. To subdue the enemy without fighting is the height of skill.'?*

And the great Machiavelli? Despite encouraging all manner of evils, in the end had not even he concluded:

> *'But it cannot be called true prowess to murder one's fellow citizens, betray one's friends, and to live without faith, piety or religion. Such methods may gain power, but can never win glory.'*

Sebastien watched the trace of his footsteps on the damp sand as they were erased by the incoming tide. He had been deceived. What he had most wanted was not the Mastership; it was to be like the Master. And in the pursuit of his false goal of power he had killed Tanya, the one whom he had most loved. Power betrayed those who quested for it, even as it shimmered in all its glory. Sebastien sighed. How brief human life was. How much to learn. The Mastership was not his, for he had been unable to perceive it.

Quite calmly Sebastien walked into the sea.

CHAPTER THIRTY-TWO

Subtle and insubstantial, the master leaves no trace . . . thus he is master of his enemy's fate.

Sun Tzu, *The Art of War*

Christmas Eve. 7.30pm

THE FIRE CRACKLED IN THE grate and its warm glow dispersed throughout the room. In the library in the third courtyard the Arbitrators sat back in their chairs listening to Andrew's story. When it was finished the Senior Arbitrator rose from his chair.

'Because of the enormous power inherent in the Mastership it is vital to ensure that it is never held by one who may misuse it. This is a very difficult task indeed. Since the foundation of the College, therefore, the process has always been the same. To set a contest or game, the real purpose of which is to determine exactly what people will do to secure the Mastership. In this way the Arbitrators can select as Master the most suitable candidate.'

'The initial candidates are chosen by lot?' said Andrew.

'Yes,' replied the Senior Arbitrator. 'As the Rules dictate, they are selected by lot from Fellows of the College within a certain age group. This is to prevent any person trying to influence the selection process. The Arbitrators determine the nature of the contest, in which they themselves can take no part. It rarely varies. Its purpose is to see what people will do under extreme circumstances. In particular, whether they will use evil means to attain their goal. While no one has doubted that this can produce tragic consequences, it is the only means to protect the integrity of the College and the essential purpose for which it was founded – the cause of peace.'

'The Master can take part in the contest?'

'Yes, he can,' said the Senior Arbitrator, 'but this never occurs in practice. Who would want to retain such a burden? If people truly understood the mutilation that power brings, they would not desire it.' He sighed. 'It was our dearest wish that the present Master continue in office. He wrote to me a year ago indicating that he would be unable to do so. As a result, a new Master had to be found.'

'Why could he not continue?' Andrew asked.

'It was as you supposed,' said the Senior Arbitrator sadly. 'The Master was dying.'

The Arbitrator went to the window and looked out of it. In the garden below a raven searched for food as it flitted past the snow-laden branches of the trees. He knew its medieval significance. Death had indeed come and it had come for the Master. He returned to the fireside.

'There is no game as such since what is important is not the outcome but the means employed. In this way, those who seek it by evil means, or those that crave it for their personal gain, preclude themselves. In other cases the contestants simply realise that they are not fitted for the Mastership and they disclaim it.'

'So the winner of the contest doesn't necessarily become Master?'

'That is correct,' said the Senior Arbitrator. 'In reality, the Arbitrators select the most appropriate candidate after they have determined how the contestants have sought to undertake the contest. For the Arbitrators secretly monitor the actions of the players during the contest. Sebastien realised this and the enormity of what he had done before he killed himself. I have also spoken to Tanya and she no longer wishes to continue. When she has recovered I believe she will be well suited to become an Arbitrator in her turn, for it is our wish that she return to the College, and the wisdom she has gained will help others.'

'What did the Master say to you?' One of the Arbitrators asked.

'I phoned him from Taiwan,' said Andrew. 'I was sure that Sebastien was with him at the time. I told the Master that Tanya and I were still alive. I also told him that his life was in very great danger. He simply said, "I understand." That was all.'

'He was a teacher throughout his life,' said the Senior Arbitrator. 'Even in the face of great evil he sought to show people the error of their ways.'

'What of the contest in which the Master played?'

The fifth Arbitrator leant forward. It was Jack Caldwell. 'It was the same as this contest,' he said. 'In my case, once I comprehended the nature of the Mastership, I realised that to continue would be for the purposes of self-aggrandisement only, and that the power of the office would destroy me. In the case of the Master it was very different. He understood the nature of the Mastership from the start and that there was no game as such. Rather, that the Mastership was a great burden. Thus, he took no part in the contest and only reluctantly accepted the Mastership when required to do so by the Arbitrators.'

'Then I have failed,' said Andrew. 'I only began to understand the meaning of the Chinese puzzle and of the Mastership after great trial and effort.'

'That is not for you to judge,' announced the Senior Arbitrator. 'The decision is ours. We alone determine who must bear this great burden and you did not use evil to achieve your goal.' He stood up. 'It is I who have failed. At the beginning of the contest I failed to thank the Master for all that he had done for the College. He will be seen as one of the greatest of Masters. Not wanting power, he bore it for the love of others and he would have laid it down without the slightest regret. In that way, to me, he had already progressed far on the path to mastership as described by the Tao:

"The sage . . . teaches by saying nothing . . . promotes all things without attributing them to his contribution and takes no credit

for himself when the work is done . . . Therefore the sage puts himself last but actually he stands foremost."'

There was nothing further to be said. They waited in silence for some minutes, each alone with his thoughts. The chapel bell chimed eight o'clock. Symes entered the study. On his arm he carried the robe of the Master. The Arbitrators all stood up and the Senior Arbitrator declared:

'Andrew. It is our wish that you become Master.'

They stood back and bowed.

'Master,' said Symes, 'the Banquet awaits.'

AUTHOR'S NOTE

This novel reflects on the nature of power, its corrupting influence and the lengths to which individuals go to acquire it, even though it invariably brings about their downfall. In this novel reference has been made to some political thinkers and philosophers who have considered the nature of power, in the case of Machiavelli from a Western perspective and, in the case of the others, from an Eastern perspective. For readers who might be interested in reading further, brief details are provided below.

Niccolò Machiavelli

One of the most well known, and infamous, of Western political theorists, Machiavelli was born in Florence in 1469, the son of a moderately successful lawyer. In his youth although Florence was nominally a Republic it was, in fact, largely controlled by one family, the Medici. In 1498 a fully constitutional government was restored. At the age of 29, Machiavelli became a civil servant and, until 1512, he was frequently sent out on diplomatic missions. Among others, he met the brilliant and ruthless Cesare Borgia, the son of Pope Alexander VI, who was seeking to establish a principality in central Italy at the expense of the Republic. These missions taught Machiavelli much about statesmanship and the use and abuse of power.

In 1512 the Medici returned to power in Florence. Machiavelli lost his government position and was thrown into prison. When released, he was reduced to poverty and retired to a small property near Florence he'd inherited from his father. It was there, in 1513, he produced his most famous work, *The Prince.* This was dedicated to Lorenzo de' Medici, but it failed to secure for him the return to favour for which he hoped. In 1520, after the death of Lorenzo, Machiavelli secured a minor post as official histographer to the Republic and, in 1527, he died – a few months after the Medici were expelled from Florence and the Republic was restored again.

Although an upright man himself, Machiavelli's fame has been overshadowed by the ruthless opportunism and political immorality which *The Prince* expounds and both the author and his work remain controversial. For many he is political schemer par excellence, endorsing the interests of the State above moral considerations. To others, he presents a candid reflection on the abuse of power in his time, and was a true democrat at heart. The debate continues.

Quotations in this novel are taken from Niccolò Machiavelli: *The Prince* translated by Bruce Penman (pub. JM Dent, 1981). See also *Machiavelli: The Discourses* edited by Bernard Crick (pub. Penguin Classics, 1983) and *The Art of War* edited by Neal Wood (pub. Da Capo, 1965). For commentary on the man, see, among many others, Quentin Skinner: *Machiavelli* (pub. OUP, 1981), Leo Strauss: *Thoughts on Machiavelli* (pub. Univ. of Chicago, 1958), Herbert Butterfield: *The Statecraft of Machiavelli* (1955), *Machiavelli,* edited by John Palmenatz (pub. Fontana, 1972).

Sun Tzu (Master Sun)

Szuma Chien in his *Records of the Historian* (completed 91BC) said that Sun Wu (the real name of Sun Tzu or Sun Zi) was a native of the State of Qi and that he presented his 'Art of War' to He Lu, King of the State of Wu during the closing years of the Spring and Autumn period of Chinese history (770–476BC) when the country was undergoing a period of translation from slavery to feudalism. In 1972 a manuscript on bamboo strips found in an ancient Chinese tomb disclosed that a lineal successor to Sun Wu by about a hundred and sixty years, Sun Bin, had also written on the Art of War in the Warring States period

(475–221BC). It is clear that analysing military strategy was a major component in both those times.

Whether or not Sun Tzu existed and whether or not the *Art of War* is a compilation arising from a variety of hands, the work is a profound and thought provoking study of military tactics as well as of statecraft and of power. Its essential premise is that winning is as much an exercise in skill and deception as it is of fighting; and that the highest practitioner of the art has no need to go to war at all. Instead, he should outwit his enemy through intrigue and by masquerading a superior strength and skill, whether or not this actually exists. Thus, while the *Art of War* commences with the words 'War is a matter of vital importance to the State . . .' it also declares 'to win one hundred victories in one hundred battles is not the height of skill. To subdue the enemy without fighting is the height of skill'.

Quotations in the novel are taken from Sun Tzu: *The Art of War* translated by Samuel B. Griffith (pub. OUP, 1963). See also Sun Zi and Sun Bin: *The Art of War* (pub. People's China Publishing House, 1995) and Thomas Cleary: *The Lost Art of War* (pub. HarperCollins, 1996) and Cleary: *The Art of War* (pub. Boston: Shambhala 1988).

Taoism – Lao Zi and Chuang Zi

Taoism is an Eastern philosophical tradition which later acquired religious elements. Its central text is the *Book of Lao Zi* (also known as the *Tao Te Ching* or *The Way and its Power*). It is asserted by some that its author Lao Zi (the 'old master') was the curator of the Imperial Chinese archives and that his book was written in the late Spring and Autumn Period (770–476BC). Others argue that Lao Zi never existed or that his work was written at a later date. Another classic Taoist text, *Chuang Tzu,* is asserted to have been written, at the latest, in the 3rd century BC.

The central doctrine of Taoism is the invisible and formless Tao (the Way) which is the beginning and end of all things and which can only be begun to be understood via mystical insight, not rational thought. The purpose of human existence is to be in harmony with one's inner nature, which can perceive the Tao. Only then will one be free of human cravings and have no fear of the natural rhythms of life and death. Taoism asserts that true rulers understand this. They seek an external simplicity and are uninterested in titles and power. They also realise that a pursuit of human values and wisdom is to completely miss the point – 'the further one goes, the less one knows. Therefore the sage knows without going through'. The point is to shed human imperfections, not to acquire more. Insight and humility are the true goals; and the one who considers himself superior is not, in truth, qualified for leadership.

Quotations in the novel are taken from *The Book of Lao Zi* by Ren Jiyu and from *Chuang Tzu* by Fung Yulan (English translations published by Foreign Languages Press, Beijing). See also *Chuang Tzu: The Inner Chapters: A Classic of Tao* by A. C. Graham (pub. Mandala, 1991) and the *Tao Te Ching*, a new translation with commentary by Ellen M. Chen (pub. Paragon House, 1989).